A Novel of Faith & Hope

THE
INVITATION
to the Shining City

*To Annette, Matt & family,
may you find your
"Shining City,"*

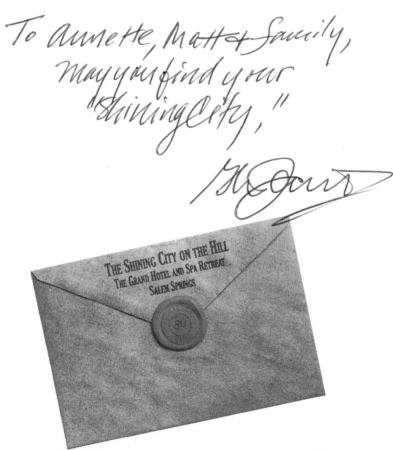

GM JARRARD

THE INVITATION
to the Shining City

BY

GM JARRARD

GM Jarrard | PO Box 95274 | South Jordan, Utah 84095 | (801) 688-5436 | gregorio1945@icloud.com. Applicable websites: www.theshiningcity.org, www.preservationbooks.com, www.latterdayradio.com (podcast)

Published by Preservation Books, Inc.

Cover Design: GM Jarrard
Interior Design: GM Jarrard (Paperback)
Ebook Design: K Christoffersen, BookWise Publishing (eBook)
Web Design & Consulting: Dustin Olsen, Cobalt Graphics

Images provided by: Shutterstock.com

Library of Congress Control Number: Pending
ISBN 978-0-9854424-8-4: Paperback | ISBN 978-0-9854424-5-3: eBook –
The main category of the book — 1. FIC042080: Fiction/Christian/Fantasy;
2. FIC042060: Fiction/Christian/Suspense. 3. FIC037000: Fiction/Political
I. Jarrard, GM.

First Edition
10 9 8 7 6 5 4 3 2 1
Version 1/06/2022

DEDICATION

THE INVITATION, a"novel of faith and hope," is dedicated to my forebears, including Stephen Hopkins and his wife who landed in Plymouth Rock in 1620 on the Mayflower, and to pioneer great-grandparents, the Campbells, the Littlefields, the Halladays (my wife's family), the Johnsons, and a single mother and my great-great  grandmother, Marie Stubbs Wiseman and her son, Richard William Wiseman (my great-grandfather whose photo appears here) who crossed the Plains from Iowa to Utah from 1848 to 1853 to find a place where they could live and worship in peace. Their faith and determination to find and help build a "Shining City on the Hill," a New Jerusalem, is a flame I tried to rekindle in this book. No longer is there an untamed wilderness for us to sail to, no place to where we can drive an ox team, or push a handcart, so I created one in my imagination. It is my hope that as children of a noble birthright we may carry on and keep this dream alive and be willing to give what they gave:

Everything!

Praise for the Invitation:

I admit that my deepest thoughts are increasingly occupied with the longing for a better world. Admittedly judgmental, I feel surrounded by greed, lies and corruption in government, business, and even college campuses. I long for that city of light upon a hill that the author so eloquently has described.

—Don Gull, Retired Broadcast Executive, Entrepreneur

I just finished The Invitation while the world around me was literally in chaos. I did not want the book to end as it gave me hope for better things to come. The author does such an amazing job of describing the scenery in the book that I wanted to jump into the pages to experience it first-hand. The characters in the book remind me of people I know. This is a must read if you are wondering what we can do as a people to rise above the mess we see around us today.

— Keri Lafferty, Sales Manager

Years ago, a Brazilian rabble rouser named Paolo Coelho saw the light and started writing spiritual novels. His gift for mixing the supernatural world and natural world in startling ways would, in time, make him the bestselling author in the world. GM Jarrard, perhaps unwittingly, has chosen to mine a similar vein with his novel, The Invitation. Driven by punchy prose, spirited dialogue, and a reality-bending narrative, Jarrard's book engages in many ways. And the story—a kind of mind-melding Pilgrim's Progress—would almost surely intrigue the great Coelho himself.

—Jerry Earl Johnston, Former Religion Editor and Columnist

GM Jarrard has created multiple characters, each interesting, realistic, and empathetic. I constantly wanted to read just one more chapter to discover what happened in their lives. The Invitation relates to our day with universal themes that compel the reader to reflect on the present, past, and future. It's a hopeful look at the world we find ourselves in today.

—Rob Bishop, former Member of Congress,
Utah's First Congressional District (2003–2021)

Jarrard's sense of humor made me smile often. The main characters, Joey and Dana, have a tender relationship that has the realistic undercurrent of tension common in most marriages. Other characters, especially Jonathan Blum, are extremely likable. I was eager to find out what happens to each of them. The Invitation is a thoroughly enjoyable adventure with a hopeful message.

—Jeffrey Kirk, Retired Former CFO

The Invitation is a beautiful mix of intrigue, history, and imagery that pulls the reader in quickly. GM Jarrard's characters invite one into a world free from the challenges of our day with messages of hope and scripture salted with history. It vividly lays out a world most long for. Especially poignant as we emerge from 2020.

—Sharon Webb Myler, Owner Capital Broadcasting

I found The Invitation to be a fascinating, fast-moving story that cleverly combined a staccato narrative style like that in The Hunt for Red October, unhindered travel through time like that in Bid Time Return, and the inclusion of historical figures and events like those in Forrest Gump, all intermixed with scriptural references to enduring truths. At the end, after a wild ride, I was left with great hope for America and for each of us as individuals.

—Neil Smith, Retired Attorney

"Today, religion in America and the constitutional protections of religion are hot topics in the courts and in the media. They should be hot topics at the water cooler and the dinner table as well. Not since the "Left Behind" book series has a novel juxtaposed religiosity against a society that seems to have lost its way. "The Invitation" takes us on a ride to a place that stirs our imagination and taps into a yearning that all people of faith share. Just as James Hilton's "Lost Horizon" took us to Shangrila, GM Jarrard's "The Invitation" takes us to "the shining city on a hill" during a time of contemporary cultural distress. Readers will share a desire and wish "if only the fantasy could be true." Jarrard describes the world we live in and the world we hope for. Perhaps, it will serve as a wake-up call to readers and leaders to create their own "shining city on a hill."

—Bruce Hough, National Committeeman for Republican
Party of Utah, retired CEO

PREFACE

ONE NATION, UNDER GOD

I first learned the Pledge of Allegiance when I was in the first grade in Sherman School on the outskirts of Salt Lake City back in the early 1950s. The last few words seemed to sum it all up for me: "One nation, under God, indivisible, with liberty and justice for all."

Those words sunk in.

They still do.

So, when I watched cities burn, rioters run unchecked through American cities, and a "free press" ignore the facts and perpetuate a Leftist agenda last year, I anguished. Lying with a straight face had become the norm and vindictiveness for others with whom one disagrees a national pastime. I became convinced that our republic is in peril. I looked for an escape. Instead of traditional media, I began binge-watching The Chosen, a dramatization of Christ's entrance onto the world's stage as he gathered followers and began teaching the Good News. The Savior tells his small band that "His Kingdom is not of this world," and it struck a chord. I recalled how pilgrims, Puritans, and pioneers, left "the Old World" behind and sought a new place where they could establish "A Shining City on the Hill" as first described by the Puritan leader John Winthrop in 1630.

In other words, I wrote **THE INVITATION** under duress.

Since I could not find an untouched, virgin place of refuge on any map to where we could sail or drive an ox team, I invented one.

That's when I began "binge-writing."

The result is the book you have in your hands: **THE INVITATION**. It asks the question, if you discovered a place where the people "were of one heart, one mind, dwelt in righteousness with no poor among them, what would you give to gain entrance to such a place?"

Put another way, would you like to live in a place that really was "one nation, under God, with liberty and justice for all?" It's an ideal that appeals to our "better angels," as Lincoln said; a place where, to quote Martin Luther King, "people are judged not by the color of their skin, but rather by the content of their characters."

In **THE INVITATION**, we get a glimpse of such a mythical place. The first character we meet is Jonathan Blum, a military attaché at the US Embassy in Israel, who still carries the burden of visiting concentration camps after World War II and prosecuting war criminals. But when he gets his invitation, his life mission and his outlook are both changed as he helps others, like Joey and Dana Kunz, find their way to the "Shining City."

When we are introduced to the Kunzes, nothing was going to stop Joey from finally getting the multi-million dollar payday due from the tech company he helped start, except perhaps his grandmother. All she wanted was a weekend of his time to help her move to a spa retreat in the mountains.

It sounded simple enough. But, when he and his wife Dana follow a mysterious hand-drawn map to take the old woman to a place no one has ever heard of, suddenly it's 1925 and Calvin Coolidge is President. Instead of the chaos and corruption of today, they discover a small-town paradise with healing waters, no crime, no sickness, and no death. To stay, they need an invitation.

Easier said than done.

It wasn't so much the suspicions cast at them, comments by the media comparing Joey with cult leaders Jim Jones or David Koresh, accusations of embezzlement, or even a kidnapping that would stop him.

Rather, it was whether or not he'd keep his $12 million payout OR accept The Invitation to the Shining City on the Hill.

That's the $12 million question.

TABLE OF CONTENTS

Part I

Return to Normalcy

Nevertheless. we, according to his promise,
look for new heavens and a new earth,
wherein dwelleth righteousness.

I Corinthians 1:9

1950

Jonathan Blum put his shoes and socks back on. "Wading in the Mediterranean would be more enjoyable if you didn't have to roll up the cuffs on your suit pants and weren't wearing a tie. This is such an odd place for a job interview," the 49-year-old lawyer said to no one in particular as he tied his shoes.

He was sitting on history, a block of sandstone, a fragment of the Roman aqueduct at Caesarea, now officially part of the nation of Israel. It was approaching dusk. For nearly ten years, all he had seen was chaos, war, and retribution, and for a brief moment, he had found peace, right here on this beach, where Herod the Great had built the aqueduct right above his head.

Captain Blum was a US military attaché at the US Embassy in Tel Aviv. Israel was now a state in its own right—already two years old. He was in the Promised Land. When he first set foot in Haifa a year ago, there was a moment when time stood still, a pause, no heavenly choirs, no parting of the sea, rather a calmness that quietly enveloped him. Israel knew him—it welcomed him. For a Jew, he was right where he belonged.

Or so he thought.

Blum turned at the sound of footsteps behind him. A man was approaching. Was he the one?

There was a vague familiarity in the man's eyes that transfixed him. Bright blue even in the dusk, brighter than any other he had seen. They were the color of the sea.

"*Sh'lam I-ken. Mah lak?*" the man said.

"Sorry, I don't speak Hebrew. Just some Yiddish. I'm Jonathan Blum," he said.

"It's Aramaic. My name's John. Nice to finally meet you."

They shook hands.

His were the strong hands of a working man, hands with history. John had long hair hidden under a headdress that could either be Arab or Israeli—hard to tell and a full black beard. But, his most distinguishing feature were his eyes.

Blum was a bit shorter and stockier than the stranger but appeared taller thanks to his halo of dark but receding curly hair. His infectious smile and the gleam in his eye had served him well, first in courtrooms and in the halls of power, then in the Army's Judge Advocate Corps.

They seated themselves on facing blocks of stone.

Blum spoke first. "I must say, I have been intrigued by your request to meet me here in such an unconventional place. You're quite the man of mystery."

John smiled. "Yes, I've heard that before."

Blum opened his small leather attaché and pulled out a recently typewritten vitae. He handed it to John.

"Let's walk and talk," John said. "It's a beautiful day turning into a beautiful night." He looked over Jonathan's résumé as they strode down the strand.

"So, you left the district attorney's office in January 1942, to join the Army? And you learned German?"

"Yes, my grandparents often spoke to me in Yiddish, so it wasn't a stretch to learn the language. I put it to good use interrogating POWs after D-Day," Blum explained.

John handed the résumé back to Blum. The sun was traveling lower in the sky, and the tide was coming in; the sand was wet, and there were now two long sets of footprints behind them.

"So, what exactly are you looking for? What is the position you need filled?" Blum asked.

"Actually, Jonathan, we are creating a position specifically for you. We need you. As I said, we've been watching you ever since law school. We watched you in Germany, first at the camps, then at the Nuremberg trials, and finally at the tribunal in Tokyo. Gruesome business," John said.

"Yes, gruesome, that's probably the right word. A stone tied around your leg would be another way to describe it. What I experienced in the camps rarely leaves my thoughts. It's so unfathomable . . . so heavy. I'm still looking for ways to lose the stone—the burden," Blum said with a sigh.

"Perhaps we have just the solution. So, here you are now, distancing yourself from Tokyo and the Third Reich, hopefully, one day, distant memories. We were happy when we heard the new ambassador to Israel needed a military attaché. We put in a good word for you. You earned your accolades."

"Who's we?"

"We'll get to that later." John changed the subject. "So, you were in-country when the Israelis finally sent the Arab armies packing, actually right in the middle of it, is that right?" John asked.

Blum nodded and John continued. "Not married, no prospects?"

"No, I'm a widower, but you probably already knew that."
John stopped near a large piece of driftwood that appeared to be part of a boat. He looked around, saw that they were alone, then pulled a valise out of his coat, held it for a moment, and then presented it to Blum.

"This may come as a surprise, but we are extending to you an offer. As you will see, it's more than just a job. It has many benefits, a generous retirement, and more than a lifetime of service. And also a list of names, a very long list, along with instructions. It provides details about the Invitation."

"The Invitation?" Blum asked.

"Yes, look in the folder. It's our offer along with our expectations. If you accept it, be at the Caesarea port Saturday night after Shabbat. Bring your duffel, suitcases, everything. We'll leave at dark. We're taking a boat ride. And, I'll be there to welcome you aboard. Go ahead, you may open it now," John said.

The envelope looked ancient, crafted out of hand-made paper and closed tightly with a large wax seal. Jonathan put the other documents, the packet of names and instructions into his attaché case and set it all down on the sand between his feet. Now, he was focused on the offer he had just been given.

The sun had set, but there was still enough light to read the invitation.

He ran a finger across the envelope, turning it over, hoping for a clue about its contents. Tentatively, he was treating it like the Nag Hammadi papyri. Carefully, Jonathan broke the seal and opened it. What he read inside cemented him in the sand. Immovable. Is this possible? He turned to John for an explanation, but he was gone. Vanished!

Jonathan Blum stared at the footsteps in the sand—two sets led back to the aqueduct where they had first met. No footprints were leading away. Where did he go?

Then and there, Blum's course was set.

DECADES LATER

Blum set the atlas on the back of the trailer, now fully-packed, bulging with law books, tools, and a few modern conveniences. He found the page he was looking for and folded the corner over to mark the spot. Bounder, his Border Collie/Poodle mix, stared at his master in anticipation, tail wagging.

"Where's Bruiser?" Blum asked the dog. "Go get him. Hurry!" Bounder obeyed. That was the difference between the two dogs, Bounder obeyed. Bruiser didn't. Jonathan mused. Brothers from the same mother still pick their own path, don't they? Just like us.

He grabbed the atlas and waited for the dogs. Bruiser had escaped to the beach chasing a couple of seabirds until Bounder brought him back, more Border Collie than his litter-mate.

"Come on, boys!" Blum yelled. He opened the back of his tricked-out custom van, the gas hog that he couldn't get rid of but knew he should. He wanted a caddy, a restored classic, and had found a few classified ads here and there that were tempting, but he dismissed the idea. It was a weakness, he decided.

"Wanna go meet the boss? Go someplace with room to run? Get in! Say goodbye to Marco Island. We're gonna miss it."

Three days, two campgrounds, and nearly 2,000 miles later—

and further away from their be-loved beach house—Blum, Bounder, and Bruiser turned down the old country road and parked below the billboard, their appointed meeting spot.

"Let's stretch our legs, boys," Blum said. He opened the van and out they ran, sniffing and marking their territory. They were out in the country on an early fall morning with the grass heavy with dew. Bruiser spooked a pheasant who spooked him back, flying over their heads. "Back in the van!" he shouted. They all scurried back in and settled down. Nap time.

Barking dogs awoke Jonathan. He rubbed his eyes and through the windshield saw a man he recognized sitting on a stump next to the signpost, just waiting patiently, a smile on his face.

"Sit still, boys," Blum commanded as he exited the van and shut the door. He hesitated, took a breath, and walked toward him as he arose.

"Happy Birthday, Jonathan," John said as they shook hands. Blum was momentarily surprised, then remembered who his mentor was; he nodded in appreciation.

John looks so contemporary, Blum thought. He was wearing a Detroit Tigers baseball hat with a capital 'D' embroidered on it and a battered, old brown leather flight jacket. His handmade goat-skin travel bag was at this feet. "Want to see your birthday present? It's a few miles down the road. Let's go. Hope you like apples."

Jonathan Blum parked "Big Brown," his oversized brown and orange van, equipped with two gas tanks, on the gravel between a red barn and a metal building where a forklift was idling just as the overhead door opened. John was talking to a big, rugged-looking man in overalls as Blum released his hounds, both overcome with canine joy. So many new smells!

First Bruiser and then Bounder made a mad dash for the orchards behind the buildings and the large farmhouse. John motioned to Blum, who walked toward the storage building. Mysterious John's unusual appearance in person piqued Blum's interest—he surmised that something important was going on.

"Jonathan Blum, meet Walter Johnson. Walter, Mr. Blum, is our attorney who has been assisting us for years," John said as the two strangers shook hands.

"Big Train Johnson?" Blum said. "You're Walter Big Train Johnson? I saw the game with Babe. Sorry about that. I'm a Yankee's fan," Blum said.

"That's okay. I think after today everyone will be a New York fan," Walter said, "at least for a while." The comment went right over Blum's head, but he'd know soon enough what he meant.

"Walter played baseball," Blum told John as they walked to the house.

"I know," John said. "I've seen a game or two. Let's walk and talk in the orchard."

For the next couple of hours, they discussed the handover of the apple operation from Walter to Blum, from a farmer-turned baseball player, then farmer again, to a lawyer-turned apple grower. Jonathan wondered what could have prompted John to make a personal appearance. It was unusual, but then, today would be unusual in many tragic ways.

"One thing I can assure you," Blum said, " is if any apple grown here ever gets into legal trouble, it'll have the best representation any fruit has ever had." That comment drew smiles from both men, then John gave Blum an assurance of his own.

"Whatever these apples need, I'm confident you'll provide that. I hope you like your birthday present."

"Love it," Blum said. "Hope there's an apple pie somewhere to celebrate it. And it would have to be quite large to accommodate all the candles."

But what Blum didn't know was that there wouldn't be many celebrations anywhere today, except maybe in Tehran or Kabul.

It was September 11, 2001.

PRESENT DAY

Margritte Kunz was just one of a couple of dozen residents waiting for dessert in the dining hall at the Columbus Independent Living Center.

But she was the only one of the inmates, as she called them, who could pronounce apfelstrudel correctly.

Today's dessert du jour had always been her favorite.

What's more, she was the only one in the dining hall who knew how to send emails and text messages, which was what she was doing while waiting for her strudel.

Technology wasn't the only thing that separated her from the rest of the white-haired crowd. The others knew they were old and accepted it and what was to come afterward. She accepted none of those things.

"Life was made for living," she would always tell family and friends, and especially Joey, whom she raised from the time he turned ten.

Wiry and sporting a wild mop of white hair that would go crazy 'Einstein' if she didn't take precautions, Margritte walked, hiked, and went to the gym as recently as five years ago. But once she turned the corner on 90, even her iron will wasn't enough to forestall the inevitable.

And that angered her, especially since the management of her old-age hostel wanted to upgrade her lifestyle, which is why she was determined to finish her long, rambling text message on her new Surface tablet, a gift from Joey Kunz, her grandson.

Texting was a fairly recent discovery, and she was not afraid to let her views be known to politicians, talk show hosts, and—much to the chagrin of her recipients–to them as well. But, Joey? He usually ignored many of her texts and emails or just didn't see them.

She raised Joey after his mother died, while his father, a Vietnam veteran, had worked overseas doing unmentionable jobs for the government until he died a few years ago. Joey still harbored some resentment toward his father for leaving him with his grandmother after his mother died and often complained about it to his grandmother. "Why is his job more important than me?" he would ask.

She would try to explain that "It is complicated–a lot of people in high places depend on your dad–his only option would be to quit, and he doesn't know what else he would do. He loves you very much, Joey. Besides I need you–we'll have fun, you'll see."

She had been true to that promise. Ever since he was a teenager, Joey had followed in Oma's footsteps, often literally. One summer years ago, the two of them hiked the Adirondack Trail from northern Georgia all the way to the Shenandoah Valley. And when she took a summer-long sabbatical in Germany, Joey went along too.

She really made an impression on him. Much of her summer sabbatical in Germany was spent in Heidelberg at the university where she finished her Ph.D. thesis on Mark Twain's famous satirical essay, *The Awful German Language*. Despite the difficulty in learning it, Joey could speak a little German when he left, he loved the food and the teenage German girls who all loved him in return!

He always said that the summer in Europe with Oma was his all-time favorite.

But, that didn't mean he was going to drop everything, read and reply to every text, email, and phone call from his grandma that came his way. He was already overwhelmed with the daily demands made on him at the start-up that was growing by 10 to 15 percent every month.

Just the same, she was unrelenting in her demands.

Joey's wife Dana shamed him into at least acknowledging messages when he received one from Grandma, whom he was supposed to call Oma (German for grandma). So far, he had resisted both Oma and Dana. He was presently swimming in alligators and being chewed up by piranha every day at work. So usually he would ignore the trivial. In this case, the email from Oma. He didn't have time to do what he wanted, given the unpleasant people for whom he was currently working.

Oma was convinced that today would be different, that he'd get right back to her once he read the subject line along with the 'highly persuasive content' she was just finishing. She was confident of that. So, there she was, just about ready to send him her digital masterpiece while in the cafeteria, multi-tasking. She was focused. She was possessed, even more so since the center's management informed her that because of her age and health, she needed to move to the assisted living section for her well-being. She didn't just say no, she said hell no!

"Charging me nearly $6,000 a month from now on, instead of my usual $2,500 isn't for my well-being, it's for yours," Margritte told the manager. She wanted to tell him what she really thought but that would be unbecoming of someone of her education and upbringing!

Sure, the money was one thing, but she had an even more compelling reason to make the Great Escape—Virginia Tracy. Oma and Virginia had been best friends since their college days. They both were attendants at each other's wedding, sent cards and gifts at the birth of every child, even though they lived a thousand miles apart, and showed up when each was widowed.

She explained to Joey in detail how a week ago last Sunday afternoon, Virginia showed up at the center. Oma was getting ready to head to the dining hall for paprika chicken breasts and fettuccine Alfredo (two of her favorites) when the front desk called her.

"An old friend's here to see you," Miss Elizabeth said. "And, her name . . ."

Oma interjected; she was in a hurry so she could get the table by the window. "Well, tell 'em I'm just on my way to the dining hall. I'll buy dinner if they meet me in the cafeteria."

Oma wasn't sure who her guest was, but she hoped it was Virginia; she had heard that Ginny had recently moved back from Illinois. She grabbed her cane so she could get there sooner. Her favorite table was over on the right side of the hall between the window and the salad bar because, as she told her guests, the patrons were so slow that if you didn't get in the front of the line you'd be wheeled off before you got to the pickled beets.

She put on her glasses and scanned the perimeter. No hunched-over Virginia in sight! Oma looked right, left, and the only person standing there was an attractive middle-aged woman in a pretty red dress. The woman was waving at her. Not to be impolite, she waved back. The woman made a beeline for Oma's table.

When she yelled, "Maggie, it's me! it's me!" Oma thought, "No you're not, you imposter!"

The woman had Virginia's voice and the nicely-formed legs of a young Virginia, the bright smile and flashing white teeth of the coed Virginia she knew seventy years ago, but this was impossible.

Just the same, it WAS Virginia!

For the first time in her life, Margritte Müller Kunz, Ph.D., aka 'Maggie' and 'Oma,' was speechless.

"What's wrong, Kiddo, cat got your tongue? Did you have a stroke or something?" Virginia asked.

Oma didn't answer.

"I'm starving," Virginia said. "Worked out this morning. What's good here?" Oma didn't answer, but Mrs. Littlefield at the next table answered for her, "Nothing. Nothing at all."

Virginia was worried. "Maggie? You okay?"

Finally, Oma was able to form words. "I thought I was okay—until I saw you. Now I feel like I'm one of those walking dead people in those movies, what are they called . . . ?"

"Zombies, Mrs. Kunz," Littlefield's loquacious table-mate said. "They're zombies. Look at us–we all are!"

Oma gave her the old mind-your-own-business look. That seemed to work.

Finally, Oma regained her focus, looking her old friend up and down. "Ginny, how much did you spend on all of this? Did you go to a wax museum? Will you melt?"

"Dear sweet Maggie, my oldest and dearest friend, in good times and bad. I'm here because I love you, and because I am allowed to give you this." Virginia handed Oma a 5 by 7 antique-felt envelope shut tight with a wax seal. "This is for you."

Maggie examined it and looked baffled. "What is this?"

Virginia beamed, tears welling in her eyes. "It's your invitation!"

"To what?"

"A way out of Zombieville," she said as she twirled around as if she were revealing a brand new outfit. "To this!"

Oma held the envelope up to the light and even smelled it. "Should I open it?" She was more than just curious. Excited? Apprehensive? Afraid? Maybe all of the above.

"Not yet. There are instructions inside, including a map and contact information explaining where you are to go to take the next step. Sometime soon, you'll meet someone who will tell you more," Virginia explained as she handed her a much thicker packet.

"Why should I accept an invitation when I have no idea what is expected of me at the party or event where I'm invited or whatever it is going on. I like mysteries and puzzles, but I don't get it."

"Neither did I, but here I am. You have to take a leap of faith. If you're happy with your current situation, then just forget about it. But, here I am, your best friend since the fall of 1948—look at me. As you can see, the results are, well, life-changing. I'm 89 years old, and I feel 50 and look maybe 60."

"So, what are you doing there?"

"Taking classes, painting, and learning to play the cello. But I'm doing what I really love to do. I opened a little boutique making and selling quilts. Always loved doing that."

"You always were the queen bee of quilting," Oma said.

"That's what I'll call it!"

"What?" Oma asked.

"My shop! Queen Bee Quilts! What a great idea!" They were now back in their old groove. They covered the last 70 or so years in less than 70 minutes. When they were finished, Virginia remembered what Jonathan Blum had asked her to do. 'Send me a note after Maggie gets her invitation." Will do!

It was coming up on harvest time at the Blum apple operation. Jonathan was checking orders when a long-awaited message arrived.

"M. Kunz given invitation." Good! He had known the Kunz family for decades now, ever since Professor Müller, Margritte's father, had taught him German at the Army's Language Institute. She was a pistol as a teenager and hadn't changed much since then.

So, now it was her time. That meant all the pieces had to be in place. He would have to get a message to Walter. The Kunz family was integral to their plans. Events were taking place faster than Blum had anticipated. With the apple harvest coming on. he would need to get more help.

After she considered the conversation she had with Virginia a couple of weeks ago, Margritte Kunz had made the tough decision. She had decided to jump off the bridge with Virginia. She pushed the SEND button. Now, it was Joey's turn. She crossed her fingers.

2

Of all the common characteristics that Margritte, or Oma, and Joey Kunz shared, one stood out above all. They were both tough when the situation demanded it. Yes, they were reasonable when someone made a rational argument and defended it well. Fair and funny. Patient, up to a point, but when a lot was at stake, they both were willing to make the right call—even when it was painful or even frightening. So she hoped Joey would understand and comply with her request.

She didn't realize that he was under immense pressure. When she had sent her request, he and his young assistant, Rachel, were huddled over a schematic for a new hierarchy that the software engineers had developed, a way to process documents and requests faster and tie them directly to the content that he and his crew were developing.

He didn't like it.

"You can't just automate this step. Content developers have to make the final decision before we download their courses. They must have the opportunity to talk directly with the client beforehand."

Rachel wasn't sure. "But, Gunderson wants it all to go faster. Let AI (artificial intelligence) do it," he said.

"Tell them to find a way for a staffer to have the final sign-off before it goes to the client, okay?"

"Okay."

Just as they were finishing their conversation, he heard his laptop chime . . . "incoming email . . ."

He looked at the ID. "Not Oma; not today!" he blurted out.

"Who's Oma?" Rachel asked.

"My grandma," he admitted.

"You better answer her. How old is she?"

"Just turned 90 she's a real pill. I love her, but she can never accept no for an answer . . ."

"Joey . . ." she gave him the official eye-roll generally employed only by wives.

You too? he thought. "Gimme a second . . ."

"Are you the only person in the family who can help her? What about your parents, a brother or a sister?" Rachel asked.

Joey was silent for a moment. "It's a sad story, actually," he admitted. "My mother died when I was 10 years old. Then I went to live with my grandma. Thank goodness for her!"

"What about your dad?"

"That's a good question. What about my dad? His secret work with the government was more important than me, I guess. My mom was dead and buried before we could even find him, and he still didn't come to see me that year until Christmas. I was hurt and mad then, and I'm still mad now. He died about 20 years ago on assignment in the Philippines; he must be buried there. It doesn't matter now, does it?"

She didn't say a word . . . just looked out the window. What could you say?

But, he needed to clear it up for himself as well as Rachel. "At the end of the day, she is the only person I know who ever loved me unconditionally and put me first, before anything else, so, yes, if Dana agrees, I will do as Oma asks," he confessed.

"Yep, gotta keep the wife happy," Rachel agreed.

They were still in the conference room, in the corner of a new building with a great view of the river and downtown. The company, OJT Partners, occupied three floors and needed more. They pioneered new techniques to help employers train employees on the job, primarily those in technology applications and specifically new hires in online sales and customer service. They also gave him a similar responsibility for the training of their help; and for good measure, had him take on the HR responsibilities, too. So far, he had just been bending under the weight; soon or later, he feared, he might just break.

Joey's clients had been using the curricula he had developed which were making the founders of OJT millionaires, but his salary hadn't changed. For each employee in various training programs, clients were billed on the average of $25 a month. Do the math. He did every day. The company was now close to 150,000 subscribers, generating almost $3,750,000 a month, projected to grow 15 percent more by the end of the year. He was hoping to cash in on the company's success. His assistant Rachel was hungry for scraps too and was attached to him like a suckerfish riding on the back of a Great White.

Finally, he opened Oma's email and started reading her essay in earnest. It looked as long as a novel, and it had attachments! How did she know how to do that?

And, this was the kicker. Oma wanted him to drop everything and take her to a spa-living center somewhere upstate by Friday! She had to vacate her tiny three-room living quarters at the center because, in her words, "They're kicking me out. They think I'm going to fall and break a hip or something just because I'm 90! Management says that because of my health and age, I need to move to the Assisted Living wing and pay $6000 a month instead of $2500. Joey, I don't have that kind of money!"

Joey slapped his forehead. She had the money, and he knew it. She was an eternal Depression-era miser, and it was supposed to elicit sympathy from people like Rachel, who was standing right there reading the email over Joey's shoulder. It worked.

"Why that's terrible," Rachel said.

He gave her a shaded look. "You're right. It is terrible. I guess I better go talk with Gary. I'll need to take tomorrow and Friday off and drive back over the weekend. Can you please wrap up all this for me? Send out memos to everybody, just let me see it all first."

He put his laptop in his bag, grabbed a few files, and made the long walk down to the corner office to see if the High and Mighty Gary Gunderson was accepting visitors.

Rachel saw this as a great opportunity to shine, to put her newly minted MBA to work.

She just hoped Joey would read her email before she had to distribute it. What if he didn't?

That evening, Joey sat on a folding chair with his laptop on their new $2,000 dining room table; he grumbled that if they had been a little less extravagant, they might have been able to afford some chairs to go with it. But in a brand spanking new house out in the tony suburbs, you couldn't sit around an Ikea table, now could you?

Their big, new 84-inch Samsung smart TV was playing in front of them, revealing the latest in burning cities, riots, Neo-Marxists, and the Cancel Culture advocates tearing everything down. What was the world coming to? No wonder Joey and Dana were both experiencing a dark moment. An ominous cloud was hanging over everything. No place to run, no place to hide.

"Dana, would you please grab the remote and turn that garbage off? Please take a look at Oma's crazy text message. She says it's an email, but it's really a text message with attachments if you can believe it. Shouldn't have given her that Surface tablet. Anyway, it sounds like she's got herself involved in some kind of weird scheme. I can't make heads nor tails out of it," he shouted.

"I'm fixing dinner. Can't overcook the salmon, you always say!"

"And you always tell me not to ignore Oma's requests. She practically raised me. Remember, you remind me of that whenever she comes up."

"All right, all right." She didn't want to, but she came anyway. He pushed the Power Book over to her and pointed out all the fine print that Oma had included in her lengthy memorandum.

"Where's Salem's Crossing?" she asked.

"Upstate? I dunno. Never heard of it, but that's what she says." She pulled out her iPhone and opened up Google maps.

"Look, there's nothing here, nada," she said, puzzled. "Maybe she's been hornswoggled by some con man; she says it's near a sanitarium, a rejuvenation center, and hot springs resort; a spa for geriatrics at a place called Salem Springs. Look at this. She sent them a $5,000 deposit . . . to the Cayman Islands! I'm going with you. She needs a lawyer, so this lawyer is going with you. Just gotta be back Sunday. I have another pointless appointment with my new OBGYN . . ."

"Pointless? You gotta try."

"Easy for you to say. You don't have to be poked and prodded. Back to Oma. If someone's trying to rip her off, I'll bet my $300,000 law degree that I'll be paying off for years to come to some good use," she ranted.

"Easy now, Johnnie Cochran . . . you don't know . . ."

"Don't be such a smart ass; it sounds like a scam to me. Besides, you're the one who was all worked up. The fish is probably salmon jerky by now!" She stomped off. He yelled after her, "Well, I have to be back early Monday too."

An hour later, they had dinner out on their newly-poured patio, sans sod, fence, and landscaping . . . just a couple of spruce trees to shade them from the late afternoon sun.

"When is this going to get all this finished? You said your college buddy was starting any day now," Dana said, motioning at the bare ground in front of them.

He paused to try to keep things civil. Nobody wants Johnnie Cochran coming after you. For an instant, he empathized with OJ Simpson; but only for a fraction of a second.

"I called him before I came home, told him I'd get back to him Monday after Oma is properly locked up and out of trouble."

She grunted and left.

"You can clean up." Hangdog, he nodded in acceptance, tail between his legs.

Way to go, Oma! Joey thought as he sent his grandmother a text informing her that they'd be there bright and early the next morning. His three-year-old marriage was starting to slip a bit downhill due to baby problems and the lack of prospects from any law firms, at least until she passed a looming bar exam. Dana had only been around Oma a few times now. Joey usually took care of Oma by himself because she was in the Center, except for holidays. He was convinced that his wife would regret coming along.

Maybe Dana will learn a lesson . . . to let sleeping Oma's lie.

"Yes!" the old lady exclaimed when she got Joey's answer. "What to take? What to take?" she asked herself. Gotta take my books, some household items. But she wasn't sure what. She added three suitcases of clothing, a set of instructions, and some legal documents, along with letters and photos. All of that she would leave right there on the countertop for Joey when he returned to clear everything else out.

Per Oma's instructions, they brought the Explorer with all its rear storage room. Before they drove off with her to Shangri La, it was packed to the ceiling, including four boxes of books, dishes, and 90 years of memorabilia which included photos, souvenirs, and clothing filled to the ceiling in the back, and several suitcases stacked on top. Good thing Joey always kept bungee cords stored in the SUV.

"Diana, it's so nice of you to join us," Oma said as she squeezed into the backseat with a carry-on bag, a sack of groceries, and a box of kitchen utensils.

"Her name is Dana, Oma," Joey corrected her.

Oma didn't miss a beat. "I know that. Dana is a nickname for

Diana."

Dana replied with a smile. "First time I ever heard that. Thank you!"

Joey engaged his seatbelt, drove out of the parking lot, and turned left, but hesitatingly.

"Oma, where exactly are we headed because we can't find Salem Crossing, or whatever it's called, on Google maps."

"Not to worry. I have a real map printed on paper right here. Head north on the Interstate, drive 75 or 80 miles to the Centerfield exit, turn east, go 12 miles more to the old Sinclair station, and then call this number. We can't drive the car all the way there. Is this a car or a truck . . . ?"

"It's an SUV, Oma," Joey said, clearly frustrated. "Please let me see that!" He pulled the Explorer over next to a 7-Eleven. He studied the map.

"You don't have to get huffy, young man!"

"I'm not huffy. How do we know this place is even real, Oma? You sent these people $5,000, and they can't even be found on Google maps!"

"Joey, Google's maps are not real. Everybody knows that. Google is run by the CCP."

"The what?" Diana, 'er Dana asked.

"The Chinese Communist Party," Oma answered. Joey slapped his forehead.

"The CCP? Come on, Oma!"

"And you sent the check to the Cayman Islands? Only drug dealers and the mob bank in the Cayman Islands," Dana interjected.

"Diana, these are good people. Their Republicans. Their town hall is called the Coolidge Center, you know after President Calvin Coolidge. 'Return to Normalcy.'"

"Man, would I love to return to normalcy," Joey muttered.

"It's all real. Remember my old Canasta partner, Virginia? She mailed me the postcards and the newspaper clippings. And two weeks ago, she gave me the map, the instructions, and my invitation. See for yourself."

"Oma, this postcard has a 4-cent stamp on it. It was postmarked 1925!"

"Well, she sent it to me less than a month ago!"

"What about the invitation? You haven't even opened it," Joey said.

"Not supposed to yet. I need to wait until I get there."

"And, here's a letter with a phone number. I'm supposed to call when we get to a Sinclair station. See here on the map?"

Dana turned pale. "Oma, this number is Hunter 75210. There's no area code. It's like a number from sixty years ago!"

By this time, Joey was back on the highway about to take the on ramp on to the Interstate and had bent his will to hers. "Hope you know 'vat you are doink, Oma. I'm just following ze orders, Frau Oma Leutnant,'" he said mockingly in a German accent.

"*Mich nicht verspotten, Junge!* (Don't make fun of me, boy!) According to Virginia, Salem Crossing is very retro, like Plimouth Plantation. Remember when we went there? The residents were all in character, never deviated. In Salem Crossing, it's like the 1920s, cars, and everything. You'll have fun. We all will."

"What about Salem Springs?" Dana asked.

"Well, according to Ginny, they're close together. It's up a hill through the forest. She called it 'The Shining City on the Hill.' She said that Norman Rockwell once lived there."

"Norman Rockwell, the Saturday Evening Post illustrator?"

"Exactly. We'll have fun, you see."

"Shining City on the Hill?" Dana said to Joey. "That was supposed to have been Boston. Hmm. Interesting."

Joey loved this part of the state with miles of farmland, cornfields, and soybeans interspersed with old stands of forest, some large hardwoods, and lots of conifers. He was happy to leave the pressure cooker of the new start-up and the arrogant, young Millennial trust-fund brats. They're trying to kill me. Maybe that's their real plan!" Oma was practically in a coma. Thank goodness for Joey, while Dana was acting as navigator following the real paper map, not a digital one by the Chicoms.

"What'd you say about 'brats'?"

"Just bellyaching about our youthful management team and wishing I hadn't signed the non-compete clause. I could have done it all myself."

"Right, you just didn't happen to have $10 million of your daddy's money for the start-up. Details, details," Dana corrected him with a smile. He softened. Why be so impatient with everybody; why be such a crank?

Then he remembered why he married her—her smile. It was entrancing. With those black eyes, big eyelashes, and long curly black locks, she had him in her power. And, her laugh! He stared at her, bewitched momentarily. Determined to get pregnant at 41 while she still was young enough to do so, Dana had been working out like a zealot, and it showed. Joey liked what he saw.

She smiled again. "What?"

"You know, I'm powerless around you when you smile, especially when you laugh. And it drives me crazy!"

"I know. That's why I love you, my little Pinocchio. I love to pull your strings and watch you dance."

"Why don't you two get a room?" Oma wisecracked from the backseat.

"We thought you were asleep," Dana said.

"More than asleep," Joey added.

"You wish," then the old lady added, "Are we there yet?"

Dana checked the real map.

"Hmm, shouldn't we about be to the offramp?" she asked.

"Look. It's coming right up. Gee, almost missed it."

He slowed down quickly and heard the luggage on the roof slide forward a bit, then turned right onto the highway.

"Twelve miles or so to the old Sinclair station, according to this hand-drawn map," Dana reminded him. Oma nodded.

Twenty minutes later they were there. It was a real old-time service station, all right, with two working pumps that looked to be fifty years old—regular and ethyl. No credit card payment mechanisms.

They entered the small C-store that looked rather retro itself. The sign at the register said, "cash only–no credit." Not "no credit cards, just "No credit." There was a phone booth in the back. Joey looked around. Beeman's and Blackjack chewing gum. A barrel of apples. Jars of penny candy. Joey approached the friendly old duffer in the overalls behind the counter.

"Hi, I'm Walter," he said with a smile. "Need to change plastic into cash? If so, there's a machine across the street by the bus stop, inside that brick enclosure that looks like an outhouse. Never been in there," Walter said. "You all going up to the Hot Springs spa?"

"Yeah, why?" Joey asked as the women returned from the restroom.

"Because you need to call them from over there in that phone booth. You know the number?"

"Got it right here . . ."

Joey studied the big-boned man in front of him. He seemed different somehow. His aura was warm and friendly. He had big calloused hands, rough from hard labor. He was tanned and looked to have good muscle tone, probably from working outdoors a lot. His hair was grey with a touch of brown. While he was wearing work clothes, overalls with a plaid flannel shirt, he looked robust. It was hard to tell how old he was. Joey was momentarily transfixed.

"Excuse me, you'll need a nickel—for the call. If you don't have one, I'll spot it for you. Pay me back when you return," Walter laughed.

"A nickel, then. Okay, thank you." Joey was truly puzzled now. He walked to the phone booth with the map, the phone number, and the nickel in hand.

The old man spoke up again. "And if you plan on buying anything in the town, they don't take cards or checks. Just cash. Get what you need from that money machine across the street."

"Okay, thanks! Is it like most resort towns, really pricey?" Joey asked as the women joined him.

"No, it's no resort town. It's not like any town you've ever seen. And the prices? Well, you can get a cup of Joe for a nickel and a

BLT for 50 cents. And the meatloaf and mashed potatoes at the Main Street diner? It's a buck twenty-five. Like everybody says, you won't want to leave."

As they left to go to the money machine, the old man added, "One more thing. You can't take those walkie-talkie phones with you. There's no service anyway. And no photos. We have a safe in the back for all your 'trappings of modernity,' including your car keys, electronic watches, and stuff. I'll give you a receipt and a key in case I'm out. Oh, and you might want to take a roll of nice soft toilet paper, unless you like Sears catalogs, just suggesting. They're a buck-fifty for a package of two."

Oma thought it was so funny when she saw "Diana's" face.

"I told you this was going to be fun."

The women walked across the street to get some real money and returned to the C-store and deposited all their trappings of modernity with the codger while Joey called the Salem Transportation Department and told them they were waiting behind the Sinclair station. They unpacked the Explorer and laid all of Oma's earthly possessions out on the gravel. The site was surrounded by groves of old-growth trees with a meadow and a narrow gravel road leading through it up the hill. The meadow was enclosed by a field fence topped with barbed wire. Twenty minutes later, a 1920s style bus, followed by an old pickup with wooden-slatted sides came down the farm road, stopped behind the building, and two young men in overalls. They loaded up everything and everyone into their particular mode of transportation and slowly made their way up the hill, kicking up gravel and dust behind them.

They entered a narrow drive surrounded by pines. Forty-five minutes later, they passed through a covered bridge and entered into a lovely wooded pasture area lined with fruit trees of all kinds on either side. In the pasture, a couple of college-age boys were loading hay bales onto the back of a 1920s era Studebaker flatbed truck. Then, a wagon load of farm produce—apples, pumpkins, and corn from what they could determine—crossed in front of them pulled by two huge black Belgian workhorses.

Oma was delighted, grinning from ear to ear. Joey and Dana were next to her, in shock. Joey spoke. "I think we're in a Budweiser commercial, and I sure could use one right about now."

The driver slowed down, turned around briefly, and spoke. "There's even more up ahead. We can stop if you want to."

Then, they turned a corner revealing some incredible sites.

Joey answered, "Absolutely. Let's stop here for a minute if that's all right." The driver stopped the bus, looking at his watch. "Sure, but only for five or ten minutes. I have a scheduled route up to the Grand Hotel."

"Thanks!"

Dana and Joey jumped off. Joey helped Oma down the stairs.

"Look at this!" Oma said, beside herself, almost giddy. "I told you this was going to be fun!"

"It's more than fun! It's incredible," Dana said.

On the right side of the narrow country road, 10 or 12 men were raising a barn, assembling it timber-frame style, where the posts and beams were held together with pegs and mortise and tenons— no nails, bolts, or staples. Joey watched as they dropped a beam on a post, pounded a huge peg into it to hold it fast, as another couple of workers were tying two joists together, dropping a tenon into a mortise slot that the first man had just finished. Then, two pieces dropped down onto the framework. The site was surrounded by several of the most beautiful flowering trees Joey had ever seen that were also bearing green and ripe fruit.

"What kind of a tree is that? Is that fruit?"

"Yes, it's our variety of sapodilla fruit. Here it's bigger and everbearing," the driver said.

A young boy who was gathering them off the ground in a basket walked over and handed the driver four of them.

"They look like kiwi, but much bigger," Joey said.

"Don't know what that is, but here, try some," he said, taking out a small penknife and quartering one.

"It's delicious! Tastes like a caramelized pear." He turned to give Dana and Oma a bite, but they weren't there. He walked around the front of the bus and couldn't see them. Just beyond a hedgerow and the road, there was a little incline and a break in the hedges. He walked through an archway and found Dana and his grandmother on the other side, both transfixed and observing a very unique scene.

They were sitting on a stone bench near a cart loaded with boxes and boxes of different kinds of fruit. In front of them were dozens of people of all ages using scaffolds and planks, as well as ladders picking, boxing, and gathering off the ground all kinds of different fruit. Some were typical orchard fruits you'd find all over America. peaches, pears, and plums, as well as cherries, all ripe at the same time with blossoms on the trees as well. A dozen or more other carts loaded with their pickings were scattered all over an area at least two acres, maybe more. A little girl brought them a basket of fruit, including some tropical varieties, like the sapodilla fruit that Joey had sampled. Then, they noticed that off to the far right were several rows of other trees that they didn't recognize; one near the front bore large, red and pink pear-shaped fruit that smaller children were gathering off the ground.

"What kind of tree is that?" Joey asked.

"I think that's a mang, uh . . ."

"Mango tree?" Dana asked.

"Yeah, and on the other side are abracadabra trees, I think," the rosy-cheeked little pixie said.

"Avocado?"

"That's right. I don't like them. But, I love the mangos."
Joey turned to Dana. "How do they grow here?"

The pixie answered even though he didn't ask her. "Mister, everything grows here. Didn't you know that this is paradise? That's what my momma calls it. Lots nicer than where we came from."

"Where did you come from?"

"I think they call it Cantrofornia. I was real little. Hope you like our fruit. We pick it every Friday. We all take turns." Just then, the driver found them. "There you are. We need to hurry. I have to take Mrs. Kunz and others up to the hot springs resort."

"And where are we going?"

"The Roosevelt. It's very nice."

3

The green bus dropped Joey and Dana off at the Roosevelt Hotel, named after Teddy, not Franklin, and continued on with Oma, now asleep in the back. It was dark now and hard to make out a lot of detail in this part of town. Almost everything was closed and dark. There was one street lamp on the corner across the street next to a narrow, neat little gabled shiplap-covered house that appeared to be a little boutique. Hard to read the sign. It was too dark.

The hotel was an antique, four-story brick building with an impressive entry leading to an ornate counter with a small bell to summon help. Behind the counter were two roll-top desks on either side, each with a hand-cranked adding machine. A large hotel register was open on the counter, ready for Joey and Dana to supply their information. The well-mannered clerk handed Joey a fountain pen to sign the register. The concierge, Allan, handed Dana a large skeleton key with a wooden number 27 hanging from a chain.

Allan explained, "Turn right behind the dining room to your right, then turn left; it's six rooms down on the right side. It's one of our nicer suites and has a great view of the lily pond from the French doors. If you're hungry, the dining room is still open, featuring the

Thursday special, lamb stew and hot rolls. It's just a dollar. And, of course, your room's been paid for, thanks to Mrs. Kunz."

When he saw Joey's signature, Allan asked. "Are you her kin?"

"Grandson," a bewildered Joey said.

"Don't get many visitors up here. The Hot Springs and the Crossing are sort of . . . well, hard to find."

"We discovered that," Dana said, still in awe of their experience at the "paradise" orchard.

"Where exactly is she. Our driver said the Grand Hotel . . . is it here in town?"

"Who? Mrs. Kunz?" Allan queried. "Oh, your grandmother, yes, uh, I see."

He cleared his throat. "She is up at Salem Springs . . . the Hot Springs at the Grand Hotel. Didn't they tell you? They're having a reception of sorts for her tomorrow sometime. Everyone wants to meet the new German professor. The town's so excited she accepted the invitation to join us here."

"The invitation?" Dana asked, puzzled.

"Yes, how else do you think you all found this place. That's the only way you can get here, you know. You have to be invited. The college has been searching for a German and literature professor for so long. Finally, we have one!"

"But she's 90 years old!" Joey said.

"So?" Allan replied, then continued. "Enjoy the stew. The dining room is closing in 15 minutes. Breakfast is from 7 to 9. Someone from the rejuvenation center will pick you up between 9.30 and 9.45 in the morning to say your goodbyes to Professor Kunz. The bus back to the high-way generally departs at 3 pm. The last bus out of town, I'm afraid. Sweet dreams!"

Joey turned to Dana and whispered, "So?" She was puzzled.

He explained. "He said so when I said she was 90! What's that all about . . . ?"

Dana was engrossed by the furniture and decor. Allan turned to answer the ancient telephone hanging on the wall. "Hotel Theodore Roosevelt! Let me check . . ."

Dana and Joey shuffled to the dining room wondering about everything, including the lamb stew.

"That's it? Only lamb stew," Dana asked bewildered.

"Don't forget the hot rolls," Joey reminded her.

After their meal, they were both surprised and baffled.

"That was good lamb stew!" Joey said.

"Best I ever had," Dana added.

Room 27 was just around the corner. The plaque on the wall said "Bridal Suite." They opened the door to a museum, an antique shop with a large four-poster featherbed, an elaborately-carved dressing table with a settee and ornate high-backed chair, an over-stuffed ottoman, and a reading table and lamp next to a huge walnut wardrobe; and, of course, as promised, a pair of French doors opening to a veranda with the lily pond just beyond. The moon was just coming up, reflecting off the pond.

Dana saw two swans paddle away, a small fawn peeked through a wall of lilacs at the edge of the woods, then ran back in when she opened the doors. Dana seemed very pleased with their accommodations, but then looked around.

"Where's the bathroom?"

"There isn't one," Joey said slyly.

"What?"

"Everything's so authentic, it's probably outside."

"No, not funny . . ." she insisted.

"There's just a WC."

"A WC?"

"Right there, in the cove by the entrance."

"Oh, a WC—a water closet. How authentic. This place is growing on me."

"You'll be happy to know there's real toilet paper in there, too, not a Sears catalog."

"Things are definitely getting better!" Dana disappeared and then returned in a minute, grabbed her bag, and announced.

"I'm taking a bath in the largest, deepest tub I've ever seen. It's sitting on carved, wrought iron legs; I hope I can get in."

"I can help you . . ." he suggested.

She smiled and said, "I'll use the dressing bench, thank you."

While Dana was indulging herself in gallons and gallons of hot water, Joey was checking out the bookcase, the magazines, and newspapers. In the rack next to the bed, he found a magazine, one he'd never heard of. "The Connecticut Yankee." On the cover was a photo of President Calvin Coolidge with the headline. "Happy 53rd Birthday, President Coolidge, Silent Cal, the Sphinx of the Potomac."

He turned to page 25 and picked through the article and learned a few things about the Sphinx. He had made war on the Ku Klux Klan, appointed Blacks to high government positions, and advocated for anti-lynching laws; and in 1924 signed the Indian Citizenship Act. And a pull-out quote from his first Inaugural Address seemed very timely for the era that Joey and Dana just left.

It read: *The fundamental precept of liberty is toleration. We cannot permit any inquisition either within or without the law or apply any religious test to the holding of office. The mind of America must be forever free.*

He put the magazine down and found the local newspaper, *The Hot Springs Bugle.*

They're really putting on a show here, he thought. Why don't more tourists come up here for just the lamb stew?

Like the magazine, the newspaper seemed, well, legitimate. Both had timely ads; the magazine was new. And the Bugle had all kinds of sales, even coupons, along with national and international UPI stories about the rise of Mussolini in Italy and President Coolidge's continual refusal to recognize the Soviet Union.

Then, he saw it, the schedule of weekly events in *"Salem Springs and Crossing."*

At 6 o'clock on Saturday, there was to be a welcoming event at Emerson College for the new Dean of Languages and Literature, Dr. Margritte Kunz. On the same day, President Coolidge himself was going to be visiting in the annual Founders' Day Parade with a band and fireworks that night. *"Come One, Come All,"* the headline announced. He walked over to the French doors, opened them, and walked out onto a little veranda surrounded by lilacs with a small wrought iron table and two matching chairs. The veranda led to a brick path. He walked 20 or 30 feet and sat on a small bench. The sky was brilliant with stars; the last time he remembered a night like this, he was in the Grand Canyon. He leaned back and studied the night sky. He was sort of an amateur astronomer, but as he looked around he saw nothing familiar. It was a crescent moon the night before they left. Now a large full moon was rising from where he thought south should be. It was strange. If that was east, which it must be, north must be to his left; he turned to face what should have been north and started looking for the Big Dipper and Polaris, the North Star. The constellation wasn't there. He needed to ask somebody about that.

Then a verse from the scriptures popped into his head, a line about "A New Heaven and a New Earth." Something I need to look into, he promised himself. Now, it was getting a little chilly. Better get back, he told himself. He walked back and shut the French doors. About that time, Dana came out of the WC wearing a huge red robe and a towel around her head.

"Dana, this place is getting weirder and weirder, from the barn-raising to the tropical fruit orchard, and now an unfamiliar night sky. Plus, take a look at this!" He showed her the announcement about Oma's new position as the head of the Department of Languages and Literature.

She glanced at it, but she had something else on her mind and said, "You're right, it is weird here, but I like this place, even the stew."

Then, she dropped her robe and said, "And I'm liking you better too."

He dropped the newspaper. "It's nice to be liked," he smiled. Dana turned off the light.

They slept in until almost 8.45.

Joey awoke first and shook Dana.

"We're late. If we want any breakfast and want to catch the bus up to the spa or hotel or whatever it is, then we got to dress fast and grab some breakfast. Hurry! Let's go!"

The sun was shining right into the French doors, the pond was stirring from all the waterfowl, and deer were munching on lilacs. As Joey was brushing his teeth, Dana was taking mental pictures. There were apple blossoms and lilacs in August! The path outside was lined with daffodils and tulips and wild roses. A hummingbird streaked by, stalled, and looked through the glass at her. Such brilliant colors!

Joey opened the door to leave, but Dana was frozen in place in front of the French doors.

"Where are we?"

He was in a hurry. "We're late, and breakfast is down the hall. Like you said, let's go!"

She followed him but kept looking over her shoulder through the French doors and out into the garden.

Come on," he said, key in hand ready to shut and lock the door.

"Where are we?" But, Joey was hungry.

"Could be a new heaven and a new earth, I dunno. Maybe we're just crazy." He turned around and grabbed the newspaper on the settee. He locked the door.

"You gotta read this," he said as they hurried into the dining room. Time for breakfast.

Not only did they oversleep, but they also overate. Joey took two plums with him and dropped them into Dana's bag. Just in case.

"Man, those are great plums," he said.

"They're nectarines," Dana corrected him.

Allan opened the door for them as they stepped outside.

They weren't ready for what they saw. It was more Disney than Disneyland, except this was real, wasn't it? Flowers filled window boxes practically on every building, including tropicals and long-hanging blossoms they'd never seen before. Rather than just two or three-story brick-faced and clap-board structures lined up like dominoes in a long row, typical of the late 19th or early 20th-centuries, each building was graced with unique features like landscaped alcoves at the entry, covered with ivy, climbing plants, or even a fountain. To the right of the hotel was an arched bridge you might see in any old town in Europe with a walkway on either side, leading up to a hillside lined with pines interspersed with flowering trees. Pure eye candy! It was the exit up the hill where the bus would later take them to Salem Hot Springs Resort and the Grand Hotel where Oma would be expecting them.

There they were, standing with their bags at the bus stop outside the Theodore Roosevelt Hotel, eyes wide open, not believing what they saw right in front of them as history rolled by. But not the history you'd expect from looking at old black-and-white photos from the 1920s. Yes, there were still horse-drawn wagons on their way to the General Store across the street. Newspaper boys hawking their wares, "The News for a Nickel, the News for Nickel!" Dana pulled a quarter out of her pocket and motioned to the boy dressed in knickers and high topped shoes worn down to the soles.

He gave her the paper and was sorting through his apron for change, and she waved him off.

"Just keep it," Dana said, smiling.

"Thank you, ma'am. You are first class! Hey, look what I got," he yelled to his compadre. They looked at the quarter, and one boy bit it. "Is this real?" They walked away, talking to them-selves, looking back at the strange couple.

People were walking by, smiling and greeting them, on their way to shops or their places of work, doffing their hats, and wishing them a beautiful day. Dana began to wish she had dressed up for the occasion. But weren't they just on a three-day vacation? Hmm. Or was it something much more?

Joey marveled at the nearly century-old ornate architecture and everything was so clean! The shops were filled with the latest merchandise with window dressings that were appealing, but not gaudy; nothing over the top, not appealing to vanity. In the two-story brick building across the street from the bench they were occupying, a potter and his apprentice were shaping vases and crocks at their respective potter wheels; next door, a young black man was at a lathe turning a large piece of what appeared to be oak. Occasionally, he would stop the lathe, inspect his work, sand it here and there and start spinning again. It looked to be almost finished.

In the bakery next door, a young girl filled a display case in the window with a rack of challah bread. Was it Yom Kippur? No, that's next month. Next to it was an assortment of marble rye, sweet rolls, and croissants.

Joey checked his pockets for change. He came up empty.

Dana paid him no attention; she checked her watch. It was almost 10. She reviewed her to-do list and made a note or two when a matronly lady in a long, flowery cotton dress who had been watching from a nearby bench approached her, hesitated, and then said, "Excuse me, but you're strangers in town, aren't you?"

Dana acknowledged her but remained sitting. "Yes, ma'am. Why? Do we look strange?"

She hesitated, "Well, yes, but in a good way. I saw you sitting here, but the bus isn't coming. It's been delayed, you know; because of the President. It's at the train station. Are you here for a reason?"

"Well, yes, we brought my grandmother here. She's up at the spa, hotel; that's where we're headed." Joey explained.

"And just who might she be?"

"My grandmother, Margritte Kunz . . ."

"Oh, the new professor at the college." She smiled. "The whole town's been waiting for her. Too bad you can't be here for her inauguration," the older woman said.

"Inauguration? I thought it was just a reception . . . tomorrow."

The woman sat down by Dana and then spoke in a very low voice, "You can't be here that long. No one from the, uh outside, can stay more than a day. Besides, with your attire, you'll be sure to attract attention."

She tried to select her words carefully, but still, Dana was getting annoyed. "Maybe you should take a look inside at Banberry's, the clothiers. They're pricey, but their products are well-made and are the latest style." She motioned to the store across the street.

Dana whispered, "How pricey?"

"Well, you'd both have to have at least $50 to get anything respectable . . . for the reception, you know. I know the assistant manager, a very nice young man; lives near me. His name is Gerald. Gerald Greenwood. He comes to my boarding house frequently. Tell him to show you 'his specials.'"

She winked and started to walk away.

"Where is it?"

"My boarding house? Oh, not far. Just two blocks north, one block east. At the corner of Adams and Roosevelt."

"Like President Roosevelt?"

"Yes, like most everything around here, those streets are named after presidents. We get quite a few coming through."

Quite a few Presidents. Really? Joey looked at her queerly.

"And, if we wanted to stay at the boarding house? How much?"

"For you two, the upstairs suite, let's say ten dollars a night. Is that satisfactory?"

"Okay," Dana said, "Maybe we'll drop by later."

As she waved and walked away, Joey asked. "Quite a few presidents? That's weird. And, what's wrong with the hotel? I thought you loved it."

"Don't you get it, Joseph? Wherever we are, we're not in a touristy spa town. We're out-of-time outsiders who dropped in from a hundred years in the future. We need to fit in. Who knows how long we'll be 'permitted' to stay here. We gotta figure out what this place is, and where the hell we are! And why is everybody putting on a show just for us? They're not just 'in character.' This isn't like Plimouth Plantation. These people don't go home at night, take off their costumes, and watch Netflix. They're not role-playing. They're real."

Joey smiled. "Wherever it is, it's not hell. Check out that bakery . . . and the potters across the street."

Dana stood, looked around, and peered into her giant purse. "Come on."

"Where are we going?"

"Shopping. We need to find Gerry?"

"Gerry who?"

"Gerald Greenwood, the assistant manager at Banberry's across the street."

He mumbled to himself as they dodged a panel truck and a bright green two-horse hackney. "Most elaborate excuse for a shopping spree I've ever heard of . . ."

"What?"

"Nothing, nothing at all," he said resignedly, as most husbands do when being dragged into a store.

They left Banberry's by the back door about an hour and a half later. It led to a courtyard which led to an alcove of grass, shrubbery, and tree—a park by any other word—and a finely manicured one at that. It was lined on all four sides by tall, well-formed sycamores with elegant brownstones, galleries, tea houses, and cafés here and there, and an occasional cottage set back from the main square. In the middle of the garden was a fountain with winged cherubs, fairies, nymphs—figures from Greek mythology—all carved in marble and arranged in cascading levels, surrounded by an incredible assortment of rhododendrons, azaleas, various succulents, and peach colored tea roses.

Dana stood there mystified by what she saw. They were dressed to the Nines in the latest fashions of the Roaring Twenties. Joey wore an olive-colored tweed suit with a cap and a pair of suede oxfords. But, he wasn't just mystified—he was captivated and enchanted by the 21st-century beauty that stood in front of him garbed in a long navy blue dress with a wrap-around bodice, over-sized sleeves, and an angular-cut hem which started out calf-length on her left leg and rose to just below her right knee.

"Beautiful, isn't it?" Dana exclaimed as she took in the fountain and the surrounding garden.

"Breathtaking!" Joey said, paying little attention to the landscaping, gawking at his wife. "No words for it."

She smiled. "Quit staring! It only cost $40. Not as much as your Bobby Jones signature outfit."

"Who's Bobby Jones?"

"I thought you were a golf aficionado. You know. Best golfer of a hundred years ago, Bobby Jones?"

"You're the golfer, not me. But, you don't look like a golfer right now. Something much more elegant."

She grabbed his arm, gave him the sack with their clothes and her other outfit, and pointed to the little tea room across the square.

She smiled again and asked, "You hungry?"

"Always," he said, still star-struck by his gussied-up wife.

In a few minutes, they were seated outside the open door to the tea room, cozied up next to a hedge of lilacs in full bloom—rich with white, pink, and violet blossoms. Below them was a row of lavender plants hovering over pansies and shading miniature begonias and succulents that avid gardener, Dana, didn't recognize.

They sat at a small wrought-iron table accompanied by matching chairs with a view of the whole square. Soon, a 1920s' parade passed by them consisting of two little girls, one pulling the other in a small red wagon, obviously sisters, a mother in neat flowery cotton dress and bonnet pushed a huge, black baby carriage behind them. Two college-age young men sauntered by in lively conversation, but caught a look at Dana and had to turn, pause, and take a mental photo of her. Joey nudged her under the table and smiled.

"Are you too old or too young for them?"

"Hard to tell," she said with a grin. Joey loved her smile, and today he was getting a lot of them. They enjoyed lemonades, a couple of crab-filled croissants, and an unusual beet salad with chickpeas, celery, and raisins.

She handed Joey a hundred-year-old ten-dollar bill, not a Federal Reserve note, but a $10 silver certificate to pay for lunch.

"This is worth more than $10, a lot more," he said. "We ought to take back as many of these as we can."

She gave him an odd look. "Who wants to go back?" Dana said. "Not me. Pay for the meal. I'm going next door to the stationery shop. The other side of that is a barbershop. Look, a shave and a haircut . . ." she tapped twice on the table . . . "six bits." She laughed and left him there with the bill. He scratched his head. She is an odd wife!

The waitress brought Joey the bill and paused awkwardly for a minute, "Sir, do you have any smaller bills?"

He looked at the tab–$1.95. "How much do you have in your cash bag?" She thumbed through it. Just four dollar bills and some coins.

"Give me, let's say, $2.50 back, and keep the change—as a tip."

She beamed. "Thank you, sir! Thank you!" She almost skipped back to the kitchen.

"What a different world this is here in this little piece of paradise," he muttered to himself. "If only we could stay."

Although his conversation with himself was barely above a whisper, an older gentleman sitting behind him with ham-sized hands wearing a straw hat and drinking tea, interrupted him. "You can, you know, remain here—if you're invited . . . if you know someone or are related to someone already here," the stately-looking man said. He pushed his reading glasses up, smiled, and began counting out change from a small coin purse. Joey wanted to ask the gentleman exactly what he meant, but just then Dana returned. "Joey? Hello!" She surprised him, and he looked back for the man with the straw hat, but he was gone—disappeared.

Dana touched his shoulder. "Got any change?" she asked.

"What change?"

The change from lunch—I left you a $10 bill. Should be enough for a haircut. I have some more exploring to do. Where is it?"

"Let's see," he said as he examined the contents of his pockets. I left a tip . . . a great big $5 tip. You sound like Oma," he said. "About three bucks and change, I guess."

"She must have been cute."

"Who?"

"The waitress."

"Dana, she was close to 120 years old—at least!"

She laughed. She was having fun, just as Oma had predicted. "Come on, let's get you a haircut. Let's get you in style. I'm walking down to the library and museum while you get trimmed. Hurry! What's wrong with you?"

Joey was still looking around for the big man with a straw hat.

After a shave and haircut "for six bits" plus a dollar tip, they began making friends all over town. Dana returned with more items from 1925 loaded in her Banberry bag.

"We need to catch a bus or a ride up to the spa. It's 3.30," she explained to Joey, who was now much more relaxed after his 45 minutes in the barber chair.

"And, what about our bags at the hotel?" he asked.

"Shoot, you're right! We better get over there. Let's hurry."
Half an hour later, they hurried past the same green hackney that almost ran them down before lunch and hurried to the hotel to find Allan, the concierge.

He was waiting for them at the entrance. "Well, here you are finally! We were worried. You've made friends, it appears."

There they stood, staring vacantly at the small prim and proper man, reminding Joey of Inspector Clouseau. He stifled a smile.

"What?" Dana managed.

Allan interrupted her. "The mayor or the judge must have put in a good word for you. Your bags are in the green hackney outside, and you're on your way up to the Grand Hotel at the Hot Springs. It's an hour's ride, so chop-chop!"

"Hackney?" Joey asked.

"The green carriage outside. It's all been arranged."

They stumbled out of the hotel, looking behind them at Allan. Dana poked Joey. "Give him a tip."

She handed a fifty-cent piece to Joey, and Allan gratefully accepted it, bowed slightly, and curled his mustache.

It was time for a carriage . . . make that a "hackney" ride.

$$\textbf{4}$$

There was no AC in the hackney, a fancy weather-tight carriage, but thankfully, this model did have windows that slid open–or closed–plus self-operating fans. No batteries required.

"You know, you'd pay a lot for a ride in a carriage like this in Central Park," Joey observed. Dana paid no attention; she was preoccupied. She grabbed her purse out of her carry-on and began fixing her makeup and hair. Joey mused about how much time women spend on such activities over a lifetime. Fifteen minutes later, Dana was finally satisfied with her artwork.

"Okay then. Let me show you what I found." Dana opened her bag from the clothing store, grabbed her carry-on, and started repacking everything. "It'll blow your mind!"

Just then, the hackney slowed down and stopped near a gated entrance to a large three-story manor at the end of a long wooded lane. The door was opened and another passenger stepped in.

It was the man from the tea room, a judge, it turned out.

He introduced himself. "I'm Judge Stone, Harlan Stone," and pulled out a small pocket-sized notebook. He addressed Joey. "We met briefly at the Tea Room today, didn't we?"

"Very briefly. I looked back to reply, and you were nowhere to be found. Vanished," Joey said.

"Probably late for a meeting. I have many of them; busywork, mostly. Pretty quiet place." Dana stared at him, and Joey nudged her. She winced and gave him a look of warning.

"Harlan Stone, you said?"

"Yes, as I said."

"I thought you were . . ."

"A Supreme Court Justice?" He laughed. "I hear that a lot. This is a lot more, uh, peaceful."

Dana was now suspicious. "Not much crime to speak of here?"

"None whatsoever."

"So, how do you keep busy?"

"Well, as you know, there's more to the law than criminal justice," he said with a slight smile.

She returned the expression.

"And how would you know that I would know?" Dana cross-examined him.

"Because Mrs. Kunz, you were fifth in your class at Vanderbilt Law, specializing in business law, focusing on contracts, deeds, and estate law. And, I was particularly interested in your re-search on the ancient Code of the Ur-Nammu, the legal framework of ancient Mesopotamia. Speak a little Sumerian, do you?" Stone asked with a laugh.

Dana offered no answer; just a vacant stare. Joey laughed.

"What's so funny?"

"I've never seen you speechless before. Your first appearance before a judge and you have nothing to say!"

At that moment, they all broke into laughter. Judge Stone had tears in his eyes.

"The jury rests, ma'am!" Judge Stone managed to get in between guffaws.

"How do you know all these things, Judge?" Dana asked.

"No outsiders ever spend more than a couple of hours here before they are driven back to the highway. We like our privacy," the judge explained.

"And, yet we wonder if all of this is real. Is it?" Joey asked.

"Well, you'll see that for yourself tomorrow when we meet the President of the United States himself, Calvin Coolidge. Your grandmother will be there too. She is very excited; she said her father was a great fan and a great Republican," the judge said with a smile.

"So, I've heard," Joey said. "Over and over and over again."

"The hackney was now on a smaller, unpaved country lane, about to pass through thick forest. And it was bumpy. They were all hanging on tightly to their handholds.

"It's beautiful here," Dana said. "I couldn't help but notice that while people are harvesting apples, some of the trees are also in bloom. There are tulips, daffodils, lilacs, ducklings, and goslings while the wheat is being cut and the pumpkins are ripe. How can this be?"

"You haven't seen beautiful yet, my dear! And, its real beauty isn't in the outward appearance of nature, it's in the people who live here. What does a judge do here? Well, one of the things I do is make judgments about people who may be joining us . . . people who will need to decide if they can give up everything they had at home and take a leap—a leap of faith."

As he spoke, Dana saw a peculiar light in his eyes. He seemed to radiate; he appeared illuminated. She felt tears flowing down her cheeks. She wiped them with her sleeve.

"Judge, what is this place? Is it really 1925?"

"Doesn't it look like it's 1925? It seemed like a good year. People of the 20th century, or even the early 21st century, can blend in here, make a life for themselves . . . a simpler life. The fact is, it's 1925 here all the time, week after week, month after month. In January, it will be 1925 again. No world wars, no Spanish flu, no firebombing in the streets . . .

"No Antifa, no crime?" Joey asked.

"Well, as I said earlier today, you have to be invited to come here. Here there are no poor and no lavishly rich people. We all consider ourselves to be rich. And as you get to know people, you'll discover that we are of one heart and one mind and do our best to love one another and live righteously. So, to answer your question, no. There's no crime. Sins of omission, of course. We all can do better."

"Of one heart and one mind? That's an interesting thought. So everybody's in lock step, no dissent, no discussion? Everybody's a 'yes' man, or woman?" Dana asked.

The judge looked away, considered her question and then replied. "Well, it takes a lot of effort, but if you really are meek and lowly of heart, you listen to others and consider each person to be someone of great worth whose opinions and point of view count for something. You'll see. We'll talk about this later. This is where I get off."

The carriage came to a halt. They were at a wrought iron gate leading to a long tunnel of trees. The gate was covered with all manner of climbing flowers and vines—jasmine, wisteria, clematis, and morning glory covering the trunks of tall oaks and maples. Through the trees, they could see a large English-style stone manor. Waiting for the judge beyond the gate was a young woman holding the reins to a bright red, two-wheeled hansom pulled by a bay.

"My granddaughter's waiting. Dinner is being served . . . and I'm the chef. Nice to meet both of you. Oh, and Mrs. Kunz, I almost forgot." He reached in his vest pocket and pulled out a dark felt envelope sporting a wax seal. "This is for you. Please don't open it until we see one another again at the Grand Hotel. Mr. and Mrs. Kunz, it's been a pleasure."

He stepped out of the hackney, waved, and stepped into the hansom for a carriage ride to the manor house. As they started back up the hill, Joey and Dana just sat in the carriage and stared at each other. Joey finally broke the ice.

"I think you just received your invitation."

As the sun lowered in the western sky, the shadows in the forest grew darker and darker, and for a very long time, Joey and Dana just held hands and said nothing. What was there to say?

They must have lost track of time. That can happen when you fall asleep, especially deep sleep, because when the hansom emerged from the forest, they were back in the light. But where was it coming from? It was past dusk, early evening, but just beyond the meadow on the hillside they were climbing, there was a warm glow lighting the sky. The trees had given way to vineyards and orchards. Trees and vines almost seemed to groan under the weight of the fruit on their branches. Peaches, pears, plums, and apples, grapes and raspberries, loganberries, blueberries, and even gooseberries, all adorned the hillside.

The driver slid his small window open and poked his head inside for a moment.

"You two doing okay back there? I think you must have taken a cat nap! Sorry to wake you, but we'll be down to the Kurhaus in a few minutes."

Joey rubbed his eyes. "Believe me, sir, it was more than a catnap. We're fine though, thank you." Dana stretched, brushed her teeth with her finger, and popped a piece of Trident into her mouth.

"Want some gum?" she asked Joey. He shook his head.

"What's a 'Kurhaus'?" Dana asked.

Joey answered for the driver. "It's German, for Kur House."

"Funny," she muttered.

"Germans love to go "ins Kur," as they say, to help their '*Kreislaufstörung*.' They go to the spa resort to help their circulation, in other words. Learned that from a summer in Heidelberg."

The driver interrupted him. "He's right, you know. I heard Germans originally built the Grand Hotel and the hot springs resort, but it was a very, very long time ago."

He turned back around to steer his team and passengers to the right through a hedgerow and down a narrow gravel path. Leaves and branches were rubbing up against the carriage and only thanks to the warm glow in the sky could they see the team ahead pulling them through the brush. Dana peeked through the small window over the driver's head.

"It's growing brighter. We're coming out of the bush. I think I see the Kurhaus ahead."

They both huddled next to the small sliding window; Dana

opened it so she could talk to the driver.

"By the way, what's your name?"

"Krämer, Hans Krämer, and I believe you are the Kunzes, no? The professor's kin?"

"She's my Oma," Joey replied.

"*Ah, Sie sprechen Deutsch!*" Hans exclaimed. "Did she teach you some?"

"Only *ein bisschen.* Just a little," Joey admitted. "But she always insisted I call her Oma ever since we took a trip together to Germany when I was a teenager."

"Well, good for you, good for you." Hans snapped the reins to get his team moving faster. They had a small climb ahead of them.

Now that they had finally arrived at their destination, Joey and Dana looked at each other. The envelope was still on her lap.

"I guess we better not open it. It is sealed, after all," Dana said.

"What does it all mean? Again, where are we?"

"Maybe we should also ask when are we? The judge went off script and revealed that they know all about you—and probably me too. And they invited you, not me. So, I don't know what that means," Joey said.

"I know exactly what it means. It's a test. They want to get to know us a little better. And, what I—what we want to know is who is behind all of this?" Dana exclaimed.

"We both know, or at least suspect, that it's run by a higher power," Joey admitted.

"Well, you're the religious one in the family. Me? I'm just, what did your cousin say, a secular Jew? Well, at home we participated in the family celebrations. I even had a bat mitzvah. But not much more. However, it did intrigue me enough to learn Hebrew and Greek and then led me to explore ancient religions and languages like Sumerian."

"And that ancient codex, which the judge knows all about. But, why? I always asked you what that was all about . . . exploring history from 4,000 years ago. And your trips to Egypt—a Jew in a Muslim country. What was the draw?"

"Well, I went to Israel too, as you know . . . to study there. Then, I met you and knew I had to contribute, so I went to law school because, as you like to remind me, I can't cook!"

"I never said that, besides, with a microwave and Costco you evened the playing field!" She feigned a smile.

He paused for a moment and then grew serious. "I can't stop wondering if this is all real. Could we give up everything at home—our lives, our new unlandscaped house?" Then he answered his own question. "I guess it depends on what this place holds for us," Joey said.

"Looks like we're about to find out."

They both leaned out the window, astonished at what loomed ahead of them.

"That's more than a hotel and resort. Holy Moley!" Dana said.

They were glued to the small window of the carriage like two school kids at an amusement park. And for good reason. What was supposed to be the "Grand Hotel" was much grander than grand; it looked more like Versailles—brilliant white with gilded edges and framed by 100-foot high trees, like redwoods, set behind sycamores and oaks with flowering bushes and an immense garden surrounding a circular driveway which had half a dozen carriages queued up to unload passengers.

Behind the "palace," thousands of soaring paper lanterns, each with its own candle, were floating and slowly ascending from the lake that nearly surrounded the Grand Hotel. The paper lanterns, as well as light reflecting from the palace, lit up the sky. Dana opened the access window.

"Hans, what are these lanterns? What is going on?"

"Beautiful, isn't it? It's the annual Toro Nagashi, a Japanese ceremony representing souls ascending to heaven. It's very popular. If there's time, you may even be able to release your own lantern. Look, it's time to get your bags ready—we'll be there shortly, and here come the bellhops. They're expecting you," he said as he pulled the team up short and put on the hand brake. "The service here is excellent!"

Hans was correct. The Kunzes thanked him and tipped him with a $10 bill—which they hoped was appropriate—probably more than appropriate given the smile on his face. Two young bellhops approached them, a young man and a young woman—about college-age—who took their bags and asked them to follow them; they already knew who they were.

"Your grandmother is expecting you; her reception is in half an hour . . ."

"Oh, good, we feared we'd missed it. The carriage ride was longer than we thought," Dana said.

"No problem. Everything you need has been laid out for you in your suite. Follow us, please."

As they made their way down a corridor to the elevators, Dana admitted it wasn't "your typical opulent Five-Star hotel." Murals on the walls were reminiscent of Carl Bloch's religious paintings. A string quartet was playing an adaptation of "A Poor Wayfaring Man of Grief" in a reception area near a series of French doors against the far wall as they entered the corridor. Through the glass doors and full-length windows, they could see a dimly lit pool with people in dark robes talking as they were being served drinks and finger food. Dana whispered to Joey, "This is more like a cathedral than a fancy hotel. There is a feeling of reverence here."

"No kidding. I think we're in for a culture shock here," Joey responded.

"I'm already in shock." As they approached a foyer where a bank of elevators awaited them, there was a floor-to-ceiling Bloch mural depicting his painting of A Wedding at Cana. "What is that?" Joey shook his head.

The young woman answered, "'The Wedding at Cana' is one of Carl Bloch's most famous works. He was amazing, wasn't he?"

The young man spoke up." He still is." The woman shot him a warning glance.

The elevator opened and an older, very pleasant man greeted them warmly. "Which floor?"

"Twelve," the young woman said.

They showed them to their suite—a large, comfortable room with 19th-century French furniture in subtle tones. On the bed were two piles of clothing. Dana wasn't sure what they were seeing. Then it hit her. This is swim wear! Laid out for each of them were a huge dark terry cloth wrap-around robe and modest black swim wear which would cover them from elbows to knees.

"What is this?" Dana asked in shock.

The young woman was somewhat perplexed. "Well, it is customary when new guests arrive, particularly outsiders, that they are privileged to be welcomed into the hot springs; it's very. . . uh, efficacious."

"I guess we're being thrown into the pool," Dana said.

"It looks like it," Joey said, resigned to their fate, not realizing what it would mean to them for years to come.

T hey stood by the edge of a large pool and could feel the heat bubbling up from where they were standing. They hadn't talked to anyone so far that they had met in town, but everyone who had talked to them tonight had been very friendly. The water seemed very buoyant and people floated with ease. A wide set of four stairs provided plenty of seating space for anyone who just wanted to luxuriate in the hot water.

So far, neither Joey nor Dana had even stuck a toe in the pool. Then they heard a familiar voice. A woman with a polka-dot bathing suit was dog-paddling about twenty feet out. It was Oma!

"Joey, Dana, come on in. As they say, the water's fine. Not too hot."

They knew they couldn't resist. Even Dana felt powerless, so they dropped their terry-cloth robes on a recliner lounge and carefully stepped into the water.

"It's hot, Oma," Dana cried out.

"Don't be such babies. Look at me, I'm 90 for crying out loud, and you don't see me whining. This is like the waters of Bethesda in the Bible. Everyone tried to get in when the water stirred. This water is constantly stirring."

"I don't know that story," Dana said.

"Of course you don't. Joey can fill you in you later."

Finally loosening up, Dana whispered to Joey, "I think she got me down here to get me baptized. You Christians can't fool me!"

He laughed, and then they both stepped in and found they were able to float. Instantly, Dana could feel "the stirring" Oma mentioned.

"It's like seltzer water; very warm, bubbly water . . . soothing."

An older woman floated by, partly doing a very casual backstroke, and spoke to Dana. "Just think about what ails you—anything. Focus on that, and you just might find yourself a miracle." Then she was gone. Dana reflected on the woman's comment and leaned back in the water and then turned to Oma.

"Who was that?" Dana asked her.

Oma turned to her and patted her arm. "No idea. But, it works. Already working on me." She stood up, stretched her arms behind her. Dana and Joey both noticed that the skin on her arms that had been hanging like rags on old bones previously now looked smoother. And her face, especially around her eyes and mouth, was tighter, fuller.

Oma looked at Dana with tears in her eyes. "I know what you wished for. I wished that for you too. And I've been praying for you as well, ever since we embarked on this crazy journey."

They reposed in the water for another half an hour, listened to the dean of the college introduce Margritte Kunz and her family, and then advised everyone to try the blue crab cakes, shrimp cocktails, and the melon cups.

An hour later, exhausted but relaxed, Dana and Joey just lay on their bed and watched the finale of the Toro Nagashi through their floor-to-ceiling windows as the last of the paper lanterns disappeared into the night sky. This hotel room was not as big as the one at the Roosevelt Hotel, but it had an even more impressive view of the hot springs inlet and the lake beyond it. Much of the landscape below them was lit up from lights from the resort and the lanterns.

Joey turned away from the window. "Tell me now that we're alone, what exactly did you discover at the museum that was so earth-shattering?"

Dana sat down on the bed, kicked off her shoes, grabbed her bag, and opened it. She retrieved a small sack filled with booklets, fliers, and a city directory, or what looked like one.

"Is this it? What's the big deal?" Joey asked, disappointed.

"Joey, it isn't what I found. It's what I DIDN'T find!"

"And, what didn't you find?"

"This directory has a listing tied to the city map that unfolds from the center that shows businesses, city offices, names, addresses and phone numbers of residents, and public areas, like the parks."

"So?"

"So, there are no cemeteries, no mortuaries, no undertakers—nothing for anyone that deals in death. I couldn't find any listings in the city records either. Given how Oma looks—like she's rolled the clock back 20 years—the big question is what if . . . what if nobody dies here? What if there is no death in this place?"

Joey sat there in stunned silence.

She continued, "And, what's more, along with a dead president scheduled to be in a parade tomorrow, there's an art show with artists who have been gone to the other side for sixty plus years. For crying out loud, Norman Rockwell, practically the town's patron saint, has an exhibit tomorrow. He'll be here in the flesh, I suppose!"

Joey nodded, "You're right! These people don't look like ghosts. They're solid! At first, I thought that the citizens in Salem Crossing were just ringers, you know, actors playing a role like in Plymouth, Massachusetts. But, now we're faced with a new reality. You can't have life without death! Entropy is a law of physics that you can't simply rollback. Everything and everybody eventually runs out of whatever it is that keeps them going. But, we're here, now. So let's allow it to play itself out and find out what's really going on. I'm game. Maybe this is just a very realistic dream," Joey said.

"A dream that we're both having, together? I doubt it. I just wonder what have we got ourselves into? I guess there's no turning back," Dana said as she turned off the lamp.

Oma was late for their breakfast meeting in the Tuscan Room. "Nine o'clock she said. It's 9:20. That's not like her," Joey said.

"She's 90 years old, Joey."

"She didn't look 90 last night. More like 60."

"Maybe she got lost. This isn't the second floor. It's the mezzanine. This place is so huge; it's easy to get lost."

"It's a palace, like Versailles; very European," Dana said, still in awe of her surroundings.

Just then, a waiter approached their table with a note.

"Excuse me, are you the Kunzes?" They nodded. "This is for you."

Joey handed Dana the note. "She's up at the "Rooftop Café and wants us to join her."

"On the roof?"

"Where else?"

They thanked the waiter and hurried to the bank of elevators, a long walk down a corridor past incredible works of art and statuary.

"You know what this place reminds me of?"

"The Vatican Museum, but not so Roman and over-the-top?"

"Exactly!"

Just as there was last night in town at the hotel, there was an elevator operator who was just as kind and pleasant as the previous one. He took them to the top.

They walked out onto the rooftop patio, more of a garden really, with small tables set up for four, each shaded by a red umbrella. Oma was at the far end and waved.

But they were more occupied with the view. Now they could see the geography and topography surrounding the hotel.

"This looks just like Montreux, Switzerland on Lake Geneva, with mountains practically rising out of the water. We were there, weren't we, Oma?" Joey said, "We certainly were! Quite a view, huh? Sit down. The Eggs Benedict is great. Haven't had hash browns in a long time."

"Delicious!" Oma raved on.

"Oma, you ate all this?" Joey pointed at all the empty plates.

"Yeah, been really hungry ever since I got here. They're bringing some bran and blueberry muffins, not that I need them. They're for you, too. Went swimming this morning. Must have worked up an appetite."

Dana and Joey exchanged smiles.

"She's a teenager!" Dana said.

"What?" Oma said.

"You're aging well," Joey replied.

"I'm not aging at all. I did deep knee bends this morning with my therapist. Haven't been able to do that in 25 or 30 years. Y'all better order, because I want you to go with me to the Farmer's Market. We got a full day ahead of us. Chop, chop! Better get some breakfast," Oma ordered.

They did as they were told.

An hour later, they had joined others on the boardwalk at the lake's edge where the merchants had set up their displays and handmade goods.

"Wow! Quite a setup," Joey said. Three rows of tents and tables backed up with shelves and displays extended along the edge of the lake about two hundred yards or so with every kind of artisan and vendor imaginable.

"It reminds me of Paris; vendors stretching along the Seine," Dana said.

"Or, Koblenz, set up along the Rhein, with the cable car passing overhead to the Festung on the other side. Remember that, Joey?" Oma asked.

"I think so. You were buying all kinds of old books, especially anything by Goethe." That's when Oma saw her best friend, Virginia, showing a quilt to a young woman. She ran to her. Ran! She didn't ramble, didn't jog. She ran!

Dana and Joey looked at each other. "What in the . . . ?"

They followed her over to Virginia's booth. Joey remembered

her from decades earlier. She looked the same!

"Ginny, this is my Joey, and the beautiful . . . DANA, his wife. You all go ahead," she said to them. "Maybe I'll get a quilt. I'll catch up."

As they walked away, Joey whispered to Dana, "That woman is a year younger than Oma! Can you believe it?"

"No, not really. Maybe I do. I guess I do. Not sure what I believe."

They kept walking along past the displays viewing hand-made pottery, bakery goods of all kinds, getting little samples of this and that. Joey looked back but couldn't see his grandmother, so they continued on ahead.

There were craftsmen and artisans of every kind. It reminded Oma of the Renaissance fairs she'd seen in Europe. She even found a craftsman demonstrating his skills as a puppeteer.

Two children were watching with interest. Behind him, there were dozens of marionettes hanging in the booth gazing into the distance as if they wanted someone to take them home.

Then Oma recognized the 'Master of the Marionettes.' "You are definitely a man of many skills, Judge Stone. So this is what you do when you're not handing out those sentences," Oma laughed.

Judge Stone turned and smiled. "Ever since I read Pinocchio as a boy, a funny series by the Italian Carlo Corrodi, I was hooked. I begged my Papa for a marionette, but it wasn't to be. Too expensive. After years carving toys for my children, I thought I'd try my hand at creating marionettes myself," he said, waving a hand at his menagerie of little wooden people.

"I started making them for my grandchildren too, until, well, time ran out, as it always does back there. But here I have all the time I need—and kids love them," the judge explained.

"Well, there they are," he said, grinning broadly as Dana and Joey approached. "We need to talk soon, maybe for lunch. Have you looked in the envelope?"

Oma asked, "What envelope?"

"We met Judge Stone on our carriage ride, and he gave me this," Dana said, pulling the envelope out of her purse as she answered the Judge's question. "Of course not, Judge, we know better!"

"Why don't we talk about your invitation at lunch?" Stone asked. "There's a little fish and chips place farther down the lake by the boat harbor—about a mile away, right on the beach. You can open the envelope there, and I'll explain what it's all about. Then I have to be on hand when the President arrives, so I don't have a lot of time. How about a quarter to twelve?"

They smiled at each other and nodded. "Good. We were hoping to talk to you before this evening."

"We will. I'll explain all the details," he said as more shoppers congregated around him to watch a wooden boy dance on strings. Joey, Dana, and Oma moved on. Dana was looking for the artists' corner.

"I think it's down at the end, arranged in a square. Heard about it this morning," Oma said.

"I can't wait for lunch with the judge," Dana said. "Once and for all, I . . . we want answers."

Oma smiled. "Dearie, these are eternal questions mankind has been asking since the dawn of time. I think you know the answer; you're just not sure you want to look it square in the eye."

Oma turned and went to the next booth, one filled with very old books, her favorite things to buy. Dana stood waiting for Joey to leave a display on First Century hand-painted icons, a collection being displayed by an Orthodox priest. She stared at her husband, encouraging him into get-ting a move on. He got the message.

For the next hour, they continued their tour through a living museum with artifacts, artwork, baked goods, toys, even cooking utensils, some antique, some recently handmade, and all on display.

Dana was growing impatient. In an hour, they were to have lunch with the Judge and get the answer they were waiting for. She was insistent they spend the rest of the time in the Artists' Square. It was well worth the wait.

It was a museum-goer's dream, the best of the 19th-century and early 20th-century's foremost artistic geniuses, but no modern impressionists. No Gaudy's, no Picasso's, mostly painters of romantic and religious subjects. Of particular interest to Dana were the Medieval interpretations of a British painter that focused on chivalry. A self-confessed feminist, she nevertheless liked the idea of knights in shining armor. And, they were on display here; several works by British painter Edmund Blair Leighton along with the painter himself, who was born in 1852, but died in 1922.

But here he was in living color, having a lively conversation, mixed with good portions of laughter in his east London accent, with a tall, angular man, apparently both enjoying their debate over paint and technique. The tall man turned toward Dana and revealed himself to be none other than Norman Rockwell, a favorite in the little town where they had just spent a day and a half. She recognized him from his self-portraits in old reprints of the Saturday Evening

Post. He died the same month in which she was born, November 1978. He was 80. But, today at the Artists' Square, he looked about the same age as everybody else, about 45 or 50.

Speechless, Dana stood there, staring at two dead men, both enjoying a lively debate over color and humor in paintings. Rockwell was the funny one; Leighton was British, and very old school.

"I guess we'll agree to disagree," Rockwell said to the Brit. Joey approached him. "Got any Boy Scout prints?"

"Do I ever! Let me show you. Heard what they did to them, the Boy Scouts, what a shame, what a shame. Let's see what I have here," he said as he sorted through a bin of magazine covers and small first attempts. "Here's one, a sketch with a wash of color, not completed by any means."

"How much?" Joey asked.

"Whatever you can afford. Didn't anybody tell you how things operate here at our market?" Rockwell explained. "You pay the balance forward. You'll see." He smiled.

Joey hesitated. "I thought 'pay it forward' was new . . . hmm."

Oma interrupted Joey's train of thought and explained for Mr. Rockwell, "They're having lunch with the Judge in about an hour."

"Oh, good. He'll set everything straight then. Were you a Scout?"

Oma proudly spoke up, "Eagle with two palms . . . scads of Merit Badges."

Joey looked uncomfortable. Rockwell explained a little more.

"The only caveat is that you don't resell it. You can keep it or donate it. In any case, as the Judge will tell you, just pay it forward. That's what we do here. Look at me. I died at the age of 80, had a great life, did what I loved, but here I am . . . still have an eternity to pay it forward, and still painting. What's your name, Eagle Scout?"

"Joey Kunz."

"So, the professor's your ma?"

"My Oma, my mentor, and my German teacher," he said as he put his arm around his grandmother.

"Well, we hope you can find your way back here," he responded as another customer approached him.

"Let's get some lemonade or something," Oma said.

"And, some place to sit. My feet are killing me," Dana added.

They didn't want to keep the Judge waiting so they hurried down the beach to the small harbor and the dock; they found it, but no little fish and chips stand. Instead, the Judge was waiting for Joey and Dana next to a sailboat. He was wearing a blue blazer and a captain's hat.

"This is my little "Fish and Chips" stand; I wasn't entirely forthcoming. It's a sailboat, as you can see, something else I always wanted to do before but was too busy trying to make a name for myself in America's courtrooms," he confessed.

"Well, you succeeded at that," Dana said.

"Maybe so, but at a high cost. One of the things about living here is that you can spend more time doing what really matters. Perhaps you figured it out already, even if you can't quite accept it, that time has no real boundaries here. Nevertheless, there is still no time here for procrastination, at least in this part of our reality."

The Judge noticed that they were more confused than ever. "Never mind, have some fish and chips; I caught them in the lake and made them right here in the galley," he said, welcoming them aboard.

As they passed the bow of his tidy 30-foot sailboat, they saw the name emblazoned on the front. "Fish and Chips."

The Judge laughed as they passed it. "You'll see, it's my specialty."

He was right; they all filled up on some unknown swimming vertebrate and had fried chips, washed down with cider.

The Judge's captain and cook, Almo, announced they were shoving off now that their next passenger, Oma, was scurrying up the dock.

"Man, look at her go!" Dana said. Almo helped Oma into the cabin.

"Sorry, I'm late. I met the President . . ."

"Which one?" Joey asked.

"Coolidge, of course," she answered.

In five minutes, they were cutting through the clear blue waters of the long lake surrounded by mountains on all sides, a lake not found on any map of the state that Joey and Dana lived in. They were trying to get used to "different."

Or so they thought.

Once the meal had been cleaned up, it was time to get down to business. The scenery reminded Joey of his European trip with Oma thirty years earlier.

"This looks a lot like Lake Geneva in Switzerland," he said.

The Judge commented simply, "It has the same designer. It was always one of His favorites."

Dana looked at Joey and then looked away.

The Judge addressed her, "Did you bring the envelope?"

"Yes, right here."

"And, the Bible?"

"It's in my purse."

"Let's see what's inside."

Dana broke the seal but then handed the envelope to Joey.

"Why me? It's for you . . ."

"Well, I'm not going anyplace without you. Look inside."

He pulled it out, unfolded it, looked at both sides, puzzled, and then handed it to Dana.

"It's blank, Dana. There's nothing on it! Is this some kind of cruel rejection notice?" he asked the Judge.

"What do you think? Would we bring you both out here, to a different world with a completely different reality to reject you, even ridicule you? Now as I understand it, Joey, you analyze, evaluate, and train people for a living, using the latest tools at your disposal. Then you help employers find the right people for the job, and then you train them for it, am I right?"

"I guess so."

"Don't be so modest. You're paid a handsome sum to do that."

"Well, that's debatable," Dana said.

"Okay. So what kind of people are you looking for?" Joey asked.

"Oh, we're not looking for them. You are."

"What?" Dana asked as the boat was catching some waves and making a sharp turn. "How are we supposed to know?"

"That's what that book is for. There are three place-marker ribbons in there; two in the Old Testament, one in Psalms or Proverbs, I think, and the other in Isaiah 53 . . ."

"Ahh, the forbidden chapter," Dana said, "at least for Orthodox Jews."

Joey picked up the Gideon Bible and opened to the last ribbon which marked Matthew, Chapter 5.

"The Sermon on the Mount. All the recruitment clues you need are in there," the Judge explained.

"Well, do you need a butcher, a baker, or a candlestick maker? What?" Joey said, growing frustrated.

Dana rubbed his shoulder to calm him down.

"How many? How do we get them here?" Dana asked.

"The old green city bus that picked you up has a capacity of 36 passengers, including you, the driver excepted, of course. That's just one way. You just need to gather them up and have them with two suitcases ready by no later than by early spring, preferably earlier. There is a deadline; things are happening back there where you come from. Send us a note. Use the self-addressed envelope inside your envelope, and soon you'll get a postcard from us. Look inside the envelope."

Dana found the self-addressed envelope to an address in Upper Michigan.

"Take the invitation, fill it in with the names, ages, and addresses of your candidates, and mail it to us. But, be discerning. That Gideon Bible is your guidebook."

"What do we say to 'our candidates?'" Joey asked, still perplexed.

"What did Jesus ask of his disciples?"

"Follow me," he said. "But, I'm not . . ."

"No, nobody is. But, look at all the modern technology you have at your fingertips. Find referrals, names of people recommended by others, use your best judgment, and prayerfully include their names on your list of candidates. Then send us the names of your prospects. And remember, we have our list, too. That's why you are here. We'll send the invitations or have you deliver them. We will tell you when and where we'll pick you all up."

"What's the common denominator of our candidates?"

The Judge thought for a moment and then responded. "They need to bring with them 'a broken heart and a contrite spirit.' "

They let that sink in.

Judge Stone could see that Joey was confused.

"So, we're not returning to Salem Crossing?" Joey asked.

"No, it's a way station, a pleasant little place, though isn't it? As its name implies, it is a place where outsiders like you 'pass through,' coming and going. You'll return there after you've completed your assignment, bringing others along with who are seeking 'the Shining City on the Hill.' Is that clear enough?" Dana and Joey nodded in agreement.

"Any suggestions on whom we might invite, how we ought to get started?" Joey asked.

"Did you ever do any hiking as a boy?" Joey looked confused.

His grandmother answered for him. "All the time, didn't we Joey?"

"Yes, Oma. How could I forget what a hiker you were? Left me behind a lot!"

The Judge explained, "Do you know what they called those piles of stones that you came across every once in a while?"

"Trail markers?"

"Yes, trail markers, but they're called cairns," Judge Stone explained.

"In our lives, on our trails from then until now, there have been people along the way that kept us, for the lack of a better term, 'on the straight and narrow.' It could have been a teacher, an uncle, a very good friend, . . ."

"A grandmother," Joey said.

"Exactly! Think back on those moments and the people who were in the right place at the right time. Put them on your list first. Find them and send us their names. We'll do the rest," he concluded and looked out the window.

"We're getting close to shore–I'll tell you more later. Look at that," he said pointing at the horizon.

"A storm is brewing, and you have to get down to the highway very soon. You're running out of time. So, we're going to have to take a shortcut."

"But, our luggage is all back at the hotel," Dana interjected.

"No, it's here. The professor had it all loaded onto the boat. We're leaning toward the shore now. There are usually fast hansoms awaiting passengers," Stone said.

"Handsomes?" Joey joked.

"Not 'handsome;' a hansom is a fast, two-wheeled, covered carriage where the driver sits behind you. We'll get one onshore. It's the fastest way down that's not motorized. And, the path you're taking? Well, a car, bus, or truck wouldn't get you through."

In ten minutes, they had pulled into a small harbor with a few small boats and a couple of sailboats like Judge Stone's.

"Ahh, they beat us here," the Judge said as he tied up the boat and helped the ladies onto the boardwalk.

"Who?" Dana asked.

"The Sphinx, but don't call him that to his face. I think it's kind of endearing, but the Sphinx doesn't.'"

Joey followed behind with the luggage in tow. A large 40-foot double spinnaker sailboat was unloading at the next pier.

"Follow me," the Judge said. They hurried over, following the Judge until he caught up with the entourage.

"Mr. President!" the Judge announced.

"Oh, Harlan, you can just call me the Sphinx like you do behind my back, because, as the papers say, I'm so dour and taciturn," President Coolidge replied. He laughed. Just a little.

"Do you have my boat bugged?" the Judge asked.

"I'm not sure what that means, Judge. But, if I understand you correctly, that would be illegal. It's a good thing I didn't hear all your razzmatazz about me, or I would have thought twice about naming you Chief Justice."

"That was Roosevelt, Franklin D. I was just one of the Nine," he said with a smile. It was obvious they were enjoying each other's company.

Dana spoke up, "Well, things may have returned to normalcy here. But, where we're from, I'm afraid things have fallen on hard times. I'm Dana Kunz, and this is my husband, Joey, uh Joseph. And Mrs. Margritte Kunz, Joey's 'Oma.'"

"I know about the professor, heard a whisper that she was bringing some 'moderns' with her. Should give us a new perspective," Coolidge said.

Now emboldened by Dana's interjection, Joey spoke up.

"Frankly, Mr. President, I and millions of my fellow citizens are yearning for a 'Return to Normalcy' and for a God-fearing leader like yourself, not trying to be obsequious or anything . . . just sharing the facts of the situation as I see them."

"Obsequious. You sound like a lawyer . . ."

"I'm not, but she is," he said pointing to Dana.

"In any case, we wish you the best on your quest and hope you can join us as soon as possible on a permanent basis."

"We do, too, sir," Dana said.

Coolidge turned to the Judge and smiled:

"Guess what, Harlan. Just as you suggested long ago, I'm taking tennis lessons. You should drop by and see for yourself. Cal Junior and I play every Friday. Isn't that something?" He smiled and the Judge understood how much that meant to his old friend. The President and his group walked toward a waiting parade of carriages, some motorized, some horse-drawn. They watched in awe as the group walked away. Joey and Dana were stunned. Joey turned to his wife:

"What do you mean, we do?" Joey asked his wife in a whisper. She shrugged her shoulders as if to say 'who knows?' She was processing the whole event. What does this mean FOR US?

"This seems so . . . uh, natural. After all is said and done, maybe we're the ones from the weird times, the weirdest of the weird."

"Anyone that would use the word 'obsequious' in a conversation with the President is weird in my book," Dana said jokingly, trying to change the subject. The reality of dead men walking was still hard to fathom.

"Well, what would you have said?"

"How about beginning with, 'Seeing that I am a fawning syco-phant, a brown-noser . . .'" Then she started laughing and so did he. The Judge and Oma joined in. She slugged Joey in the arm, and they held hands and walked to a bench to wait for a ride, still mulling over the new reality they were facing,

"Judge," Joey said, "we have no idea where we are, how we get back to the 21st-century, and then return with our 'catch.' I can only assume that if we are to fulfill our assignment, you'll help us 'be fishermen,' right?"

"Exactly, to be fishers of men," he added. "And, they're not all that easy to get aboard, but, yes, you'll get help."

Dana still looked confused, pulled one way and then the other, and she was still in shock. Joey wondered, Am I just being obsequious again, do I just want to curry favor? I don't know. But, deep down, he realized that the sacrifice would be tremendous. If we do this, we have to be all in, both of us.

Judge Stone flagged down a shiny, well-kept hansom hitched to a big powerful steed approaching at a fast gait. The driver pulled up sharply and addressed him.

"Are you the Judge?"

"Yes, sir, I am. Are you Roberts?"

"No, I'm Hopkins. Don't know where he is. I'm the replacement. Nobody could find him." The Judge gave him a note with instructions as Joey and Almo loaded up the luggage in the boot.

After a tearful hug with Oma, Joey and Dana climbed in and waved goodbye.

"Come back, you two. I don't want to be here without you!" Oma said.

They were in for the ride of their lives, clueless as to what they were facing, that is, if they really went through with it.

PART II

RETURN TO THE 21ST CENTURY

7

Dana and Joey became concerned the minute they left the sight of Judge Stone. Hopkins, the driver, stopped frequently to check Judge Stone's instructions and a hand-drawn map. For about an hour, they hugged the shore of the lake across from the Grand Hotel and the Kurhaus. In the two-wheeled hansom, the driver sat behind them overlooking the roof of their cabin.

He reined in the horse and directed it where to turn, when to stop, and so on. Its advantage was its speed; its disadvantage was its stability. As long as they were traveling along a path through pastures, or even the forest, no problem.

They remembered the moment they encountered a covered bridge on their way to Salem Crossing; it was peaceful, safe. Now, as the storm, wind, and rain beat down, they became more and more concerned for their safety, as well as for the young driver perched upon the seat behind them. Something had changed. They no longer felt the protection that had surrounded them and everyone else back in Salem Springs and the Grand Hotel and spa.

Dana spoke first. "Do you feel a bit uneasy, like we've been kicked out of Paradise?"

"I do. It's like we're back in the cruel world." Joey opened the small, sliding window behind him and yelled to Hopkins over the din of the wind and rain, which was growing in intensity. "How are you doing back there, Hopkins?"

"As best as I can, sir. It's kind of exciting. I think I now know why I had to drive for Roberts. We've left our safety zone, but we have a good strong horse carrying us along. Don't you worry."

But, they did worry—and for good reason. They had left the shelter of the forest and were now slipping along a ridge on a muddy road; more of a trail in reality. On the left side, they could see the edge of a ravine with treetops just below them. Then they were climbing up a rocky slope. Five minutes later, they headed downhill, picking up speed.

Occasionally, Hopkins would lock the wheels to slow down their descent. Then, they heard barking. Suddenly, a huge black dog, possibly a wolf-mix, was running alongside the carriage followed by another. Soon there was a pack of them. The horse and the passengers had become prey, and the big black horse was galloping in fits and starts; he was the wild dogs' objective, never mind the human passengers inside and the driver.

The driver yelled above the storm, the howling dogs, and the clattering of hooves on loose shale. "Hang on! The bridge is out." They saw no bridge. Now, they were really accelerating. What was Hopkins doing? Dana looked back through the small window and screamed, "The driver's gone!' Dana yelled.

The horse suddenly turned to the left now that his blinders allowed him to see there was no bridge ahead.

In a fraction of a second, the carriage's tongue broke, the horse was freed from his harness and halter, and they passed the horse as it was struggling to get back on its feet. But, since the rig only had two wheels, it cartwheeled over and over into the flash flood below them.

Dana and Joey were hanging on to each other as they landed upside down in the water, then popped back up. The roof was bent, and since they had bolted themselves in, they still had air to breathe. Then, just as they caught a breath, the carriage hit something hard, flew into the air, landed hard, and rolled.

Everything went black.

Three County Deputy Sheriffs were exchanging notes at the accident scene as another ambulance drove up and screeched on its brakes, allowing three paramedics to rush around to the back of the vehicle to pull out a gurney. Two ambulances loaded up their cargo and closed their back doors. Everyone jumped and burnt some rubber, leaving the scene all lit up and screaming down the street on their way to Country General, some fifteen miles away.

The Sheriff himself arrived and walked over to Deputy Davis.

"Pretty bad, huh?"

"Yeah. Don't know where the accident happened. It's like they were washed overboard or something. A man and woman are on their way to County General, probably family members. The two must have been thrown clear. Weird, though. They're wearing strange clothing as if they'd been to a costume party or something. And, they were soaking wet. A Ford Explorer is over behind the stand of aspens, wet and muddy with the front doors open. But, how did it get there? A passing motorist luckily saw the car, gave CPR to the man and woman, and got them breathing again."

"Will they make it?"

"Hard to say. Hopefully. When–if–they wake up, they'll be able to explain how they got there, just lying in the pasture behind that stand of trees. It's a mystery to me."

Rachel Clawson, Joey's assistant, had been waiting outside Mr. Gunderson's office for nearly half an hour. She checked again with his assistant, the Bosnian woman, Martina Ilić, but she held her hands up in surrender. Just as she was about to return to her office, she was buzzed. Martina gave Rachel a "thumbs-up" sign; Marta, as her friends called her, was disgusted with Gunderson; he reminded her of the despots she left back in the old country.

"You can go in now, but he's only got five minutes or so," she said.

Rachel had never spoken directly with Joey's boss, the CEO, before but she'd heard about the so-called "trust-fund brat"–not from Joey, but from everyone else who had dealt with him.

"And, who are you?" he asked as he stayed focused on his spreadsheets.

"I'm Rachel. I work for Joey Kunz. We've found him, sir."

"About time. Is he ever coming back to work? He's been gone now for what, five days? Since he's my only HR guy at the moment, I guess I'll have to fire himself," he laughed.

Rachel could feel the hair stand up on the back of her neck. Her first impression of Gary Gunderson confirmed everything else she had heard said of him. He was a jerk, no doubt about it!

"Mr. Gunderson, he's in a hospital upstate, in a coma. So is his wife!"

"Car accident?"

"Not sure. It looked like they had been caught in a flash flood, but they were found by a small stream."

"And what have you been doing for him?"

"Helping with HR matters, training protocols and client interface and testing."

"I've been looking for his personnel records, his employment contract, and so on; can you get them for me? I don't know why we don't have those things in this end of the building."

She was getting hot under the collar now. This guy had no idea about how Joey kept the company together the first six months before Gunderson and his partners took over, and what he'd done since then. She had to think fast–his passwords. She knew them, but this jerk didn't know that she knew them.

"Sir, his personal files are all password-protected, but if I could talk to him–when he can talk, that is–I could ask him, discretely and then return and open those files for you."

"When can you leave?

"Tomorrow."

"Leave tonight. Have Marta give you the company American Express card. Stay up there until you get the passwords. Do you have a laptop?"

"Yeah, sure."

"Then, take it with you, find the docs, and email them to me. All right?" And then Gunderson added, "Oh, and when he wakes up, call me, nobody else. Just me. Okay?"

She nodded.

"Then go." And, she did.

Rachel arrived in Culver City about 10 pm, found a hotel, and called the hospital, but because she was not a relative of the Kunzes, they wouldn't tell her anything. She did bring her laptop and opened up the files for which she supposedly didn't have the passwords. She found all the pertinent documents, but realized she would need to get them notarized. They were all signed electronically and saved as PDF files. In the wrong hands, namely Gunderson's hands, they could be changed, and Joey would be out everything. Right now, he had 10,000 shares, and if he couldn't exercise his options because of his incapacitation, maybe, just maybe someone else could act on his behalf. Now her business law class she had hated at the University of Iowa was paying off. Maybe her MBA could actually help some-one else rather than just make her money.

It was so unfair! She fretted about it for a couple of hours and didn't get to sleep until well after midnight.

Rachel now had a righteous purpose, and she had new energy. Joey was so good to her; in the words of her grandma, "He's a real Mensch!" Maybe she'd be fired too. Well, that's not as bad as what could happen to Joey.

So, she was off and on her way to the hospital by 9 am. At first, no one would talk to her until she bluffed them into thinking that their corporate lawyer said millions of dollars were at stake, and the hospital would be at risk for damages if she couldn't talk to Joey when he awoke. After all, his wife was in a coma too, and Rachel didn't know anyone else in the family. She was all he had!

So, she waited. And waited.

She returned the next day and waited some more. The hospital room was nice enough, but why were they always painted green? This one needed a make-over, maybe some wallpaper.

Finally, about 4 pm on the second afternoon, a balding man with a pocket protector (she didn't think people used those anymore) came into the waiting area and asked her if she was "family" of the Kunzes. She answered like any good politician would, "In a way, I am. I represent them legally," she prevaricated.

"Well then, here. This bag is for you. It was found in the back of their Explorer, and some of it was scattered around the accident site. We don't know what to do with it. The Sheriff's office checks in once in a while. There's a card in there from a deputy. This is all yours now," the bald man said as he hurried out.

There was a big red bag, obviously a purse, probably Dana's. It was zipped up tight, beat up a bit, and damp, but after a look inside, it seemed to have weathered the storm. She also found their cell phones, but they were dead. Luckily, she had her iPhone charger in her purse, so she plugged one in and then the other. She found a small package of postcards from a place called Salem Crossing.

There were two packages of gum, a Beeman's and Blackjack, a city map, an old newspaper—it didn't look old, wasn't yellow, but was dated August 20, 1925, and a business card from a judge, Harlan Stone. The telephone number was short several numbers with no area code. But, there was an email address written on the back after an SOS. This situation was definitely an SOS situation in her mind, so she sent a "to-whom-it-may-concern" message about the plight of Joey and Dana and added a plug about how his employer was going to "do him in."

Finally, it was getting dark and visiting hours were up, so she gathered the items from the bag, including the cell phones. I'm going to listen to their last voicemails and read their text messages when I get back to the hotel, she promised herself.

And, she left.

Rachel was back at her post at 10 a.m. the next morning in her usual spot in the corner of the waiting room. First, she checked with the supervisor at the nurse's station, the one closest to Joey's room, and second, the one nearest Dana. She had sent a couple of emails to Gary the Great just to let him know that so far, "no news is good news." That wasn't the news he wanted to hear. He told her to press the doctors. Little did he know that nurses really run a hospital, so she had an idea. Why not put Dana and Joey in the same room? She figured that in their subconscious states, they might get the "vibe" from each other that their life partner was right there with them.

She was told by the nurses that they didn't believe in "vibes," since it was not a proper medical term, but, heck, what would it hurt? So, the floor manager bought it. Good job, Rachel, she told herself. Later, when she was in their room sitting between their beds, she asked a nurse whom she had befriended what their diagnoses were.

"To be honest with you, their brain functions, from what we can determine, don't show any impairment. I'm surprised they're not coming around," the nurse confided to Rachel.

"What about stimulation? I have both their cell phones. What if we played back voice messages to see if we can get their 'juices flowing,' so to speak?" Rachel asked.

"Couldn't hurt," the nurse said. "Go ahead."

Rachel explained that she had found two or three longer exchanges they had about buying a dining room table, another about taxes, and finally one about going to Salem Crossing. Dana was certain it didn't exist as it didn't show up on Google Maps. Then Rachel remembered the city map she had found. So, she played it a second time and noticed Joey's lips move. She rang for the attending nurse.

"Watch this," she said. She played it again and again. Joey's fingers were moving, then his lips again.

"It's like he's trying to talk," she said.

"But, he's intubated, so he can't. I'm calling the attending physician," the nurse said. He did not answer, but he called back and said, "Remove the intubation and play it again."

This time, Joey opened his eyes, turned toward Rachel, and smiled.

"I told her it was a real place, and now she knows, too," he managed to whisper. "Where is she?"

"Right here, Joey, waiting for you. She's, uh, taking a nap."

A look of fear and anxiety came over him, and he tried to sit up, but couldn't. Just then Dr. Wiseman appeared.

'Hi, Joseph, I'm Dr. Wiseman, and you're in the Culver County General Hospital. You and your wife were badly hurt, but you're both on the mend, looks like."

"She looks to be in a coma," Joey said.

"We've been a little more cautious with her because of her . . . condition."

"Why, what condition? Tell me!"

"Well, it's good news; we've been regulating her dosages very carefully because she's pregnant . . . don't want to do anything risky at these early stages," the doctor explained. "About ten days or so. It showed up in her urine. It's too early to hear anything like a heart-beat."

He sat up, burst into a smile, and laughed. "The hot springs worked, just like Oma said they would! Thank you for sharing this with me. Wow!"

The nurse stepped in at this point, pointed to Rachel, and spoke to Joey. "This young woman has been here all week; she's the one who suggested we put the two of you in the same room. And, she's the one who insisted we play your voice messages in the hope it would stir something in you, and it did."

Joey whispered, "Rachel, Rachel, you're the best. You better call the office . . ."

"Oh, I will, but not right now. We have to talk first."

Dr. Wiseman intervened at this point and suggested that they take Joey down the hall. "We need to conduct some more tests, take some fluids, so if you could excuse us."

Rachel got the cue, grabbed her purse and the cell phones, and exited toward the waiting area. On the way, she bumped into an older man in work clothes who watched her leave just as they wheeled Joey out.

"Excuse me, but did you happen to send an 'SOS' yesterday to an unknown party?"

"Yes," she responded.

"Are you Rachel?"

She nodded.

"Can we go sit for a moment and talk?"

They did. His name was Walter, and he introduced himself as a "friend of a friend" who was sent to make sure that Joey and Dana were doing okay.

"Fill me in please on the situation." She did the best she could and explained the whole sorry reason she was sent to extract his password. After a few minutes, she was struck by his honesty and his desire to do what was best for the Kunzes.

He gave her very explicit instructions regarding what to say to Gunderson and not to tell him that Joey was now awake and talking. "Just tell him that he's improving, then don't do anything about his contract or his stock options until we get back to you. Just sit tight, okay?"

She nodded. Just then, they wheeled Joey back into his room, sitting up and sipping a drink.

"Can you wait here a minute? I have a message for him, then we can leave," Rachel said to Walter.

Walter followed her into the room, looked at Joey for a minute, and smiled.

"I know you," Joey said, "but I can't remember where."

"Did you forget that you owe me a nickel," Walter laughed.

"So, it's all true! It's not a dream," Joey exclaimed.

"No, it's not a dream. It's real, every bit of it, and we have work to do," Walter said. "How's Dana?"

He answered with a big smile, "She's pregnant. Isn't that great? Hey, I don't even know your name. I'm Joey."

"Maybe you forgot. I'm Walter, but some folks call me "The Big Train." Well, they did anyway. Used to farm and play a little baseball."

Then they shook hands. Walter then gave him his "card" from

the 1924 World Series.

Joey looked at the baseball card and laughed. "I guess there's no bubble gum with it."

"After a hundred years, it'd be a little stale! But, maybe the card's worth a little money."

Walter left in a hurry as Rachel was waiting for him.

They had work to do.

The next morning, Joey was up and taking his first steps with the help of a CNA and a walker. They were up on the 3rd floor in a large gym-like room referred to as the Rehab Studio when Sheriff's Deputy Brady Owens and a plainclothes sergeant by the name of Bleazard entered the room.

They were all business.

The young black officer with an athlete's physique, Deputy Owens, addressed the nurse's aide. "We need a few minutes with Mr. Kunz; have some questions to ask him.

The "Certified Nurse's Aide," Mrs. Gregory, an imposing black woman with an attitude, told the officers that he was scheduled for another half-hour of rehab, "So he can get back on his own two feet," and they could wait in the visitors' suite, "Right over there by the entrance, where it says on the door, 'patient and staff only.'"

The Deputy was about to put her in her place, but the sergeant complied. "We'll wait for him outside." She and Joey exchanged a smile.

"I'm glad you're my nurse," Joey muttered.

"I'm just a CNA trying to move up in the world," she said.

"I think you will," Joey said.

Right on time, Mrs. Gregory delivered Joey to the officers who had grown impatient from their confinement in the visitors' suite, and since the three of them were alone, Sergeant Bleazard proceeded and explained why they were there.

"Mr. Kunz . . ."

"You can call me Joey, everybody does."

"Okay . . . Joey, in your words, please tell us what happened on that mountain road, how the accident happened; everything you can remember, including where Margritte Kunz is. Her care center called us when she didn't come back. We were told she left with you. Deputy Owens is recording this, uh, aren't you Brady?"

He nodded and pulled a digital recorder out of his pocket, tried to turn it on, and started to check the batteries when Bleazard grabbed it from him and pushed the ON button.

"Am I under oath?"

"Not exactly, but we expect a truthful response," Bleazard said, taking over the conversation.

"Margritte, that's my grandmother, I call her 'Oma,' asked us to drive her to a health spa out in the country and up a small road. We were following her map. We went to a small town, a retro town like in the 1920s, and then took a carriage up to where the Grand Hotel and spa was. We said goodbye to Oma by the lake, and the rest of it is still foggy. I don't know how we got here and have no idea how my car was found there because I wasn't driving it."

"What?" Bleazard asked, "You weren't driving?"

"No, we'd left it off the highway, parked behind an old Sinclair station, and took a bus up a narrow, gravel road through the woods. We passed over a covered bridge until we reached the resort town of Salem Springs. Oma had left ahead of us, and then the next day we joined her up at the resort," Joey explained.

While Joey was talking, the uniformed deputy grabbed his cell phone, started to make a call, and left the room. Then, Joey shared most of the events that happened with Bleazard, but without the "fantastic" details about the age of the town, the historical context, and people they met, especially President Calvin Coolidge.

He continued, "Anyway, it was a very neat, old-fashioned place. It seemed time had stopped. We met Oma at the resort, and the only way we could get back to our car was by taking a horse and buggy."

"Horse and buggy?"

"Yes, it's called a 'hansom,' a two-wheeled buggy pulled by one horse with the driver seated up behind the cab and passengers. It was pretty fast for being horse-drawn. But, the driver was young, inexperienced, and we squeezed through some pretty tight spaces—4-wheel drive country, really . . ."

Bleazard quizzed him. "Why didn't they use some other 4 x 4 or off-road vehicle?"

"Well, I'm not sure, but maybe they were Amish or Mennonites," he answered, stretching the truth a bit. "Anyway, we were chased by a pack of dogs, it was raining hard, we were on loose shale, and then the horse broke loose, and we went careening down a flooded river, and over the edge. That's all I can remember until I woke up here."

"So, you weren't driving? You left your Explorer parked behind a Sinclair station . . .?"

"A very old, antique Sinclair station. I even got a package of Blackjack gum there."

About this time, the deputy whispered in Bleazard's ear, and he turned off the recorder, put it in his pocket, and stood up to leave.

"That's quite a story, Mr. Kunz. It really is. We'll check out things but reserve the right to return. We were contacted by people from your grandmother's care center who were worried she had left so quickly and didn't completely vacate her suite. Two other residents have disappeared from the care center without leaving forwarding addresses in recent months. We're all concerned."

"Who's concerned? The center because they're losing tenants? Is that it? Maybe they shouldn't try to gouge their clients!" Joey replied angrily. "I already told you. We left Oma back at the spa, and as I said, I did not drive the Explorer down the mountain. I do not know who was in the vehicle. It's all true, as best as I can remember," Joey said as he balanced himself on the chair and stood up.

"I'm sure you believe it's true. We'll get back to you."

Joey waited for Mrs. Gregory who grabbed his walker as the officers left.

Bleazard turned to Owens. "If it was an accident, it was an accident. Period. End of story. But, what's he hiding?" He took a breath and stopped. "So, what did you find out?"

"Found nothing. No town, village, or bump in the road called Salem Crossing or Salem Springs. And no lake! Nothing on GPS. Nada. Sinclair left the state decades ago. I guess I'm going have to do some web sleuthing back at the office," Owens answered.

"Ahh, sleuthing! I like the sound of that. Very detective-like; you'll go far," Bleazard quipped. Owens wished he'd become a paramedic like his mother wanted him to ever since he had been assigned to be Bleazard's tote-and-fetch boy!

Nevertheless, he was intrigued by Joey's story; it had the ring of truth, as fantastic as it sounded. It was a mystery and that's one thing he and his dad liked to do years ago, watch a mystery movie or share a who-done-it and compare notes. So, he was going to dig into Joey's claims. Let the truth fall where it may! Who cares about snarky Bleazard and his constant sarcasm?

Back on Joey's floor, Mrs. Gregory took Joey's walker as he opened the door, and when he did, Dana was gone, her bed, her bag, her tubes, and electronic gear—all disappeared!

"Nurse Gregory?"

She turned around and hurried back.

"What's wrong?

"My wife's gone. What is going on here!"

"I'll find out!" Mrs. Gregory ran over to the nurse's station.

"Where's Dana Kunz?"

"They moved her. She tried speaking a bit, and according to the orders from 'higher up,' she needed to be apart from her husband. Once she starts talking, an officer needs to be present–before she and her husband can compare notes. The order came down yesterday, and before those officers went back to find you and Mr. Kunz, it was all set in motion," the nurse in charge said.

"That is ridiculous!"

"Francine, you are over your depth here, okay?"

"Well, if she's talking, she and Joey need to have a conversation."

"A short one, with someone else there. They can't talk about the accident, get it?"

"Yes, ma'am." She went in and settled Joey down. "I'll watch out for you," she promised him.

"I need to find out more about this Mrs. Gregory. I like her, Joey thought," then he asked her: "Where is she? When can I speak to Dana?"

"I'm working on it," Mrs. Gregory said and hurried away.

$$8$$

Walter and Rachel agreed to meet at a roadside diner north of town on State Road 94 for lunch at 1 pm. He asked her to bring her laptop because the lawyer was coming. They were both already there.

And, Rachel was late.

Walter and his booth mate, Jonathan Blum—officially a retired attorney, but now an apple farmer—were worried. They were huddled back in the corner of the diner in the one place where they could have a conversation without being seen or overheard. How could they be, really? The diner's occupancy consisted of a trucker, an older couple, a likely sales rep in the opposite corner, the waitress, and the cook. That was everybody. And, yet Walter looked concerned. Blum was getting impatient, but that was his nature, a bad trait for a farmer.

"Walter, I have honey crisps to pick, and the Jonathans are coming on, too," Blum said.

"Your apples carry your name?" Walter asked jokingly. They laughed.

"Walter, she'll be here, or she won't," Blum said. "I just have to be back by this evening. Got a crew coming to pick tomorrow, and a long drive. My trees are overloaded. Plus, I don't see any nefarious characters in here, except for me, being an attorney and all."

"So, what's the problem?" Walter asked.

Blum sighed and leaned back. "Well, here in this world of light and shadows where we find ourselves now—a world that I find more distasteful by the day—the shadows are growing longer, and the light is receding. Joey and Dana are behind in their assignment. They haven't even begun, haven't even been able to talk together, and commit 100 percent. We are all facing forces of darkness that are growing in strength." Just then, something caught Blum's eye.

"Look, is that her?" he asked, pointing to a pretty red-head grabbing a bag from the backseat of an Audi.

"Yep," Walter said.

Rachel walked in, looked around, spotted them in the corner, and hurried over.

"Sorry, I'm late. I got a whole chain of text messages from Gunderson as I was getting ready to leave; I had to respond in some way. He tried to call me earlier, but I let it go to voicemail. I feel like such a cheat. I hate to lie, after all, he's still paying me. I didn't want to say anything until I talked to you," she said, almost in a panic. She brushed her hair back and took a breath as the waitress brought her a glass of water and a menu. The waitress waited for a second and then wisely left.

"Rachel, this is Mr. Blum, an attorney, who does a lot of work for us; favors, really, in situations like this. He is up to speed, but may have a few questions for you," Walter said.

"Well, what should I do?" she asked.

Blum spoke. "Reply to the text message from Joey's boss—his

name's Gunderson, right?'

She nodded.

Blum continued. "First, tell him you'll send him a detailed email only after you talk to Joey since you haven't really had the chance yet. Then, make sure that Joey knows what his boss is up to; we don't trust him. Second, be very careful what you tell Gunderson–we're sure that he doesn't have Joey's best interest at heart. Joey and Dana are very important to us . . . "

"They're important to me, too," she replied.

"Good," Blum said. 'Maybe it's best NOT to tell his boss that he's awake and talking, at least for now."

"Okay. Do we have Wi-Fi in here?" Rachel asked.

Walter shrugged his shoulders.

"Why?" Blum asked.

"I'll send you the email so you can review it first. Then, I'll send it off once you okay it. So, tell me: exactly who are you guys?"

"Rachel, I think Jonathan and I would rather hear about you. We're old, and as they say, 'over the hill,'" Walter said. "Not much to tell. You go first" (If she only knew, Walter thought).

Rachel pushed her hair back and began. "Well, I finished my MBA last year at the University of Iowa where I was also working as an assistant coach for the women's softball team. I played softball at Florida State, where we came in second at the College World Series. We lost to a California team–I hate California; I majored in Agronomics, which is why I went to Iowa where they grow stuff. People always have to eat, you know.

"But, then I got an internship at OJT. Joey brought me on; he was so good to me. And, when the internship ended, he hired me as his assistant. The pay's good, Joey's great, but when the new 'trust fund brats' came in last January, as we call them behind their backs, the attitude of management changed, and so did ours; they're not there for the long haul. We believe they're going to strip it down and sell the remaining parts to someone else. In short, they're vultures—vultures of the worst kind. So that's it."

Blum turned to Walter. "Okay, Walter, your turn."

Walter squirmed a little, but told the truth, as much as he could. "I was born and bred in Kansas on a farm, played a little ball myself . . . (Blum nudged him under the table and Walter nudged him back) . . . then I returned to farming when I wasn't helping a team here and there. And then retired . . . but, Jonathan Blum, here, made a name for himself in corporate law, mergers and acquisitions, and along the way, acquired a beautiful apple orchard. He even named the apples after himself," he said, teasing Blum.

Jonathan smiled and wrapped it all up. "Well, the fact is, there were Jonathans long before I came along. I've got some honey crisps, too. In all, there are about 750 Jonathan trees; altogether about 3500 trees in production on 12 acres. I brought some nice crisp ones with me in the car for both of you. Anyway, let's order some lunch now because once you hit the send button, we are on our way; I already have my copies of Joey's contract notarized, certified, and sanitized. Push the button!"

She hit SEND, and Blum concluded, "Okay, let's order. Our business here is finished, I think."

"Sorry," Rachel said. "No time to eat. I still have to get back and talk to Gunderson before he leaves. And I have the last game of the year to coach on Saturday. They depend on me, and I'm really attached to them. Too busy!" She put her laptop in her bag and stood to leave.

Walter grabbed her hand and smiled. "You'll do fine. Go knock it out of the park, kiddo!"

Rachel turned to him, "What? My grandpa always said that whenever I came up to bat! I'd love to stay, you two are great, but I'd better run. Thanks for everything!" She stood up and shook their hands.

"Your grandpa must have seen your potential. Travel safely," Walter said. She walked away, waved, and gave them a big smile.

"Cute kid. Do you think she knows?" Blum asked.

"Not a clue, absolutely not," Walter said as he watched her go out the door. He turned toward the window and kept watching until she drove away. "I'm so proud of her!"

"Shoot, I forgot to give her a bag of apples," Blum said.

Walter smiled. "Maybe we can give her the apples on Saturday."

"Saturday?"

Walter answered Blum, "Yeah, at her game."

Rachel still had her biggest task of all to do before she returned to the office. She had to tell Joey about everything. She checked out of her hotel and drove straight to the hospital. Joey was still in rehab when she arrived, but in ten minutes, there he was walking slowly but unassisted by Mrs. Gregory back to his room.

Joey went straight to the nurse in charge.

"I appreciate everything you've done here, but I need to talk to my wife now! I don't know why you moved her or why we've been separated, but either you take me to her or I'm calling my attorney!"

he demanded.

"You don't have to call her. I'm right here," Rachel said, walking up behind him and looking straight at the nurse.

The nurse was frazzled. "There are instructions here . . . let's see, from somebody named Bleazard . . ."

Rachel spoke directly, but with a smile. "He's just a deputy sheriff, not the DA. There are no charges filed. What room is she in?"

The nurse turned and whispered, "D-14, third floor. But, I didn't tell you . . . go!"

Joey and Rachel walked around the corner to the elevators and were on their way. They found Dana asleep in her room, but stirring; Rachel waited outside.

In a moment, she heard Dana's voice. "Joey, you're okay. You're okay! I've been kind of out of it, and nobody would tell me anything. You're walking around. That's great."

"I'm better than okay. I have a secret to share with you, so listen closely," he said and then whispered in her ear.

She screamed, "I am? We are? How did this happen?"

Joey was mockingly slow and deliberate. "Well, you see, my dear, when a mommy and a daddy love each other so much, then Mr. Stork comes . . ."

They both started laughing, and so did Rachel, still eavesdropping outside the partially open door.

Dana said, "It was Oma's magic water. She practically dragged us into the hot springs. That did the trick. It worked. Well, first we worked, and then it worked."

"It didn't seem like work to me," Joey joked.

"You better close the door all the way," she said.

"I can't. Rachel's standing out there listening to everything. Rachel, come on in and shut the door. You have something to tell us?"

She slipped in fast, shut the door, and switched on the DO NOT DISTURB button.

"Dana, you remember Rachel?"

"Of course, I do," Dana said.

"Well, she's been doing some undercover work for us. Share your secrets, Rachel."

She did. And it took a while to explain everything she and Walter discussed until someone finally knocked on the door and ended their confidential conversation. Dana told them to come in. It was just a nurse to take her vitals, but it did alert the attending nurse outside.

"Maybe we better get you back, Joey," Rachel said, "I have to return to work and face the 'Trust-fund Brat.' But, don't you worry, Walter and Mr. Blum have the ball rolling, and it's a big ball," she said.

"Walter? Mr. Blum?" Dana asked.

Joey interjected. "Walter is the older gentleman at the Sinclair station, remember?" Dana nodded, trying to remember.

Rachel continued, "And Jonathan Blum is the attorney Walter hired." She gave Dana a large Macy's shopping bag. "By the way, here's as much of the stuff as the deputies could find: cell phones, laptops, wallets, and other stuff. It's all here in the bag, along with your big red purse," she said as she hid everything in the closet. "I got everything charged up, ready to go. And, Dana, you keep it hidden, lest Officer Fife starts snooping around in Joey's room."

"Why would he care?" Dana asked.

"Because I suspect he thinks I know something about several old ladies who disappeared from the care center–Oma included–who went into the mountains and poof, just like that, vanished."

Dana was puzzled. "But, she's up at the spa retreat . . ."

"But, as you pointed out on our way up, nobody can find the place . . ." Joey said.

"Right, the old green bus wouldn't be there to pick them up and take them the rest of the way!" Dana finished his sentence. They both glanced at Rachel who was totally clueless, like the proverbial deer staring at the oncoming semi.

"It's complicated. I didn't believe it either. But, guess what? I'M PREGNANT!" she shouted.

"And I'm late and have got to go. Gary's waiting," Rachel said as she turned to leave.

"Thanks for everything. You saved us," Dana said.

"Absolutely, you did," Joey added.

Rachel smiled and replied, "I haven't done anything yet."

She was right. It wasn't over. It was just beginning.

Now, they had to get out of the hospital. No time to waste.

Just as she was getting in her car, Rachel remembered she needed to call Mr. Blum. She dialed but got no answer. She confirmed her meeting with Joey and Dana on a voicemail message and added, "You've gotta get them out of the hospital. Officer Bleazard is determined to keep them there." And, I need to get out town and make sure Gunderson does not destroy Joey and Dana's lives, she muttered She sent a text to Walter and warned him about the investigator, too. Then, she squealed out of the parking lot.

❑ ❑ ❑ ❑ ❑

Deputy Owens was still irritated about Bleazard's snarky comments—what an unpleasant man to work with! It was like the Inspector was playing the role of the bitter alcoholic P. I. in a run-of-the-mill TV cop show. Owens wished he could change the channel.

Instead, he was doing some serious sleuthing, world-wide-web-style—looking for old Sinclair stations, buggy accidents, spa resorts, and anything else he could find in the area. Then, he remembered something he saw in the bag of odds and ends found at the accident site, a magazine cover that had been torn loose and was found blowing around. The date was 1925, August or September.

So, now he narrowed his date range and put in "buggy accident, flood" and a few other descriptors.

Then, he found a hit. "Out-of-town couple missing in flash flood" from an old newspaper. He drilled down into the story. "No bodies found, hansom driver badly injured, horse killed in fall . . .." And, there was the report of the wreckage of a carriage, described as new and bright green, that was discovered later near the spot where the Kunzes were found; however, over 95 years later. That's a long time to lie unconscious in a meadow!

Now he was talking to himself out loud. "It all adds up. They were telling the truth, except the truth is impossible! He had to talk to someone about this, but certainly not Bleazard. The only evidence Bleazard wanted was proof that confirmed his preconceived notions. Maybe he should talk to Joey Kunz or the older man who gave him a card, the one with the odd text address. I'll find the card and text him tomorrow,."

❏ ❏ ❏ ❏ ❏

The next morning, Thursday at 10 am, two weeks to the day that Joey, Dana, and Oma took the old green bus up the mountain to Never, Neverland, Jonathan Blum was in the hospital administrator's office. He had a court order, a habeas corpus, stating that he was forcing their release and taking them home. Period.

The administrator's name was Green, an older man, portly, with a comb-over. Blum was frustrating him. "But, sir, they need to be released by a physician. I just can't let them walk out of here," Mr. Green said.

Blum held his ground. "Look at the third paragraph where it says our firm is releasing the hospital from any legal responsibility resulting from their so-called 'early' departure. They both are walking, talking, and feeding themselves. They are fairly young, 40 and 41 respectively. They're physically active and want to get out of here. They gave you their insurance information. But, I understand you have had conversations with Sergeant Bleazard from the County Sheriff's department. He confirmed that they were not in the car . . ."

"But, they were nearby . . ."

"Are you an officer of the court, sir?" Blum asked.

"No, but what I have is an affidavit which I received from the County that says new information from Mr. Kunz's former employer."

"Former employer?" Blum asked.

Green continued, " . . . that says due to Mr. Kunz's alcohol and drug problems, he has had numerous warnings about DUI's . . ."

By now Blum noticed Mr. Green was sweating and flushed, so it was time to cut to the chase. "Mr. Green, first of all, those claims are bogus; second, we don't want to sue the hospital. It's costly, takes way too much time, so here's the deal. You let them go with me, or I am filing this . . ." He showed Green a large envelope filled with blank pages and continued, ". . . because there are no charges filed against Mr. or Mrs. Kunz. They were the victims of an accident, as you well know. I know you conducted a blood test, and I have a subpoena to see it. You know and I know there will not be any evidence of his impairment at all therein. Additionally, we suspect that you are under political pressure from his employer and from people in County government who simply don't like their story about a Shangri La somewhere up in the hills," he said, pointing out the window.

He continued, "And if you have any communication from Mr. Kunz's employer, I will not leave nor relent until I have a signed, notarized copy of any correspondence between the two parties. Am I clear?"

"Yes, clear as glass, but you don't have to get huffy."

"Oh, you haven't seen me huffy. Not yet, whatever that means. Can we please take care of this right now, Mr. Green, so we can all leave, and you can make their rooms available for really sick people?"

"Sure," he said and called the Medical Director. "Excuse me."

Blum stepped out, and he heard Green raise his voice and tell somebody, "I don't care who said what. Release them. Now!"

After a couple of minutes and four ibuprofen, Green stepped out and smiled. "Mr. Blum, if you pull your vehicle around to the west entrance, you can pick them up there."

"As soon as I have that copy of the communication from OJT, his employer, I'll leave and go do that."

"Very well, give me five minutes or so."

While he was waiting, he texted both Rachel and Walter and let them know the Kunzes were leaving. And, he included a sentence about Gunderson's treachery.

Forty-five minutes later, two orderlies wheeled out both patients, smiling broadly, to Blum's vintage Cadillac with a trunk big enough to hide a camel. They both hopped out of their wheel-chairs, wearing their recently cleaned 1920s outfits, appearing as if they were cast members of a Jimmy Cagney gangster flick, with their bags as well as the sack that Rachel left for them. There was plenty of room in the trunk for their gear.

Joey introduced Dana to Blum as he opened the giant back door of the Caddy. As they got in, Blum apologized. "Sorry, no seat belts in the back. I'll try not to get you into another accident."

"Hey, there wasn't one in the hansom either, and look at us; we're fine and dandy," Joey said.

"That reminds me of something. Let me check my messages. I got one from that Deputy Owens, remember him? He followed up on your Never, Neverland story."

Dana bristled. "Don't call it that."

"Sorry, it's code we use. Anyway, he has a question for you. What color was the carriage you were in when you careened into the river?"

They both answered at once, "Green."

And, Dana added, "Brand new. Looked like it had just been painted."

"Thanks. Let's see if that's the right answer."

Later that afternoon, Jonathan pulled into a long driveway in a neighborhood of older, estate-like homes hidden away among im-

posing stands of hardwoods–maple, oak, and chestnut trees surrounded and concealed behind lilacs, wisteria, and all kinds of other
well-manicured greenery. Dana and Joey woke up.

"Where are we, Mr. Blum?" Dana asked.

"I guess you could call it a safe house," he obliged them.

"Safe house? What for?"

"We have a physician and a nurse inside to ensure your continued recovery, and there's been some buzz about you on social net-
works and so forth. Walter's on his way and so are some friends. And,
later Rachel, as soon as we can reach her, will join us. We left her
some messages. She's probably being fired, right about . . . (he
checked his watch) . . . now. I imagine she'll probably call us soon.
Let's go make you comfortable.

Rachel wasn't fired, not yet anyway, but people were avoiding
her, afraid to look her in the eye. When she called Gunderson's office,
all she got was voicemail. Marta wasn't answering. Probably already
gone, given the cloud hanging over everyone at the office.

Finally, she received a text message from Paolo, Gunderson's
comptroller, who told her to bring her laptop, collect Joey's personal
belongings in a box, and come down to the small conference room
on the second floor.

Then, she realized that her text messages were also stored in her
"Messages" app on her Power Book, so she turned off the Wi-Fi
connection, found the three or four text messages and the accom-
panying chain of communications, and deleted all of them. After
quickly gathering up his photos, diplomas, and knickknacks, she
packed it all up and started down-stairs. She remembered that she

had her own documents on her laptop which she sent to the Cloud and then deleted them. I'm ready, she thought.

When she walked in, Gunderson, Paolo, and a small man in a dark suit were waiting for her. They were not smiling, but then, Gunderson never did smile.

"There you go," she said putting the box on the table, but she remained standing. "Make yourself comfortable," Paolo said.

"Sit," said Gunderson.

"I'm fine, thanks."

"No. You're not," Gunderson said. "You were sent upstate to get Joey's password and files off his laptop, and we didn't get that information until yesterday. Explain yourself."

"There's nothing to explain. He was still unconscious for the first two days, and when he regained consciousness, the hospital staff wouldn't let me see him. When I finally was able to speak to him, I sent you exactly what you asked for."

"Do you have his laptop?"

"No, I suppose he still does. I just asked him for his password and told him I needed some files to send to you. Now you have them."

"But, you sympathize with him."

"Of course, I do. He hired me, he trusted me, and he trusted you. He's been through a lot. He and his wife were in comas for days. I don't know why you don't sympathize with them."

Paolo interjected, "His own grandmother is missing!"

"How do you know that? What makes you think so? They made it clear they left her at the spa resort, and then someone else drove them down the highway when they got in an accident. They don't remember any of it. How do you know these things, because Joey doesn't? I did what you asked, and I don't know what more you want. I have a lot to do upstairs until Mr. Kunz returns."

Gunderson then dropped his pretense. "You know, you should take some time off, figure out what your place is here and where loyalties lie, because, frankly . . ."

She stopped him in his tracks. "Frankly, I've had enough of this mealy-mouthed attempt to besmirch Joey and rob him of his shares, and I've had enough of you. We all have. Here's my laptop," and she put what looked like a hockey puck on top of it.

"What's the hockey puck for?" Paolo asked, bewildered.

"It only looks like a hockey puck," she moved it around on top of the laptop and added, "It's a magnet, for degaussing. Just put my check in the mail."

The little lawyerly man stood up to stop her. She stepped toward him.

"Please try to stop me, please! I'm a former All-American shortstop for Florida State. I've knocked over people tougher and bigger than you before sliding into third."

He backed off, and she left. She looked behind to make sure no one was following her. So far, so good.

9

Rachel enjoyed the beautiful ride in the woods and vales, pastures and cornfields, through a countryside that looked like a Currier and Ives print. She enjoyed her free time. *I did just lose my job. Or did I quit?* Either way, she felt free after seven-and-a-half years of college, while working at various jobs along the way.

Finally, she arrived at the obscure address Walter had given her. It too looked like an Americana poster. She drove up the long driveway to the house, knocked, and Francine Gregory, Joey's CNA answered the door.

"I know you. Where do I know you from?" Rachel asked.

"We passed in the hallway once at the County General Hospital, and I came to Joey's room just as you were leaving. Today's my first day, thanks to Walter. He said he has an eye for talent," Francine said.

"And, yesterday was my last day at my job. In any case, it's nice to finally make your acquaintance," Rachel said.

The grand old house had high ceilings, archways over every entrance, and solid, carved-oak doors. Since it was September, there was already a chill in the air and a blaze was spitting out sparks from the huge fireplace. Everyone was seated around an antique ten-foot table in the dining room except for Francine; she was attending to Dana who was in a recliner near the window.

Everyone that is, except the guests from Atlanta whose flight had been delayed.

Blum got a text that said they had found the turn-off and should arrive momentarily. Around the table sat Joey, Blum, and Walter; then Martina, "Marta," Ilić, recently discharged from OJT, next to her. Rachel, even more recently discharged, was in attendance. And a certified court reporter, Swarupa, freelancing at Blum's request, was recording and verifying what was about to happen.

A few minutes later, Glade Peacock and his brother Keith arrived. They were the owners of an Atlanta-based investment firm that focused on up-and-coming technology firms and were eager to acquire the technology and processes Joey and his firm had created, not only to teach courses and test students of employers studying online, but also to issue them college credit and tie it to other coursework they had earned elsewhere.

Blum made all the introductions and then explained what was on the agenda. "In a nutshell, my friends, we are here today because the members of the firm that acquired OJT last year are bad actors. We suspect they are about to fraudulently change the employment agreement with Joey so that they can void his agreement that includes 10,000 shares or 15 percent of the total. What are they valued at, Martina?"

She replied in a slight Bosnian accent, "Stock price estimates for owners' shares if they were publicly tradable, would be between $300 and $350 per share, given the company right now is worth about $35 to $45 million if it were to go public. And it's growing about 15 to 25 percent per year and is estimated to generate more than $100 million per year in four years. At least, that's what the company's financial advisers say, and that should be reliable information."

The Peacock brothers looked at each other. Keith, the younger one, seemed to be the talker and more marketing-oriented. "We've looked at the numbers and, given the interest of our partners, I think we can make the numbers work. The original owners can't understand why Gunderson and his partners want Joey gone. It can only mean that a third party, likely a competitor who covets their customer base, is behind it, and they don't want to share any profits of the sale with Mr. Kunz. We feel we ought to move quickly before they break it all apart."

And Blum added the kicker. "If they try to falsify his agreement, we can take them to court, where they would most likely face criminal charges, and any interest they may have accumulated since they took over could revert to the original owners, making the deal even sweeter. Anyway, that's something to consider. Shall we have a bite and let the Peacocks think about this overnight?" Everyone agreed to that.

It was now late afternoon and, although Joey knew off the record that he was no longer employed, Blum wanted to get the official notification straight from the source. He sat down with Joey and Dana in a small library in a nook just off the dining room overlooking the garden to inform them what was about to happen. First, he told Joey to send Gunderson a message telling him that he wasn't yet cleared to drive, but that he believed he would be in the office later in the week. If they terminated him, then Joey could cite his validated employment agreement, meaning they would have to cash out his shares.

Blum explained, "They have dug their own hole. We just need to wait and let Gunderson fall into his own trap. And then," he added, "if they try to produce their doctored document, the courts will have fun with them. They would most certainly be forced to walk away from the ownership of the company and possibly even face criminal charges."

Joey and Dana liked what they heard. Now, they needed to decide what course to take. In the meantime, Walter and Blum gave them the chance to decompress in the beautiful hideaway for a few days until they were ready to restart their lives.

After the other parties left, Joey asked Francine, Martina, and Rachel to stay behind and talk with him, Blum, and Walter. They were waiting in the study when the three came in with Dana in tow.

"Sorry to keep you. We had some legal issues to discuss regarding the Gunderson partnership. We've been waiting for the other shoe to drop," Joey said. "So far, nothing."

Martina wanted to share her insight with the others. "First, I think something else is wrong at OJT, and it has nothing to do with you, Joey. The owners started having long meetings almost a month ago, before the accident, with people I'd never seen before. They came and went. The strangers appeared to be in control. The partners seemed to be backed into a corner. I suspected that they had to acquire your shares to get bargaining power or all was lost. That's why I hid their copy of the agreement so that they couldn't alter it and why they needed Rachel to get your copy. I knew they'd try it. They're very conniving . . . is that the right word?"

Blum nodded in agreement. "It's the right word."

"But, wouldn't the law firm have the originals?" Rachel asked.

"The problem for them is they have new lawyers," Marta explained. "I am sure I'm the only one who knows where the documents are. I considered bringing them with me when I was forced to leave, but then that would put me under suspicion and put Mr. Kunz in even more jeopardy."

"Marta, that was a very smart decision," Blum said.

At that point, a housekeeper brought in some snacks and drinks just as the afternoon sun sunk into the western sky. Floor-to-ceiling windows revealed a beautifully maintained garden and a small pond. Dana watched as a covey of quail fluttered about near some pyracantha bushes along a terraced walkway. She squeezed Joey's hand and pointed outside as if to say signs of life!

Then at Walter's urging, Joey began his explanation of what happened when they made their trip to Salem Crossing and up to the Hot Springs.

"What I am about to tell you will sound, fantastic, unbelievable, like a UFO abduction or something akin to that, but when I'm finished, you'll know why I asked the three of you to join us."

Dana stepped right into the conversation. "It's an unbelievable story. But it is true, because if a skeptical, sarcastic Jewish girl like me is convinced, then you ought to give it serious consideration. It has far-reaching consequences for all of us here, doesn't it, Joey?"

He nodded and looked to Blum for help. "Mr. Blum has mentioned a place he calls the 'Shining City on a Hill' . . . what is it again in Latin, Dana?"

"*Civitate Dei's Lucet*, which means God's shining city or *Splendidis-*

sima Civitas Super Montem. It was posted on signs at the Grand Hotel."

Joey then continued, " . . . and what we're telling you is that we found a *Civets Super Montem.* It's a great story. Jonathan can explain more about it."

Jonathan Blum leaned forward and looked at Dana. "Like my new friend Dana, I was raised in a Jewish household, very Jewish, so we weren't schooled in the religious background of the country's founders–Christian pilgrims and Puritans largely from England.

But, thanks to my exposure to this place and the concept, let's just say I became more 'illuminated' and was given a new chance at life after a harrowing beginning.

He continued. "You probably all know about the pilgrims, Plymouth Rock, and the first Thanksgiving. But, what most people overlook is that farther south from Plymouth another group of English settlers landed some ten years later, in 1630, at the place that would eventually become Boston. They were the Puritans. They wanted to purify the Anglican Church of all its vestiges of Catholicism, like holidays and rituals for saints, while the pilgrims, on the other hand, held completely different Protestant beliefs.

"But, the one thing that gave the Puritans a unique appeal that eventually made Boston the center of everything in New England, instead of Plymouth, was the vision of their founder, John Winthrop. He shared it with everyone back in England . . . a vision that attracted the gaze and attention of everyday Englishmen–a New Jerusalem in the New World. He called it the "Shining City on the Hill." This whole idea was incorporated by the English Colonies and then later by the newly-founded thirteen United States of America. Today, it's symbolized by the Statue of Liberty in New York harbor.

In 1980, Ronald Reagan held up this ideal as the lofty standard for what America symbolized . . . of what it could be," Blum said.

"We read in Genesis about such a city, the City of Enoch, for example, which the Bible said was a place filled with such righteous people that it was taken up, off the Earth . . . 'it was no more.' There are stories and rumors about places, hidden places like this all around the world. Shangri La, for one."

Then Dana added, "The unbelievable thing is, we found such a place, Salem Crossing, and the place it leads to higher up the mountain that they call the Grand Hotel and Spa, but I suspect there is another 'official name.' You'll see their motto, 'One Heart, One Mind,' inscribed here and there. The ideal they embrace is a place where people are of 'one heart and one mind, live righteously and have no poor among them.'"

Blum picked up on that. "The thought of an ideal place like this exists everywhere, sometimes with horrific results. You all know that the world has experienced 'false prophets' expounding on how to create a fair and just society for at least two centuries now—from Marx and Engels to Lenin, Pol Pot, and Stalin, to Castro and his copycats in Venezuela—these are devilish counterfeits. And not surprisingly, when you reflect on recent history, they were generally based on class conflict, covetousness, violence, and force of arms.

"What the Kunzes saw—and what I experienced—is no such thing. It's not another secular application of Social Darwinism, it's not dialectic materialism, it's not based on government-run redistribution of income or property. Rather, it's founded on love and sacrifice, with people willing to serve others and to make free-will offerings to lift everyone else up. While the early apostles were still alive two millennia ago, the early Christian church practiced these principles, as have other groups here and there in modern times," he explained and then turned to Dana and Joey.

Dana was the first one to speak up. "Let us tell you how we first found the little town of Salem Crossing that looks like a Norman Rockwell painting, a slice of America taken out of 1925, and second, a virtual Shining City on the Hill that can't be found on any map. A place that offers life-giving waters and unbounded brotherly love. We thought it was a spa resort, a Grand Hotel, and a rejuvenation center, but it is more than that. I'm evidence of it, now three weeks pregnant, but I'm just one example," Dana added.

Then, Joey described how Oma got a postcard from a friend, an invitation to join her in a place that couldn't be found on any map, followed by a personal visit from her friend Virginia. The two of them persuaded Joey and Dana to drive his grandmother to the Shining City where she remains.

Dana then said, "Mr. Blum mentioned the Plymouth settlement. Well, Joey's Oma first characterized the place as a representation of the Plymouth Plantation where residents role-play as if they were pilgrims right out of the 1620s with period clothing, houses, even accents, and modes of speech.

"But, that's not what it was. It looked like life in 1925, but is probably cleaner, with real homes, hotels, businesses, shops, and stores with real people running lathes, baking bread, and shoeing horses. The streets were filled with antique buses, Model T's, horse-drawn wagons, and carriages, which is how we ended up in the hospital. Our carriage lost its horse, and we were tossed into a swollen stream, deposited in a meadow, and found by a passing motorist.

Now we're here," Dana finished.

It was silent for a couple of minutes as the group absorbed the incredible description of such an unbelievable place. But, before they could make any comments or ask any questions, Dana added her own, very personal story.

"The most unbelievable part is that I have had dozens of visits to my OBGYN in the past year and various clinics. I missed one because of our accident. They all told us our chance of ever having a child was slim to none. They were going to tell me about another new experimental process, but then we found a better one; we visited the hot springs and a miracle occurred. The doctors at the hospital told me I'm expecting! Can you believe it? So, I'm a believer, I guess. Miracles will do that to you."

The women were very touched by what they heard, but they seemed troubled. Francine was never at a loss for words, so she asked the obvious question.

"I think this sounds wonderful. We're happy for you. But, what does this all have to do with us?" Marta and Rachel nodded in agreement. They had the same question.

"Yes, why are you telling US of all people?" Rachel asked.

Walter drew in closer to them. "As the Marines say, we are looking for a few good men. In your case, women." The women seemed stunned by that revelation.

Then, Rachel interrupted Walter. "I don't know these other ladies really at all. I've worked with Marta for a year or so, and I just met Francine at the hospital, so I don't know their qualifications, but I just barely finished my internship. Yes, I have a brand new MBA. However, my life experience is limited. I played some softball . . ."

Walter interrupted her, "Tell them what's on your schedule to-morrow at 11 a.m.."

"What? Well, I'm set to coach a softball game . . ."

"Go on. Not just any softball game; tell them about your team," Walter said.

"It's a Special Olympics softball team of girls with various dis-abilities; most are Down Syndrome kids. We are in the playoffs . . ."

Walter interjected, "And, how did you get started in this?"

"I had a little brother, Jeffy, who was born with Downs Syn-drome, and who loved to come to my games. He never missed them. I did a lot of biking, and I had a bike trailer. I'd pull him along on long rides. It was a good workout. And, then when I was a freshman at FSU," she hesitated, choked a bit and wiped her tears away, "he got pneumonia, and he died. He was seven-and-a-half-years old."

Walter turned to Francine, "Mrs. Gregory, you were in the news . . . the national news last year. Tell the others about what put you into the spotlight."

She hesitated and looked at Blum. He nodded. Encouraged, she went ahead. "Well, a few years ago I finished my CNA and was try-ing to get accepted into a program to get my RN. But I wasn't ac-cepted anywhere, so I accepted a position at a women's clinic in Chicago. The pay was really good, and for the first couple of months it was okay, but there was a lot of stress and turnover with the women 'in the back.'

"Then, I was sent there, and to my horror, I discovered it was like a scene from Schindler's List. It was a human butcher shop, an assembly line run by a modern-day Dr. Mengele with tiny baby parts everywhere. I knew I had to leave, but if I did, I'd just run away like everyone else had done without doing or saying anything. We had to sign a non-disclosure agreement, so I did, but not before speaking with an assistant Federal District Attorney. Soon, I was the government's 'snitch,' taking pictures, recording conversations, and so on.

"But, the best part was, I was able to rescue three different full-term babies—babies, not fetuses—that had been set aside on a shelf where we were just supposed to just let them die. I couldn't do that, so I was able to clear their air passages and hide them in a closet covered by an infant-sized electric blanket. And, on three different occasions, I spirited them out in a big gym bag just as I was leaving work for the night. Friends helped me, the DA offered assistance, and so did a colleague who worked for a pediatrician. Two of them survived, and I'm raising them with help from my sister and my oldest daughter who's 14. Here are their pictures. Natasha and Chloë." Francine took photos out of her wallet and passed them around.

"Natasha just turned 5, and Chloë is 3. Two years ago, I testified for the prosecutor, and Dr. Mengele, as I call him, is now serving three consecutive life sentences. And, he's getting better treatment than any of his patients ever did!"

Finally, Blum and Walter looked at Marta or Martina Ilić, fifteen years now a US citizen. "Marta," Blum asked her, "tell us about yourself."

"I haven't talked about this to anyone in years—I try to forget it. I was born in a small village near Sarajevo in what was then Yugoslavia. The area I come from is the Balkans, a collection of many small countries, languages, religions, and ethnic origins. And the word 'Balkanization' came to mean places forced to be one country where the various inhabitants wanted to be separate. And when push comes to shove, they do exactly that. I was 15 years old when the Serbs under Milosević started bombing the beautiful city of Sarajevo, the capital of the province in Yugoslavia called Bosnia. Now the country is Bosnia-Herzegovina, but then it was a hell-hole with murder and slaughter, rape and destruction.

"At that time, I was attending a prestigious girls' school in Sarajevo, but my family was in my village farther east from there, right in the path of the Serbian destruction. The village was destroyed: my family, my home, my friends, everything was gone. I do not know what happened to them, and I don't want to think about it. We had to flee, so one night, one of our teachers found a bus and a driver, and we headed south toward the city of Mostar. There we had trouble. The Croats had declared themselves independent of Serbia; they never liked each other much, mostly they hated each other. The Serbs were moving on to the coast so they could shell the Croats and move on the coastal cities of Split, Makarska, and Dubrovnik, so they could have Mediterranean ports.

"Anyway, our driver was shot at a stop point; our teacher ran out to try to protect us and pacify the soldiers and let us through. But, they had seen a busload of teenage girls, Bosnians, some Muslims, some Orthodox, and like me, some Catholics, so you know what they were thinking. All of us got along fine. We loved each other. Then, they shot our teacher. We had no choice. We had to leave, and since I knew how to drive and had family in Dubrovnik, I figured if we could get there, I could talk our way in.

"The bus was still running, there was so much confusion out there. But the way ahead had cleared, so I jumped in the driver's seat, drove through the stop point, and hit a couple of soldiers as I drove away. Bullets struck the bus, but the soldiers had problems of their own. That evening we were in another traffic jam, but the checkpoints were manned by Croatian soldiers, and I told them we were all Croatian students being chased by Serbs. I gave them my name as well as the names and address of my aunt and uncle.

"We all eventually came under U.N. protection, and eventually I was able to contact my mother's cousin in Chicago, got a ticket, and here I am. I'm no hero."

Blum spoke up, "Actually, the 32 girls on her bus think she is; the commander of Dutch forces as part of the NATO forces called her a hero, and as a result, she got sponsors, a scholarship, and earned a degree in accounting and international business."

Francine scratched her head. "Well, I gotta say, these are couple of choice persons, and I hope we can all become friends, but what do we really have in common? I still don't understand."

Joey provided the answer. "I can tell you how we see it from our point of view. When we were on our way to Salem, we were given this by a man named Judge Harlan Stone." He held up their invitation. "It's an invitation. We thought it was simply a ticket or a pass allowing us to come to the Grand Hotel and the Hot Springs, but it was blank. But why, we asked ourselves, would anyone invite us to such a remarkable place? The judge reminded me that my background in recruitment and instructional development might come in handy, and Dana's training as an attorney and expert on ancient languages, and the law would be helpful. He then asked what kind of contribution we could make and told us 'to fill in the blanks on our invitation.' So, what did we see as our responsibility? To find people who, in our estimation, would contribute to such a divine place. The judge asked us to seek them out, write down their names and submit them as candidates to receive an invitation . . . enough names of people to fill another bus, much like the one that Marta just described, and then send the list on to the 'Higher Ups.'"

"In other words, if these people are willing to apply, to let us put their names on our invitation. Then they too can enter the Shining City on the Hill," Dana explained.

"And you are the first ones we are considering," Joey said in conclusion.

"What is required of us?" Marta asked.

"To leave everything behind. Handle your affairs here and say your goodbyes to the world we all will leave behind," Dana explained. "And to give your all, because you'll all get so much more in return. To join people who are of one heart and one mind."

"That's a hard thing, isn't it?" Marta asked. "How do you do that?"

Blum almost whispered: "For starters, to esteem your brother—or your sister—as yourself."

Everyone chewed on that for a moment. Francine broke the silence.

"What about family, kids? I have three, and there's my sister who helps me raise my girls; what about them?" Francine asked. Dana and Joey looked to Blum for an answer.

"Give Dana and Joey their names. They'll be put on the list too," Blum answered.

Francine beamed. "Nothing this good has ever been offered to me in my entire life! I hardly have anything to give up, All I have is my family. I say 'yes, yes, and yes.' Tell me what you want of me!"

Walter smiled. "Just your heart and your mind," that's all."

"You have it," Francine said.

"Mine too!" Marta said.

Rachel looked away, tears in her eyes. "I don't have any family to speak of anymore; my dad passed, and I don't know where my mother is . . ."

Walter leaned toward her. "Do you remember your father ever talking about his grandpa, his mother's dad?"

"Yeah, he did. He said I got my pitcher's arm from him. Why?"

"You know his last name?"

"Johnson, I think. Yes, Johnson."

"Do you know his first name?"

"I don't think he ever told me, but he played baseball, I remember," Rachel said with growing interest.

Then, Walter took an old baseball card out his pocket–his last one–and gave it to the young woman seated in front of him. "Does this ring a bell?"

She took it, studied it, and then looked back at him. "Yes, that's him. His name was Walter, Walter Johnson. I saw his–your bust at Cooperstown! It's you, isn't it? Why you're my great-great-grand-father! But, this is . . . is impossible!" Rachel screamed with delight and rushed to hug him.

Walter embraced her and replied, "Rachel, get used to impossible."

PART III

GONE FISHING!

Rachel and her college hunk Tanner Hutchings, an NCAA football standout still trying to land an NFL contract, were unloading their bikes from his Dodge Ram and locking them to a nearby bike rack as members of her team were arriving at the park. None of them could resist running up and hugging her.

Tanner was touched. "Rachel, these girls love you, but then that's really an easy thing to do."

"What is?" Rachel asked, distracted.

"Loving you . . . "

"Tanner, these sweet creatures love everybody! That's why I love to coach them, They're non-judgmental. They only see the good. People call them handicapped, but I think we're the ones with the disabilities."

She put on her cleats, grabbed a large bag of bats and balls, and started the long walk over to Field Four and her team's dugout.

Both teams were warming up when a couple of fans took their seats a few rows up in the bleachers behind the "Wolverine's" dugout, where Rachel was running her team through its drills.

Walter and Blum settled into their seats. Blum opened a sack of goodies he bought at a 7-Eleven on his way to pick up Walter. He shared his favorite weakness with his friend.

"These are good! What are they?" Walter asked.

"Like it says right here, Red Twizzlers. Got some black ones, too."

"Too bad they don't sell dogs . . . a dog and a Coke would be good," Walter said. "It was fun to play, but the spectators had even more fun. The only games I saw were hers, but I was merely there in spirit, literally. No Twizzlers or Chicago dogs for me, with sauerkraut and hot mustard. This is great," Walter said. "Too bad I have to return."

"Yeah, but you have been a great help to Joey and Dana and especially Rachel," Blum said.

"It was a treat. I hope she can make the journey. It looks difficult, complicated."

"Kind of gutsy to reveal your real age. When exactly were you born, the first time I mean?"

"Would you ask a woman that question? I'm kind of sensitive about that . . ." They laughed and then saw Rachel. She had just spotted her 'fans' in the bleachers.

"Hey, come on down here for a minute! I want you to meet somebody."

Walter and Blum tiptoed down and then around to the stairs behind the dugout. Rachel was calling out the starting line-up, checking off names.

"Stay with us We don't start for another 15 minutes," Rachel said. "Let me introduce you guys."

She grabbed Tanner and pulled him over to meet Walter. "Tanner, this is my grandpa, Walter Johnson. He played some ball a few years ago. And, Grandpa, this is Tanner Hutchings, a friend from college." They shook hands.

"Just a friend?" Walter asked.

"We've been busy," Tanner said, smiled, and then looked at Rachel. "Too busy."

"And, Tanner, this is Jonathan Blum, sort of a family attorney . . . an extended family attorney," Rachel said. "Walter, Jonathan, I'm so glad you came."

"Our pleasure," Walter said and then pulled her aside for a second. "Rachel, we have to leave soon, and I might not be able to talk with you after the game. I've been called back to the City, and I just wanted you to know that whatever happens, I hope you can, uh, make the trip . . . the, uh, the whole family does."

Rachel felt a lump in her throat; she just found a family member, and now he's leaving?

"I'm going to do all I can. I just don't know what's going to happen with Tanner and me. I haven't told anyone about what I've learned. Who would I tell? I'm not sure what is required of me . . . but, right now, I've gotta get back to the team."

"Rachel, just remember, everybody writes their own invitation. Now just go knock it outta the park, Kiddo!" Walter said as he and Blum made their way back to the bleachers.

"What's that all about, Rachel?" Tanner asked.

"Family stuff," she said.

"But, I thought you didn't . . ."

"I did, too, Tanner. I did, too, and now he's leaving."

Tanner immediately recognized how crestfallen she was. He had to fill the gap!

Rachel and the Wolverines were able to slip by with a 3-2 victory, thanks to a double in the top of the 9th. When she looked up to see if her great-great-grandpa saw her girls finish the game with two strikeouts and an infield pop-up, he and Blum were gone.

Tanner and Rachel put their gear in the truck, unlocked their bikes, and set off toward the lake. She needed to burn off some calories and clear her head.

The next 24 hours would prove to be more heart-wrenching than anything she had ever faced.

Back at the manor house in the woods, the safe house as Blum called it, Joey and Dana had grown accustomed to their comfortable circumstances. Dana especially fell in love with the library and all the ancient classics lined up, floor-to-ceiling on two sides of the reading room. Joey had been conferring with Blum who returned about noon about the strategy of what he would say to Gunderson.

Despite his numerous emails and text messages to his old boss, he wondered what was happening at OJT Partners. Blum advised Joey that he should accompany him as his attorney if and when he got an appointment.

Then, Joey decided he would just show up with Blum at his side Monday morning. It was Saturday, and he was feeling better every day now. He and Blum were hiding out under the terrace watching the quail and sipping on Cokes.

"What do we have to lose?" Joey said.

"I'm coming around to your thinking. That way, we could force him to play his fraud card and paint him into a corner; sorry for the mixing of metaphors. The longer he strings this out, the harder it will be for you to make your claim," Blum said.

"I can't wait any longer . . . we can't wait any longer. Since we're certain now that no one is watching the house, Dana and I need to go home, straighten up some things, and get our clothes, because Wednesday, we're going fishing."

"Fishing?"

"After the two-legged variety. No time to waste. Dana has a list. She is 100 percent on board now. We both are," Joey said, crossing his fingers; at least at that moment he was.

"She says, that to be successful, we need our own bait and lures."

"What kind?"

"I have no idea."

Sunday morning back at home, Joey discovered what Dana had in mind: a website, a blog, and a podcast. First thing last night, she sequestered herself in her cubbyhole of an office upstairs, acquired a URL, set up a simple blog, and posted her story. Then, this "secular Jewess" pulled out a few verses of the Sermon on the Mount and included them in her first post.

"Magic words," she called them, "especially on Sunday morning when pious Christians search the Net for inspiration. Fairly well versed in SEO strategies, she plugged into a word-search tool she'd used during her law school days and hoped for a few bites.

"What exactly are you doing?" Joey asked her. She was seated behind a 100-year-old roll-top desk she had inherited from her father that looked out the attic window in the cozy little nook above their bedroom. It was still piled high with books and research materials from law school and was squeezed in between two tall filing cabinets;

the one to the right was devoted to the ancient world: her favorite subject was the ancient library at Alexandria.

"What?" Dana was distracted.

"You can't divulge the details of our trip to the Grand Hotel and making friends with dead people! Everyone will think we're crazy," Joey said in frustration.

"I'm just browsing the Web," she answered as she dusted off the antique world globe in her office and adjusted her Mona Lisa print.

"I really need to tidy this place up," Dana admitted. She was dressed like a co-ed with a tattered Vanderbilt sweatshirt and an oversized pair of warm-up pants. Still, he couldn't take his eyes off her.

"I look terrible, don't I? Go ahead, be truthful, I can take it."

"Dana, you be truthful. What are you up to?"

"I used to think religion was just the vain imaginings of weak minds, the insecurity of old people grasping for hope. But, I saw with my own eyes where religion met reality! We both did. At first, I figured we had shared a bad dream—or a good dream. I'm not sure which, and that the accident warped our perception of what's real and what's not.

"And, then we met Judge Harlan Stone, Hall of Fame pitcher Walter Johnson, and Norman Rockwell who captured Americana in his paintings that graced the cover of the Saturday Evening Post for decades. And, of course, there's President Calvin Coolidge himself. And, they asked us to join them . . . and, all of them deceased for decades."

"But only if we finish an impossible task . . ." Joey added with a sigh.

She turned back to her computer, put it to sleep, and continued to tidy up her cluttered attic office. Joey joined in.

"Nothing is impossible to them who believe. You see, not only did I read Matthew, Chapter 5, and the Sermon on the Mount, but I found Luke, Chapter 24, and read about 'Doubting Thomas.' And here I am, 'a secular Jew,' quoting the New Testament to my Christian husband while I'm chumming."

"Chumming? What are you talking about?"

"I'm throwing bait over the side. I'm hooked up to three different Christian chat rooms right now, asking readers to help me with my blog to find 'saintly people' whose lives embody the principles illustrated in the Sermon on the Mount and who deserve some recognition, and perhaps even an invitation to the Shining City," she said.

"Look, I've already received three hits and a list of nine different recommendations just since last night. And, what's more, someone at the hospital has put our story on a couple of social media sites, and people are asking about us. 'Who are these people? Do they have any proof? Why don't these people come forward? Where is this place?' It's starting to pick up steam, Joey. Please tell me if you are getting cold feet. Remember, I was the skeptical one, and I don't want to go any faster than you're willing to go. I don't want to drag you along."

"No, that's not it," he said as he lifted a big box of books and put them on the wardrobe. "Tomorrow, I have to face Gunderson at the office. Blum's going with me. I just can't walk away from what I helped start and at least collect what's owed me. Plus, I need to make Gunderson pay. That would help finance our mission or whatever you call it."

Just then, she got a beep on her iPhone . . . a plea for help from Rachel. She opened the text and stopped Joey as he was carrying trash downstairs.

"Joey, stop. Rachel's at University Medical. There's been a terrible accident . . ."

"Was she hurt?"

"No, her friend she was biking with was hit by a truck. She needs to see if Blum can contact Walter; he's her only family."

"Funny, I just checked my messages and emails to see if she contacted me, and I've got a strange one, too from that officer."

"Bleazard?"

"No, the kid that was with him. He said, 'Call me, I've got some information you might need.'"

"Looks like we've got miles to go before we sleep . . . and a lot more hurdles to jump over."

Joey started back down the stairs. And garbage to take out. There's always more garbage.

Bleazard thought he was punishing his trainee, Deputy Brady Owens, by having him sent back to the evidence room, but it was like when Fox threw Brer Rabbit into the briar patch as depicted in the now banned 1946 Disney cartoon classic, *Song of the South*. As his grandma who raised him said, "Boy, you're back where you wanna be, where you can use your skills with technology to dig into all kinds of stuff other people ignore. Plus, take your new 40 pound dumbbells to your 'cage' with you and keep on pumping up, baby!"

Unlike most young black athletes his age, Brady always wanted to be in law enforcement if he couldn't play football. A badly torn

ACL that never did heal right ended his dream of getting a football scholarship. But, he loved the pursuit of the truth; he loved the hunt, and he was good with computers. So, for the last ten days or so, he had a lot of time in between manning a desk behind a chain-link cage to look into the Kunzes 'wild claims', as Bleazard called the story told by Joey and Dana.

"There's something to this," he told his granny, "and I found a smoking gun."

"A gun?"

"No, a green carriage that crashed almost a hundred years ago, just like the one they claimed to be riding in. I think Bleazard wants to ignore their story because he's been talking to people down in the big city. He wants to move up in the world and out of this 'one-horse county' as he calls it. But, it's not fair to the victims, in this case the Kunzes. Plus, what if their story is true?" With his granny's encouragement, he pushed forward.

He thought about that conversation when he sent an email to Joey Kunz and attached a large file to it, including images from newspaper clippings from 1925. He loved the stuff you can find on the Web if you just took the time to look and if you don't care where the search takes you!

Joey and Dana arrived at the University Medical Center about 8:30 pm after visiting hours but sweet-talked their way to the waiting area where they found Rachel. Her eyes were red and swollen, and she looked like she hadn't slept in 24 hours. She hadn't.

"So sorry to pull you away after all you've been through. Seems like we're always meeting in hospitals. Did you talk to Blum?"

"We tried. We left a message. What happened?" Dana asked her.

"It's my friend, almost fiancé, Tanner. We went biking up the canyon road toward the lake; he was way up ahead on the incline, and I had problems with my shoes leaving the pedals for some reason. I came to the turn-off . . . the fork that I thought was the turn-off and took it, and after a mile or so realized I'd turned too soon. So, I flipped a U-ee and went back down to the junction when a police car, a fire truck, and an ambulance screamed up the canyon with lights and sirens blazing. I immediately had a bad feeling and hurried to get to the scene, but it was uphill, and I couldn't pedal very fast.

"Then, I came on the scene; a pick-up was off to the side with its hood smashed in and its windshield broken. Tanner's bike was up against a tree on the other side of the highway, its frame and front tire bent out of shape. That's when I turned and saw the paramedics strap Tanner onto a stretcher with one of the medics holding a bottle of plasma; his head and neck were secured in some kind of brace.

"The officer prevented me from seeing him, and when I finally got to the other side, the ambulance sped off back down the canyon. I had to wait for the officer to clean things up, issue a ticket to the driver who ran the stop sign and wait for the wrecker. An hour later, he took me down to the hospital, here, where I've been ever since. My bike is still up the canyon, chained to a tree!"

Rachel collapsed on the sofa, and Dana sat with her and comforted her.

Seeing Rachel was still in her biking clothes and hadn't changed since embarking up the canyon, Dana talked to the nurse in charge and got her a pair of hospital-issued scrubs. The three of them stood in front of the nurse's station.

"You can take a shower here," the nurse said, "and change into these. What have they told you about your boyfriend?"

"Not much. Just that he has a compound fracture of his right leg and spinal injuries. He had a couple of surgeries last night, but they haven't told me much. I don't even know why I'm still here. I haven't seen him, since I'm not family, they won't let me in.

"They called his parents who are set to land here later today; I've never met them. We had agreed to announce our engagement before your accident, and by then I hadn't seen him for a of couple weeks. It's a real mess." They started walking to the visitors' lounge. Dana looked at Joey for approval and then said, "Why don't you come with us? We have an extra room, and tomorrow I can take you to your car . . ."

Rachel interrupted her. "Actually, it's his truck, and it's parked at the ball field. Maybe you can take me there. But, I don't have the key. Let me talk to the nurse."

A few minutes later, she returned. "First sign of cooperation. They found his keys in his pocket; I told the nurse to give his wallet to his parents. I'll take you up on your offer. I'm sick of hospitals."

"Not any more than we are," Dana said. "We can check back here tomorrow. I'll come with you."

$$\textcircled{11}$$

After Dana had tucked Rachel safely away in their guest room, she and Joey were back in their own familiar surroundings, but something was different. It was late, and they had a lot to talk about.

"Does this feel like home to you? Joey asked.

"Now that you mention it, I'm not sure. It feels more like a hotel room or an AirBnB."

"I wish I knew what was up with the company. I had hoped to get an answer to my text," he said, "but, so far nothing."

"Have you tried your email? I mean your corporate email. Or Slack?"

"Slack! Why didn't I think of that? I never did use it much."

Joey went downstairs to the kitchen where they'd dropped their stuff from the hospital, grabbed his MacBook, and hurried back to the bedroom.

"Good call, Dana. Here it is. Terse but definite. 'Appt. set with Gunderson and partners in the second-floor conference room at 1 pm Monday. Please respond upon receipt.' Not exactly warm and friendly, no 'Hey, glad to have you back. Hope you're feeling okay.' It's like Robo-Mail."

Then, he checked his text messages. "Look, a text from that

young deputy. Says Bleazard is planning on being at the office on Monday. Looks like some sort of a trap. Whaddya think?"

"Better call Blum," Dana said.

"I'll send him an email. And a text. I've got to talk to him early. Are you taking Rachel up to her boyfriend's truck in the morning?"

"Yeah, after I talk to a Realtor. We need an appraisal."

"A reappraisal of everything, don't you think?" Joey said.

Brady Owens didn't mind his new schedule in "The Cage," as everybody called the watchman's job in the County's evidence room. He worked a three-day, 12-hour shift one week, usually Thursday, Friday, and Saturday, and then a four-day, 12-hour shift the next week, from Tuesday through Friday; one week swing shift, the next week the night shift. That way, he could stay on schedule with his online courses in forensics and criminal law.

So far, so good. He had three semesters to go to get his BA. He had just started new courses in cyber-crime and second-year forensics when he got sideways with Bleazard. Something smelled bad whenever he was around that guy, and he wanted to find out what stunk. So, when he discovered the business card with Blum's name on it, he called him. And that resulted in a three-hour meeting that afternoon at Blum's apple orchard that included some very good barbecue.

They had been getting along very well. Brady didn't have a dad, and he and the old lawyer had bonded, which was good for both of them. They clicked.

"So, you're telling me this is a real place, this retro town in the hills, and the Grand Hotel up the mountain?" Brady asked.

"Yes, the Shining City. It's real. I've been there. Spent an afternoon and an evening there with a family member," Blum said. "I help them from time to time, usually pro bono. They pay my expenses, but my real pay is being able to work with some extraordinary people."

"What do you mean?"

"All I can say is, they're saintly people . . . the kind of people you read about in the Bible. I've seen miracles by the dozens," Blum said guardedly.

"So, my discovering an article about a green carriage, a missing couple presumed drowned in 1925, and an injured driver is a miracle that fits Joey's story to a 'T', is that what you're saying?"

Blum nodded.

"But, there's nothing that could be used in a court of law to prove any of it, right?"

"Well, since you are still assumed innocent in this country until proven guilty, we don't have to prove anything. Bleazard has to show that a crime has been committed, then make the case with the DA, and convince him to file something against Joey," Blum explained.

Blum jumped up from his Adirondack chair and hurried over to the Traeger grill and dumped more wood pellets into the hopper. They were spread out on the patio table behind the "Apple House," as he called it, where he stored his produce. In the adjoining Cider House, Blum had recently set up his apple press and a bottling line.

"This is a great place you have here, Mr. Blum," Brady said, admiring the covered trestle and deck where they were sitting and waiting for the brisket to be finished. He was hungry!

"Sure is. I'm even starting to make some money on the operation instead of just breaking even and pouring more money into it.

"So, if I catch your drift correctly," Blum continued, "you have a hunch that Bleazard has something going on besides an unexplained grudge toward the Kunzes . . . that he's up to something, but we just don't know what it is, right?"

Brady nodded and then pulled a laptop out of his backpack.

"I originally thought that he was just following up on a claim by the care center about missing residents, three in total, with Mrs. Kunz being the third. But, I've been wondering if there's something more to it than that. I might have done something that could get me in trouble since I found Bleazard's schedule for the past ten days or so; we're all supposed to log in our appointments and official inquiries as well as travel records. From what I've been able to glean . . . hang on for a second."

Brady pulled out a $10 bill and set it down on the table next to the barbecue sauce and continued. "That's to retain you as my counsel so that I can share this with you." They smiled. "You know, attorney-client privilege."

"Yes, Brady, I'm familiar with that point of law," Blum said with a chuckle. He really liked this kid! Then, he added. "So, this $10 bill is all mine, and I can spend it any way I want to?"

"Yes, no strings. Spend it on something nice . . ." They both laughed at that and Brady continued, "Anyway, as I was saying, yes, Bleazard had a couple phone calls with the Columbus Care Center, but he has also met with Gunderson—well, I think it's Gunderson—both in person or on the phone at least five different times, the first one being after we met you and the young redhead . . ."

"Her name's Rachel. That's probably right after she left Gunderson a text message . . ."

"So now, look at his phone records," Brady said as he handed Blum three pages of telephonic details. "He got a call in the office from a number belonging to Gunderson's firm where Joey worked a day later; the call lasted for nearly an hour. Then, two days later, after Joey woke up, they talked again.

"And, the kicker is the day after that, about the time he had been pulling my chain and getting me sent back to The Cage–which I appreciated, by the way–he drove to the city and met with Gunderson again Friday. And had a sleep-over; he's staying at a hotel on the riverfront this weekend near their offices and booked another night there. He's not checking out until tomorrow morning. I think that's because, as I told you in my text, I assume he's planning on being there when you and Joey are supposed to show up at the office."

Blum scratched his chin and then turned toward the grill.

"Just a second!" Blum said, as his grill was sending a lot more smoke. He turned it down, raised the lid, grabbed the corn and vegetables in a tray, and set them aside. Blum wiped his hands on his apron and returned to the table.

"Hmm. I'm sure glad we've had this talk. I think it's better that I go there by myself and give them a demand letter and then encourage the Kunzes to get on the road and hurry out of town.

"But first, let's eat. Then we need to load up and clean out my Winnebago. I hope the battery's not dead. And put some gas in it. Ever driven a bus?"

Brady shook his head.

"I've been thinking about my Winnebago for a while. I hardly ever use it anymore. We'll drive the Winnebago over to Glenmore, close to where they live. We can stay in it tonight and then take it over to Joey and Dana early tomorrow morning. We have lots to do. Things are getting even more complicated. We continue to face serious opposition.

"After we've finished eating, if you'll clean up, I'll call Joey and Dana and break the news."

Blum and Brady had a short, nearly sleepless night in the Winnebago parked in a Costco parking lot. A security guy woke them up about 6:30 am and gave them the boot. All they'd had to eat or drink was warm bottled water and some Kit Kat bars that Blum had stored there since last Halloween. Brady didn't complain.

"I don't mind," he told Blum. "I love Kit Kat bars."

"I can see that," Blum said, pointing to the empty package near the sink. "There's a wastebasket under the sink." Brady got the message and started cleaning the place up. Before they left, Blum gave him a list.

"Listen, as you can plainly see, this antique rolling penthouse needs some TLC."

"TLC?"

"Tender loving care. There is a dealership owned by a dear friend of mine–an old client actually–who gave me this rig to satisfy a $75,000 legal fee that he couldn't pay; you need to drive this over there after we go see the Kunzes. They need to see it and agree to their accommodations."

"Maybe we better get it detailed first," Brady said.

"We'll let them have a quick look, and then you drive it off to Quigly's."

"Who's Quigly?"

"My buddy, the RV dealer. So, here's the list: new fridge, toilet refurbishment, waste-water filter, two propane tanks, one hooked up, plus an extra quilt, sheets, and pillows. And, yes, I want the whole thing detailed. Super detailed."

"How do I pay for it?"

"You don't. He still owes me another $26,000. I'm that kind of a guy."

"So, you're a sucker?"

"Yep. You could say that."

"So, you won't be around?"

"No, remember, I have to go face the organized crime group. Maybe that's unfair to call them that, the folks at Gunderson's office, and set them straight about Joey. I'm giving Gunderson a demand letter to buy Joey out. Per your suggestion, I'm going early, and Joey's not going at all. I hope he and Dana are ready to hit the road; they took it well last night on the phone. They're just worried about Rachel."

Brady was puzzled. Blum explained, "Rachel, the cute little redheaded softball player; you first met her at the hospital, remember? Dana told me her boyfriend was badly hurt in a bike accident—could be paralyzed. She stayed with Joey and Dana last night. Anyway, we better get going. Here's the key."

"What if I wreck it?"

"Don't. Besides, I'd rather drive the Caddy. And, I DON'T want you to wreck the Caddy! I know I shouldn't be so attached to material things. But I love it! Let's get going."

With Brady taking care of the Dinosaur (the RV), Blum was in the Caddy on his way to see Gunderson. He had the demand letter ready even before he decided to go it alone. Joey texted him and said they were taking Rachel to the hospital. But, per Blum's invitation, everyone was meeting at the Cider House at 5 pm. By then Brady would be back with the RV, and everyone could get started on their various assignments. That included himself, Dana, Joey, Mrs. Gregory, Martina, and he hoped, Brady, and Rachel. Blum loved it when he had everything prepared like clockwork. They could put Gunderson in a vise so he'd have to settle with Joey, giving Joey and Dana the capital they needed to finance their mission. But as some say about the "best-laid plans . . .. "

Blum would soon discover that arriving two hours earlier than the appointed time would pay off–big time!. The thing about plans is, you have to consider what to plan for when unplanned debacles undo your ORIGINAL PLANS. Blum was good at that.

Dana left Joey to pack everything for a long road trip. Then she was set to meet with a Realtor and tie up loose ends with Oma's estate. The last Oma told Joey before he and Dana left Salem Springs was to clean out the things she had left back at the center and resolve matters with management. Now that he had the Explorer road-ready again, he drove to Oma's old place.

Joey was annoyed when the manager wanted him to pay for another whole month, but he promised to do the final cleanup if they'd reduce the amount to two weeks. Happy with the outcome, he got her key and went inside. On the countertop, he found a personal treasure: piles of photos, letters, and documents that Oma had saved for him, including many things which he'd never seen and some that had never even been opened. The first one was from his dad, Charlie Kunz, on Joey's 12th birthday.

"I don't remember seeing this before!" Joey said to no one in particular.

It had a 1992 postmark from Manila, The Philippines.

September 25, 1992
Manila, Philippines
Happy Birthday, Buddy!
You only turn 12 once, so I wanted you to know I'm thinking about you. I'm working in the Embassy here and have lots of good friends. In fact, one of them, a comrade-in-arms, Pete Scofield, dropped by to see me today; heard I was here, I guess. We were together in 'Nam when the platoon made its escape by "rubber duckies," down a river and finally into the mighty Mekong. We had the job of rescuing a group of freedom-loving villagers who had saved dozens of our pilots. You know the story—they made it, I didn't. Those of us who stayed on the river- bank didn't find our way back to Saigon until just before it fell. Anyway, Scofield gave me some photos of our unit which I've included here. You can see me right next to Big Red One, our lieutenant, my best friend, Carl Jewell. I was happy to learn from Scofield that they all made it back.
I hope someday you can meet him. He's got a farm in the Midwest somewhere, Scofield said.
Gotta run. Save these photos, and if there's ever a letter from Jewell, please tell Grandma to get his address and let me know where he is. Love, Dad!

The other letter was unopened. Since it was postmarked in 2000, he figured it arrived when he was away at college. He opened it; it was from an Army buddy of his dad's. Joey didn't know who

Pete Scofield was. It was a long account telling of his dad's time in Vietnam.

Joey had never heard any of this before.

December 20, 2001

Washington, D.C.

Dear Joey,

I'm Pete Scofield, a friend of your dad's from Vietnam. He saved my life and the lives of some fifty other people when he and four other guys jumped off our rubber rafts and stayed behind to fight off the Viet Cong who had attacked us. They covered our escape. Maybe you know that we had volunteered to go back and get about thirty Vietnamese villagers to safety.

I was so sorry to hear that he passed away. He was a hero, and I wanted you to know that.

When he and I met in Manila almost twenty years ago, he was kind of blue because he hadn't been there with you when you needed him. He said he never shared the full story with you of what happened, so I will.

We called our lieutenant all kinds of names, and not just behind his back. Big Red One, Carrot Top (no relation to the comedian), Carl the Carrot, Red Mop, or just Sir. Mostly we called him "Sir," even though he was younger than most of the noncoms, your dad included. Jewell and your dad, his first sergeant, kept us one step ahead of death and dismemberment. They were Cheech and Chong, Abbot and Costello, Laurel and Hardy. Couldn't separate them. They both went to DLI together and learned the natives' language.

But, that night was different. Darkness was overtaking the jungle, no moon with clouds and drizzly rain. The Viet Cong and the NVA, or the North Vietnamese Army, were hunting us. Time was running out for South Vietnam in the fall of 1974.

158 | GM JARRARD

We were somewhere northwest of Saigon right on the Laotian border with the villagers who had been saving our pilots who ejected, radioing in for help and getting them to safety.

There were seventeen of us and the Vietnamese villagers from a place the Americans called "Big Talk," where originally a squad of Green Berets had set up a listening post. I remember your dad sneaked back to talk with Jewell because the natives were getting restless. They wanted to know when we were leaving. It was hot and muggy, even at night. The sounds of the night, crickets as big as your index finger, little yellow poisonous frogs, and jungle birds can easily drown out a squad of Viet Cong. We were on high alert.

We had to navigate this tributary of the Mekong River and take the correct tributary to the river so we didn't end up in Cambodia. That was a "no-no."

I ran back and told your dad that the rubber duckies were now all inflated and ready to go. He assembled the villagers and told us we all had to be very, very quiet. Truh Hoc was the unofficial mayor of the group and as pro-American as they come. He hated the Communists; they nearly killed all of his family, except for his daughter, Binh.

Your dad was given one of the first night vision scopes ever used in combat. Back then, it was a big, clumsy telescope, but it could be mounted on a rifle. He was the only one who knew how it worked; thanks to the scope and your dad, I am here today to write this to you.

Soon, we were floating down the small river until we could navigate to the point where it separated and flowed into the huge Mekong River.

"Stay low," Charlie whispered to us. Jewell was a couple of rafts ahead of us. "I saw movement on the other side," your dad said. It was passed down the line to all nine rubber duckies. The GI's were in three boats: the lead, the middle, and the end, but with an armed escort here and there down the line; three young Vietnamese men had M-16's too.

Then, a child started crying back behind them. Suddenly, automatic fire rang out from the opposite shore. The lead boats made a turn around a bend ahead of the others. The distinctive sound of AK-47 fire was unmistakable. M-16's fired back from the last two rafts. All you could see were muzzle flashes. There was more firing, but by then we had our oars in the water.

Somebody cried out for your dad behind us. It came from the shore. Their rubber duckie was kaput. Most of them got out. They said that Hansen took rounds in his ankle and foot, but they bandaged him up and put him on raft eight, just behind us. They abandoned their boat, but made it to shore, firing across the river until they finally caught up with us. We were hugging the opposite bank, moving way too slow. Your dad jumped out and waded to the bank to join them.

Because he had the night-vision scope, he decided he had to stay with the squad on the bank so he could fire back across at the enemy. Only he could see them, thanks to the scope.

Jewell objected and said he needed to get back on a raft.

And I remember what he yelled back to us. "If we don't stay here, everybody could die. I can see them! Y'all paddle as fast as you can. We'll be alright!"

That was the last I heard from him until we talked years later in Manila.

We did as he said, paddling furiously now that noise protocol was no longer important. The other rafts, loaded with men, women, and kids, and all their property followed, paddling with all their might and picking up speed, now all of us out in the middle of the river.

The battle grew fiercer behind us, with mortars going off with increasing rapidity. Minutes later and about half a mile away, we could still hear automatic fire. Then, we were on our own, and so were they. Your dad—Sergeant Kunz—and his squad of four.

By 7 am, we had arrived at a US depot and heliport on the Mekong. Jewell said goodbye to his Vietnamese friends and took extra-long with Binh. I remember he told her that they'd be home by Christmas. He admitted to me that he gave her his address and parent's phone number and told her about his farm, and promised her that the government would fly them to America. He always worried that the government wouldn't keep its promise to them.

The Vietnamese got on a Navy boat and continued down the river.

Jewell had "chartered" a Huey to go retrieve Charlie and the boys. He was sure he could find Charlie and his men. I jumped on the chopper with him, and we took off north, while Binh, the spunky 5-foot Vietnamese 'saint', her father, and the others sailed south. He would finally find her back in the US of A, but not for more than a year.

But, he would never see Charlie Kunz and company again. I'm just happy that I did. We had a great time, had dinner, and I gave him some photos of our group to send to you. I hope you got them.

Good luck to you in your life's pursuits. If you're anything like your dad, you'll go far.

Your brother in arms,

Pete Scofield

He was stunned! Joey just sat there in Oma's old kitchen all by himself for half an hour, trying to put all the pieces together, and then he said out loud, "Sorry, Dad, I've never heard any of this. I had no idea. I've been so critical, so unfair. I wish I could make it up somehow."

In time, Joey Kunz would have that opportunity.

He gathered all the documents and paperwork Oma had left for him, put it all in a box, and locked the house. He glanced down at this watch. He still had his assigned chores at the old house to take care of. Wonder where Dana is, he asked himself.

At that moment, Dana was in the parking lot waiting for Rachel who was in the hospital trying to talk with Tanner. Then, they planned to drive up the canyon and get her bike. So far, no one had heard anything from Jonathan. Had Blum seen Gunderson? Did he deliver the demand letter? Were they free to move ahead with their plans? She called Joey. It took him a while to answer.

"Hi, it's me," she said. "Hear from Blum?" He told her about the "treasure" he had found and then glanced at his messages.

"Looks like I got a text from Jonathan. He said something was going on at the office; he still hasn't gone in yet. He said he had to call Brady first who was at the RV dealership getting the toilet re-placed on the Winnebago."

"Oh, dear! Okay. Gotta go. Rachel's coming, then we're driving up the canyon. Call me if you hear anything. Love ya!"

"You, too, baby," Joey said.

They were all waiting for Blum. And it looked like Blum was in trouble.

Rachel got into Dana's Subaru, dabbed her eyes, lowered the visor, reapplied her makeup, then turned to Dana and simply said, "Thank you." Rachel turned and just watched the scenery for the next ten minutes or so as they left the town's suburbs and headed to the ballpark where Tanner had parked his truck before his accident. Dana decided not to ask about Tanner's condition because it was obvious it wasn't good. It was clear that Rachel had already shed buckets of tears; no reason to start it all over again.

It was Rachel who finally broke the ice. "So, you're really pregnant? How did that happen?'"

"Yep, and I asked Joey that same question when he told me about it because I didn't believe him," she started laughing. "I'll give you the same response he gave me. 'When a Mommy and Daddy love each other so much!'"

And then Rachel laughed, too–for the first time in days.

Dana continued, "We had lost hope. We spent over $20,000 in the past year on tests, procedures. I even tried in-vitro; the doctor said at my age and in my situation, it just wasn't going to happen. Nevertheless, I had scheduled one final appointment with my OBGYN for the Monday after we were supposed to have returned from taking Joey's Oma to the spa resort, but as you know, I was in a coma and in the hospital. But, the night before, I had taken a dip in the magic waters, and when I came to on Wednesday, Joey shared the good news."

Rachel nodded. "I know. But, sometimes, we are fortunate because we get good, sometimes incredible news, like my being introduced to a great-great-grandfather born 110 years before I was even born.

"And then other times, we're hit with bad news, really terrible news, like I was, after the good news. I was hit square in the face with the shock of seeing Tanner all bloody, his leg bent out of shape, watching him being loaded onto a gurney, and whisked off to the hospital. They cancel each other out. I don't know which one to accept," Rachel said.

"Well, lately, I've been learning a lot about faith—and hope. My advice to you is to not focus on the negative, but focus on the positive. You know I'm a Jew, right?"

"I'd heard that."

"Except for maybe the ultra-orthodox among us, we're generally skeptical people—and sarcastic, often irritatingly so. And, for three thousand years, we believed we were 'the chosen,' then we went about stoning the prophets, chasing after false gods, and finally 2000 years ago, we sacrificed our Messiah. Then, we complain and wonder why we've always been dispersed, cast out and persecuted. That's a lot of self-defeating behavior, and it's time to quit it because, as my grandma used to tell me, you can't keep doing the same thing over and over again and expect different results. So, I have a suggestion for you," Dana said.

"What's that?"

"Help us. Help Joey, Blum, and me. How many people do you know who are in the same boat as you and me—people who have lost parents, had a bad accident, been fired, or afflicted by this or that, and would love the chance to be welcomed to a place where the people are of one heart and one mind, share and share alike, and then are invited to soak themselves in healing waters. Do you know people like that?"

"Dana, everybody's like that in one way or another," Rachel replied.

"Yes, they are. But, how many are willing to make the required sacrifice to be invited? Are you? Am I? That's what we are about to find out."

Blum had been sitting in his classic, baby-blue Caddy watching police and movers and other people come and go from the OJT office building for nearly an hour now. He had to find out what was going on in there, but he didn't want to show his hand or reveal himself until he knew what the situation was. He had no idea what he was walking into. And, he was getting hungry. He had skipped breakfast, which made him cranky.

Then, he thought. Maybe they're hungry, too!

Across the circle from the complex of new buildings where OJT was, he could see a strip mall and several stand-alone retail establishments, including a Domino's pizza shop. He drove over there, ordered several family-size pizzas and a small one for himself. He removed his tie and coat and waited for his order. When it was ready, he took a $20 bill out of his wallet, plus money for the pizzas, and approached the gangly teenager who was at the cash register and took him aside.

"Hey, I want to surprise everybody at the office with the pizzas, and since they haven't seen me since I retired, I wanna have some fun. You got an extra hat?"

"What?"

"An extra Domino's hat, like what you're wearing."

"Yeah, but . . ."

"Listen, I'll rent it from you . . . for twenty bucks, and I'll bring it right back. Is $20 enough to use it for half an hour?"

The kid smiled. "Hang on. I'll be right back." He returned a minute later. "This one was Luke's. He either got fired or found a better job, I'm not sure. But you can keep it. Twenty bucks is fine." He looked around and put the bill in his pocket. First tip he ever got working at this crappy job!

Blum thanked him and left with hat and pizzas in hand, plus an empty pizza box specifically for Gunderson.

❑ ❑ ❑ ❑ ❑

Dana got out of the Subaru when they arrived at the ballpark. Tanner's truck was there, tires and all, including the bag of gear behind the front seat. She could see that Rachel needed some comfort and reassurance as she unlocked the door to drive the truck and head up the canyon to retrieve her bike.

"Want me to come help you find it and load it up?" Dana asked.

"No, it'll either be there or it won't. I can handle it."

"So, you're joining us all at the farm, right? At 5 pm sharp? Blum wanted to give us the news about what happened at the office and where we go from here."

Rachel thought for a second, then straightened up and smiled. "Why not? I got to 'buck it up' as my coach always said. You strike out, then you do better next inning. I got a few things to do, check my mail, put my bike in the garage and get some clothes. I'll be there!"

"Before you leave, let me check with Joey." Dana took out her cell phone, checked for bars, and then saw a text from Joey. She read it to Rachel. "Blum said he left the demand letter with Gunderson after poking around at the office. He has some interesting news."

"Well, that sounds hopeful," Rachel said. "I'll be there at 5. I hope Gunderson feels the heat."

Blum especially loved the pineapple and ham with mushrooms pizza he was eating, now finishing his third piece. "I'm sure glad I'm not kosher anymore," he said to himself. He loved ham sandwiches, ham and eggs, especially Hawaiian pizza with ham. He drove the Caddy to a nearby park and watched the waterfowl come and go; a good place to eat a pizza.

When he was finished, he called Joey.

Joey answered immediately. "I've been on pins and needles here. I thought you would have called an hour-and-a-half ago. What happened?"

"Relax, I tried the old pizza trick, and it worked like a charm," Blum explained.

"Pizza trick?"

"Who turns down a Domino's Pizza delivered hot and delicious and paid for by an old friend, an old employee?" Blum asked.

"What old friend?"

"You, Joey, you! Your old compadres really appreciated a free lunch and asked how you were doing, when you were coming back. But, Gunderson, he wasn't so happy when he opened up his box, and it was empty—except for the demand letter! I guess he didn't like the toppings!" he said with a laugh. "So, you're all still planning to come out to the farm, right?"

"Sure, at 5, right?" Joey said, still puzzled by Blum's "pizza trick."

"Five it is," Blum said and hung up.

12

Gary Gunderson didn't appreciate his pizza. It wasn't the toppings. There weren't any. It was the other thing in the box that upset him! He was more determined than ever now to make Joey pay. But, Joey's friends and co-workers down the hall not only loved the free lunch, they were even more gratified when they heard what was waiting for Gunderson in the pizza box.

The accounts payable clerk, Betsy, wasn't supposed to eat pizza—or carbs at all for that matter—but was delighted to break her self-imposed celery and carrots diet.

"I can't think of a better way to fall off the wagon than to enjoy a pizza while watching Gunderson eat crow," she said.

"That was a good idea to take the extra pepperoni pizza into them. Gary had a small Domino's box on his desk, but nobody was eating anything. No pizza! I just barged in and said, 'Hey, I guess Joey's coming back. We're all so excited. Here's an extra pizza for y'all.' I turned to leave just as Gunderson yelled at me, 'He's not coming back!' And, he threw down a big yellow manilla envelope in front of Cassiday and told her to 'take this to the attorneys.' By then, just as I slipped away, I heard her say, 'Why me?'"

"What about those cops and the pickle-faced guy, Abe Lincoln-looking guy in the bad suit; probably the detective?" a skinny programmer asked.

"They had left before the pizza got here. I saw 'em earlier in the hallway waiting for an elevator. Weren't happy dudes."

Betsy and her comrades returned to the remaining pizza.

"Maybe he's coming back . . ." one man said.

"Who?"

"Joey, of course!"

"And, maybe they're on their way out. Wouldn't that be sweet?" Betsy added as she took the last veggie piece.

Gunderson skipped lunch that day—no pizza for him. His appetite was gone—his appetite for food, maybe, but not for vengeance. He sat there brooding all alone in his window office, surrounded by photos of himself with the rich and famous: Steve Jobs, Mark Zuckerberg, even Barack Obama. Gunderson was reading a copy of the demand letter and trying to find someone else—anyone else—to blame for all his troubles.

Of course, Gunderson knew that the company's SEC problems had nothing to do with Joey. But, days earlier, when Bleazard told Gunderson that the care center manager was asking questions about the disappearance of Margritte Kunz, a light bulb went on. Apparently, she was the third former resident who had just vanished into thin air from the Columbia Center with no forwarding address, nothing. And, after some research, he learned that Joey stood to inherit much of his grandmother's estate. Joey had both motive and opportunity! He sold Bleazard on the idea.

But, he was still in a bind. He knew the company's private equity lenders wouldn't keep faith with their second installment, and without Joey's shares, he couldn't get approval from other stakeholders to okay the sale of the company to their chief competitor.

He sent a text to Bleazard hoping he could shake something loose. "We heard Joey was his grandmother's primary beneficiary. He stands to benefit if she's dead. So if he did have something to do with her disappearance, then you have a suspect. If we learn anything, we'll fill you in."

The question then was where in the world was Joey?! He didn't know. But, he knew someone who probably did; the 'pizza delivery man/attorney' who gave him the demand letter, that's who!

"Find the deliveryman, find Joey," he texted again to Bleazard.

"Then maybe you can find out what happened to the old lady."

Gunderson didn't care what happened to 'the old lady'—or any old lady, for that matter—he only cared about how he could get Joey's shares away from him.

And, being convicted of murder, extortion, and elder abuse would do the trick—even if Joey were just accused of it, that would be legal justification enough to cut him off.

Gunderson was running out of options. Joey was his exit plan.

Out at Blum's apple orchard, Joey saw his exit plan pull up in front of the Cider House. The Winnebago looked a lot shinier than what he had seen out his window earlier that morning. A young black man jumped out of the RV and gave the key to Blum. Where had he seen him before?

That's the Sheriff's Deputy who accompanied the obnoxious detective! What gives? Joey said to himself. He stepped away from the grill he was attending to see what was going on. Dana had already taken a peek inside. A moment later, she exited, gave Joey a "thumbs up," and returned to the house where she was preparing the rest of the meal with the other guests.

An hour later, Blum had gathered everyone into the Cider House where he had set up chairs and a large table with a whiteboard standing behind it. In the background were several palettes of large containers with his 'Avalon' brand of cider emblazoned on the side. A couple of gallon jugs of cider and muffins were on the table and after a prayer, Blum began.

Seated around the table were the Kunzes, Joey and Dana, Brady, the county deputy, Francine Gregory, along with her sister, Georgia, and Marta Ilić, along with Judge Stone, who had come down the mountain to make a surprise appearance. Blum began by having each one introduce themselves since not everyone knew Brady.

"Thanks for being here. I hope Rachel arrives soon. She needed to go to the hospital to talk to her friend, Tanner; her text said she'd be late, " Blum said. "Let's get started."

Blum began his presentation in earnest by writing several odd names on the whiteboard. Avalon, Arcadia, Cockaigne, Lemuria, City of Enoch, Paititi, Lyonesse, Shangri La, Zion.

"Who knows what these names or places have in common?" Blum asked.

Francine said, "Lost cities, synonyms of paradise, I suppose."

"Yes," Blum said, "and, Wikipedia calls them myths or legends from different cultures and places throughout history. For example, my little house-brand of unfiltered apple cider is called 'Avalon,' a mysterious island where King Arthur is buried, an apple-growing paradise. There are dozens more of these fantastical places, called 'myths and legends' all over the world, practically in every culture. John Winthrop, the Puritan leader and founder of Boston, had his own name: the 'New Jerusalem' or in his words, 'A Shining City on a Hill." While on a ship, one of eleven sailing west from England in 1630, he delivered a sermon about where they were going and what their purpose was. I've asked Dana to review it and give us a short summary of his vision."

"Thanks, Jonathan. I found what he had to say most interesting after reflecting on our trip to Salem Springs and the Grand Hotel and Spa. It was, as you know, a life-changing event for Joey and me," Dana said.

Just then, Rachel poked her head inside the door and, discovering she had finally found the meeting, rushed in, followed by Walter who spoke. "Sorry, my fault. The train was late."

They took their seats, and Blum continued. "We'll make more formal introductions later. In the meantime, let's hear what Dana discovered."

"I was amazed to read what John Winthrop wrote almost exactly 400 years ago. It seems that good, honest people through eons had heard about places like these, yearned to find them, and in some cases, like Winthrop, actually did find them," Dana explained.

"Joey and I, the Judge, Walter, and Jonathan all know and assure you that such a place really exists!" She walked around near the whiteboard and grabbed the marker. "May I?" Blum nodded. "Of course."

She began outlining her key points on the whiteboard.

"Winthrop postulated that God created mankind with the purpose that there 'must be rich, some poor, some high, and eminent in power and dignity; others mean and in subjection.'

"Then he describes the reasons why. First, he says it was 'to show forth the glory of his wisdom in the variety and difference of the creatures . . .'

"Diversity, in other words, but not for diversity's sake, rather because he wanted to provide people with the opportunity to see to the needs of others, to care for the poor and the needy, and to be stewards, counting himself more honored in dispensing his gifts to man by man, than if he did it by his own immediate hands.' God wanted us to learn how to be more like Him by observing and empathizing with others, not just to test us, but also to teach us.

"Secondly, He wanted to demonstrate to His children 'the work of his Spirit, first upon the wicked in moderating and restraining them, so that the rich and mighty should not eat up the poor, nor the poor and despised rise up against and shake off their yoke.' Winthrop was no Rousseau. He abhorred the class warfare that is being demonstrated on our streets today in this country. Rather, he proposed that the poor be lifted up, in that the rich were made low through their own voluntary benevolence.

"And 'thirdly, that every man might have need of others, and from hence they might be all knit more nearly together in the bonds of brotherly affection. From hence it appears plainly that no man is made more honorable than another or more wealthy etc., out of any particular and singular respect to himself, but for the glory of his Creator and the common good of the creature.' Those were his exact words. Winthrop gave this speech aboard his ship, one of eleven carrying 750 people to New England to find and inhabit such a place, to build a city. After a couple of trial landings, one in Salem, another farther, they settled on the area that he eventually named Boston. This was to be his great 'Shining City on a Hill.' Human nature, as it is, proved to be a stumbling block to achieving Winthrop's dream. I guess the question is, can we find people who have proven themselves ready to populate such a place? But are we that kind of people?" Dana put the marker down and returned to her seat.

Blum looked around and could see that the group seemed greatly affected by her presentation.

Joey got Blum's attention and asked, "Don't you think it becomes harder and harder for someone to sign on as they get richer and richer? The more you give up, the harder it would seem for people to sacrifice what they have."

Judge Stone had a ready answer. "Of course it is, as the rich young prince discovered when the Master advised him to sell all that he had, give it to the poor, and come follow Him. And, Winthrop warned that there would be consequences for a people who covenanted to do this and then fell short. But, he said 'to avoid this shipwreck'. And remember that when he said this, they were sailing on the Atlantic. In his words, people needed 'to follow the counsel of Micah, to do justly, to love mercy, to walk humbly with our God. For this end, we must be knit together, in this work, as one man. We must entertain each other in brotherly affection.' But we err if we think this only has to do with material things.

"Even the poor have sacrifices they can make, as Mother Teresa did. She had nothing in terms of material wealth. She gave of herself, all of herself. And Winthrop explains this when he says that 'we must delight in each other; make others' conditions our own; rejoice together, mourn together, labor, and suffer together.'"

Blum waited for the group to absorb what the Judge had said and asked again. "What other questions do you have?"

Rachel and Brady both raised their hands at the same time. Blum saw Rachel first. "I don't want to be skeptical because I believe what Joey and Dana said, and I certainly trust anything Walter has said, but I'm sort of a 'Doubting Thomas.' How can we know with certainty that this is a real place, this Grand Hotel and life-giving hot springs, this Salem Crossing—whatever it's called—can be found, that we can actually see it?"

Brady spoke up. "That's my question too."

Francine couldn't stay silent anymore. "Well, I don't need to see it! I was there when Dana found out that she's pregnant after modern science did nothing for her. That's good enough for me."

Her sister Georgia nodded in agreement. Martina Ilić looked like she was praying.

Judge Stone looked to Blum and Walter; they both nodded, and the Judge pulled an envelope out of his pocket.

"Have any of you ever taken one of those old-time railroad rides, like the one in Durango, Colorado, where you board a railcar pulled by a steam-powered locomotive and go clickety-clacking down an antique rail line, maybe visiting an old mining town or something?" Now he had everyone's attention, including Martina's.

He opened the envelope and removed several small items and set them on the table.

Brady was curious. "What are those?"

The Judge smiled. "What do you want them to be?"

"A railroad ticket," Martina said.

"How many do you have?" Francine's sister asked.

"As many as you need, but they expire soon."

"Can we have five?" Francine queried. The Judge peeled them off and handed them to her.

Soon everyone had at least one, except for Rachel. Walter looked concerned.

"What about you, Rachel?" Walter asked. She hesitated.

"I have to be close to Tanner. He can't walk, his leg is in a cast . . . and he's paralyzed."

The Judge smiled and looked at her. "It's just a half a day. We leave at noon and return that evening." She looked at Walter who moved over by her and held her hand.

"I'll make sure you're back by evening. I'll be with you."

"May I still have one?"

"That's why I'm here," the Judge said and gave her a ticket.

As their session came to a close, Blum stood and explained what was next.

"You'll notice on your tickets that they are all good either for tomorrow or a week from tomorrow. We have directions as to where the train leaves from. You need to be there an hour early because we have a special car that we will all board together; the Judge must return tomorrow; he'll be with you; I'm going next week. But Joey and Dana will be on the road beginning tomorrow, so if you want to say goodbye to them, tonight's the only chance for a while."

Cider glasses in hand, the group, one-by-one, came up and wished Joey and Dana Godspeed. Brady took a moment and drew them aside.

"I wanted you to know that Bleazard has concocted a theory that not only you, but others have conspired to have their grandparents or other old relatives disappear so that they can accuse you of attempting to claim that they died and get their inheritances."

"Well, that's hard without a body, isn't it?" Dana said. "Besides, we're not trying to grab Oma's money."

"But someone else is accusing you of doing her in, hoping you would be exempted from inheriting anything from her estate and taking it all for themselves; that person is in contact with Bleazard; I think with Gunderson's help."

"Who?" Joey asked.

Brady looked at a note. "Someone named Trudy."

"Oh, Trudy, your troubled tattooed cousin," Dana said. "She must be out of rehab."

"You better secure your other accounts: bank, retirement, etc.," Brady said.

"Why is that?" Joey asked.

"Because Bleazard is trying to get a judge to have your funds frozen so you can't skedaddle."

"Well, Blum is telling us we need to be RVing down the highway by tomorrow."

"Then, you better get your money and get out of town," Brady advised.

"What about our house? We haven't settled that," Dana said. Blum heard what she said and interrupted her. "I have asked Rachel to house sit for you, and with the power of attorney you gave me, I can negotiate a sale and take care of your payoff."

"We're not ready to do this . . . we need to go through our stuff,"

Dana said, now clearly upset. Then, she calmed down and faced the music. "I guess it's one thing to preach about sacrifice and totally another to do it." She looked at Joey who clearly had reservations of his own. "What do you think?" she asked him. "Either we're all in, or we're out."

"We're in," he said.

She nodded. "What about our stuff?"

"When the time comes, I'll bring it here. Store it with the apples," Blum promised.

"Then, rest assured. We're all in," Dana said. "It's settled. We have to move our money where Bleazard can't find it. I'll do that tonight, and we can leave early tomorrow morning."

Twelve hours later, Joey was sitting at the helm of the Winnebago, aka "The Dinosaur," steering it like the captain of the Titanic keeping the huge-wheeled behemoth from hitting an iceberg. From where Dana sat in the back at the kitchen table working on her laptop, she could hear a curse word every once in a while when a big rig passed by.

"Just stay in the slow lane," she advised her very nervous husband.

"There's just passing lanes and our lane, the slow lane, Dana! And everybody passes us when we come to one. Look behind us. It's like Game Day at the Coliseum; cars and trucks queued up for more than a mile. You wanna drive?"

She didn't, so she turned back to her spreadsheet. Already she had assembled more than 150 names of prospects, and then with the help of Google Maps, she had created a route that zigzagged all over the country. Their first stop was right off I-80 in about 150 miles. They would stay there for the night. She had found an RV park in a small town named Butlerville, population 3,500. Her prospect was a widow: the ex-mayor who was appointed to her position when her predecessor, her husband, died.

He had been a veteran who often complained that there was no VA clinic in the town as the closest one was 200 miles away. She had lobbied Congress and the Veteran Administration to set up a clinic in the little farming community where they lived, the County seat for other towns and villages in the area. With her daughter, she had written a book about her husband, Carl, and his Army platoon in Vietnam called Forgotten Heroes, who helped rescue and relocate an entire village before Saigon fell.

She had been one of those villagers; they married after she and her family came to the United States as refugees in 1975. Her name was Binh Jewell, but most people called her "Mayor Bee." She was an accountant who played the cello but had worked as a nurse when she was in Vietnam, the article that Dana found online explained. Binh, Dana learned, meant "peaceful" in Vietnamese.

Dana looked at her picture. She must be tiny, Dana thought. Dana tried to call her but got no answer. She now lived with her son and his family who had inherited a wrecking yard and used-car lot when her husband died. The son sold used cars and especially liked restoring them. Dana figured she would employ her newly-found calling as a podcaster to introduce herself.

The next morning, Dana had learned a lot of new R-rated words that were unfamiliar to her as Joey was exposed to the wrong way to connect to a sewage line from the Winnebago. Then she thought he was going to blow the big rig up when he messed up connecting the propane tank to the water heater and the stove.

They had cold cereal for breakfast, her favorite Quaker Oats granola with raisins and almonds. Joey had nothing; he said had no appetite.

They had towed her Subaru behind the Winnebago and, per Blum's instructions, Joey had removed its rear license plate. He had detached the car from the RV and was now putting the license plate back on.

"Why did Blum make us do that?" Dana asked.

"To prevent state police from identifying us as fugitives, I suppose," he said. "But, now that we're out of state, we can leave it on," he surmised. "So, where are we going?"

"Just to the outskirts of town. She lives with her son and his family. They have a wrecking yard and car lot in front of their small farm. I finally got an answer; she's there but was back in the office working when I called. Let's drive over."

The morning after the conference at Blum's Cider House, Inspector Bleazard got a FAX from the family of another "missing woman," Virginia Tracy. Her daughter said in "no uncertain terms" that her mother was not missing, but changed residence from the independent living center because she found a spa "upstate" that provided more services for less money and that the center was stirring up trouble because they were perturbed by people moving out due to their raising prices.

"In fact, the woman said, "my mother came to town about six

weeks ago and looked terrific. The spa had really helped her. So quit bothering us about this!"

Hmm. Bleazard was still not satisfied. Then why can't I find the address or even a phone number for this place?

Gunderson had even offered him more expense money to find Margritte Kunz dead or alive. He suspected Gunderson hoped she was dead. Still, Gunderson's offer for him to handle the security consulting for his company sounded great.

He called the lieutenant at Internal Affairs and asked him to look into a rumor he had heard about Brady Owens snooping about and looking at his emails.

"Hi Jackson, this is Bleazard down on the second floor. Is there some way to track down who may have been snooping around and looking at another officer's emails?"

"You mean, your emails?" Jackson asked.

"Yeah, my emails."

"Only your superior could—or us if you were under investigation and you're not—is authorized to check on other officers, except for HR, of course, to verify travel or other expenses. They are the only ones who are authorized to peer into personal files, and that's the magic word—authorized. But, if someone else you've worked with somehow gets access to your password, well, then that's when we step in. And, if that were the case, we'd open a file on that and do some digging of our own. Who could possibly know your password?"

"Brady Owens might. He's back in The Cage in the evidence room after I complained about him. He works various shifts down there," Bleazard said.

Jackson paused for a moment and then replied, "Let me check his IP address and see if he's been looking somewhere he shouldn't; according to his schedule, he's finishing his midnight to 8 shift right about now. I'll check on him."

"Thanks, Jackson." Bleazard reflected on the day when he had been summoned to Gunderson's office because Joey was due to be there at one, and an attorney showed up an hour earlier instead—with pizza!

"He must have been tipped off by someone, and I'll bet it was Brady Owens who did the tipping. Damn him!" Then, Bleazard spoke to himself out loud. "I'll go right down there and confront that little snitch myself!"

"Who?" his co-worker in the next cubicle asked.

"None of your business, Taylor." Then, on his way out, he asked the day sergeant who the officer was in charge of The Cage.

"That's McMullin," the sergeant said. Taylor overheard that and called Brady, who was getting ready to clock out for the day.

"I think Bleazard is on his way to confront a snitch. If that's you, you better leave early."

Brady got the message. He needed to go and get some sleep before he had to catch an old mountain train. He had more important places to be than in The Cage!

By the time Joey and Dana finally got in to see Binh, Dana was dizzy and nauseous. Maybe it was the Vietnamese food that was cooking in the backroom, nevertheless, she asked for some water. Binh had her sit down. Binh was indeed tiny but full of energy and human warmth. She and Dana bonded almost immediately.

"You having baby?" Binh asked softly. Dana nodded, trying to swallow some water.

"You must drink water, no beer, no cola. I make some ginger tea with peppermint for you, okay? You say you have something to share with me. Let's walk to the house and you tell me. Come."

Half an hour later, they were in the kitchen of an old farmhouse decorated by both old Americana and Far East artwork and novelties, with framed photos, including one of a platoon of GIs in the jungle. Binh pointed to a tall, redheaded gangly officer on the right. Up to this point, Joey's head had been elsewhere, worrying about Gunderson and Bleazard, and all the time he'd spent building that company just to have it all taken away. Then he looked at the photo and gasped. Dana glanced at him as Binh continued.

"That funny redhead man is my Carl; miss him lots every day. Look, we have three boy and two girl, two look like redhead Vietnamese. We laugh a lot. He love my noodles with swine . . . uh, pork. So, please tell me why you come here."

"Just a second, somehow I missed your last name. Is it Jewell? That sounds so familiar. I remember a picture that came with a letter from my dad. Could it be?" Joey asked, trying to recall something. He took a closer look at the framed photo on the wall.

Now he had both Binh's and Dana's attention. "There's a copy of this same picture somewhere in Oma's albums, I'm sure of it. I just need to sort it out when we get back." He pointed to the man next to Jewell. "That's my dad! No wonder we're here. Einstein was right!"

Both women looked at him totally befuddled. "What?" Dana said.

"Remember what Oma always used to say about coincidence?"
Dana was still clueless.

Joey quoted her in German and then translated, *"Der Zufall ist wie Gott anonym bleibt!* Coincidence is how God remains anonymous!"

"My Carl and your father were best friends in the war. I know. I was there! Charlie jumped out of the boat to save us. Your name's Kunz?"

"Yes, Joey Kunz. My dad was Charles, Charlie."

Binh became emotional. "Charlie save my Carl, he save me, my father, all the GIs, too. He save us all! That night we were in rubber duckies, they call 'em, and after a bit, Commies started shooting at us, and they sink one boat. The GI's get out, and they shoot back.

"They stay on the shore to keep us all safe. Charlie jumped out of Carl's duckie to help because he had a camera to see in the dark, and we waited and waited, but they never come back. Oh, Joey, Dana . . . this is God's hand for you to be here. For years, Carl asked about Charlie, but he found nothing about his death. We went to the memorial in Washington and look for Charles Kunz name on the wall. It wasn't there. Carl flew back to look for him in a Huey. Viet Cong shot at the chopper. No sign of him, no sign at all. Where is Charlie now?"

"He died, Binh. I'm sorry," Dana said.

She smiled. "So, your Charlie and my Carl bring us together! That's what I think."

"Maybe that's why when I saw your name on my list, I knew we had to find you," Dana said.

"What list?"

"The list of people who read my blog and responded . . . on the

Internet," Dana explained.

"I don't know what blog is. I don't do Internet," Binh said. "I send texts and emails; I don't surf the web."

"Well, that makes this even more interesting. Binh, we are here because we know of a special place for special people . . ."

"I'm not special . . ."

"Well, we think you are. You are a Christian, right?"

"Yes, that's why we had to run from the Viet Cong. Carl, Charlie, and his soldiers saved our whole village. We help find American pilots. And, I liked Carl right away. I guess he like me too. We have five kids," she laughed.

"As a Christian, are you familiar with the Sermon in the Mount?"

"The preaching on the mountain, yes, the bread and fishes place. Yes."

"Yes, may I read some of it to you?"

"Yes, I love the Bible. Carl was Methodist, and I am Catholic, so we kind of go halfway—meet in the middle. I make compromises. That's why they think I can be the mayor after Carl die. Both Carl and me, we tell jokes and laugh. People like that. But, people in the town learned that I hold my ground when it comes to doing the right things. Carl got cancer from Agent Orange, but there was no VA here. So, I got mad like a wet chicken . . . I mean, a wet hen, until President Bush said, 'Okay, Binh. We make you a clinic!' But for my red-head Carl, it was too late. He had such beautiful hair," Binh said looking away through watery eyes.

Dana opened her Gideon bible to Matthew, Chapter 5. "When I first read your story, I thought there were verses in this chapter that applied directly to you, the first one being in verse five, where it says, *'Blessed are the meek for they shall inherit the earth.'* Followed by others like verses six through ten. *'Blessed are they which do hunger and thirst after righteousness for they shall be filled. Blessed are the merciful for they shall obtain mercy. Blessed are the pure in heart for they shall see God. Blessed are the peacemakers for they shall be called the children of God.'* And, then verse ten, which says, *"Blessed are they which are persecuted for righteousness' sake for theirs is the kingdom of heaven.'* And finally, verses 14, 15, and 16 apply to our destination and the people we invite to go there. *'Ye are the light of the world. A city that is set on a hill cannot be hid. Neither do men light a candle, and put it under a bushel, but on a candlestick; and it giveth light unto all that are in the house. Let your light so shine before men, that they may see your good works, and glorify your Father which is in heaven.'"*

"May I see your bible?" Binh asked. "Please wait, I will get my Vietnamese bible." She returned in a minute and opened her bible to Matthew. She beamed. "Yes, these are my favorite verses, too." She showed Joey and Dana her copy where the same verses were underlined in red.

"You really think a goofy Vietnamese lady who speaks not-so-good English belong there?"

"We can't think of anyone else who belongs there more," Joey said. "We'll put your name on the list."

"What list? What about others," she asked.

"We will submit your name, and if they accept you, they will send you a card and an invitation."

"So, you are putting me on a list to inherit the earth? Me?"

"Yes, you, Binh. The salt of the earth," Dana said.

"Wow! Such a long way from my tiny village in the mountains.

I wish Carl could be there, too."

"Me, too!" Dana said. And then she thought, Maybe he will. They stayed there for another half hour, writing down her particulars, then said goodbye, and returned to the RV park. Dana had a long to-do list before they moved on to their next stop, a much larger city with several prospects and an appointment with a popular Christian podcaster and blogger.

Later that evening, Joey got a troubling text message from Brady. Among other things, he said. "Watch your back!"

13

Brady Owens and his grandmother arrived just 15 minutes be-fore departure time. She was dressed like she was going to church, and Francine soon discovered she had found a kindred spirit. The two black women were happy to meet one another; inside the coach were Francine's three girls, Natasha, and Chloë–the little ones Francine had rescued and adopted–along with her daughter Liz, a teenager who appeared to be there under duress until she realized she would miss school, and Georgia, Francine's younger sister. Brady was carrying his grandmother's small bag.

In a moment, the Judge and Walter walked through the door from the car in front of them, looked back, locked the door behind them, and pulled the curtain down. They introduced themselves to each person warmly, taking each one by two hands and thanking them for their willingness to investigate something so "improbable," as the Judge described it.

Once they were underway and making their uphill climb through a narrow canyon with a river below them, Judge Stone asked, "Anybody have any questions?" At first, no one dared–not even Francine–and then Brady raised his hand.

"Judge Stone, I do a lot of online research, and I found this photo of the Chief Judge of the Supreme Court, Harlan Fiske Stone, first appointed by President Calvin Coolidge to be the Attorney General of the United States with the task of restoring faith in the Justice Department and then second, a year later this same Harlin Stone was appointed to the Supreme Court . . ."

Judge Stone then interrupted him. "But not as Chief Justice—that was Franklin Roosevelt who did that."

"So, this Harlin Fiske Stone, the Chief Justice of the United States, was he your grandfather, because you look just like him, except uh, thinner and younger?"

"No, he wasn't my grandfather."

"Your father then. If so, you'd be in your 80s," Brady said getting more nervous.

"No, he wasn't my father." By now, Brady had passed the photo around of the Supreme Court Justice, taken in the early 1940s, a picture of a man with a lot more bulk than the trimmer, younger-looking man who was answering Brady's questions and having fun doing it.

"You're him!" Francine said. "But you died in 1946!"

"Hey, that was the year I was born," cried out Brady's grandma.

"And I'm the same age as the current president!"

By now, both the Judge and Walter were laughing.

"Oh, that's nothing. Next to me is 'the Big Train, Walter Johnson, one of the first five baseball stars inducted into Cooperstown's Baseball Hall of Fame. When was that Walter?"

"1936, along with Babe Ruth and Ty Cobb. It was a long time ago."

Their audience was stunned.

"Is that why you locked the door, Judge Stone, so we wouldn't jump off the train?" Georgia, Francine's sister asked. The Judge just smiled and shook his head.

Walter could see that Brady's grandma was now clutching her Bible. "Are you Mrs. Owens, same name as Deputy Owens here?"

She nodded. "Take a moment, if you don't mind, and read from Luke Chapter 24," he said. As she was looking it up, Walter continued, "Read verses 36 through 39."

In a shaky voice, she did as she was commanded and began reading. *"And as they thus spake, Jesus himself stood in the midst of them, and saith unto them, Peace be unto you. But they were terrified and affrighted and supposed that they had seen a spirit. And he said unto them, Why are ye troubled? And why do thoughts arise in your hearts? Behold my hands and my feet, that it is I myself, handle me, and see; for a spirit hath not flesh and bones, as ye see me have."*

"We're just the first evidence of what you'll find in the Shining City," the Judge said, "no need to be afraid. Even the apostles were frightened. But there is one thing you'll learn this afternoon that's more important than anything else you'll witness, including us—something you'll never forget. It's that God really is love. Faith and reality will merge together. You'll see!"

At that point, Francine's daughter Liz began weeping uncontrollably. She hugged her mother as tears just rained down both of their faces.

"Oh, Mama, I'm so sorry I never believed you and gave you such a hard time, every time you dragged me to church. People always said you were a saint, and I thought they were crazy. I thought you just wanted to control me, control my life, and keep me from my friends. Please forgive me, Mama, for not believing you."

Her little sisters both comforted their big sister. There wasn't a dry eye in the coach.

"I guess there are no more questions, because, for now, we're out of answers," the Judge said with a chuckle.

Georgia whispered to Francine, "I really like these old white guys!"

The lights were on in the Winnebago late into the night. Finally, Dana had the time to explain to Joey what her strategy was and what people and places they would visit in the next month or so. Before they left, she was able to successfully transfer their funds from all their accounts into her deceased mother's credit union checking account—some $325,000. She had her mother's debit card and had used it to pay for her mother's various memberships and charities, and property taxes for her cabin. It was now their lifeline. Blum sent them an email earlier that he had met with a Realtor who was getting an appraisal and a work-up. Rachel was there watching things and trying to get Dana's various houseplants and her roses back into the land of the living. So far, so good.

Then, Joey read Brady's warning, namely, that somehow he found out that police were on the outlook for a big RV pulling a Subaru.

"Hmm, how would they know about that?" Joey asked.

"They must have had someone watching the house. The Dinosaur did stop by that one day, and that evening we left in the Subaru, not to return. Gotta think about that one," Dana said.

"Okay," Joey said, "show me your master plan."

She leaned forward and complied. "Well, the plan has changed a little bit since the revelation that the Subaru is on the wanted list. I was thinking, you've always wanted a pick-up. Maybe we ought to dicker with Binh's son and trade in the Subaru. We don't owe any money on it. There were older Ford pickups he had restored. I liked the bright orange one because it has a camper shell."

"I see where you're going with this," Joey said.

"We could find a central location, park the RV, load up some gear, get a mattress, and then drive without the burden of the RV. We have six different locations where there are people who responded to my initial email. We have my little Handy audio recorder if I want to record on the road for my podcast. By the way, I have a time to meet Emilie Johnson, the podcaster, on Saturday in Ames. We're right here, outside of Milford, and I have more leads in five other towns heading north. We can park the RV up at the KOA campgrounds near Panorama Lake after we drive to Binh's and trade the Subaru for the pickup. We'll make a grand circle right back to the lake, right here," she said, pointing to Google map.

"And, I was thinking. The article that I found about Binh came from their weekly newspaper. In between appointments, we could stop at local newspapers and ask them about special people out here in America's farm belt. These folks, like Binh, are the salt of the earth. We tell folks we're on a human-interest sojourn for my podcast. We stay overnight in the truck at KOA parks—we leave no credit card trail for Gunderson and Bleazard to track; and the weather's good, not too hot or steamy, not cold yet. And while I have a little morning sickness, if we stay close to bathrooms, I should be fine. In the next ten days, let's see if we can find at least ten more recruits.

After the podcast on Saturday, I hope more will come streaming in," Dana said and then folded her map.

"Boy, I have to hand it to you, you're quite the zealot!" Joey said. "Didn't think you liked camping."

As Dana was getting ready for bed, Joey was feeling anxious and sent Blum a text message. "Got any line on the buy-out yet? Getting my money would be nice."

No answer right then, but unfortunately, Jonathan wouldn't be the only one who would see Joey's message.

Brady, Francine, and company were still experiencing some culture shock after their encounter with the "immortals," Judge Stone and "Big Train" Johnson, on their rail trip to Salem Crossing. But, then the fun began.

They disembarked at the train station where everyone but Brady's grandma was picked up by a hay wagon.

Natasha, Francine's 5-year-old, asked the driver. "Where we goin', Mister?"

An old farmer dressed in overalls turned and smiled. "We're joining a whole bunch of other folks in the upper field. We're picking pumpkins and squash, or gathering acorns, depending on what they need. Then, they're goin' to feed us right out in the field at harvest time. Everybody takes a turn at gathering and reaping."

Brady spoke up. "What about my grandma?"

"Most likely, they're taking her to the Fall quilting bee, maybe choir practice. We'll see."

As their wagon made its way through town, people were decorating Salem Crossing for the Fall Festival. They had put signs up all over; one announced a Kids' Fair with apple bobbing, pumpkin carving, and a barn dance. Another invited residents to a brass band concert.

Francine and Georgia took in the nostalgia of the 1925 shops, the wagons, cars, and fashion with wonderment. But Georgia looked concerned and asked the driver, "Is everything here just like it was a hundred years ago. Everything?"

He knew what she was asking. "Do you mean, do some people here have to ride in the back of the bus and have their own . . . segregated accommodations? Look at the sign over the top of that hall right there." She glanced at the clock tower in the opposite square.

"I see it."

"What does it say; rather what does it mean?"

"One heart, one mind . . ."

"Exactly. It's not skin color that gets you here, Ma'am. It's the content of your character."

The driver loosened the reins and encouraged his team to get a move on; they had a hill to climb. The sisters exchanged smiles.

About 5 pm, the whole group of harvesters was gathered in a meadow ready to take seats around dozens of tables surrounded by wagon loads of produce they had picked and gathered. The tables were set like a Currier and Ives poster with all kinds of things grown, harvested, and prepared right there on the spot. Judge Stone took a moment to introduce his guests and invited Francine to come up to the front.

"This fine woman is Francine Gregory, and she and her family are our guests today. She is somewhat famous where she comes from for the many infants she has rescued. And, today, I am presenting her and her family with her official invitation."

Francine stood there in shock while everyone clapped and cheered.

"But, there's one thing you have to do first before we eat. Would you mind saying grace?" He winked at her, and she folded her arms and did what she always did before every meal. Then, they all got their fill.

By 6:30, everyone was all back on the train except Brady's grandmother. Brady was worried. About ten minutes later, a carriage rolled in at a good clip, the driver exited and helped the older woman out. She thanked him and managed to get herself and a huge sack up and into the car. She turned and waved to the driver.

The train's whistle blew a long and then a short warning note as if to say, "We're leaving now—you better hurry!" The station was painted a bright red and green with vendor carts rolling up and down the platform. Folks dressed in their finest, carrying neat leather bags and occasionally pulling a trunk, talked, bought newspapers, and said goodbye to family and friends. It was like a scene from a 1925 movie, except it was in color, and there was sound.

"Pinch yourself, Brady! You have any idea where we are, where we've been today?"

"I have an idea, Grandma."

Sitting across from them, Francine, Georgia, and their girls were eating candied apples and holding onto their little gift bags full of hard-tack candy, nuts, and a handmade toy. Both Francine and Georgia each had a bag of produce in front of them, and Brady's grandma pulled out a new hand-tied quilt and showed it to the others.

"Look what my new friends gave to me. Isn't it beautiful?"

The train pulled out of the station, puffing as it went back down the mountain, leaving a trail of steam behind it.

Standing on the platform and watching them leave was the Judge, along with Margritte Kunz, and her best friend, Virginia.

Margritte asked Virginia, "Did she like her quilt?"

"Loved it and maybe enjoyed helping tie it even more."

Oma turned to the Judge. "When will I see Joey and Dana again? You promised."

"Give 'em time. They've gone fishing, and I hear the fish are starting to bite."

❏ ❏ ❏ ❏ ❏

Joey loved his new rebuilt orange 1980 Ford F-150 pickup with its big tires and sleeper cab. There was a small fridge back there, but no headroom and, unfortunately for Dana, no commode, unless you counted the bucket. She didn't.

"Hey, don't complain. This was your idea, a rather good idea, I think," Joey said. They were traveling northeast on a two-lane road with lots of farm equipment. Their first stop had been a bust.

A lady at a gray, rundown farmhouse told them in no uncertain terms that she didn't appreciate traveling salesmen and asked Dana if she was illiterate. "Don't that sign on the door say 'no solicitation?'"

Dana didn't bother her to ask if she could use her bathroom. She was glad she didn't ask after they turned around and saw that it was one of the "free-range" kinds, standing out back all by itself.

Joey should have known better not to pour salt in her wounds, but he couldn't help himself. "You could have got some slivers!" She gave him the pirate look, one eye closed, the other one with a raised eyebrow. Then, he quickly changed the subject.

"Hey, good news though. We're only about five miles from Fort Dodge, the town with the newspaper; they'll have a restroom."

"Really? You think?" Men too often learn things too little, too late.

Joey hated her pirate eye; he worried she could cast some kind of spell over him. Wait! She'd already done that! He was powerless in her presence

So back to her route plan. They had just passed Moorland, then it was on to Fort Dodge and the Messenger newspaper; after that, Dana had another name in Coalville to investigate. Joey was now driving as fast as he could.

Mrs. Halladay, the librarian at the Messenger, was as nice as she could be. But, many of their old copies were still on microfiche. Only the last ten years were on their web archives. But she had found several heart-warming human interest stories where some local person had done something extraordinary.

The librarian was gracious enough to call three of them; the first one was in a rest home, the second one simply said he wasn't interested in talking to anybody he didn't know, but the third one was a special-ed teacher who had received a life-saving kidney from a young accident victim . . . and that victim, her donor, had been one of her students years earlier. She said she would talk to Dana.

Before they left the Messenger, Mrs. Halladay gave Joey and Dana names of nine other people in the area. Mrs. Graham, a single woman living in an old farmhouse in the small farming town of Otho, south of Fort Dodge welcomed them.

"Thank you for allowing us to talk with you, Mrs. Graham. I'm Dana and my husband's name is Joey. We're collecting stories and meeting people like you. I do some blogging and am just starting a podcast. My website is still under construction, but you can read about why we're here at our website, *www.theshiningcity.org*," Dana explained.

Mrs. Graham turned around and grabbed her iPad from a bookshelf behind her. "Do you mind if I have a look while we talk?"

"Not at all," Joey said.

She read it for a moment and then stiffened a bit. "You're not missionaries, are you? Jehovah Witnesses or anything?"

Dana laughed. "No, actually I'm Jewish and my husband is a Protestant. Jews normally don't do a lot of proselyting." The woman kept scrolling through her website and seemed to be interested. Joey looked at the books in her bookcase behind her. She had several titles by Stephen Ambrose, including *Band of Brothers* and *Undaunted Courage*, the story of Lewis & Clark. "I see you read history," he said. "Ever read about John Winthrop, the founder of Boston, Massachusetts?"

"Yes, the Puritan."

"That's where we got the name for our website," Dana said and then asked, "Do you know about his reason for his leading 750 people in eleven ships to New England?"

"No, but I bet you're about to tell me," she said now smiling.

"With your permission," Dana said.

"Give it your best," her student, the teacher said.

And, she did. She related the story of the Shining City and John Winthrop's sermon on the ship and about myths and legends of similar places throughout history. Then Joey explained how they found themselves in Salem Crossing, the Grand Hotel, and their experience in the hot springs of healing water.

"It sounds wonderful, but why are you telling me, a stranger, this? I don't know you. I don't know if you're selling herbal supplements. Maybe you're from Amway or something." Dana could tell she was skeptical, but her interest had been piqued.

"I was skeptical, too until I woke up from a coma and learned that after years of testing and trying, I was finally pregnant. Then we were invited to go to the Shining City and leave everything behind, Give it all up."

"Like the rich young prince," Mrs. Graham said.

"Exactly. Given the way this world is going, with acrimony and riots and burning cities, and even family members who won't talk to each other anymore, I yearned for someplace where the people were of one heart and one mind. And, when we were there, I found peace. I'll show you our invitation." Dana pulled it out and handed it to her.

"It's blank!"

"Yes, it's blank. We were invited, but there was a stipulation. We were asked to fill it up with the names of people we find–like-minded people of good faith, who have demonstrated by the kind of lives they have lived that they yearn for such a place where inhabitants are of one heart and one mind.

"After we read your story in the newspaper, you seemed to fit the bill. We wanted to meet you and see if you feel the way we do; as such, we are authorized to bring others back with us once they're invited. We submit their names, we send them in, and then if they are selected, they get their own invitations . . ."

"To the Shining City?"

"Yes," Joey said.

"Well, ever since I retired early last year due to my surgery and everything, I thought I'd like to do some traveling. I was thinking about Italy, but then everybody goes to Italy. How many people get to see a Shining City?"

Dana and Joey were beaming, and Mrs. Graham seemed more than intrigued. Dana got her name, address, and details and said their goodbyes. She was on the list.

Jonathan was up early taking inventory of his apple harvest now that most of the picking was finished. He paid off the last foreman for the work his crew just completed; the forklift was back in the storage area where it belonged. It had been a great year for apples. He sat down in his small cubby hole office in the storage barn and checked his email and messages.

The most recent one from Brady got his attention.

"BLZD knows J&D R in IO. Frosty here. B."

"That's awfully cryptic," Blum said to one in particular. "BLZD is Bleazard; Brady is B. And Joey and Dana are J&D. So they're in Iowa. That's a long way from home."

Then, it occurred to him. Bleazard must be tracking Brady's phone, but he couldn't possibly have Dana's unless she's been calling or texting Joey. Maybe they have my phone's IP address too. Francine was due in soon; Jonathan had hired her, he was paying her, and she was as loyal as a hound dog. I'll have her drop Dana a note and tell Joey to get a burner phone. Why won't Bleazard let this go? It's not just because he can't find Salem Crossing or the missing grandmas, is it? He must be moonlighting for Gunderson; that's the only explanation.

And, what did Brady mean by 'frosty here?' Blum figured he'd better get some answers. And fast!

It was more than frosty at the Sheriff's office. Brady was sitting in an interview room on the 4th floor next to the office of Internal Affairs. He'd been there for nearly 45 minutes as requested. A moment later, Sergeant Miller came in.

"We want to clear up a few things, Brady. We've had a complaint."

"From Bleazard, I know. We didn't exactly see eye-to-eye," Brady admitted.

"He was your training officer. You noted you've always wanted to do more serious investigative work . . ."

"Mostly, I was just driving his car, getting him coffee, and carrying his clipboard. I've seen some things . . ."

"That's what he's complaining about; that you were snooping," Miller said, raising his voice.

"Well, I was doing what I was supposed to do, which he wasn't doing. He had a specific agenda regarding Joey Kunz, and I suspected he was doing the bidding of Joey's boss, Gary Gunderson. I found this," he said. He handed Miller a print-out of an ongoing SEC investigation of OJT Partners.

"Okay, fill me in. Who's Kunz? Who's Gunderson?" Miller asked. Brady gave him a quick explanation about the accident, the Kunzes' hospitalization, and the missing grandmother. Then Brady shared his suspicions about Bleazard.

"When we were at the hospital to question Joey Kunz and his wife, Bleazard immediately began treating Joey as a suspect when he was clearly the victim of an accident. I looked into what the Kunzes claimed and, although their story seemed fantastic about going to a city no one could find on a map, where was there a crime? Now, Sergeant, you may want to reprimand me for what I am about to show you, but take a look at the real improprieties here. They're not mine, they're Bleazard's."

He handed Miller another couple of pages of phone records and travel records, along with a confirmation about Bleazard's overnight stay and appearance at OJT. Joey explained. "I don't know Bleazard's motives, but he spent all this time on the phone with OJT, probably Gunderson. He spent a weekend there at the same time as the company was being visited—probably audited—by the SEC. I'll bet you dollars to donuts that he did not file for reimbursement for the hotel room. Do you know why?"

Miller shook his head. He looked confused.

"Because OJT paid for his night's stay a week ago Friday night."

"Have you told anyone else about this?"

"No, I thought if there was anything to this business, you'd call me. And you did," he said as he handed him the documents. "Keep all this. They're copies."

"How did you do all this?" Miller asked.

Brady smiled and shrugged. "I'm good at computers, and I like to solve puzzles. And do you know what's the oddest thing about the Kunzes' story? I found a story about their accident, how they ended up soaked and nearly drowned in a meadow next to a stream. Every detail matches what they told us."

"Well, let's have it," Miller demanded.

Brady pulled a folded-up printout out of his pocket and handed it to the officer. "It's all right here from a newspaper clipping . . . from 1925. It's amazing what you can find on the web if just have an open mind and ask the right questions: a young couple gone missing in a flash flood near the wreckage of a bright green two-wheeled carriage near the same place but in 1925. How about that?"

"Well, I'll be damned!" Miller said. "I'll get back to you on this. Go back to The Cage now."

Brady nodded, knowing full well that no one would get back to him. But, he also concluded that not only was Kunz still an active target, but he was, too. And probably Blum as well. They all had to be very careful from now on.

❑ ❑ ❑ ❑ ❑

Joey and Dana were still driving around in the pick-up that Joey had come to love, hidden in plain sight from anyone looking for them. Now almost two months pregnant, she was quite tired of sleeping in the camper shell on a six-inch mattress. She was homesick already for the Winnebago and having a flush toilet at her beck and call.

They had been town-hopping for three days now and, in addition to Binh and Mrs. Graham, they had three more recruits: a husband-and-wife team who knew the Jewells–the husband had been a medic in Vietnam with Carl Jewell and Charlie Kunz and was now a retired podiatrist. And then there was Mr. Hardy, a handyman and school bus driver who was in the news because he performed CPR on the principal at a high school in Ft. Dodge and saved the man's life by driving him to the hospital with a busload of the school's marching band.

"He was a character," Dana said. "And a pretty good tuba

player," Joey laughed.

They were almost to Ames, Iowa. It was Saturday and Dana had an appointment with a Christian blogger named Emilie Johnson.

"You sure you want to do this?" Joey asked as they turned the corner on their way to the Blogger Lady's house.

"A little late to back out now, don't you think?" Dana said.

"Well, I mean, generally, to broadcast an unbelievable story, making us sound like real nut cases . . ."

"Hold on a second. Was it real or wasn't it? Did we have some kind of hallucination?–Correction: Did I have a hallucination? And were you someplace else? In my dream, you were there too. We both had an accident, we both bathed in magic healing waters, and we both will be parents soon–of the same child! And, we both met President Calvin-freaking-Coolidge who supposedly died in 1933; and if he didn't, he'd now be about 148 years old. He looked pretty darn good for being nearly a century-and-a-half old, don't you think?"

"I'm sorry. I can't stop thinking about what I put into that company, and how I got double-crossed by criminals. There must be some justice. He's gotta pay. They all do!"

"And you've got to get your money!"

"You bet I do!"

"So, that's it. It's all about the money, is that it? What can you do with that money in a hundred years from now?" Dana asked, pressing him.

"What?"

"A hundred years from now, in 2121, how much will you have? What will you buy with it?"

"I don't know," he replied flatly.

"Well, if you stay here, 'where moth and dust doth corrupt,' you'll be pushing up daisies, but if you join Oma and me, you won't need it; but I think you should still get the money—all of it."

"You're not making any sense," he said now, really backed into a corner by his lawyer wife. "Why?"

She softened. "Because we saw with our own eyes and were beneficiaries of how others used their money, and how we can use ours as well to 'pay it forward' for countless other people like Brady, Francine, her sister Georgia, and those little girls, you know the ones she saved from the abortion butcher, and Binh, the little Vietnamese former mayor of Butlerville, Iowa, and the wife of a true friend of your dad. What do you say, Joey?"

He was speechless.

"Well?"

Finally, he managed to utter a few words. "I know 'you can't take it with you,' but why . . . ?"

"Why what?"

He was speechless again.

Dana answered for him. "Because He wants to see if you love Him and others enough to give it all away . . . you know, like the rich young prince who was asked to sell all that he had and give it the poor. That's why."

"Low blow," he laughed. "That's so unfair—using the rich young prince thing."

Now Dana was laughing too. Joey continued. "What a knucklehead he was! And I know for certain, you'd never marry a knucklehead or want a knucklehead to be your kid's dad. So, let's go do a podcast, whatever that is."

"You're kind of sexy! You know who you remind me of when you talk about knuckleheads?" Dana asked Joey.

"No, who?"

"Charles Barkley. Start the engine."

Blum spent the whole morning with an old student of his, a former federal attorney and an expert on securities law now working as counsel for his son's law firm. They were in an exclusive "old men's club" surrounded by antique furniture and floor-to-ceiling bookcases filled with old classics. Each man had an iced drink as they sat around a small cocktail table. The man, Jack Lee, was shocked to see Jonathan after all these years.

"Jonny, you look great! I know you're at least ten years older than me. How do you do it?"

Blum laughed and reached into his leather satchel. "Apples. I'm an apple farmer now. Brought you some," he said and handed his old friend a small sack of freshly picked honey crisps.

"They must be special apples," Lee said.

"Grew 'em myself," Blum said.

"So, what can I do for you?"

"I just found out that a young friend of mine, in a way a client, has been set up as a fall guy by his unscrupulous former employers for a serious SEC violation, when he wasn't even around when the supposed deal took place."

"What's the charge?"

"The owners who took over late last year claim that my client somehow diverted funds from an investor's account to his own, but he was in a hospital when that happened . . . in a coma. The lag time from when it would have been moved is generally two to three days to the day when it actually appeared in the account. He was up and around when it was deposited in his account but not when it would have been moved. How would he have accessed it from a hospital bed? He had no computer at the time."

Lee thought about it for a moment. "With electronic transfers, that money may have been moved a couple of times before he got it. Here's another question, since your client is a former employee, did the company use direct deposit for payroll? If so, then they already had access to his account."

"But, with direct deposit access, that wouldn't mean they have the ability to make withdrawals, would it?" Blum asked. Lee shook his head.

"Listen, give me what you have regarding the accounts involved, and I can have our investigations unit look into it. I'll bet this was a stalling action, anyway," Lee said. "They should know they couldn't make it stick. Maybe they just needed to show it in his account for a couple of days and knew they could put it back in short order to pull the wool over a third party's eyes, especially if buyers were looking at the company; or to show a third party that there was money missing from a client's account. See if the amount corresponds to some other significant figure . . . that's what accountants do when something else is awry in an account.

'That's when they get those 'aha' moments, you know like when you find a missing number when you're balancing your checking account."

"Hmm, that's interesting. I'll text the account information."

"Thanks for the drink, Jonnie. I got to get some more of those apples."

Dana got a short text from Blum on her new burner phone. "Jonathan says Gunderson is trying to convince the SEC that Joey has violated some securities law." She showed Joey,

"Good luck to him. I haven't touched my account in almost two months since they're not paying me anymore. You handle all the money, remember?" Joey said. "Phone the podcaster lady again, and tell her we're just outside her house. I'm gonna stretch my legs. Dang, I love my new orange truck so much better than the Subaru!"

As he opened the door and stepped out, she contradicted him.

"Since we traded my Subaru for the truck, it's mine!"

"I don't think so," he said under his breath.

"What was that?" she said.

"Nothing."

Just as she was walking up to the big red, two-story house, she got a text. Joey caught up with her. The podcaster was waiting for them on the steps. The home was nestled among several large maple and oak trees that looked to be at least a hundred years old. Emilie Johnson invited them in.

She had an infectious grin. A couple of small children were playing a board game in the corner.

"You little pups hush now. Me and these nice people are going to make a podcast. And, when we're done, if you're really quiet, we'll go to DQ and get you something really bad for you," she told them, and they started to laugh.

"You can't laugh, or all you'll get is a salad—without dressing. So zip it, buckaroos!" She turned to her guests. "Follow me up to the attic. I'm all ready for you."

She set up the mics, did a sound test, set her levels, gave them each headsets, and adjusted the microphones in front of them. Her attic recording studio was not much more than a closet with her equipment crammed into the corner under a tiny window. It was kind of stuffy, but their host wasn't. She was a firecracker with all kinds of personality.

The recording light turned to red, she made her regular introduction and introduced herself and her guests. Emilie got right into it.

"When I first read your blog, I thought you'd come here wearing tin foil hats and tell me about *Close Encounters of the Third Kind*. But, somehow, you don't strike me that way. Dana, you seem very NVG," Emilie said.

"NVG?"

"Nature Valley Granola girl, you know, works out, college-educated, loves the environment, and is no one to mess with."

"You got that right," Joey said. "She speaks a bunch of dead languages, has a law degree from Vanderbilt, and I'm smart enough never to get in an argument with her, at least one that I couldn't win."

Dana gave Joey the pirate eye, but a good-natured one.

"Man, folks! He's right. She gave him a look that even scared me!"

Emilie asked them about what happened, and Dana explained how they found Salem Crossing, the Return to Normalcy, about the trip to the Grand Hotel, how they took a dip in the hot springs, and meeting several dead people, including President Coolidge. But, she held off explaining the accident and their hospital stay.

Instead, Dana wanted to talk about "Normalcy" because she had been doing some reading about Coolidge, his 1924 campaign for the White House, and the kind of President he was.

Emilie took the bait.

"So, you actually met President Calvin Coolidge? He wasn't an actor or a Cyborg or an animatronic, wax dummy?" Emilie asked.

"Nope, none of those things. We were on a boat on a body of water that shouldn't have been there, in a state without ten-thousand-foot peaks rising out of an alpine-type lake . . ."

"Like Lake Geneva in Switzerland," Joey added.

"Really?" Emilie asked.

"Yes," Dana said. "You may ask, why did we happen to fall into the year 1925 when Calvin Coolidge, called the Sphinx of the Potomac, or Cool Cal, was President? If I may, please let me share some things about the man. He was the first "equal opportunity president" of the 20th-century. Unlike Woodrow Wilson, he made war on the Ku Klux Klan, and he did not make excuses for it; he appointed Blacks to high government positions and advocated for anti-lynching laws. And in 1924, he signed the Indian Citizenship Act. Here's a quote from his first Inaugural Address, which we need in our public life today more than ever:

"'*The fundamental precept of liberty is toleration. We cannot permit any inquisition either with-in or without the law or apply any religious test to the holding of office. The mind of America must be forever free.*'

"Here was a man who wasn't so politically correct that he couldn't talk about religion and government at the same time. Like the Founders, like John Winthrop, the Puritan founder of Boston, he recognized, as did Adams, that this Republic can only function when its citizens are God-fearing people," Dana said, then she referred to her notes.

"I have some excerpts from speeches he gave in 1925, both his inaugural address and one he gave to a group of religious leaders later that year. Remember, when he was elected as Harding's vice president in 1920, the country was only two years removed from the end of World War I; the Spanish Flu had taken more than 50 million lives around the world. So, when he campaigned in his own right in 1924, after assuming the presidency when Harding died in 1923, he wanted a 'Return to Normalcy.' I think what he meant was a nation of God-fearing people who embraced the notion of 'One Nation, Under God'. Great message for today, no? These words I think are really prescient for our time. In this segment, he was reflecting on what America learned after its participation in World War I.

He said, '*Peace will come when there is realization that only under a reign of law based on righteousness and supported by the religious conviction of the brotherhood of man can there be any hope of a complete and satisfying life. Parchment will fail, the sword will fail, it is only the spiritual nature of man that can be triumphant.*'

"In talking about the government's helping the human condition, Coolidge clarifies that it cannot replace personal responsibility or excuse people who cannot accept the rule of law. He said that '*there is another and more basic reason why the Government cannot supply the source and motive for the complete reformation of society. In the progress of the human race, religious beliefs were developed before the formation of governments. It is my understanding that government rests on religion.*' Then, he got to the core of the matter, and he wasn't timid about it. Let me read it. He explained that *'The claim to the right to freedom, the claim to the right to equality, with the resultant right to self-government—the rule of the people— have no foundation other than the common brotherhood of man derived from the common fatherhood of God.'* That pretty sums it up for me. Now listen to this," Dana continued quoting Coolidge. " *'. . . society reverts to a system of class and caste, and the Government instead of being imposed by reason from within is imposed by force from without. Freedom and democracy would give way to despotism and slavery . . .'"*

"That's why I am a big Calvin Coolidge fan when, just a month ago, I knew nothing about him," Dana added.

"So, in a nutshell, tell us why you are on this tour of America's heartland. Are you missionaries? Are you starting a new congregation? What?" Emilie asked.

Joey spoke up to answer this question, "No, nothing like that. We're simply asking people to recommend the heroes in their lives to be invited to the Shining City on the Hill."

"Invited to WHAT city?"

Dana answered. "To the same kind of city that John Winthrop proposed to the masses in England in the early 17th-century. Come with us to 'The Shining City on a Hill,' where the people are of 'One Heart, One Mind, Dwell in Righteousness and There Is No Poor Among Them.'"

"So, what is the catch? How much does it cost?"

Joey was now ready to answer the Big Question. "Everything. Just like the rich, young prince whom Jesus asked to sell all that he had, give it the poor, and come follow Him."

Dana clarified. "But, it's also nothing. Somebody else paid for us, you know, they 'paid it forward.' Others paid for us, and before we go, we'll give all that we have and 'pay it forward' so others can follow."

Finally, Joey added his own observation. "If you read Matthew 24 and other so-called 'apocalyptic' verses in the Bible, you might be asking yourselves the question, as we have, how long can this go on, this poisonous climate, this class hatred, these riots and burning cities and division? How long do we have until the Messiah returns?

"As far as I'm concerned, all the politicians, all their promises, and all the money in the world can't fix human suffering and injustice until people are finally ready to live in a place where all the people are of 'One Heart and One Mind' and are willing to pay the price to be there. Anyway, that's what I think."

Emilie added her closing remarks quickly, mixed in the music, and said, "Until next time."

Afterward, she asked them to follow her downstairs; she wanted her children to go in their bedroom, "because she wanted to talk to these nice people for a minute."

She offered them a couple of soft drinks and some cookies and took a seat across from them. "I have a question. What do I have to do to put names on your list, and if, by chance, somebody invites me, could I bring those two characters with me? Oh, and how much time do we have?"

They smiled, got her information, put it in the envelope, and got back on the road. Regarding her last question, Joey said simply,

"We'd all like to know the answer to that question, but there's only One Who knows, and He's not telling!"

Blum had his hands full, but thank goodness, Francine was with him in the cider house. He was on his way to meet another attorney to uncover exactly what schemes Gunderson and Bleazard had cooked up; he still couldn't figure out what burr was stuck under the inspector's saddle.

"Mr. Blum, you know I'm just trained as a nurse's assistant, I can run Excel, had some accounting, and I can talk on the telephone, but . . ."

"No, 'buts' Francine. You have something that most doctors, lawyers, and Indian chiefs lack—you have moral courage, and that's a rare commodity these days," he said. "Let's contact the produce buyers on this list and the fruit-stand distributors. What we can't sell fresh, we'll juic—that's the backup plan. You have the price list: the apples are graded, boxed, palletized, and marked in the warehouse. Make sure any orders match the price and grade marked on the pallet. Text me if you have a question or problem as I might be in a conference."

"Will do, Mr. Blum."

"You can drop the Mister. Just don't drop the apples. Call me Jonathan," he said as he hurried out. Then he turned, smiled, and just said, "Thanks."

In a moment, the big blue Caddy was kicking out gravel as he turned onto the asphalt and sped away.

He had reminded her to keep an eye on the monitors in the back; he had four cameras watching things around the house and the barns, along with motion detectors. And, now she could watch activity on her phone, too. You can't be too careful these days, he thought, and she knew it wasn't the apples he was worried about. Darkness was seeping in everywhere like fog quietly creeping in on a cold, rainy night, on little cats' paws.

The truth was the only antidote; light the only antiseptic.

Truth and light seemed a little hard to come by on the road back in Iowa, too. After a few initial successes, Dana and Joey found the welcome mats locked up and put away. They had already made about a dozen house calls, follow-ups from Dana's blog post, and had yet to get any feedback from the podcast. They were on their way back to Binh's to get the Dinosaur when they stopped to stretch their legs at a park in a small farming community.

"Look, is that a farmer's market, booths, or a harvest fair over there? Let's stop. Maybe we can get something to drink and find a bathroom," Dana said.

They were low on gas anyway. Good idea.

Farmers, artisans, bakers, and a couple of used-book dealers were set up like soldiers in formation with two rows facing each other, offering free samples and answering questions to passersby, eager to show what they had grown or made. The Wounded Warriors had a booth telling their story about soldiers who lost limbs in wars in Iraq or Afghanistan; AL-ANON was there, too, explaining how their 12-step program worked for people with alcohol or drug problems; and a young woman sat silently behind a table selling CD's she had produced to raise money for battered wives.

Joey sat down at a picnic table across from her canvas-covered booth and munched on a churro as people walked by the booth without even acknowledging her. Dana was talking to a bookseller at the next booth, paying for an old book. When she was done, Joey motioned to her.

"Sit down for a moment and watch and see if anybody buys a CD from that young woman while I get you a Coke Zero," Joey said.

"Make it a light lemonade, if they have it," she responded.

He waited in line for a few minutes, and when he returned, she was sitting with the girl, listening to her story. The young musician was wearing a pair of jeans and flip-flops with a tunic and flowers in her hair. A guitar stood behind her just waiting to be played.

"Do you play?" Dana asked.

"Yes' play and sing, sometimes with friends, sometimes it's just me," she admitted.

Dana could see she needed some encouragement. "Play me something, please." When she reached for her player, Dana held up her hand. "No, you play me something. I like to hear it live."

Her name was Blythe, and she lived in a trailer park west of the little farming community with her mother, who was currently in a 30-day rehab facility. She told Dana she just turned 18, but she looked more like 15 or 16; she had ten or so CDs she had produced herself, and the "battered wife" foundation she was working for was her own mother. As she was tuning up her old nylon-string folk guitar, a Goya, a left-over relic from the 60s, she admitted as much.

"I don't mean to cheat anybody. And my mom's not really battered, except by circumstances and life and by being a single mom, but I do this whenever I can 'cause people tell me I have a good voice," Blythe explained.

"Well, let's hear it! What are you singing for us?" Joey asked.

"My version of Sheryl Crow's 'Wildflower' but in a 60s folk-style, usually with bongos, but I'm just by myself . . . " Dana interrupted her.

"No, you're not! I'll bongo for you!"

She smiled and started with a few bars as Dana tried to catch on to her cadence.

Blythe began singing, slowly at first, until she warmed up. In a moment, Dana was keeping up with her on the bongos and whispered to Joey, "Never one lesson!"

He smiled. "Really?" They listened to Blythe who sang with real conviction as other passersby listened too.

"Quiet eyes

"You have always been my wildflower

"Showing up wherever beauty's lost its way

"Your heart must break

"I was free ,,, "

She picked up the pace, and soon she had attracted a fairly good crows.

She started on the second verse as people stopped to listen. Dana was really bongoing away now—Joey tried not to avoid eye contact with his wife; was she on LSD? He stifled a smile.

"Burning faster than the closest star... "

By now, even more people had gathered to hear the teenager finish the song. "She's really good!" Dana whispered to Joey. Blythe finished.

"And everything I know just fades away

"Everything, everything, everything . . ."

When Blythe had finished, more than a dozen people were applauding, and Joey had collected $80 for her remaining CDs, he then added $50 in tuition monies for allowing Dana to learn how to bongo along with her. It was the least he could do. He promised himself never to bring bongos up in public. It would a secret he would keep to himself. Good thing she went to law school!

The crowd dispersed, and Blythe was putting her guitar in its case when she looked up at the highway. A bus had just stopped, discharged passengers, and started again on its way.

"Oh, dear!" Blythe said as she started to scramble to leave.

'You miss your bus?" Dana said.

"Yeah, and another won't come for an hour, and I have to be to work." Dana looked at Joey who nodded.

"Where's your job?"

"At a diner in Minersville. That way," she pointed west. "About ten miles."

"Don't worry, honey, we can drive you. We can grab a bite there. How do you get home? Someone coming for you later?" Dana asked.

"I work until 7 am. I bus dishes and clean up. I catch the bus right in front. It works out okay."

Joey gave her the $80 and the $50 for the "bongo lesson." They helped her clean up her stuff and packed it into a little backpack as she secured her guitar. They all walked over to "Orange Crush," the blazingly bright orange pick-up, and hit the highway.

"Since we're driving by my place, can I leave my stuff at home?"

For the next few minutes, they learned more about Blythe Hunter, a high-school dropout whose dream was to be a recording engineer and produce music for "up and coming young people" and eventually move to Nashville. But she admitted her mom needed to be on her feet first and gainfully employed somewhere, anywhere.

"She's never been the same since my dad failed to home from Afghanistan. His body came home, but he didn't. It was a really nice funeral, though. We even got a letter from the President, and my mom gave me the flag. She didn't want it. Oh, here's the trailer park. I'll be just a minute." She ran out to the trailer.

Dana looked at Joey. "What can we do for her and her mom?"

"I don't know. I guess all we can do right now is get all their information and stay in touch."

They drove her to the 24/7 Diner on Highway 169 on the way to Carroll where they needed to turn south to Binh's place to get the Dinosaur so they could get back to Blum's and process everything they'd done so far. Maybe Emilie, the podcaster, might have stirred up some interest by now. After a burger and a bathroom break at Blythe's diner, they stayed on the road until late that night when they finally arrived at the scenic spot, Binh's family wrecking yard, where they had left the Winnebago so they could enjoy another five-star experience cuddled up in the Dinosaur (Joey hadn't yet got the hang of getting the propane heater to work).

"Oh, that was romantic," Dana muttered as she was stretching out at the edge of the Dinosaur's bed the next morning, trying to work out the kinks. She was feeling a little bloated and off-kilter. She knew why. It wasn't the thin mattress. And, Joey smelled odd! "What was that? Oh, yeah, almost forgot. I'm pregnant." How long can I drive around in the Dinosaur? she asked herself.

"And, I always thought it would be great cuddling, no matter where we were. I was wrong!" Joey said.

'You don't find me attractive?" Dana asked, trying to put a humorous twist on it, her hair sticking up like the Wild Man from Borneo, the proverbial side-show attraction.

He kissed her on the forehead. "That's never been a problem," he confessed.

"I think we need a shower," she observed. "Both of us."

"Then, we need to find a KOA and get hooked up to water and sewer," he replied.

"Let's go talk to Binh."

After they had a moment with Binh to say goodbye, and everybody made promises to reunite very soon, Joey and Dana gassed up and were back on the road again.

Dana was reading text messages on her burner phone (Blum had advised her to take the chip out of both of their iPhones and store them to avoid being tracked).

"This changes things!" Dana said as Joey was trying to pass a semi.

"What does?"

"Blum sent us an epistle, longest one I've ever seen," she said.

"And I got another one from Emilie."

"Emilie?"

"You know, Emilie Johnson, the podcaster."

"So, fill me in," Joey said as he got the Dinosaur under control. This part of Iowa wasn't exactly flat; it went up one hill and down another with ripe corn on both sides interspersed with little stops on the road and the occasional grove of trees. Joey remembered a line from a movie: "This isn't Heaven, it's just Iowa," the character said. It looked like heaven, he thought.

Dana gave him the Reader's Digest version.

"First, it seems that Gunderson and his partners are in some serious trouble, and in the process, they tried to blame you for embezzlement!"

"What did I do with that money?" Joey laughed and turned to her. "You're not kidding."

"Nope, but the crafty old Blum had an investigator, another old friend attached to a law firm, do some serious snooping."

"Don't tell me. It was someone who owed him a favor," Joey interjected.

"How'd you guess? Anyway, they contacted the SEC who has an ongoing investigation that is coming to a head, and the information Blum gave the Feds was the final piece to put the nail in their coffin. That's the good news."

"And, the BAD news?"

Bleazard's people found the body of a missing woman who disappeared from the Columbia Center . . ."

"Where Oma was . . . ?"

"Yes, where Oma was, and Bleazard convinced Blum to have you come in and clear up a few things," Dana said, trying not to upset the driver of the Dinosaur.

"And Blum agreed?"

"In a way; but he has a plan that he didn't share with us. However, it has something to do with another old-time train trip up the mountain, which leads to the other text from Emilie, you know, the podcaster."

Joey was starting to flush. "You don't want to see my head explode, do you? What is going on?"

"Emilie has had more than 300 hits on our podcast, and she's getting more every day. There's a Fox 13 TV station that wants to talk to us . . . in Omaha."

"Wait a second!"

"There's more. She wants to have a look at Salem Crossing, and she has more than a dozen friends and relatives who want to go with her. Blum had already arranged to take Rachel and Martina on his Paradise Express up there over the weekend while the train was still running, and Blum okayed my idea to take Emilie's entourage with them. Jonathan is texting her the details. Binh, too," Dana declared.

"Along with Blum, Walter, Rachel, and Martina, they'd fill up an entire railcar."

"So, you've done all this texting while I've been driving happily down the highway?"

Dana set him straight. "Well, you can't text and drive; you're barely keeping the Dinosaur going in a straight line."

"Well, I suppose I need to take the next exit and get onto I-80 and head to Omaha."

"Omaha it is," she said. "I have the address for a KOA that's right on the way."

❏ ❏ ❏ ❏ ❏

Jonathan and Francine sat back, relaxed outside the Cider House as the last produce truck left. All the apples destined for distributors and local produce stands and grocers were gone. What was left would be made into cider, and everybody loved Jonathan Blum's unfiltered, all-natural cider.

So, now it was on to the business at hand: the last train of the season to Salem Crossing for the passengers whom Blum called the "witnesses."

"Okay, Francine, let's go over this list one more time now that we have the final podcaster's contribution," he said. They had left the cider house, and thanks to unseasonably warm fall weather, they were sitting on the patio with a laptop and a clipboard, making sure everybody on the list was accounted for. All around them fall was in its full vibrancy. Behind them, a big maple was dropping multi-colored leaves everywhere.

"So, you're sure that the passenger car has 40 seats, or was it 36?" Francine asked.

"Let's stick to the smaller number, but remember, these are facing benches, not individual seats. What's the total as of right now?" Blum asked.

"Joey and Dana submitted six specific names but said they'd have more after lunch. Emilie's list contains 27 or 28. And, then, of course, there's Rachel and Martina, but Rachel said she might bring a friend. That's 36 or 37 with eight of them being small children. Now what?"

"We forward the names on to Walter who gives them to the Judge so the invitations can be prepared. Walter's bringing them Friday night. Then there's one more surprise person I'm bringing," Blum said.

"Should I include the name on the text to Walter?"

"No, he doesn't know about it, but he'll find out when he's on the train."

Francine furrowed her brow. "What's going on?"

"You'll see."

16

There's nothing like a hot shower to bring you back to life, even if the shower stall is smaller than a broom closet. The hot water tank in the Dinosaur, of course, was not much bigger than the brain of a Brontosaurus, but that's why Joey let Dana go first; he got the leftovers; whatever hot water remained, that is.

Soon, they were ready for their TV interview. Their KOA campground was east of the Missouri in Iowa, and the interview was set for a park across the river at a historic site called Winter Quarters.

It was near a pioneer cemetery surrounded by ancient cottonwood trees. Joey saw the van for the Fox station parked near the entrance with a perky little reporter huddled in a parka sitting on a bench with a microphone in her hand. Dana and Joey were back in the "Orange Crush," the name Joey gave his newest and now most beloved earthly possession, his 1980 Ford F-150.

"Is it cold? Look at her," Dana asked.

"Well, probably not for you, ever since little 'No Name' decided to join our family," Joey said, commenting on Dana's new proclivity to open all the windows and sit in a draft whenever she could. Joey did have a sweater and offered it to his wife, but she declined, even though the producer was wrapped up like an Arctic Fox. "She must be from California," Joey said.

Sure enough, she was from Huntington Beach, they would later discover, and her name was Carol, the station's human interest rookie reporter who never, ever appeared on screen after 5 pm. She was not yet ready for prime time, but she hoped this day would prove different.

It wasn't really that cold, just windy, but that caused all kinds of audio problems. Anticipating that, the producer had arranged with the visitors' center at the cemetery to let them use a small conference room that had floor-to-ceiling windows looking out at the cemetery. The place was empty, so she started her interview using the cemetery as a backdrop.

Remembering that it would be Halloween at the end of the month, Dana and Joey figured what she was up to once she began her opening statement.

"One of my favorite movies, especially this time of the year, was the classic horror flick written and directed by the 'Bolly-wood' film-maker M. Night Shyamalan and released in 1999. Of course, I'm talking about *The Sixth Sense* starring Bruce Willis, Toni Collette, and the young clairvoyant played by child actor Haley Joel Osment, whose line, 'I see dead people,' made him—and the movie—famous."

Joey felt the hair stand up on the back of his neck and whispered to Dana, "Let's get out of here," and started to get up and leave, but Dana pulled him down.

The reporter then began her introduction of her "guests."

"Today, we have a couple who not only see dead people, but they actually talk to them, including the 30th President of the United States, Calvin Coolidge. So, what better place to conduct this inter-

view than right here near the Winter Quarters Pioneer Cemetery?"
And then she got to the question she wanted them to answer.

"So how do you talk to the deceased. Is it like séance. What
happens exactly?"

She stopped, then the cameraman recorded a second version,
got the 'okay' from her producer, and turned to Dana and Joey with
a repressed a smirk, flashing them a phony smile instead. "Let's bring
you two into the shot here at the table. I'll introduce you, and then
we'll have our conversation. You okay?"

Dana whispered to Joey, "I have this. Just sit and watch. She
doesn't know it, but she has really stepped into it. As Oma likes to
say, 'this will be fun!'" Dana nodded.

The producer filled in as the make-up and lighting person wired
them both with lapel mics and set them together on one side of the
table with Carol, the talking head with the big blond hair, opposite
them. Then, the cameraman framed a wide shot with Dana and
Joey on the left to capture their response to the "gotcha question."
The shot was wide enough to show Carol on the right, so he could
not only get her reaction and record additional questions she might
pose but also so he could reveal the cemetery outside behind her.

Dana turned on the charm. "Carol, that is an interesting way
to get our conversation started, but, maybe we can answer your question WITH a question. Is that okay?" Joey could see Carol instantly,
stiffen. "From your perspective, do you believe there's life after
death?"

Carol hesitated. "Well, I don't know for sure . . ."

Now Dana got going. "But, you've thought about it, though,
when you went to church as a child, correct?"

"I didn't go to church as a child," she admitted. "I've moved on from childish things like Santa Claus and the Easter Bunny."

"And, life after death. Okay, I get it. Ever read the Bible, Old or New Testament?" Dana asked.

"No, sorry," she added. "I know that's how most Christians look at things, clinging to their Bibles . . ."

"No, Carol, actually I'm Jewish. So, according to your viewpoint, what happens when we die? Do we go anywhere, experience anything at all?"

"I don't know, but I've come to grips with the reality that when we die, the lights simply go out."

"That's a rather bleak outlook, don't you think?" Dana asked.

Now, she was getting defensive as Dana had turned the tables on her, and the interviewer had become the interviewee. Rather than answer the question, she drew her finger across her throat to tell the cameraman to stop filming. She was now hot under the collar.

"Wait a second! I'm supposed to ask you the questions, not the other . . ."

Dana interrupted her, " . . . the other way around, is that it? So, you ask me a 'gotcha' question to make us look foolish. Now you're ending the interview and returning to the station . . . with nothing, is that it? Do you think you're Mike Wallace now? Come on, Joey, let's go," Dana feigned a departure, and as they were ready to stand up, Carol had a change of heart.

"No, you're right. Let's start over," Carol said.

"Trust me, people will love this interview when we're done. You'll get some national hits from this, I promise." Dana said.

Her eyes lit up. "Really? What is your training, actually?"

"I'm a trial lawyer," Dana said, exaggerating a bit, even though she still had the bar exam coming up.

"All right, what was your question again?"

Dana repeated her original question. "That's a rather bleak outlook, isn't it?" Dana gave her time to let her give a reasoned response. She waited a bit more. Then Carol composed herself and replied.

"Yeah, it's bleak, but that's why we have to make the most of the time we have here."

"In this realm, in this reality, right?" Carol nodded.

Dana continued, "For sure, yes. But wouldn't it be great to get a glimmer of hope and hear a first-hand witness describe face-to-face conversations with people, like a former President of the United States, a Chief Justice of the Supreme Court, or one of the first inductees into the Cooperstown Baseball Hall of Fame, the last two of whom died in 1946? Don't you think your viewers, and viewers around the country, even around the world, want to hear what they had to say?"

"Certainly, I would!" Carol said, seemingly very interested, sincere even.

"Then, let us relate the experience that happened to us when we simply took Joey's grandmother to a rather odd address, down an old country road, not knowing beforehand where we were going, and then found ourselves back in 1925 where we met some very interesting people."

Then, Dana turned the interview over to Joey who described their first encounter with Walter "Big Train" Johnson, then meeting Supreme Court Justice Harlan Stone, famed American Saturday Evening Post illustrator, Norman Rockwell, and finally the 30th President of the United States, the Sphinx of the Potomac himself, Calvin Coolidge.

Dana then brought the interview to an end by describing her experience in the hot springs, 'the stirring of the waters,' and her miraculous pregnancy against all odds.

An hour-and-a-half later, they said goodbye to the Fox News crew, jumped in the Orange Crush, and headed back across the river to hook up with the Dinosaur and get out of town.

When they were back on I-80 returning to Blum's orchard, Dana suddenly grew pale and turned to Joey and said, "What have I done? Why didn't you stop me? What if the story grows legs and crawls out from under a rock?"

Suddenly, she had Joey's attention. "What if it does go national? We have 36 seats on the bus, and if by rail, maybe room for 40 or 42 passengers, kids included? You're right. What have you done?" Joey said.

"You? Don't you mean we?"

"Yeah, I guess. Don't forget, I got up to leave, and you pulled me back down."

"Why didn't you resist me?"

"Are you serious? How in the world could I ever do that?

They drove through most of the night, but before they had crossed back over into Nebraska, Dana texted Jonathan who told them to park the Dinosaur somewhere at a campground ahead of the apple farm and then drive the Subaru the last 20 miles or so. "But be careful not to get pulled over."

He was happy to hear they had sold the Subaru station wagon

and replaced it with the truck. "Good thinking!" Blum told them.

They pulled in about 4am, and per Blum's instructions, came in through the garage and camped out upstairs in the spare bedroom. They padded downstairs about 10 am, still bleary-eyed. Jonathan was making bacon and waffles. The smell woke them up. Blum turned when he saw them shuffle down the stairs.

"Good morning! I like the truck," he said. "It's a cherry piece of machinery. What year is it, '78, '79?"

Joey rubbed his eyes, processed the question, and finally answered him. "It's a 1980 Ford F-150, completely restored and with a Power Stroke V8 engine. It's a gas hog, but in that smaller, lighter frame, it really moves," Joey said. "So, counselor, what do you have cooked up?" He and Dana were all ears.

"Well, you got my cryptic text message. I told Bleazard you're ready to sit down and answer all his questions," Blum said.

"What? Why? There's nothing to say," Joey said, irritated. "I told him already everything I know, which is nothing. Oma's in Paradise in Salem Springs or wherever we left her. It's simple. We got in a carriage, took a ride down the canyon, fell into a river, and woke up in a hospital. When and where is this supposed to happen?"

"Saturday. Just be here at 8 am, and I'll take care of the rest," Blum explained as he burned himself on the waffle iron. "Dang!" He piled the new waffles onto the stack.

Now Dana was perplexed too. "That's not much of an explanation. What's going on?"

Blum smiled. "Turns out, the body of an old woman was found near the canyon and, as a result, we learned why Bleazard has been so OCD about the whole thing. His own mother disappeared about a year ago; she was a resident at your grandmother's facility as well, and she was a friend of Margritte's friend, Virginia. She was likely the one who invited Virginia. When Bleazard heard about the body, he feared it was his mother. That's when it was reported that Bleazard's mother had disappeared."

"And . . .was that her body?"

"No, it was an older woman, a dementia patient, who went on a little camping trip with her grandkids a couple of years ago, wandered off in the middle of the night, and must have walked for miles. The body was found when Bleazard's search crew went back to find anything he could on you."

"So, where is Mrs. Bleazard?"

"She runs a boarding house in Salem Crossing," Blum said.

"We met a woman who ran a boarding house," Dana said. "On the street: the woman who told us we needed to buy new clothes to fit in," she explained.

"Oh, yeah. So, Blum, what do I do? Fill me in," Joey asked.

"Just show up on Saturday. For you to sell it, I don't want you to give anything away. Just be there," Blum said. "And, Dana, what happened in Omaha?"

Oops, here it comes, she thought to herself. "Why?"

"Because you and Joey made the national news. You are on the Web and on Fox's subscription site, Fox Nation. Do you want to know how many views you've had? Have you checked your website for inquiries since you returned?"

"Jonathan, we just woke up."

"Well, you'll probably want to spend the next three days answering the nearly 4,000 emails you've collected since the broadcast, not to mention a few hundred more from Emilie Johnson's podcast. You and Francine can work on that together. We have a couple of laptops set up in the Cider House, Francine got in at 8 this morning, and she was here last night until 10."

"Jonathan, I am so sorry! I just wanted to get the word out . . ."

"Sorry? It was fantastic! It couldn't have come at a better time because we don't have much of it left, " Blum said, grinning.

"Much of what left?" Joey asked.

"Time, that's what! The schedule's been moved ahead, and you have provided our needed jump-start. It's our chance to catch up. This train trip on Saturday may very well be the last one. We want to fill up the seats in our train car so, Dana, good work! Francine can fill you in."

Blum continued. "In the meantime, Joey and I need to take Orange Crush back to retrieve the Dinosaur. Rachel and Marta will be here this afternoon to help. Plus, we have to be back in a couple of hours to meet Brady; he's been doing some great work, and then the whole team will be on hand here at 3 pm. Let's go, Joey. I'll drop you off, and then I have to go into the city."

17

Blum and several associates from a local law firm were sitting with a judge along with the creditors in the suit versus OJT Partners, specifically Gary Gunderson. The SEC had already slapped the firm with fines and criminal charges were pending, including charges against Joey. The Feds had joined the meeting. The Peacock brothers were supposed to be there shortly, so Blum had to be on his toes. The group was huddled in a meeting room in the ancient courthouse that smelled like old books and aged leather. Blum was up.

"I appreciate the opportunity to speak for my friend and client, Joseph Kunz, who helped the original owners establish the company, and who, as you can read from about a dozen depositions that are enclosed in the package that we gave you, can vouch for Mr. Kunz, both in terms of his integrity, his work ethic, and his contribution to the firm. It was his algorithm and his contacts that created the process that has been successfully used to grow this company, which was growing by double digits per month in just the first year. You can see that graphically on page 12.

"And while sales still grew after Gunderson and his group acquired majority ownership a year ago January, so did expenses, and profit margins slipped as a result. They were bleeding it.

"We have no standing nor evidence as to what took place, but I know others here do. They can address that. But, I will just make note of two things.

"First, for the representatives of the Securities and Exchange Commission, we have depositions and evidence, including doctors' statements and a police report, that when funds showed up in Mr. Kunz's account, he was in a coma in a county hospital upstate.

"Second, all employees were paid via automatic payroll, so the company had access to his bank account, and on at least one occasion, due to a payroll mistake, he had authorized them to reverse a deposit and redeposit a corrected amount, so they were authorized to deposit funds for his salary and, in at least one instance, make withdrawals as needed. And that happened while Mr. Kunz was hospitalized, as the bank records show. It was a rather clumsy attempt to implicate him in something that they did. That is their only justification for filing embezzlement charges against Mr. Kunz, and we can show it was fabricated. He was framed, pure and simple.

"Now, in regards to the viability of the company due to malfeasance of the Gunderson partners, we are offering a solution to the creditors, namely, an offer to acquire the company by a third party to restore its reputation and goodwill with its growing list of clients.

"Excuse me a moment while I text them; they are waiting outside, I believe."

The door opened seconds later and Glade and Keith Peacock and their attorneys entered. Blum introduced them and gave them the floor. About an hour later, the conference came to a close. Blum and the Peacock brothers took a moment while everyone else filed out.

"Well, Jonathan, I think we all made a case for a nice clean resolution. Everyone should be happy, and we hope we can sit down with Joey and resolve matters with him. With his 10,000 shares, we'll have a majority position in the company and take it to the next level; the original owners bought our proposal! As soon as we hear something, we'll call you and make arrangements to sit down with Joey," the older Peacock brother said.

Blum knew that most of the people–those at the meeting–looked happy. But he knew that Gunderson and his people wouldn't be. What more trouble could they still cause? Joey wasn't out of the woods yet.

❏ ❏ ❏ ❏ ❏

Martina Ilić had been sitting outside the hospital in Rachel's car for nearly 45 minutes waiting for Rachel. Finally, she texted her to remind her they would be late for the meeting at Blum's farm.

Some ten miles away, Brady was waiting for his grandmother to get in the car. She was packing two suitcases after she had received her invitation from Walter. Brady had a couple of boxes of her mementos in the back. She was leaving on the train tomorrow.

A thousand miles east, several carloads of guests invited to take a ride tomorrow were on their way too. Binh, Emilie Johnson and her children, Blythe and her mother, and Mrs. Graham. The podiatrist and his wife were coming too; they were taking Binh. And, Mr. Graham, the high school's handyman from Fort Dodge was ready to go.

Francine had been following up on replies from Dana's website, talked to many people on the phone, and sent them emails; she received twelve confirmations, including three couples. The folks on the road were due at the old mountain railway's depot tomorrow at 11 a.m. for a 1 p.m. departure.

Blum, Francine, Joey, and Dana had everything ready in the cider house when Brady and his grandmother arrived. By 3 pm everyone was there—everyone but Rachel and Martina.

Blum got started.

"Almost everyone's here, and I received a text that Rachel and Martina have left the hospital. So let me tell you what I know. Dana and Joey have put everything on the line and stirred things up but in a good way. They've become online celebrities and even had 40 seconds of fame on a cable network due to their claim of 'seeing dead people,' right in time for Halloween. But, that's okay because we've had tons of hits on the website. Francine, how many leads do we have now?"

Francine had a whiteboard ready and flipped it around revealing numbers of names listed by state and even country. She had handouts for everyone and passed them all around.

She now took charge. "Thanks to Dana's website, the Kunz's podcasts, and the TV interview, there have been more than 7,500 inquiries so far with more coming in every day. We've sent them emails, talked to about 300 people so far, and have almost a hundred commitments from people who want an invitation. These have been forwarded on . . .."

"Forwarded on to where?" Brady asked.

Blum answered. "They've been simply been forwarded on. We don't extend invitations from here; they come from higher up." That was enough of an answer for Brady.

"Oh."

The door then opened, and Rachel and Marta entered. They sat in the back; Rachel's eyes were red and swollen.

Francine finished. "So, I handed out the packet for each of you with different assignments on them. We're asking you to call these people, follow the script and then, in your own words, describe your visit to Salem Crossing. We have a couple of phones here, two iPads, and two laptops. Or you can work remotely. But our time is short. Jonathan can now answer your questions."

Blum took a few more minutes answering questions, explaining what was happening next, namely the last trip of the season set for the next day when he expected to fill up a couple of train cars. After the group dispersed, Rachel was waiting to talk to Blum.

Martina waited at the door for her ride home as Rachel bared her soul with Blum; she had a tough time at the hospital with Tanner. She had told Martina it was doubtful she could take the train tomorrow.

She didn't say much on the way home, but Martina could see she was calming down, still anxious, but much improved.

It was 10 a.m. Saturday. Blum and Francine were standing next to the Caddy parked right in front of the Old Canyon Creeper depot. The big 1901 steam engine was taking in water now that the coal car was fully loaded. The train ride through the gorge and over the bridge always attracted a of lot out-of-town visitors even in October. This was to be the last run up the mountain before it snowed and the possibility of avalanches made it too treacherous, at least that's what the insurance carrier claimed.

Fall colors were ablaze across the landscape. The aspens were a bright yellow but fading fast, giving way to a cool breeze wafting down the canyon. The river in the gorge below had slowed to a meandering stream, but if you looked over the edge, you could see a few fly fishermen trying their luck. The maples and Gambel oak trees added the real color thanks to a wet spring. They were showing off but not for long. Someone in the canyon had a campfire going strong, the smoke rising in the distance. Was that coffee and bacon I smell, Francine thought. Probably just my imagination.

Blum had arranged for one large Pullman passenger car to be attached at the end behind the caboose. At a particular stop ahead another locomotive was waiting for their mysterious trip to a side-track through a long mountain tunnel and ending at a place no one ever traveled to unless Jonathan had arranged it.

He checked his watch. It was twenty after 10. He got Francine's attention. What a godsend she is, he thought, especially now that the pace was picking up!

"Are we ready for them?" Blum asked.

"I hope so. Ready or not, here they come!" Francine pointed at a convoy of three cars and a van, all with Iowa plates, that were just parking.

A small Asian woman hopped out of the van and looked around. Must be Binh, Francine thought. She waved at her.

The next car belonged to Emilie Johnson and with her were two small children and an older man. Francine looked at the spreadsheet under "Iowa." Just then, four Harleys came rolling in, each with a driver and passenger, eight in all. Francine thought they had Iowa plates too, but she couldn't figure out from the list who they might be.

In a minute, she was checking off names and handing out train tickets. Binh introduced the bikers. "They are my friends who help at the wrecking yard. They bring us old cars and stuff. They are good church-going people." Francine noticed the light in her eyes; it reminded her of a scripture. "Behold, an Israelite in whom there is no guile." Once they were aboard, she grabbed Blum, panicked.

"That's eight people we didn't expect! What if there are more?"

Blum smiled. "We've made contingencies. It's okay," he said. "Just make sure you get everyone's information. When we're aboard, put it all in the iPad." She nodded.

Then Brady and his grandmother arrived with what appeared to be all her earthly belongings. "Jonathan, look!" Francine exclaimed.

He just smiled again and waved to a porter pushing a dolly who hurried over to her. Her luggage went into a baggage closet at the back of the car.

"She is not returning," Blum whispered to Francine. "Hers is a one-way ticket."

As Brady helped his grandma up the stairs, a Winnebago—the Dinosaur—pulled into the back of the parking lot and found a spot near the picnic area under some lodgepole pines. Dana and Martina got out on the passenger side, and Joey walked around the front carrying a small briefcase. As they were walking to the train, a passenger van with a cross emblazoned on the side drove in, and eight nuns disembarked. Francine quickly totaled up her passenger list again and looked at Blum. He was unconcerned.

Soon, more cars and family vans arrived, an SUV, a Mini Cooper, and several other cars; most of the passengers were going to the end of the line, not diverting off to the spur through the tunnel, but some found their way over to Blum and Francine. They had come because they had heard Dana's podcast or the interview or someone else had suggested they come take a look. And, they'd come to take a look!

It was past twelve, and still, there was no sign of Rachel. She had told Martina to ride with Joey and Dana because she needed to visit Tanner at the hospital. Blum was standing with his clip-board waiting near the caboose. He was looking for another latecomer. Joey and Dana waited in the Dinosaur until Blum called them.

At nearly 12:45 p.m., a van pulled in right by the train. Rachel jumped out and motioned to Blum who hurried over. From the window, Brady and his grandmother saw the whole scene unfold.

"She made it!" Brady said. "Look at that!"

Heads on the left of the passenger car turned and watched as an older man removed a wheelchair, then with a woman's help, probably his wife, they lifted out a young man in a leg cast and put him in the chair. He and Rachel were talking as they pushed him to the train. Brady jumped out to help.

It was Tanner, Rachel's fiancé. The older man, likely his father, and Brady carefully carried Tanner and put him on the first bench. Rachel sat with him. His parents took their places across the aisle. They all looked anxious, but hopeful, holding hands as the locomotive began letting off steam and blowing its whistle.

The passengers' attention then turned to a Sheriff's car that had just arrived and parked near the concessions stand. Blum finished a call on his iPhone, put it in his pocket, and hurried out to greet Inspector Bleazard as he got out of his car. Bleazard looked irritated, but Blum was at his best, put his arm on the inspector's shoulder, and guided him toward the train. In a moment, Joey hurried out of the RV, put on a cap, and came in through the back door of the car and sat in a backward-facing seat.

Bleazard and Blum were the last ones to get on the train. With all the latecomers and recruits, Blum had to fork over some more cash to the conductor and cashier and filled up two cars, not just one, with about ninety people.

Blum and Bleazard were sitting together in the first car, and Joey was in the back of the car behind. Bleazard was irritated, but still curious.

"So where is he?" Bleazard asked Blum. "He is going to tell me his secrets."

"He's close by, but we have to have some privacy, some alone time, away from all these people," Blum said. By now, the conductor had yelled, "All aboard, final call," and shut the doors.
Bleazard was trying to get up, really upset now.

"What are you doing, Blum?"

"Trying to show you the truth! If that's what you really want, sit down. If you want to learn where your mother is, take a ride with us."

Bleazard froze and sat back down. "My mother?"

"Yes, she started all of this. Now obey your mother and quit being such a knucklehead!" Jonathan said with a smile.

"How did you know that she always called me a knucklehead?"

"She told me, now enjoy the ride. Joey's in the car behind us. We're taking you to a very special place. Do you like fruit?"

"What?"

"Fruit, do you like it? I heard you love Piña coladas and smoothies with bananas, mangoes, and strawberries."

"Who told you that?

"Your mother did; she's waiting for us. After you two talk, then you and Joey can have a long conversation. But, I think once you arrive in Salem Crossing, you'll find most of your answers. So enjoy the ride, and welcome to Disneyland."

Bleazard went silent and just stared out the window.

Everyone else was on a train ride steaming up through the mountains now except for Dana and Francine who were busy on a couple of laptops in the Winnebago.

"This is hardly Technology Central," Dana said. "We could download a lot of new inquiries if we only had a decent Wi-Fi connection."

"Or more bars on our phones," Francine said. "You know, given what we know and what we're trying to do in our own small way, I still feel like we're wandering in the Sinai desert waiting to finally get to the Promised Land."

"Think it'll take forty years?"

"Well, it's already taken 2000 years, what's another forty?" Francine said with a chuckle.

"It's good you can laugh about it," Dana replied and then thought to herself. I sure like this woman, and then decided to share her feelings out loud. "You know, Francine, I feel like you're my sister. I'm so glad we can do this together."

Francine patted her hand. "Me, too!"

Dana pointed to the total on the last line of the spreadsheet. "Wow, look at our totals now; more than 10,000! What are we supposed to do next?"

"I've been thinking about that a lot too, and I've been worried about how the children of Israel needed a miracle to walk through the Red Sea on dry ground, and then when they arrived in Sinai, they had forgotten how they got there. They were worshipping a golden calf, for crying out loud! And then when you related the story of John Winthrop and the eleven ships he led to New England, I recall you said he had told his followers that they were about to establish a 'Shining City on a Hill.'

"Now, Boston is a pretty place," Francine said, "but it's not what he imagined his city would be. People through the centuries have always been looking for a new Promised Land, for deliverance. Abraham left his home to go to Canaan. My people 150 years ago were looking for delivery from servitude; we identified with the children of Israel in bondage in Egypt; in one of our Gospel tunes, we sang the refrain, 'Let My People Go.'

"After my horrific time at the abortion doctor's slaughterhouse, I kept praying for a new destination, but I assumed there was no more 'undiscovered country' where we could pack up our wagons and flee to until you and Joey showed me the way. I thank you for that," Francine said.

"You know, at first I thought the judge wanted us to just find another three dozen people to fill that little old green bus. Then, today I saw how Blum just arranged for an additional passenger car for the train . . . just like that," Dana admitted. "Seating is unlimited."

"The same thing occurred to me. What we're doing isn't exclusive. We're not soliciting people to join a country club for a privileged few. However, I can't stop thinking about a couple of verses in Matthew 24 where it says that '*Then shall two be in the field; the one shall be taken, and the other left.*' Maybe they won't be beamed up magically. Maybe they'll just get there in an old green bus," Francine said, "or in a 19th-century steam-powered train."

"The key thing is that they simply accept the invitation offered to them and then act on it," Dana added.

"Exactly," Francine said.

Dana nodded and then added, "Our job is to gather and organize the information on those seeking an invitation and then submit their names. I just worry that we haven't yet come face-to-face with our opposition."

Francine looked out the window of the RV and turned back to Dana. "Me too."

They were wise to be worried.

Gary Gunderson and his colleagues may have been ousted from managing OJT partners, but that didn't mean they were finished with Joey Kunz. They had a score to settle with him. Gunderson was at his beach house plotting with the other members of his former management team about how to do that. They were not all on the same page.

The diminutive lawyer made the case for everyone to just keep their heads down and maintain a low profile. The other two were unsure. They were focused more on flight than fight.

"Gary, I'm pretty sure that we have more charges pending against us, criminal charges. Let's not rock the boat!"

The lawyer was connected to them via Zoom from an undisclosed location; not even Gunderson knew where his attorney was. He was definitely in hiding. Gunderson looked out at the sea from his perch above the harbor and was happy to talk about that metaphor.

"Don't tell me about boats! I sail all the time on my yacht. I can see it from here. In stormy, windy conditions like today, you stay in the harbor, but when you're out on the water and a storm comes in, you don't abandon ship, you can't drop anchor. You sail through it," he said.

His older partner sitting next to him tried to calm him down. "Gary, we don't have any options. We can't undo what we did. We warned you about this after Kunz's accident, and you made matters worse."

Gunderson countered. "Remember Staley & Staley, the PR agency that we helped and still owes us money? They were cash poor and gave us a $50,000 credit; have you forgotten about that?"

Everyone looked puzzled. Gunderson took another swig on his drink, put his feet up on the ottoman, and pointed out to the sea. "Out there unseen and unnoticed to us all is an ocean of skeptics, people who don't do the 'Jesus Thing' and recognize a scam when they see one. Do you know what Kunz is now up to? Do you remember who Jim Jones was? Let me read what Google says about him, and I quote, 'James Warren Jones was an American cult leader, preacher, and self-professed faith healer who, with his inner circle, orchestrated a mass murder-suicide of himself and his followers in his jungle commune at Jonestown, Guyana on November 18, 1978.' Does this ring a bell? Rob here is old enough to remember the whole episode. We were all infants or still a twinkle in our dads' eyes," Gunderson smiled.

The older partner, Rob, was catching on. "So Joey is the new Jim Jones resurrected? A cult leader willing to lead others in a scheme to bamboozle people?"

The other partner in the room, Rob's son, nodded.

"Exactly," Gunderson agreed. "A storm is coming, and the only way for Kunz to weather it is for us to call off the dogs . . . but, of course, they will already be tearing him to pieces. It's all set in motion. Nobody can stop it now. And when it all hits the fan, we will have sued Joey for damages, and no one will believe what he has to say."

The timid lawyer exited the Zoom meeting; Gunderson did not even notice, but the other two did. They were not all in agreement, but as Gunderson said it was too late anyway.

Gary Gunderson was confident he could pull this off, but if he thought he could push Inspector Bleazard into going after Joey, he was about to be mistaken.

The canyon late at night was a spooky place, spooky but incredibly beautiful with moonlight throwing long shadows, its light reflecting off the river below. Joey estimated that they were about 200 feet above the water but now slowly descending. Even though it was now autumn, you could still hear life above and below.

Occasionally, Brady saw bats zig-zag around their car in search of flying insects. The train was clickety-clacking along the rails and every so often, the train would let out a plaintive cry, its whistle echoing off the canyon wall. The interior light had mostly been extinguished except for in the passageway between the cars, and when a restroom door would open and close.

The "pilgrims" on their way back from the "Shining City" occupied parts of three passenger cars with a baggage car following behind. Jonathan had been moving from the first car, then to the second talking to the travelers and finally to the third carriage where he found Joey on the last bench with an open book, Gulliver's Travels, that he had found in a used-book shop in Salem Springs, lying face down on his lap, now that it was too dark to read. He was staring out at the enchanting scene passing below them. He was all alone. Jonathan sat down on the bench opposite him. Joey looked at him, smiled and then continued gazing out the window. He said nothing. For a long moment, Jonathan joined in the silence. Finally, he spoke:

"Joey, you OK?" Joey nodded, still silent as a sphinx.

Jonathan paused, then leaned forward and asked him very softly:

"Something on your mind?"

"This and that."

Jonathan waited.

Finally, Joey sat back, closed the book and sighed: "You know, I was really confused today when Bleazard came aboard the train and proceeded up the canyon with us. Did he get an invitation?"

"Well, he did see what all the rest of saw, experienced what we experienced and witnessed what you've now witnessed twice. Why, don't you think he should get one?"

Joey looked out the window and turned back to his mentor.

"I don't know. I don't know what to say."

"So, you have a problem having what you have, benefitting from a future life in a 'loftier sphere'?"

Joey shrugged his shoulders.

"Ever hear of the parable of the householder and the laborers in the vineyard?" Jonathan asked.

"No, doesn't ring a bell," Joey answered.

"Look it up later. It's in Matthew Chapter 20; seems a master of the vineyard, a 'householder' as Matthew describes him, needed some help on the farm. So, he goes to the local marketplace and finds a few 'idlers' standing around waiting for work and offers them a penny a day—a guess a penny bought a lot more in those days—and sent them to his vineyard for the day. In fact, the master said *'whatsoever is right I will give you.'* And Matthew records... *'and they went their way.'* But, I suppose the workload was more than he expected, so he returns to the marketplace the third hour, the sixth hour and the ninth hour and hires even more. Even at the eleventh hour, he still finds *'others standing idle and asks them 'why stand ye here all the day idle?'* They respond, 'hey, nobody hired us!' Finally, night falls and the master asks the foreman to gather everybody and pay them their wages. If I recall it correctly, in verse 9, he tells his foreman, 'pay everybody' and send them off: Everybody gets a penny. So, what do you think the men hired at 7 a.m. said:

"Well, I know what I'd say..."

"Exactly. So, would most people. Matthew writes that *'they murmured against the goodman of the house.'* They complained that the latecomers just worked for an hour, and they got the same wages as we did, and we were there all day long!"

Joey smiled and sat back in his seat.

"Then, the boss reminds them that he didn't wrong them—they agreed to the terms when they started early that morning. And, in

Matthew's words *'Take that thine is, and go thy way: I will give unto this last, even as unto thee. Is it not lawful for me to do what I will with mine own? Is thine eye evil, because I am good? So the last shall be first, and the first last: for many be called, but few chosen.'* "

Joey let that sink in.

Again, Jonathan waited.

"It's about being of one heart and one mind, isn't it?"

Now Joey smiled. "It's never easy, is it?"

"Never has been," Jonathan said. 'Now you know it's not just about sharing wealth, is it? I'm still learning that.

"Yes, and I suspect you are older than you look." They laughed. "Come with me. Let's move up a car and talk to Brady and Bleazard. We all have SO MUCH to do!

They found Brady and Bleazard sharing a pair of facing seats in the middle car. This was a different man than Brady knew when the inspector was barking out orders to him. And a changed man for Joey, too. It wasn't the same Inspector Bleazard. Like everyone else on the return trip to the 21st century, Bleazard was both wistful and peaceful. He had said very little the whole trip up and back, except when Brady and Jonathan observed the tearful reunion he had with his mother.

Finally, Bleazard spoke. "She was so young, looked younger than me! I'm pushing 50, and she looked like she was maybe in her early 40s." They knew he was talking about his mother. Blum was now in front of them, talking to the nuns. Bleazard looked at Blum. Joey sat down with them.

"How can I ever thank him? This is such a miracle," he said as he turned to Brady. "And, I wanted to apologize for not trusting you.

You have great instincts. You'll make a superb chief of detectives someday, hopefully in a city with a bigger budget."

Brady thanked him and smiled, then added. "But, where I'm headed, they don't need detectives."

He pulled out his invitation from his satchel. "As you can see, I've been invited to the 'Shining City.' As we heard from Judge Stone today, there is no crime where we've just been. They've made us cops irrelevant relics unless we get an assignment like Blum's."

"Blum?"

"Yes. His assignment running the apple farm will be coming to an end soon, then he returns. Would you like to know more about him, just between us three?"

Now Joey perked up, too. They both leaned forward to hear more of what Brady had to say.

It was difficult to make out what he was saying as the train was still clattering down the rails, picking up speed, and he didn't want anybody else to hear. Moonlight bounded around inside the passenger car as it poked through the tops of the 100-foot lodgepole pines outside. His voice was barely louder than a whisper.

"Jonathan Blum was born in 1901. He graduated from Columbia Law School in 1927 and worked for the district attorney's office in Albany, New York, until the outbreak of World War II, and then he joined the JAG Corps. In 1945 after the war in Europe ended, he served as an assistant prosecutor at the Nuremberg trials, and when it ended in October of 1946, he went to Japan to help with the Tokyo trials. For nearly four years, he put war criminals on trial and helped sentence many of them to death, and sent others to prison. Now you know why he loves apple farming so much."

Joey was very curious. "So, when did he, you know, 'pass on?'"

Brady shrugged his shoulders.

"Don't know. Why don't you ask him?"

"No thanks," Joey said. Brady reached back into his satchel and pulled out some print-outs from a website.

He had piqued Bleazard's curiosity. "What's that, Brady?"

"Something interesting about the place we just came from. Remember when I told both of you about the story of a young couple that went missing when a carriage was washed away in a flood that matched your story, Joey . . . remember, a green two-wheeled carriage called a 'hackney?'"

"Yeah, of course," Joey answered.

"I remember it well," Bleazard said, "thought you had gone bonkers!"

"So did I. Then I found there was a small mining town where the story originated, a town that a year or two later disappeared when a dam broke, and it was supposedly buried under a huge mudslide. They never found any remnants of the place. Earlier today, I did a little snooping around at the town library and learned that some of the people who are still alive lived in that town, and to them, there never was such a slide, just some flooding from the small river that passes through it. It wasn't destroyed, it was 'moved,'" Brady said. "And, to them, it wasn't all that long ago."

"And?" both of them said.

"And . . . that's it. That's all I know. I guess it's our little secret."

The problem with secrets, of course, is that they don't remain secrets very long, especially in the era of universal Internet access when everyone can publish what they want, whether it's true or false.

Gary Gunderson was counting on the latter.

The next morning Joey, Dana, Francine, and Blum were going over the latest feedback from their web outreach efforts from Dana's website, Emilie Johnson's podcast, and the Fox News interview in Omaha. While Dana and Francine were looking at new blog hits and responses to emails, Joey was running some "SEO" searches. . . looking for anything that rose to the top of things about "The Shining City on the Hill."

Almost in unison, they all muttered, "Uh oh!"

"So, you're the new Jim Jones, are you?" Dana asked Joey.

"Apparently, and you're Mrs. Jones."

"What are you talking about? Who's Jim Jones?" Francine asked.

Joey let her see his laptop screen.

"This is Jim Jones, the Reverend Jim Jones who led his group of gullible followers 'to drink the lemonade' in a mass suicide event in 1978. Check it out," he said as he pushed the laptop over where Francine could read the post.

"The narrative comes from a YouTube video which ran on MSNBC yesterday evening and is being picked up and parroted all over the mass media: Twitter, Facebook, everywhere. And, of course, CNN did their own version. You wonder who they attribute it to," Dana said as she also looked at it. "Maybe it was the Russians!"

"Those dang Russians!" Joey said in jest in an attempt to whistle in the graveyard.

"It all has a common source," Blum said, "and we all know who probably got the ball rolling."

"Who?" Dana asked.

"Gunderson," Blum answered. "I was expecting something like this, and we are prepared."

"How so?"

Blum continued: "My source tells me that it came from a public relations firm that does a lot of political dirty tricks smearing campaign opponents, a firm that helped the Gunderson Group about five years ago when they wanted to take over a Christian broadcasting company and 'make some adjustments.' So, tomorrow morning, we're going to file a defamation lawsuit against Gunderson's group for millions; it's really a lot! I learned he's planning to sue Joey later this week anyway, so we're going to go on the attack, rather than try to answer his groundless charges."

"How do you know all this?" Dana asked Blum.

"From the lawyer-partner of Gunderson's who has been fighting him all along, the little guy who tried to confront Rachel when she went to meet them. He is being excluded from our suit and will testify to everything if it comes to that. He has distanced himself from Gunderson. He has been talking to Bleazard for some time now, and earlier today, the inspector called him. What's more, the Peacock Brothers want to meet with you Joey, but I told them we had some complications and put it off until a week from tomorrow.

"I hope Gunderson's other partners will also abandon him," Joey said.

"We'll see," Blum smiled, crossing his fingers.

$$\textbf{19}$$

At first, Joey figured all his problems with Gunderson were just
about money. That was it, he thought; just numbers on a P&L,
figures on a spreadsheet, maybe even a briefcase full of Benjamins.
But when he met Greg Gunderson, Gary's dad, he saw his old boss
in an entirely different light. Gary had all the money he needed, even
wanted. Greg Gunderson made billions, billions with a capital "B."

Joey concluded that if he looked up "trust-fund brat" in the dic-
tionary, Webster's would probably have dedicated an entire page to
Greg Gunderson's heir apparent, little Gary.

That would explain why Gunderson had come after him with
such vengeance, even though Joey's problems all started with the carriage accident. His accident was not part of Gary's plan; Initially,
Gary wanted Joey to play ball, to make himself look good in the eyes
of his old man. But, Joey's accident didn't square with Gary's plan.
It made him look bad. It all boiled down to that.

Joey and Blum had flown in on the red-eye to Boston arriving
at 9 am. Now Joey was waiting in Greg Gunderson's palatial office
in the penthouse of one of Boston's fanciest addresses, looking down
on the Old Statehouse, the site of the Boston Massacre. Blum, Gunderson Senior, and his lawyers were in an attached stateroom work-

ing out the details. Joey was playing solitaire on his iPhone, doing quite well for himself.

Meanwhile, his reputation was being valued in the room next door. So what? He just solved the puzzle in 2 minutes and 53 seconds, a new record for him. He stood up and walked over to the credenza to pour himself a glass of ice water. He returned and plunked the glass down without the benefit of a coaster, hoping to make a lasting watermark on the desk. He concluded that this meeting was all about competing reputations, his versus Gary's. He told Blum when it came down to it, he didn't give a hoot about reputations; he had been to a place where everyone's value was inestimable, priceless, because "they dwelt in righteousness and there was no poor among them."

But, what if the offer was in the millions, really up there? He tried to put that out of his mind. But what if it were? Would it be prudent to just walk away from it all? He had put nearly four years of his life into developing OJT only to have a spoiled brat come in and practically destroy it. He was due those damages!

He took a drink from his glass and wiped the condensation off of the desk. This piece of furniture was a work of art. It wasn't his to mar. He walked over to the window and looked out over the Boston Harbor. It was about 250 years ago that a shipload of tea was dumped over the side. And it was nearly 400 years ago when John Winthrop had expressed his hopes for this place. That thought suddenly overwhelmed him, reminding him what was important. Just then Blum, Gunderson, and the lawyers returned.

"Great view, isn't it?" Greg Gunderson said. "I can stare out at the scene for hours. You're probably wondering what kind of deal we've worked out for you."

Joey cut him short. "Not really."

"So, what's on your mind?"

"John Winthrop," Joey said. Blum smiled.

"Boston's founder," Gunderson said.

"Yes, the Puritan visionary who dreamed of 'A Shining City on the Hill,'" Joey said and then asked. "Do you think he'd be impressed if he saw what we're seeing right now?"

The lawyers were getting annoyed and impatient with Joey; they had other clients to bill at $500 an hour. "Just tell us what you want, and let's see if we can make a deal," one attorney blurted out but came to a screeching halt when he saw the angry look that Gunderson just flashed him; the attorney immediately shut up.

Joey turned and looked Greg Gunderson squarely in the eyes and began. "That's a good question. I think Winthrop said it best when he was on his way to the New World with 750 settlers sailing on eleven different ships; I'll quote him as best as I can remember if I can read this," he said as he pulled a card out his pocket.

"He dreamed of a place, 'A Shining City on a Hill,' *where 'every man might have need of others, and from hence they might be all knit more nearly together in the bonds of brotherly affection. From hence it appears plainly that no man is made more honorable than another or more wealthy etc., out of any particular and singular respect to himself, but for the glory of his Creator and the common good of the creature.'* If you can do that, then we have a deal," Joey declared and set his glass down on the desk—without a coaster—and walked to the door. He said in parting, "Whatever Mister Blum works out with you is fine with me; he's been around a long time, and I'd trust him with my life. You should too."

He waited for Blum at the bank of elevators.

It didn't take Jonathan long to meet him there carrying a much fatter briefcase.

"You should do deals all day long. You don't need me," Blum replied grinning from ear to ear. "He also bought out the original partners and included that in the final deal. Want to know how much it was all for?"

"Not really," Joey said, smiling as well.

"Then, what do you want to know?"

"I want to hear about Nuremberg and Tokyo, the trials of the century, justice being served on the most monstrous people in history. You know, Jonathan, you've taught me something that I didn't understand about myself previously, namely that I love justice more than I do money. I really do. Whatever you've got in the briefcase, I feel vindicated. So let's go."

"You sure you don't want me to tell you how much it is?"

"You know, on second thought, it's not how much I'm valued or worth, it's how much he's willing to pay to protect his own spoiled son. But that's one thing I do envy—to know that I had a father who cared that much about me. Whatever you got, it's probably too high anyway.

"But, I guess you can tell me on the way down. Our elevator's here."

Brady woke up after six hours of sleep and nine hours in "The Cage." He joined Dana and Francine that afternoon in the Cider House. They wanted to know everything that happened up in "The City." And they had at least twenty hours of work sorting through

queries and requests, answering questions from bloggers and pod-
casters, and verifying names, addresses and the like. They were glad
to get his help.

But first, they asked. "Tell us what happened up there?"

"Where do you want me to start?"

"We didn't see Rachel come back? What about her and her boyfriend?"

"They're still up there. I assume they took Tanner up to the hot
springs pool to get rehabilitated; Walter met them at the train station,
and then they all left. That's all I know. But you did hear that my
grandma is staying there, right? Her health's not been good, particularly her diabetes, so she accepted her invitation, and she stayed
there. That's all I know for now," Brady said.

"And, Martina?"

"Well, she's catching a flight later today to Vienna. As you know,
there are already more than 200 inquiries from Europe, and since
she speaks four different languages, she is going to talk to as many
interested parties as she can, beginning in Austria and Germany, and
then down where she came from in old Yugoslavia, Slovenia, Cro-
atia, Serbia, and Bosnia–Herzegovina. And, guess what? There's a
'portal city' over there somewhere," he said.

"A portal city?"

"Yeah, like Salem Crossing, that leads to another 'Shining City.'
I found out that they're all over the world, basically, another level of
existence or dimension . . . a place where 'entropy is mitigated'.
That's what I was told. Different rules of physics apparently," he surmised.

"I should have studied more as a kid," Francine said.

"Never too late for that," Dana said. "Let's dig into these names and see what we've got. It doesn't look like we've lost very much momentum from Gunderson's slander. In fact, it's picked up. I have to leave by 5 because I have to pick up Joey at the airport. Then we're going to the old house. We have a lot to clean up there."

The next morning, Joey and Dana woke up to nearly two months of mail, dead house plants (Rachel did apologize), and a garage full of Oma's stuff from her tiny apartment at the Columbia Center. Good thing I paid all the bills online, Dana thought. Otherwise, there might have been a sheriff's notice of "foreclosure" on the door! There was also a collection of more than a dozen business cards from Realtors and landscapers.

Meanwhile, Joey was staring at Oma's sparse collection of furniture stacked in the garage next to the Ford Explorer, now shiny and new-looking after the accident. But, then he saw stacks of boxes of documents and photos that had been retrieved from Oma's cellar at the center. He grabbed a folding chair and willed himself to stay there until he had sorted through the boxes and retrieved things of value. He was out there in the cold garage until about 5 p.m. when he found a shoe box stored with her photo albums with his name on it.

It was dinnertime, and he could smell pizza, so he grabbed the box and carried it inside to the kitchen.

When he opened the shoe box, he couldn't believe what he saw. Up until he was ten, his mother had collected photos, postcards, and letters from all over the world and addressed to him. They were from his father, Charles Kunz, Jr. There was a whole envelope of small Kodak prints from Vietnam, including group shots with his dad and

Binh's husband, Lt. Jewell. He yelled at Dana.

"Come here, Sweetie, and see what I found!"

She sat next to him at the kitchen table as he became better acquainted with the father he barely knew and for whom he had harbored so much resentment over the years. The postcards were funny and entertaining and warm. His dad loved him! Tears formed and dripped slowly down his cheeks; Dana wiped them away with a napkin, until she too, joined in.

There was a stack of more unopened letters along with a collection of postcards bundled with a big rubber band. One looked very official. It was from the Director of the Central Intelligence Agency, postmarked 2003. He opened that one first. It was a letter of condolences regarding the death of Charles Kunz in the Philippines at the hands of the Abu Sayyaf Islamic Terrorist Group. It stated in part that his dad had been attempting a hostage rescue; there was a photo of a star on the wall at CIA headquarters in Langley, Virginia, placed there in remembrance of his father.

"Why was I never informed about any of this? I was 22 when that happened," he said.

"Look at the envelope," Dana said. It had been forwarded three times, and when it got to Oma's, Joey was away at school. "She must have held it for you and then forgot to pass it on."

"I don't know whether to feel proud or ashamed," he admitted. "He came home from time to time, spent a few days with us, took me to a couple of baseball games, and then he was gone again. I guess by the time I was in my teens, I had emotionally decoupled from him," he said. Then he pulled a snapshot out of the envelope and handed it to his wife. "And, look at this! It's Jewell, Binh, and

Dad playing cards and another older Vietnamese guy—maybe her dad. I've got to show this to her. What have we heard from her so far?"

"Not much. But, I did get a text from her just yesterday that said 'she loved her trip to heaven and was anxious to go back.' They probably returned to Iowa earlier today, I imagine," she said.

Joey finished his pizza, kissed his wife on the forehead, and took the shoe box upstairs. It was as if he had discovered a buried treasure. He pointed to the ceiling and said, "Love ya, Pop!"

About 1 am, Dana awakened Joey.

"There's a problem with the baby. I'm bleeding, and it hurts," she said.

They had come so far by this time, he didn't want to return to where they had been. Neither did she.

"I don't think I should sit. Let's take the Explorer and put the backseats down," she said, and Joey rushed to grab a quilt and a pillow, searched for the keys, and finally they were on the road to the hospital. Twenty minutes later they were in the emergency room with an obstetrics nurse who also assisted as a midwife. An ultrasound revealed that the placenta was tearing away.

The obstetrician on call arrived about 45 minutes later. "It's a good thing you came in because if you want to save the baby, you're going to have to remain flat on your back until at least 33 weeks; you're past the halfway mark of your first trimester, probably about 11 or 12 weeks. I was able to access your earlier exams on our website, and from what I saw, I don't know how you ever got pregnant in the first place. Staying pregnant may be even more difficult. Pray

for a miracle; in the meantime, stay down! I'm writing you a pre-
scription to help stop the bleeding for now."

"Thanks, doctor," Joey said. He and Dana held hands for a few
minutes. He looked at the clock on the wall. It was just past 4 a.m.

"I'm going to call Jonathan," he said.

"It's 4 a.m.!" Dana said.

"I know, but didn't you hear he's nearly 120 years old? The man
has stamina; he'd be mad if we didn't call!"

Joey was right. The man was like the Energizer bunny; he had
batteries that never wore out.

Joey got through to Blum on his cellphone. "Is it possible to get
her up to the Spa? It is? Good. How do we get there without a carriage or a train ride up the canyon? Okay. We'll be there! Thanks!"

Dana was a little groggy, looked around, and couldn't see Joey. She
tried to raise her head, but the nurse persuaded her to lie still. He
was back in a minute.

"Where were you?"

"Just arranged for an ambulance," he said as two orderlies arrived and carefully moved her onto a stretcher and belted her in.

"An ambulance? To where?"

"To Blum's, and from there to a helicopter, and then to an airfield, a very private airfield. It'll be fun, you see!"

"You really are Oma's boy! This is going to be expensive!"

"So, I'm a multi-millionaire, remember? Big deal!"

She awoke the next morning in a suite at the top of an ancient
manor above what looked like a fjord. Joey was asleep, holding her
hand in a lounge chair next to her bed. She was covered with what

the nurse called a "dynen," a Federdecke in German, or a duvet in English which comes from the French—a big, light, feather-filled, quilt-like pillow.

She overheard nurses speaking in a foreign tongue outside in the hallway; they were dressed in uniforms and looked as if they'd been stolen from a Carl Bloch painting. A young girl brought Dana a plate of cheese and sliced pears. She didn't offer any to Joey, and he was hungry. Too bad, Joey. It's only for pregnant people. Are you pregnant? No? Maybe there's a McDonald's in Norway, he wondered. "Are we in Norway?" He didn't know where they were!

"That doesn't sound like German. Is it Danish?" Dana whispered to Joey.

"It's Norwegian, and this is a health spa, too."

"How did we get here?"

"That's a secret; our craft was powered by ten tiny reindeer."

"Joey!"

Just then, a tall blond female obstetrician arrived with a leather binder; she flashed them a brilliant smile. Joey appeared spellbound until Dana gave him a warning glance.

"So, you are the famous Dana who has been making such big waves that we have felt them even this far away! Thousands have heard your story. We also. Such a good work you are doing, but even though you took a dip in our magic waters, we need to keep you here for a while longer. More dips coming for you, just to make sure. As you know, time is running out on the 'outside' and we too, are working overtime. It is an honor to have you here," she said, as Joey still kept his head down. She sure has an interesting accent, he thought.

Gawking would be impolite, he figured, especially since Dana was right there, pregnant in a hospital bed. But the doctor had such a nice smile, very good teeth. Straight and white. They must have good dentists in Norway!

A young man arrived five minutes later and motioned to Joey. "Mr. Blum has arranged for your travel home, and there's not much time. If you'd please come with me," he said.

"Honey, I'll find a way to get back in touch, to get back to you soon." He kissed her, but she didn't want to let him go. He squeezed her hand, stepped away, and looked back. "Love ya!"

Then, he spoke to his escort. "You know, I forgot my passport."

"You got here, didn't you?"

"Yes, but . . ."

"And so you won't need one to get back home either. Hurry. They're waiting."

After spending the weekend recovering from jet lag, Joey jumped in Blum's big blue Caddy to ride into town for a meeting with the Peacock brothers. It was Monday morning and a time for "Truth or Dare." He was 99.8 percent convinced that his future was up the mountain, through the covered bridge and the lush meadows, and into a real "Never, Neverland" within the boundaries of "The Shining City on the Hill." Wasn't it?

"I understand you gave the visitors at the open house quite a speech; Judge Stone was impressed," Blum said as they were entering the interstate.

"I was just answering questions," he said.

"Well, I heard it was quite the sermon that you pulled right out of the Gospel of John, and if anyone up there misunderstood what is being offered them and where it comes from, now they don't have any excuse," Blum said.

Joey looked out the window, paused, and then answered Blum's probing question.

"You're quite a wise man, you know that, Jonathan?"

He laughed. "Well, as you discovered last week, it's not that I'm so wise, but rather because I'm so old, albeit not by Methuselah's standards."

"So, does wisdom really come with old age, or does getting older just make you more bitter?"

"Probably both. So, tell me about your sermon."

"As I said, I just used scripture to answer a question, that's all. I've been reading the Bible lately . . . I should say we've been reading the Bible lately. Dana is not just a Christian now, she's a Shiite Christian! Like most men, I have to sprint to keep pace with my wife's faith and religiosity," Joey explained, trying to avoid the question because he knew why Blum was testing him, given the meeting they were about to attend.

"What scripture was it?"

"It's in John 6. That chapter follows on the heels of the miracle of the loaves and fishes, and it revealed something about how Christ reacted to the crowd."

Blum passed a pickup on the right so they didn't miss their exit to the belt route.

"Okay, go on. I'm listening," Blum said.

"Christ sounded disappointed that the crowd had left him; it was just his apostles and his closest friends who were still there. Why had the crowd abandoned him?"

"Quite simple, really. They had run out of loaves and fishes. The free food was gone. And I imagine that they were still on the shore where the first miracle with Peter and Andrew had occurred when the fishermen landed their biggest catch ever and assumed Jesus was promising them bountiful catches from then on. Referring to the 'fair-weather' followers who had left after the food was gone, or *'those who walked no more with him,'* Jesus then queried His disciples, *'Will ye also go away?'* Quoting best as I can remember, the verse reads, *'Then Simon Peter answered him, Lord, to whom shall we go? Thou hast the words of eternal life. And we believe and are sure that thou art that Christ, the Son of the living God, "'* Blum explained.

They were now at a stoplight and Blum asked Joey. "So, why are you asking me this question?"

Joey turned to Jonathan at the wheel. "I just wanted to see if the answers I gave one of our visitors to Salem Crossing were correct. On the bus, an older man asked me, 'What is expected of us who come here?' I guess he was where I was when I first arrived at the Crossing. At that time, I thought it was a re-enactment of the peaceful year 1925 when President Calvin Coolidge fulfilled his campaign promise of 'A Return to Normalcy.' I think maybe he assumed I was impatient with him, but then I came to grips with the reality of the miracles we had experienced there. My answer was, we just bring the bread and the fishes.' I thought he was going to hit me. But then I explained, 'the disciples had only brought three fishes and five loaves, not baskets of them to feed the crowd.

"Jesus Christ took what men had done and multiplied it. Men did the best they could. They donated what they had, but it's not enough, it never is. The Messiah himself performed the miracle, both on the beach 2000 years ago, and up that mountain, and through the covered bridge," Joey explained. "We do a small part; it's our sacrifice. That's what we've done. And, that's what others like he can do. The Lord does the rest."

"Good answer! So, that must have satisfied him," Blum said.

"Not really, not yet, he kept pressing me like you are now. He asked what contributions people who move there are expected to make. So I turned to John again, my favorite apostle, and quoted another chapter."

"You're becoming quite the Bible thumper!" Blum said, ribbing his apprentice just a bit.

"No, I only know a few key verses, enough to get me into trouble. This time I turned to the end of John's Gospel, Chapter 21, verse 15." Joey pulled a tattered note out of his pocket and read from it. "Most church-going people are familiar with, or at least have heard this verse, where Jesus Christ asks Peter, *'Peter, Simon, son of Jonas, lovest thou me more than these? He saith unto him, Yea, Lord; thou knowest that I love thee. He saith unto him, Feed my lambs.'* We all get it. The Savior wanted Peter to acknowledge that he loved Jesus and pressed him to serve others. But, what does 'these' refer to? So, I asked the man questioning me who had brought a small New Testament with him, the kind they used to give servicemen, to read verse 11 that explains the context of the three verses where Christ asks Peter not once, not twice, but three times, 'Lovest thou me more than these?'

"So the man read it, and it says that *'Peter went up and drew the net to land full of great fishes, an hundred and fifty and three. And for all there were so many, yet was not the net broken.'* This was the second time that Christ had filled the fishermen's nets. This time, of course, was after His resurrection. Did Peter love Jesus Christ, the Messiah, the Savior of Mankind more than these 153 fish? That's the big question for all of us, isn't it?

"When the man read that verse, he smiled, nodded, and like me—very recently—he got it. The specifics, I said, come later."

Five minutes later, they arrived at the lawyer's office where the Peacocks were all set to offer Joey more than he would have ever imagined. Now, it was Joey's turn to compare what Judge Stone had offered both him and Dana to the Peacocks' offer of 153 fish. What would he say?

In the weeks that followed, Joey was putting a lot of the miles in the Dinosaur, but this time with a new traveling companion, ex-Deputy Sheriff and computer wizard Brady Owens. Dana was ensconced in a far-away spa in a distant land, growing bigger by the day as she described in her frequent letters. No Internet access, email, or texts from her, just love letters sent the old-fashioned way. For Joey, they were a treasure.

"I guess I'm just a romantic," he admitted to Brady who was still addicted to at least one earthly vice. Classic NFL and NCAA reruns.

"What?" Brady asked as he watched the ending of yet another Brady-Patriots Super Bowl win. "Can you believe he moved to Tampa? Incredible!"

"So you must be a romantic, too," Joey said, grinning. That went over Brady's head as well. They were far more than travel companions spreading the "word." Brady was now Joey's employee–his one and only employee–in his new charity, "The Shining City Foundation," which he set up after settling with the Peacock Brothers on selling his share of OJT Partners. The Peacock's desire was to have Joey run the newly organized company while getting a handsome financial package in return. Instead, he agreed to use his recruiting skills in finding and training his replacement, to which they reluctantly agreed.

Now, Joey and Brady had a full-time mission. Brady's job was two-fold: First, to keep Dana's website outreach program going; and second, to act as the Foundation's Director of Security, protecting them from cyber and other kinds of attacks by people whom Joey described as "the ungodly."

Joey was to continue "fishing," leading the effort to find as many people as possible who yearned for a place of peace, security, and faith and were willing to sacrifice everything to get there.

According to Blum, they were about to get a lot more help. So, in the morning, they were leaving the KOA Campground in Farmington, New Mexico, and taking the Orange Crush to learn what plans Blum had in store for them at the apple farm.

Dana was more than surprised to see Margritte Kunz walk into the salon that morning, she was astonished! "Oma, is that you?"

"Who else were you expecting, Elvis?" Oma asked with a laugh.

"You look twenty years younger, no thirty years younger! How did you get here? How did you find me?"

Oma faked a German accent al a "Hogan's Heroes" and said, "Vee haf' our Vays, Fräulein."

"Seriously, what mode of transportation did you take to arrive here, wherever this is?"

"We call it the Underground Railroad; it's faster and cheaper than planes, trains, or automobiles. Doesn't matter, I'm just glad I'm here to give you a hand if I can. It's not every day you are expecting a great-grandchild. My, my, look at you. How you've grown!"

"Thank you for that, Oma."

"One of the perquisites you get when you're over 90–in my case 92–is you can say whatever the heck you want to, and nobody is allowed to get offended by it. Isn't that great?"

"And, what are you gonna say next? 'Go ahead, pull my finger?' Because I will not do that!"

They both laughed. Oma helped Dana stand up, and then they went out on the veranda to view the scene below. It was a bit chilly, but they were wearing thick sweaters. This "Kurhaus," as Professor Kunz called it, was more of an inn housed in a castle, perched high above a fjord and surrounded by towering pines.

One of the more amazing aspects of living in an "elevated" state where the laws of entropy don't apply is how wildlife behaves. A mountain bluebird landed on the table where they were sitting and just stared at them. Oma knew what to do. She pinched off a bit of a blueberry muffin and fed it to the bird.

Since she had been there, Dana had watched deer and mountain goats walk right up to people. Last week, she was sitting up on the deck and observed a young girl pet a fawn.

"I can't wait until I can watch a lamb lie down with a lion," Dana said.

"It happens," Oma said. "By the way, maybe you heard about Joey's so-called 'sermon' to a group of visitors to Salem Crossing last week, but now it's getting shared everywhere. After the visitors returned home, they put it on Facebook and Twitter. Blum told Walter that it's really growing legs."

"Oma, you're sounding like a Digital Diva, an expert in everything electronic, and here you are, living in a realm where that is all so passé, irrelevant, but it's relevant where Joey is. I wonder how he's doing. I send him letters, but he doesn't have our address. Can you find out when we can get back together?"

Oma pulled up closer to her and spoke softly. "All I know is that things are moving very fast now, faster than ever. So whatever they're doing, I hope they realize that."

Joey and Brady pulled into Blum's place in the early evening. The old apple farmer was on a call in the cider house; he sounded animated. They helped themselves to some cider and waited.

Jonathan hung up and turned to his guests. "Let's get down to business. Like I told you in my text message, we're getting some help. I'm getting urgent queries from 'Upstairs' about how we're doing, along with offers for help, so I just said 'any and all help is appreciated.' So they're on the way," Blum said.

"They?" Joey asked.

Brady interjected, "From our last train ride up the mountain we have several volunteers who want to help any way they can. They want to share what they experienced with others."

"Let's take them up on their offer," Blum said. "Go ahead with it."

"That one's already set up," Joey said. "It's scheduled for Friday in Tulsa. We got a second call too, right after the first one."

"Hang on a minute. Who was the second caller," Brady asked. "And when was the call?"

"Why?" Blum said.

"I am by nature suspicious, and since you want me to check things out, let's vet this person . . . at least compare him . . ."

"Her," Blum corrected him.

" . . . let's compare her to our master list of names and numbers and those who went on the train ride up the mountain."

Blum gave him the name and number, but Brady wanted more.

"Did you get the call on your cellphone?"

"No, only a few of you have that number. It came in on the land-line phone over there," Blum said, pointing to his desk in the corner of the warehouse.

"Let me get my laptop and do some cross-checking," Brady said.

"This will take a while."

Blum was curious. "Why so paranoid?"

Joey explained. "We have received calls from a couple of Christian cable channels that have been following us ever since Dana's interview on Fox and before that on her podcast. One of them wanted to do some interviews with us. Then shortly after that, we got another one from a woman. I think Brady's comparing the numbers, and once he has the phone's IP address, assuming the person was connected to a Wi-Fi network when the call was made, in other words, in their home or office, then we can pinpoint the location and possibly who made it."

"He can do that?" Blum asked.

"I believe he can," Joey said. "We verified the first call; it came from the Christian network's office in Tulsa. They want to get some interviews. When I asked how many people, we brain-stormed and came up with the idea to produce a group interview, something that their producer called a 'televised focus group.' We thought it would be a great opportunity to validate our message by having others share their experiences too."

Brady came back about a half-hour later. "You won't guess what I found. Joey and I have made several calls to the cider house line; so have Francine, Dana, and Rachel. After a couple of our calls, that number from the second caller phoned here, but when somebody answered, it hung up.

"Then, another call came in a few days later, and it rang and rang. That was when we were all up at the Old Train Depot, remember? I suspect that was when line could have been tapped. Didn't Francine say she thought she might have seen someone at the house a couple of weeks ago?" Brady asked.

"I'll send her a text message," Joey said. "She's home, right?" Blum nodded and then replied to Brady, "We better find it and pull it!"

Joey reacted differently. "Maybe we should let it stay there."

"And feed that person false information," Blum said.

"There could be another explanation," Brady said.

"What? they both said.

Brady pointed to the ceiling. "Maybe they can hear us now!"

"We should call Terminex," Joey said loudly. "I hate roaches!"

"I'll take care of the roach problem tomorrow," Brady said, and then added sotto voce. "But, my first guess is that it's the phone in the cider house. I can check it out right now."

21

The next morning, Blum and Joey were crunching around on the gravel outside the barn carrying on a conversation while Brady was sweeping the cider house for bugs, the electronic kind.

"Brady was right," Joey said. "Remember when Francine said she saw somebody snooping around the house and then let the dog out? He ran to the house barking, snooped around a bit, then came back. Somebody was here tapping phones and who knows what else. By the way, I've spoken with four of our visitors who took the train up the mountain and said they'd be happy to appear for an interview in Tulsa with us. I told them we'd take care of their travel expenses. I've got two more possibilities as well."

"Let's walk over to the house," Blum said. Joey followed him.

They sat on the patio while Brady finished the sweep.

"I've been thinking about something. When do you think we could do the videotaping in Tulsa?"

"This coming Friday. It works for them."

"Okay, I have an old friend, a veteran investigative reporter at a station in Las Vegas who's done a lot of unconventional stories on Area 51, UFOs, and spirituality. He's fairly well-known; maybe I'll call him on my cellphone, tell him what's up, and then call him back on the landline and pretend as if I'm following up on 'an interview' set for Friday at the same time as the Tulsa interview. Whoever it is, and my money's on Gunderson, he and/or his stooges will be in Nevada when you're in Oklahoma. If he does show up there, I want to be there to greet him; I have an idea."

Brady came out of the cider house and waved at them.

"It's all clear. Come on back. No bugs except on the phone."

With Blum and Francine's help, Joey and Brady had arranged for seven people to participate in the panel for the video interview at the TV studio. Joey had spent the first hour with the host and producer going over the questions and the format. Another reporter just arrived as they were finishing; she was not part of the staff but rather a freelancer who produced features and documentaries. She had been invited, Glen the host said, to ask tough questions and create some "controversy."

Joey was a bit on edge now, not sure where she might take the discussion. But he suspected that the producer wanted to gin up ratings.

Brady was invited in and brought in the other panelists. Joey stepped over and took Brady aside while the crew was seating the participants and wiring them with lapel mics.

"I want you on the panel; the woman at the table might be critical so be prepared; they're planning on interviewing after the Q&A with our friends." Brady agreed and found a place in the semi-circle with the other guests who were all seated on the large production stage when an audience of maybe forty people filed in.

Ten minutes later, the lights came on and the host announced the program.

"Good evening, I'm Glenn Hughes for Timely Topics, and today we are discussing a subject as old as America itself, the yearning for "A Shining City on the Hill," a mythical place first proposed by Puritan leader, John Winthrop, the founder of Boston. These people believe there is such a place because they claim they've been there.

"First, let's meet our guests. If you don't mind, tell us where you're from and something about yourself." One by one, they introduced themselves.

"I'm Mark," the first man said, a graying, thin man about 60, nicely dressed in a blazer. "I'm a retired chiropractor from Kentucky, a widower, and a choir leader in our congregation."

Emilie Johnson, the podcaster was up next. "I'm Emilie, a single mom, and small business owner and work from home. I do podcasts."

"I'm Sister Johansen, a nun in a Catholic order that focuses on people with disabilities," she said, a cheery woman in her 50s.

"My name is Binh, originally from Vietnam, now a widow living in Iowa with my son and his family; we own a wrecking yard and used-car lot."

Tom Hutchings was up next, a large powerful man and Tanner's father. "I'm Tom from Colorado, a retired attorney."

"I'm Brady, still going to school and have worked as a cop. I also work in online security, among other things."

Beth, the reporter, wrote a note and handed it to Glenn.

A bald man in a turtleneck with wire-rim glasses said, "I'm Coleman, a history professor from Texas."

"I'm Hastings. I write faith-based books mostly for kids and teens," a young man in a Beatles T-shirt and jeans said.

Glenn asked the first question. "So, this place is real, this place called Salem Crossing?"

They all nodded and agreed.

Beth interjected. "But, it can't be found on any map, correct?"

Tom answered. "Not on any earthly map, no."

"Then, how did you get there?" Beth probed.

"We were all on the train . . . an old-time train in the mountains," Binh said. "We are telling the truth, all of us."

Joey was sitting in the back of the audience, and he could feel the tension from back there. He looked over to his left and saw Walter, who nodded and smiled.

"So, you are moving there, is that right, and you have to pay to go there. What's in it for you?" Glenn asked.

The nun answered him directly. "Look around, Mr. Hughes. As it's written in Matthew 24, even as we speak, there are wars and rumors of wars, earthquakes in 'divers places,' looting, cities burning, people at each other's throats, enmity everywhere. Why would anyone want to remain here if there were an exit to a better place?"

The audience burst into applause; she had hit a nerve.

"Why is it that people of faith can't get on board with everybody else. Wouldn't there be a lot less division?" Beth asked.

"Why can't Christians see what is obvious to everybody else?" Coleman had a ready answer. "Maybe it's because we recognize that the so-called experts are not only wrong but full of themselves."

He held up a print-out of a newspaper. "The well-respected London newspaper, The Telegram, ran this headline a few years ago: '*The Future Belongs to Science. We Will Have the Power of the Gods.*' Here's another quote from futurist Michael Sherman: '*Science is My Savior.*'"

"I met Coleman on the train back from the town, which is amazing beyond description, by the way," Hastings said. "We both share a love for C. S. Lewis; mine began as a boy when I read the *Chronicles of Narnia*. What Coleman, a history professor, is talking about is the notion of 'Scientism.' C. S. Lewis hit the nail on the head when he wrote *The Magician's Twin*. Scientism is now the official state religion in this country, in western Europe, and even in repressive regimes like Communist China, Cuba, and North Korea. What C. S. Lewis says is that people can't distinguish between magic and science. They don't know how their cellphones work; they're magic. There is a total lack of skepticism regarding anything that comes out of the mouth of someone with a Ph.D. behind his or her name.

"The result is total obedience to this man-made faith along with the lack of moral judgment. When a physicist says, 'Science flies us to the moon, and faith flies into buildings,' we recognize that sooner rather than later, our faith will be totally discounted. And some politicians wonder why we cling to our Bibles and our guns!"

The audience burst into wild applause. The host announced a break for a commercial announcement which gave Joey a moment to send Blum a text message. "How are things in Vegas?"

Things were hot in Sin City in more ways than one. And the city's slogan, 'What Happens in Vegas, Stays in Vegas,' Gary Gunderson would soon learn did not apply to him. Blum was with his friend at the Fox station in the city, waiting in the reception area.

Blum saw Gunderson and his latest girlfriend walking to the door.

"That's him," he whispered to his producer friend who told him to go wait for them in the green room. Blum left just before they entered.

Gunderson looked around, puzzled.

"Can I help you?" the producer asked him.

"Uh, yes, we were supposed to meet some people for a videotaping about the secret city in the mountains," Gunderson said.

"Ahh, yes, the secret city! Come with me," he said.

Gunderson and his girl followed him down the hall and around the corner into the green room. They walked in and waiting for him was not only Blum, but a cameraman, and a grip with a boom mic and lights.

"I assume you know Mr. Blum," the producer said. "He has someone on the phone for you."

Gunderson took Blum's phone and on the other end was Greg Gunderson in Boston.

They couldn't hear what the father was saying to the son. All the younger Gunderson did was stammer and say, "I'm sorry. Yeah, I understand. No, it won't, not ever again."

Red-faced and shaking, Gary threw the phone at Blum and turned to leave, but the producer and the lighting man were standing there with a microphone.

"Mr. Gunderson, do you have anything to say about the impending SEC charges filed against you for illegal wire-tapping or the allegations of a slander suit?" the producer asked.

"No comment," he said as Gunderson and his assistant pushed their way out the door.

"That's what we thought you'd say," the man with the microphone said as Gunderson made his exit. The producer indicated they were done. They all had a good laugh.

"You're right, Jonathan; the guy's a real tool, glad we could help."

"So, how much do we owe you?"

"Jonathan, you still have a lot of credit on your account here," he said as they packed up their gear. "I'll email this footage to you; keep it as 'insurance.'" Blum smiled, and then his phone rang. It was Greg Gunderson with a lengthy apology.

"I think we made our point. No charges. Thank you," Blum said and put his phone in his pocket. When he was back outside in his rental, he got Joey's text and just replied. "Went as smooth as silk. Gunderson is chewing on a piece of crow. How's everything there?"

Joey breathed a sigh of relief. The lights went back on, and the hosts were ready to continue. Would there be more "gotcha" questions?

Beth had one at the ready. "You make it sound like liberal-minded people can't make a distinction between right and wrong, good and evil. That is emblematic of why there is so much division in our country, even over things like the reality of global warming!"

Mark, the chiropractor, had something to say about that. "Global warming is a reality? Why not let everybody speak their minds about the subject without condemning them as ignoramuses?"

Professor Coleman injected a little more wisdom from C. S. Lewis into the conversation. "When Scientism and Secularism become the state church, people of faith are criticized for being close-minded while secularists themselves are the ones who lack skepticism and never question anything in their arena. C. S. Lewis wrote another book on the subject too, called *Willing Slaves of the Welfare State*. He said, 'The new oligarchy must increasingly rely on the advice of scientists, until, in the end the politicians become the puppet of the scientists.' And why? Because they now own the public's mind and gain power as a result."

"But, you didn't answer my question about the lack of moral judgment in people who disagree with you," Beth said.

Emilie Johnson raised her hand and began, "You misunderstand what my friend said. Maybe you hear Christians say, 'I am a sinner, and only Christ can make me whole.' Why would a law-abiding, tax-paying person who teaches her children good behavior, and volunteers at the local food bank who seems so righteous say such a thing?" She pulled out a 3 x 5 card from her purse and continued reading from her card.

"We had this discussion earlier in the van when we drove over here. Quoting C. S. Lewis, here's my answer to what you asked: *'When a man is getting better, he understands more clearly the evil that is still in him. When a man is getting worse, he understands his own badness less and less. A moderately bad man knows he is not very good; a thoroughly bad man thinks he is all right. This is common sense really. You understand sleep when you are awake, not when you're sleeping. You can see mistakes in mathematics when your mind is working properly. While you are making them, you cannot see them. You can understand the nature of drunkenness when you are sober, not when you are drunk. Good people know about good and evil. Bad people know about neither.'*

Glenn saw that Beth was on the ropes and needed some help. So he stepped in. "We all know that the world today is in need of help and improvement. But why just pack up and leave?"

Brady recognized that he had to clarify some things. "Mr. Hughes, you asked a couple of questions that we still need to answer. First of all, we don't just 'pick up and leave;' we are invited,. We receive an invitation that we RSVP to. I was asked if I would like to be invited by Mr. Kunz, who is sitting in the back. I entertained the idea, and so I took my grandmother to Salem Crossing, just as he took his grandmother.

"It was beautiful beyond description, but it wasn't the fact that there were all kinds of fruit growing and ripening out of season or that there were tropical flowers and birds everywhere; and it wasn't the fact that the place looked like 1925 with artisans at work making things with their hands, bakers, potters, wood-turners, weavers, and quilters. What was unique was that they lived their motto . . . namely, that they are of one mind, one heart, dwell in righteousness with no poor among them.

"Before we left, we watched a barn-raising and participated in the co-operative harvesting of peaches, pears, and apples. My grandmother spent the afternoon making a quilt; young people were assembling hygiene kits to go to the underprivileged here in our world. My grandmother is there because she suffers from diabetes. Is it a better place? Yes, it is a Shining City on the Hill, but it's not the Shining City that everybody was anxious to visit.

"You have to be invited to go there. And the way it works is quite simple. If you know someone, anyone who has made a difference in your life, changed it for the better, or did something courageous or unusual for others, log onto the website at www.theshiningcity.org, and share that person's story with us. We'll pass it on to the people who extend the invitations. It's all on the website. Send a photo if you've got one."

"And, you haven't been invited yet?" Glenn asked.

"At that time, I wasn't, " Brady answered.

"My son was," Tom Hutchings said. "If you follow football, maybe you've heard of Tanner Hutchings. He was supposed to be a top draft pick as a quarterback; he graduated from the University of Colorado last year and was hoping to get an NFL tryout, but last month he was on a bike ride up a canyon and was hit by a truck.

"He suffered a compound fracture in his right leg, needed a total knee reconstruction, and worse, we discovered after he woke up that he was paralyzed from the waist down. The doctors told us he'd never have the use of his legs again. Then, his girlfriend, Rachel, convinced his mother and him to take a train ride.

"I thought it was crazy, but Tanner insisted I go with them. So, not only did we travel to Salem Crossing, but we went with Tanner further up the mountain to the Grand Hotel and Spa where for two weeks he bathed in the hot springs, in what they call their 'stirring waters.'

"Before I came down here to participate with you, he was walking with a cane . . ." he said, as tears streamed down his face, "and the scar from his fracture was barely visible. It's just like the healing stories from the Bible which I hadn't opened in forty years, by the way, until now."

"And what did all this cost?" Beth, the skeptic asked.

He smiled and tried to answer as best he could. "Nothing and everything," he said quietly.

"What?"

"No bill is coming. It's all paid for," he explained. "But, for us, we are selling all that we have and going there." He pulled his invitation out of his pocket and showed it to the audience.

"Someone else paid for us, and now we're paying it forward . . . for others, for people like you to come. Don't know what I'll do there, since there is no crime, no ambulances to chase, and no litigations to litigate. I think I'm going to buy a loom and do some weaving." He sat down and the place was as quiet as a cathedral.

"One last comment before we open it up for the audience to ask their questions. Why all this animus toward science and technology? It sounds rather . . . Amish," Glenn said.

Emilie spoke right up. "I was invited to a friend's birthday party a while back; there were many friends from high school I hadn't seen in years. I spoke with those I could, but many of them were chatting on their phones, sending emails and texts, or taking selfies.

"Technology is replacing human interaction and relationships. Soon, if the secularists have their way, we'll just get checks from the government and let people in faraway places or robots do the work that we should do for ourselves. What a miserable existence!" Emilie added.

Mark, the chiropractor, took out his smartphone and addressed the audience. "This seems like a rather innocent little device, brilliant in construction and beautifully designed. But look at what's happened to our communities, to our local newspapers, and to human relationships since we've all 'logged on,' dropped our landlines, and moved to these devices—phones, tablets, laptops, as well as everything else in our homes and cars, including such things as Alexa.

"Secularists make fun of people of faith when we bow our heads in a restaurant and say grace. And yet they'll yell across the room and ask Google's Alexa that's plugged in on the counter, 'Alexa, what's the meaning of life?' and it will provide an answer derived from a Google algorithm. In other words, according to the tech masters, Google can answer our prayers, but God can't, because He doesn't exist. As for me, I choose God over Google."

The audience erupted in applause and gave the group a standing ovation. Walter gave Joey a thumbs-up from his seat in the back.

Time to go.

For the next two weeks, Joey, Brady, Francine, and Blum watched as the inquiries came pouring in. Brady turned the spreadsheet into a proper database and forwarded it every day to the "office" in Upper Michigan where "Management" processed their requests. And they were happy to hear that others around the world, including Martina Ilić who was somewhere in the Alps, were also submitting names to receive invitations.

Joey kept asking about Dana, but all he got so far was just a weekly postcard from her somewhere in a north country. But, as they all learned, geography in the other realm was a whole lot different than what they had learned in school. No time for those questions now! Now he only had one. When can I see my pregnant wife again? Blum had promised to give Joey an answer, but he soon learned why everyone was in such a hurry.

Joey did something he hadn't in more than two months. The night before he spent three hours in front of his Smart TV and turned on the news. It was heart-rending.

Channel after channel, from left-leaning to the far right, from local to national, revealed a world in turmoil.

It broke his heart. Beautiful cities in flames. Looters and "peaceful protesters," police officers and their foes going at each other face-to-face were all there, one disgusting scene after another.

How long can this go on?

Warships were rattling nerves in the Persian Gulf, in the South China Sea, even Australia was in peril.

He had avoided looking at social media for some time; he used to check in with pundits he trusted. Or watched YouTube videos. The news was impossible to watch. Soon, he wondered, will any place be safe?

There was only one place he could think of.

The children of Israel had to wait on the Lord to part the Red Sea. Joey read a note that Blum had given him about the Israelites who had been taken into captivity by the vicious Assyrians, then repented of their wickedness and asked for and received a way out. Now, he and Blum were alone in the cider house in Jonathan's tiny office. There was a small window that looked out into the warehouse; Joey walked over and shut the door. Now it was just the two of them.

"I have a couple of questions," he said. Blum had a large binder stuffed full of notes in a bookshelf behind his desk. Before Joey could ask his questions, Blum hefted the binder out of the bookshelf and plopped it onto the desk. He opened to a divider toward the back and pulled out a tattered couple of pages barely held together with a staple.

"What's that?"

"Is that one of your questions?"

"No," Blum said as he put on his reading glasses. "But, it may provide you with some answers. This is a segment from the Apocryphal Book of 2 Esdras concerning the lost ten tribes of Israel; I came across it years ago right after I got my Invitation . . . when I was still a practicing Jew."

He began reading: *"But they took this counsel among themselves, that they would leave the multitude of the heathen, and go forth into a further country, where never mankind dwelt, that they might there keep their statutes, which they never kept in their own land. And they entered into Euphrates by the narrow passages of the river. For the most High then shewed signs for them, and held still the flood, till they were passed over. For through that country there was a great way to go, namely, of a year and a half, and the same region is called Arsareth. Then dwelt they there until the latter time."*

Blum then related what happened centuries ago in Palestine. "A few years later, Judah's King Hezekiah relied on the Prophet Isaiah to prevail on the Lord to save the Jews from the Assyrians. A plague swept through their ranks as they were camped around Jerusalem. A hundred years later, they were not so lucky and were carted off to Babylon. And in 70 AD, as Jesus prophesied, the Romans destroyed Jerusalem, killed over a million people in Judea, left only 100,000 Jews alive, and sold the survivors as slaves around the empire."

Joey still looked puzzled. "Arsareth?"

Blum nodded. "Is that one of your questions?"

"Not exactly, but it does pique my interest."

"So, what do you want to know?"

Joey leaned forward in his chair and put his hands on Blum's old walnut desk. "What was in your Invitation? You said you got one."

"I did."

"But is it too personal?"

"Some of it," Blum said. "Do you want to know what I gave up?"

"You didn't have twelve million dollars too, did you?"

Blum smiled. "No, Joey, I never had very anything close to that. I had been in the Army for ten years, and my wife and infant both died during childbirth. I was in Southampton in England at that time waiting for D-Day."

Joey was ashamed that he had even asked such a question; Blum saw Joey's reaction, but just smiled and continued.

"After D-Day, I followed the first wave in and began working as an interrogator, working over German–or as I saw them–Nazi prisoners of war. I hated those people. I figured it was their fault that I was a widower, had no children, nor prospects for any more. For the next year-and-a-half, I went from one prisoner-of-war camp to another interviewing prisoners. I was especially hard on SS Officers; well, we all were. Then when I heard of an opportunity to be part of the legal staff to try Nazi war criminals, I jumped at the chance–even gave up a promotion to become a lieutenant colonel to join Ben Ferencz's prosecution team. Then when I was in Nuremberg, I had an assistant, a young Hungarian Jew who was my driver; he had fought the Nazis when they finally took over their one-time ally. He gave me a book," Jonathan said, and turned around and pulled it from the shelf. It was in German.

Joey read the cover: *Gemeinsames Leben*. What does that mean, Life Together, or Living As One?"

"Something like that," Blum said. "Bonhoeffer had been a constant voice against Hitler, the Nazi's, and their treatment of the Jews ever since he returned from New York in 1931 where he had studied theology. After Hitler came to power, he recognized the threat to his life if he opposed the Führer. But, he stayed, unlike others, until finally the regime had enough and imprisoned him. But when the authorities saw the end was near on April 4th, 1945, they hanged him on a wire and strangled him slowly to death."

Joey still looked puzzled.

"I was with Patton's Third Army at the time; we liberated Buchenwald. I saw the bodies. I saw the survivors, and I saw the crematoria. I saw everything."

A tear ran down Joey's face. "So that's what you gave up: hate, resentment, vengeance?"

Blum put the book and binder back on the shelf, and with a lump in his throat, turned back to Joey and muttered, "Yes."

They went back to work. Joey understood. He knew that whatever they were doing was not enough, they needed to do more to speed things up. He texted Brady and Francine about what he had just seen and read. "Whatever we're doing, it's got to go faster. And we need more help."

What he didn't know at that time was that the opposition was growing stronger and more determined too. But he would soon find out.

The good news about the cable channel's interview in Tulsa was that it had thousands and thousands of views; the bad news was that it had thousands and thousands of views! Think of all the metaphors that apply: "Don't wake a sleeping dog!" "Don't rock the boat!"

"Don't kick over a hornet's nest!" All are valid here.

Not only was Joey being compared to mass suicide instigator Jim Jones, but now he was also labeled with the persona of David Koresh of the Davidian Compound fiasco in Waco, Texas; even to lemmings in Denmark encouraging thousands of his followers to jump off a cliff with him.

"Don't you remember what the king of the big top, P. T. Barnum said, Joey?" Blum asked.

"Never heard of him, so no."

"He said, there's no such thing as bad publicity. What's more, you have proven to have a worldwide reach. Do you know where Martina is?"

"I thought she was in Austria."

"Nope, she's a long way from there; she's as far away from here as you can get. She's in Siberia, no kidding, close to the Chinese border. I received an email from her yesterday from the 'Jewish Autonomous Region', or 'Oblast.'"

"Fill me in," Joey said, now curious.

"During World War II, Jews in the caucuses and western Russia proper had heard how the invading Nazi forces were rounding up Jews; they needed a place of refuge. At the behest of Communist Jews up the ranks, Stalin agreed to establish this zone as a 'Jewish homeland' inside the Soviet Union proper, but in a frozen desolate Siberian wasteland that could act as a 'speed bump' to invading forces from the East, like Japan, for example.

"So off these pious Jews went and scratched out a place for themselves in the Far East, like American pioneers did in the Far West. Today, it's called Birobidzhan, the capital, and some Jews who live there heard about our new 'Promised Land' on the web, and thanks to you, Dana, Francine, and Brady, they wanted to learn more. Martina caught a sleeping berth on the Trans-Siberian express, proselyting on the way, and arrived a couple of days ago.

"She met with Rabbi Oleg and others and explained that you don't have to be Christian to escape to the Shining City. All that was required was to believe in God and having lived a faithful, virtuous life with a broken heart and a contrite spirit," Blum explained.

"Along with being willing to make the sacrifice," Joey added.

"Exactly. I understand you've found some old acquaintances that you're planning on visiting."

"Yeah, it took a while, but after the Judge told me about finding my life's 'cairns', I've been doing some detective work and found several . . . at least the ones who are still alive," Joey explained.

"Cairns? Piles of stones on a hiking trail?"

"My cairns," Joey said. "They're the people in my life who were there at critical moments who helped lead me back to the trail that helped keep me safe and protected me along the way. I'm leaving in the morning to visit several of them. They know I'm coming, but have no idea why."

"Driving or flying?" Jonathan asked.

"Been trying to get a cheap flight on Southwest."

"I want you to protect your identity. I'd hope you'd drive."

"Why?"

"You've been out of touch and off the grid for some time now."

"Well, I did catch an hour of cable news two days ago, and that was enough for a while," Joey said.

"Then you haven't heard about the FFR Activists who've been defacing and even burning churches. They tried to burn down the National Cathedral in Washington and were successful in a couple of places in the Northwest. You're on their radar," Blum said.

"Who is the FFR?"

"The Freedom from Religion group that claims that Christian churches, especially evangelical and charismatic churches, have been used by White Supremacists for four hundred years to enslave people of color, to hold sway over them, and to maintain power. And being labeled as one of them, you probably have a target on your back."

"Me?"

"You! You know how many hits, shares, or gross rating points—whatever they call them to-day—that you've accumulated in the past month, especially just this week after your video went viral on YouTube? It's a lot! You're probably about as popular as a Senator from a fly-over state or a conservative commentator. So, be careful, okay?"

"Okay. Heard anything about my visiting Dana?"

"No final word yet. Maybe when you get back."

Dana was asking the same question. Nevertheless, she was so grateful to have Oma by her side babying her. What a sweetheart! Before all this drama, she had never really had a one-on-one conversation with her, but now they were together all the time, and she was learning a lot about Joey and his difficult childhood separated first from his mother, and subsequently, his father. "I miss him. I don't know why I can't go down there, or he can't come up here."

Oma sympathized but explained. "They don't exactly have direct flights to this place," she said. "Think of where we are as if it were the dark side of the moon, except that it's a beautiful paradise where you can feed the bluebirds and pet the fawns. Besides, Dana, you're getting—how should I say this—kind of big."

Before Dana could reply, her OBGYN entered her suite.

"Yes, Mrs. Kunz, as your mother said . . ."

"Grandmother-in-law," Oma corrected her.

" . . . you are extraordinarily large, and for a very good reason. You, my dear, are having two babies, not one. You will be raising twins! Congratulations," the doctor revealed.

Dana laughed, and so did Oma! "How about that!" she said.

"That's why if you were still on the 'outside,' I'm afraid things wouldn't turn out so well. Even though this environment offers special recuperative properties, we still have to monitor you very closely and limit your activity. It's one thing to speed along the healing process for fully formed adults and children, but it's different for the unborn."

"But, how do you know I'm having twins without conducting an ultrasound?"

"We just know," the doctor said, and then added as she was leaving. "Jonathan Blum is making travel arrangements for Joseph, even as we speak."

Joey arrived in San Diego in full disguise driving his beloved orange truck loaded with Blum's apples, dressed like a good-old-boy redneck farmer, wearing a Caterpillar hat, denim jacket, a pair of aviator sunglasses, and sporting a three-day-old beard.

He parked the truck in a parking lot near a farmer's market and sold his produce by the bushel for a flat 20 bucks each. Didn't take him long.

His first appointment was at noon with Mrs. Emma Schneider in Oceanside, now about 80 and widowed, his primary school teacher at the time his mother died. After he returned to school, she asked him to stay late one day, gave him some science fiction books to read, then hugged him and wept along with him.

He told Blum she was the first person he ever met who loved him and who wasn't related. She stayed late every day after school for a month to talk with him and gave him more things to read. She gave him his first Rubik's cube. He never forgot her. He hoped she'd remember him.

She did. "Oh, Joseph, look how great you turned out! I'm so proud of you. It broke my heart when I heard about your mom. Oh, and my son, remember Frankie? He sent me one of those Video-Tube things . . ."

"YouTube."

"Yes, that, where you were interviewed by the reporter with your beautiful wife. He said you were a preacher or something. Is that why you're here? I'm already a Christian."

'I'm not a preacher, but I do have a gift for you because you are at the top of my cairn list," he said, and then explained what his "gift" was. She seemed reluctant to "make such a commitment at her advanced age," but she agreed to talk to Frankie about it.

Joey had three more appointments in the area that day: a track coach, a pastor, and a boyhood friend, the best example ever of someone who always asked the question, "What would Jesus do?"

By 8 pm he had delivered his messages, given his "cairns" some food for thought, and written down their vital information. He had to hurry to the Balboa Pavilion in Newport Beach to catch a yacht to Catalina Island. Blum had sent him a lead to follow up on as well as the name of the yacht and the captain who would take him there.

But, he never made it to the island.

❑ ❑ ❑ ❑ ❑

Joey awoke the next morning on the yacht at anchor in a cool, quiet bay that bore no resemblance to the island off the coast of Southern California. All he remembered was taking a quick nap in a guest cabin on a Barcalounger. What a surprise!

"Mr. Kunz, we're here," a young man dressed in khakis said to him.

"Well, this isn't how I imagined Catalina Island would look."

"It's not Catalina Island, sir, but I'm sure you'll like it. Come with me."

"Old Blum is sure full of surprises, isn't he?"

The young man grinned and gave him a hand out of the chair. "You have no idea," he said. "He's been surprising people now for a very, very long time."

They stepped off the gangplank and walked along the dock to a small strip of sand where a group of Machiya bungalows, in the traditional Kyoto style, surrounded a small chapel. Joey took a mental snapshot of all that he saw and wondered, "Are we in Japan, Alaska, or Norway? And how did we get here on a yacht overnight?" In front of him, a thick forest of both pines and deciduous trees, some of them flowering, rose above him, covering the sides of a mountain peak rising some 8,000 feet right out of the water. The mountainside was dotted with more neat and tidy Machiya dwellings following a narrow road nearly all the way to the top.

Joey seemed transfixed by what he saw. The steward gently nudged him. "Mr. Kunz, people are waiting for us. Let's go."

They walked up the path toward the chapel. The entrance was framed by an archway covered in wisteria with potted bonsai trees on either side.

"Impressive," Joey muttered–by the people waiting for him.

There stood his wife beaming! "Dana, look at you!" he said as he hurried to her. Standing by her was a much younger-looking Oma.

"Let's go in here," Oma said, leading them into a small reception area where Judge Stone was seated, waiting for them.

"Quite a reunion I see here," he said. "Dana?"

"Got some news, Joey. We're not having a baby . . . we're having two!"

Her husband was stunned, then broke out into a big grin. "I can't believe it–one miracle after another. So are you coming back with me?"

Oma answered. "She has to stay here to make it another 22 weeks."

"Oma's right. I'd probably lose them both if I went back 'outside,'" Dana said.

"Outside?"

"That's what our old world is called here," Oma said. "But we've heard that things are moving faster there." Judge Stone got up and walked over to join in the conversation.

"That's right," the Judge said. "We were hoping for an update; we get the reports and see the numbers, but we'd like to hear from you directly."

Joey recounted many stories about other people who received invitations in addition to the first invitees that he and Dana had originally recruited like Binh, Brady, and Francine.

Joey continued, "We figure that we have contacted at least

100,000 people, mostly via texts and emails, and they continue to share it and pass it on. That includes the podcast as well as the cablecast from Tulsa. As a result, people know where to go to get more information. We've had close to half a million hits on the website. This week, I have been contacting the cairns in my life–people who touched me–like my primary school teacher, Mrs. Schneider. But things are getting so chaotic, especially in the big cities. It's not just discord and dissension. Now it's violent and hateful. As much as we have done, I am very concerned that it's totally inadequate, that we'll come up short."

Judge Stone sat back down in the big wicker easy chair and leaned back. "You know, at least one-third of mankind is aware that they received their official 'Invitation' a long time ago, when Jesus of Nazareth said, 'Come, follow me,' but most people pay no attention to His offer. One of my favorite historical figures–and I met him in 1942–was Winston Churchill. He not only kept totalitarianism at bay for nearly three years until America came to Britain's aid, but he was also a great writer, orator, and philosopher. One of my favorite bits of his wisdom was this: 'Men occasionally encounter truth, but most of them do not recognize it.'

"And why don't they? It's obvious to us, but why not to everybody? From years in the court-room, I learned that truth in the sense of obtaining justice is only arrived at by questioning in a searching way. We have to want it!

"Pilate posed that question to Jesus himself. 'What is truth?' As Francis Bacon explained 'There are three parts in truth. First, the inquiry, which is the seeking of it; secondly, the knowledge of it, which is the presence of it; and thirdly, the belief, which is the enjoyment of it.'

"Why do some people enjoy it and others don't? I believe it is directly related to the two great commandments: First, to love God with all our heart, mind, and strength, and second, to love our neighbors as ourselves. As Christ said, everything hangs on that. When we love Him, we don't want to hurt or disappoint Him. The Psalmist said it best: 'Rivers of water run down mine eyes, because men keep not thy law.'

"'To know that I caused Him pain grieves me greatly,' Scottish essayist Thomas Carlisle said. I have always found that the honest truth of your own mind has a certain attraction for every other mind that honestly loves truth. Remember what Christ said, *And ye shall know the truth, and the truth shall make you free.*' And later in the Gospel of John, He added, *'Every one that is of the truth heareth my voice.'* Joey, take heart in knowing that you've done your best–but, you are not alone. Finally, never forget that Christ purchased your freedom and mine. And, because of that, He lets us choose. Remember that word: Let! Let people hear your invitation, and if they are seeking it, their love of God will lead them there. Don't fret–just keep doing what you're doing."

Joey left that evening on the yacht believing and assuming that somehow the skipper would have him back at the Huntington Beach Harbor in the morning so he could continue his quest and return to Blum's apple farm. His goodbye meal that evening with Dana, Margritte, and the Judge was bittersweet, but memorable nonetheless. Wherever he had been, he knew he'd taken another bite of Paradise.

And he wanted more.

Joey walked along the dock, through the gate, and into the key shack to give the attendant his parking receipt; he needed the key to Orange Crush. He didn't have much time to drive north and over the Sierras to his next stop in Carson City, Nevada. Joey handed the man his ticket through the little slot in the window.

"I'm sorry, but your vehicle has already been picked up," the parking attendant said.

"But, I gave you my receipt!"

"I know that. There must be some mistake. Let me check."

"No kidding. I can't even call anybody. My cellphone's in the truck!"

"That's why we post that sign right outside to warn customers not to leave any valuables in their vehicles . . . please give me a minute," he closed the window, left the booth, and locked it, leaving Joey outside the shuttered shack with no place to even sit down.

It was almost 10 a.m., and like nearly always in Huntington Beach, it was a warm, sunny day. But Joey was anything but sunny.

He was angry, frustrated, and a little bit afraid. He searched every corner of the parking lot. No orange truck anywhere! How could this happen to him? To him?" He was on an important mission. He had to get the word out, and he needed help. He was still in his redneck disguise from his drive to the coast, wearing jeans, cowboy boots, and the Caterpillar cap; he hadn't shaved now in four days.

As he walked northward along the Pacific Coast Highway, he encountered many homeless people huddled under tents, or inside a sleeping bag on a piece of grass, under a tree, or out on the beach. When he saw his reflection in a store window, he realized that he looked just like them! The vast number of homeless living on the streets had become the new normal in California. And like them, he didn't have a wallet, a credit card, or even a thin dime.

He saw a drinking fountain across the street next to a park bench. Traffic is always heavy on this once beautiful strip of asphalt hugging the Pacific Ocean; he dodged a Lexus and a Mercedes but was almost hit by an Audi TT.

"You homeless dredge! The street doesn't belong to you," the driver yelled at Joey as he slammed on his brakes.

"Sorry, man!" Joey replied.

"Get a job and move away," the driver told Joey as he drove off.

Joey got his drink and took a seat on the bench. Shoppers, tourists, and pedestrians walked by, occasionally glancing at him. Mothers pulled their children away and walked around him. A disheveled older man pushing a grocery cart loaded with what appeared to be all his earthly belongings walked up.

"May I share this bench with you, man?" the old man said.

"Sure, it's not MY bench," Joey said.

The man on the other side of the bench had a grocery sack in his cart; he opened it up and pulled out a handful of small packets wrapped in plastic. He handed a couple of them to Joey.

"Do you like Little Debbie's? They're my favorite. They're only 49¢ a piece. They're thin wafers sandwiched with peanut butter and covered in chocolate. Very nutritious. Got all your food groups. Take a couple. You ain't had no breakfast, have ya'?"

Joey shook his head.

"Go ahead, take one! I bought 'em fair and square. Clean and sanitary!" Joey relented. The old man was right. They were delicious.

"I get 'em from the Dollar Store. Just a buck for two of 'em. I have a whole sack full, enough for two days. Ever been to the Dollar Store? No? It's right next to the VA clinic up the road a ways," Joey's new friend said. "Share and share alike, that's my motto."

"So you're a vet?"

"Yep, got out at the last moment, as they said, 'The NVA is on its way.'"

"The NVA?"

"The North Vietnamese Army, unfortunately," he explained.

"My dad served over there, spoke Vietnamese, and worked with the locals who saved downed pilots," Joey said with pride.

"You're kidding, right?"

"Not kidding. That's what he told me."

"Well, my name's Scofield, Pete Scofield, and you, my young friend, look familiar. What's your name?"

Joey smiled and put his arm on the old man's shoulder. "Kunz. Joseph Charles Kunz. I believe you sent me a letter more than twenty years ago from Manila! Oma was right! There's no such thing as coincidence."

"Agreed! God always looks over us, especially in our extremities!" They stood and shook hands.

Just then, Joey saw a 1980 rebuilt, orange Ford F-150 drive by across the street and then park; it was his Orange Crush!

"Stay right here! That's my stolen truck!! I'll be right back." Joey ran through traffic just as the driver got out and stood there waiting for him. He had thick black hair and a beard, slightly graying, looked to be in his late 50s, wearing a hand-knit sweater with a high collar, khakis, and boots. Joey was running at him on the attack.

Just before he reached him, the man called him by name and said, "Hi Joey, sorry I'm late. Get in and let's get your friend. We have places to go. I'll drive."

The man got in and started the truck. For some odd reason, Joey complied and got in the other door. They made a quick U-turn, crossed the street, and double-parked near retired Army Platoon Sergeant Peter J. Scofield's shopping cart. Joey sat there, dumbstruck, then the driver told him to open the window. He did as he was told.

"Pete, we're going somewhere, and you need to come with us," Joey said. "Throw your stuff in the back, but bring the sack of Little Debbie's up in front here."

"There's no room," Pete protested.

"We'll make room," said the stranger driving the truck. He pulled into traffic and made a left at the next light.

"Where are we going?" Pete asked.

"Don't know," Joey said.

"Who's the driver?"

"Not a clue," Joey said, staring at the man to his left.

"This is weird," Pete said

"You have no idea," Joey said as Pete threw his stuff in the back of the truck, secured it, but left the shopping cart on the sidewalk.

"Somebody else can use that now," Pete said, as Joey slid to the center of the old bench seat, making room for the homeless veteran. One of us could use a shower, Joey thought to himself. Very likely me!

"My name is John," the driver announced, "and we're driving to Garden Grove, known in southern California as Little Saigon. We have work to do there." Somehow, Joey felt like all was well, but why?

On the way, Joey told Pete all about taking Oma to the Crossing, the Hot Springs, the accident, the podcasts, broadcasts, and everything else, including his fortune.

He had Pete's interest. "So, you're kind of like Howard Hughes, an eccentric millionaire hanging out with homeless people, going to ghost towns, and snatching vets off the street for some nefarious purpose?"

"I have a purpose. I just have a craving for Little Debbie chocolate-covered wafers. Give one to John. Try one, John, they're delicious," Joey said.

Mysterious John agreed and took one. "They are!"

Somehow Joey knew not to ask John about who he was or where he came from. He had authority. Joey was certain of that. He was going to toe the line and do whatever John told him. But, Pete wasn't so discrete.

"So, tell us about yourself, John. How did you end up stealing Joey's truck—which is beautiful, by the way—and finding us on the street?"

"It's complicated. It's in the Bible."

"Yeah, where?" Pete asked.

"In the Gospel of John 21, verses 23 and 24."

"Hmm," Pete said. "My Bible's somewhere in the back in my sleeping bag, I think. I'll look it up later."

"Do that," John said. "You should read it every night before you go to bed."

"But, I don't got a bed," Pete said.

"That's okay because your new friend here is a millionaire. Aren't you, Joey?"

"Last time I looked," Joey admitted.

John parked the truck and led Joey and Pete over to the Vietnam Memorial plaza in Little Saigon where two statues of an American GI and a South Vietnamese soldier stood side-by-side in a cauldron surrounded by flames. Pete handed out bottles of water.

They sat and waited. Right at three o'clock, a group of Vietnamese walked over to them. John began speaking to them in Vietnamese; Pete could understand only a little because it had been more than forty years since he had spoken any of that difficult language. Then John introduced his two friends to the group, mostly people in their 60s and 70s with a scattering of their children and grandchildren.

They all had been shaking Joey and Pete's hands, one after the other.

"Nice to meet you, Charlie's boy!" one old man said. "And you, Sergeant Scofield, we play cards once—you teach me blackjack. You still owe me three chickens!"

And so it went until the man in charge came. He was Binh's younger brother who was about 12 years old back then.

He addressed the whole group in English. "You can all see this statue. Maybe the American politicians and the media wrote us off, but Lt. Jewell, Sergeant Kunz, and Corporal Pete here, never forgot us. They came back for us, and now we are here in a country troubled like South Vietnam was. Look at that statue with the GI standing next to one of our countrymen. Pete is the last one. Three cheers for Pete!"

And the 25 Vietnamese one-time refugees and now American citizens gave the old vet three hurrahs. Pete was touched and thanked them.

Then John spoke to them in Vietnamese. "I do not know the details or why this man (referring to Pete) is in his current situation, but he has no home. He lives on the street and pushes his belongings around in a shopping cart. Do you have any ideas?"

He let them discuss the situation for five minutes until Binh's brother spoke to Pete directly. "Mr. Scofield, we welcome you to our community. You sacrificed for us. We have a place for you. Do not say no. As far as we are concerned, you are the hero cast in bronze standing in front of us." Pete looked down, overwhelmed. Somebody cared about him!

"And, Charlie's son, Joseph," John explained, "has come far to tell you about a place being prepared for people like you . . . a place we call The Shining City on a Hill. Binh Jewell says she wants to join us, and she sent us here to invite you as well. Joey?"

He turned to Joey who told them all about The Shining City. Then John said to the group, "I see how you help one another and share each other's burdens. That tells me you would fit right in. Give Joey your information, and he'll pass it on."

When he was finished, Joey and John spent a few minutes with Binh's brother who gave Joey a card and thanked them profusely. They left about a half-hour later after all of Pete's earthly possessions were offloaded, along with Pete himself. They said goodbye to their new friends, including Pete. Then Joey and Mysterious John headed north.

Between Garden Grove and Sacramento, they made four stops and drove through two cities where rioters and looters had forced the cities into lockdowns. It was night now and many off-ramps were closed. Late that night, they stopped in Fresno to meet a retired professor and his wife, then drove past a couple of military bases that were surrounded by protesters, and through an area that had been hit by firestorms. Last month, an earthquake rattled nerves already on edge from disturbances and attacks on police stations.

Joey was behind the wheel now, and occasionally John would look over his shoulder and give Joey instructions to exit the freeway, loop around, park for a minute, and then either return to the main freeway or take a collector highway, and get back on the road. About midnight, they got gas, and John slipped behind the wheel. Shortly after that, Joey was asleep.

He woke up early in the morning as the sun lit up his face. They spent the day in Sacramento, went to an AL-ANON meeting, stopped at a school for children with disabilities, and then went to a hospital. John had messages of hope he left at each stop, and Joey found another old friend with whom he shared the story of The

Shining City. Toward evening, they passed through the Sierra Nevadas, and stopped near the site of the Donner Party tragedy, then continued toward Reno, Nevada, where Joey had planned to meet an old high school coach. But that appointment wasn't until tomorrow.

It was dark now. John pulled over at a diner and gas station just past Lake Tahoe, a beautiful setting on the downward slope of the mountains. He exited the truck, followed by Joey.

John took a moment and just stared at the view below them of Reno and the surroundings. They had passed Lake Tahoe half an hour ago. They stood there surrounded by towering Ponderosa pines.

"It won't be long now," John said, a mixture of joy and sorrow.

"What?"

"The great and dreadful day of the Lord as prophesied in both the Old and the New Testaments," John explained, still a bit melancholy. "Great for some, dreadful for others. What you are doing will be a great blessing to those who listen."

Joey felt a little uneasy, wanting to ask a question, but not daring to. John smiled. He was a slight man, with dark, curly hair, a beard, and mustache touched with grey. But his briliant blue eyes were warm and piercing. He could see things and kept everything to himself. Joey had a warm feeling come over him, a feeling of standing next to a great man.

"You have a question, Joey?"

"I have so many, and here's the first one. Why did we stop here? Do you want to go inside?"

"No, but you should. Get something to eat and gas up, but you have another more burning question, don't you?"

He nodded.

"My wife is in somewhere in Salem, I think; she is having twins, and I want to be with her."

"Yes, I know."

"As you know, I have work to do here, and I will do all that I can . . ."

"But?"

"But, I feel like Lot's wife . . . I keep looking back, and it's not just the money. Did you know that I have twelve million dollars?"

"Yes."

"So, there was a Bible in a motel room where we stayed in a while back, and I found a scripture in Luke . . ."

"Right. It's in Luke 18 when a rich young prince came to Jesus asking if he qualified for eternal life. The Savior then told him, *"Yet lackest thou one thing. Sell all that thou hast and distribute unto the poor and thou shalt have treasure in heaven, and come, follow me. And when he heard this, he was very sorrowful, for he was very rich.'* And, you're worried about that because twelve million dollars is a lot of money. Is that it?"

Joey hesitated, and then replied, "Well, yes."

John look at him directly and smiled. "Don't overlook the verses that follow. Verse 26 says his disciples asked, *'Who then can be saved?'* The Master put them at ease. He told them, *'The things which are impossible with men are possible with God.'"*

"I still need to qualify. I remember the story of Ananias and Sapphira. I need to understand how I should best part with my treasure," Joey said.

"That's for you to figure out. You did tell the Vietnamese in Garden Grove that you'd donate to their foundation, and that's good. But I believe another opportunity is coming soon. So listen closely. Be observant. And one more thing. Watch your back. I'm worried about you. Be alert and listen to the Spirit because I have to part company with you."

"Here?"

"Yes, I'm catching a ride."

Joey suddenly felt very alone. "I wish you could ride awhile longer with me."

"Me, too," he said. "What was your second question?"

"You told Pete that if he read a couple of verses at the end of the Gospel of John, it would reveal who you are and what you're doing."

"Yes. Peter had a question for the Master regarding his return; this was after the resurrection, part of the forty days of instructions that He gave his disciples. Speaking of one of the other apostles there with the Master and Peter, Peter asked *'What shall this man do?'* *Jesus answered him and said, 'If I will that he tarry till I come, what is that to thee? Follow thou me.'*

"Of course, Christians have been wondering if there is still one of his disciples roaming the earth ever since, 'tarrying.' And then verse 24 verifies that 'this is the disciple which testifieth of these things and wrote these things, and we know that his testimony is true.'"

Joey couldn't look at him, but he managed to get a few words out. "This has been a great privilege to have you in my truck, at my side, teaching me and leading from place to place. Thank you. When you go, I will have a taste of what life must have been for you since that day. I will be terribly lonely."

Joey looked up at John with wet eyes, trembling.

"Lonely is correct, but I get visits from others from time to time and am called to perform special assignments occasionally. And, I have been able to meet some very interesting people over the years . . . many, many people like you, and I help where I can."

"People like Jonathan Blum?"

"Yes, we go way back . . . back to some terrible times. But now we all have a new task. Just remember, Joey, I'm only a messenger, just like you."

"Only much older and immensely wiser," Joey said.

"With age, comes wisdom, I suppose. Now, you go in the diner, get some nourishment, and wait for Blum's call. He has some more things cooked up for you. You like Blum, don't you?"

"Yes, of course," Joey said. John started down the highway but halted and said, "Good. Follow Blum's advice to the letter. Be vigilant and watch your back! Goodbye."

He waved and walked away, down the hill toward Reno.

Part IV
Exodus

Joey finished a plate of fish and chips and a soft drink while he waited for Blum's call, and then he waited some more. He sent Blum a text indicating that John told him, "You were going to call," saying he would leave soon if the phone didn't ring.

The widescreen TV over the bar went to the news and showed footage of protesters in front of a burning police station and then another segment of a church with broken windows. The talking head came up and related a discussion between an atheist and a preacher that got heated, especially when the commentator showed footage of Dana and Joey. Joey put down his drink and listened.

A trucker at the counter turned and spoke to him.

"Hey, that's you!" He tapped his buddy on the other side and said. "We got a celebrity in here."

The station cut to a comment by Dana with Joey watching where she said, "There's not much time left, and many people are looking for a place to flee to."

"What a pile of crap," a young man with a ski cap in the corner said. The trucker next to Joey replied, "You look like Antifa. You're the dweeb driving the Subaru with Oregon plates, aren't you? Why don't you go back to your socialist paradise?"

The truckers stood up just as the Millennial in the corner dropped a twenty on the counter, hurried out, passing by Joey, and giving him a dirty look.

"Check please," Joey asked the waitress behind the counter. He settled up and walked to the door. The Subaru with the Oregon plates was gone, but a dark sedan was parked down the highway a short distance with its lights off, but its engine running.

Joey walked over to his truck, got in, and started it up. The truck barely moved. He got out and saw that both tires on the right side were flat!

He tried to call Blum, but got no answer. He went around the back of the truck, lowered the tailgate, sat down, and tried to find a tow truck. After three calls, he finally got through. It was now 8 pm and the dispatcher said he'd have a tow there by 9.

Joey sent another text to Blum. Nothing.

The truckers exited the diner and asked if they could help. He told them he had a tow truck coming; they wished him well and drove away. He went back in the diner, ordered a drink, and waited. Finally, about a quarter after nine, he saw a tow truck drive up to the diner and stop. A woman talked to the driver as Joey hurried out, just as the truck drove away.

"What the . . . ?"

The young woman in black was walking back to the dark sedan as Joey ran out in the road, waving, just as the truck disappeared. He kicked some gravel and started back to the diner when a Chrysler drove up.

A woman rolled down the passenger window and yelled out. "Looks like you're stuck here. Can I give you a ride into town?" The diner was closing up, Blum hadn't returned his call, and Joey thought, Why not?"

He got in, and they pulled out on the highway toward Reno. Less than a mile down the road, his phone finally rang. "Blum?" Joey said.

"Nope, it's not Blum. Just an old friend." It was Gary Gunderson. At that moment, Joey felt cold steel on the back of his neck.

"I'll take that phone," a deep voice behind him said. "Toss it back."

Blum had finished with Francine and Brady who were compiling lists to finish up for the day. When Blum finally got back to his phone, he saw that Joey had left a voicemail message and two texts. He also noticed that John had texted him earlier; since John only texted,

Blum texted him right back.

Instantly, Blum got a warning text from John. He ran out of the cider house to catch Brady before he left.

"Can you stay a minute?" Blum shouted to him. "We fear that Joey has met with some trouble." Shortly after that, Blum received Joey's text with the address of the diner. Blum noted that it was on the highway leading out of Reno toward Lake Tahoe. He made another call to the small private airfield and then called Brady over.

"There's a plane waiting for you at the address I'm texting you. I need you to fly to Reno; I'll text you the details."

Early the next morning, Blum and Francine were planning the day in the farmhouse in between breakfast and news snippets from all around the world. But not all the news was bad.

Blum explained: "The Good Book says the Great and Dreadful day is coming, but we need to remember that sometimes it's a Great Day! I just got some good news from Martina; she's in Romania of all places, and she has a trainload of pilgrims: Jews from Siberia, Ukrainians, Byelorussians, regular Russians, Czechs, Poles, and a collection of others from all over Eastern Europe.

"So while the Russians and Ukrainians are turning up the violence toward each other just north of there, her group is making their exit," he said.

"What about Brady? Did he find Joey?" Francine asked as she finished cleaning up the kitchen.

"All I know is that he called Bleazard, his old boss—the newer, kinder Bleazard—and persuaded him to join Brady on the plane. They should already be there following Joey's tracks."

They were already hot on his trail. Brady had been tracking the phone calls to Joey's phone from the perp as well as two calls from Blum to helped him create a partial 'bread crumb trail' for Joey. Bleazard used his Sheriff's ID to gain cooperation from the Washoe County Sheriff's Department. The waitress in the diner in Verdi did confirm that she saw Joey get in a dark sedan after the tow truck left. Bleazard convinced the Washoe deputy to file it as a possible kidnapping so that they could get statewide help.

Brady employed the Find My Phone app to see if they could get any idea as to where Joey was and if he was okay.

Joey had no idea where he was. After he felt the barrel of the gun, he was given a dark hood to put over his head, and they drove through the night to an undisclosed location. He was deposited in a locked bedroom with an attached bath and no windows; he assumed it was a basement because he could hear footsteps and conversations above him.

They left him with a package of granola bars, some old books, and several ancient copies of Reader's Digest. He got some sleep on an old mattress without any sheets, pillows, or blankets. The room had a musty smell and was covered in dust.

The furnishings consisted of a bookcase made with cinder blocks and a pair of 6-foot long 2 x 8s, a cheap lamp, and the mattress and springs. Spartan to say the least.

A while later, he heard the front door open and people walk in. A conversation commenced. There were at least four people. His captors had left a cheap walkie-talkie with him. It squawked and hissed, and a voice cracked and said, "You enjoying your stay, Joseph?"

He didn't answer. He had no intention of cooperating with them, and while there was no window in the bedroom where he was, there was a closet in the bathroom filled with old cleaning supplies: Clorox, insect spray, and even paint.

First, he pulled the bed over against the door, stacked the bricks behind it along with the few books that were in the room. Then he jammed a 2 x 8 just below the doorknob at an angle with the other end against the leg of the bed. He heard the voice telling him to cooperate, and they were coming soon to chat with him.

This ain't no chat room, he told himself and went in the bathroom, locked it, and used the other 2 x 8 to jam that door shut, too. These are Mickey Mouse, fly-by-the-seat-of-the-pants kidnappers, he told himself. Gross amateurs. Am I whistling in the graveyard? He didn't know. He removed all the contents of the linen closet, stacked it all in front of the door, but kept a can of spray paint and a can of insect killer with him.

He was certain he could kick through the sheetrock of the back wall of the closet, assuming there was another room and not concrete on the other side. The hanging ceiling in the bedroom revealed it was built in the corner of the house.

Joey heard more noise coming from the walkie-talkie. This time it sounded like a warning: co-operate or suffer the consequences. "No, you suffer the consequences," he said out loud.

Joey started working on the Sheetrock, pushing first, trying to be as quiet as he could. With a screwdriver he found in the bathroom vanity, he was able to poke a hole in the Sheetrock, revealing a furnace and utility room on the other side; he saw daylight streaming in. With the screwdriver, he was able to weaken the wall enough to punch a hole open for a better view.

By creating another set of holes on the other side, he weakened that too. He heard two sets of footsteps, then three, running down the stairs. First, there was knocking, then yelling, and a lot more noise, which gave him just the opportunity he needed to kick out the bottom of the Sheetrock. He closed the closet door behind him and locked it behind him.

Finally, he was able to bend the Sheetrock enough to squeeze through on his belly. In the other room, they were trying to break through his barricade, so far unsuccessful. But, there was another barricade behind him in the bathroom.

He pulled himself into the furnace room, looked around and

saw another set of frightened eyes staring back at him!

Blum picked up his cellphone. It was Brady. "Bad news, Boss. It looks like Joey was kidnapped, and according to the phone number we were able to trace the call, and it did come from Gary Gunderson. But, it wasn't from Nevada; it came from Oregon. We were able to follow their digital tracks heading north," Brady explained.

"You got help from local authorities?"

"We do. Bleazard used his badge and influence to get the Nevada State Police, as well as their counterparts in Oregon and California, involved too. We hope that the FBI will jump on it as well because it's now probably an interstate felony," Brady said.

"Good, I'm going to call Gunderson's daddy and get him grounded if he isn't already."

He had an idea rolling around in his head, that is, if Joey gets out unharmed.

The big brown eyes belonged to a young Native American girl about 12, Joey figured. He introduced himself, whispering, "Hi, my name's Joey. Don't be scared. Some bad guys locked me in that bedroom. I'm sorry I kicked a hole in your wall. I was just trying to get out. They kidnapped me! Are you okay?"

They both could hear the pounding and screaming from the hallway. Joey assumed his kidnappers still hadn't been able to get in the bedroom. She nodded, still wide-eyed. They were both in the corner behind the water heater.

"What's your name?" Joey asked.

"Belle," she answered.

"Is this your house?"

"It's my granny's, but she died. My aunt was tending me, and then her boyfriend came with the mean men, so I hid down here."

"I want to try to get out the window. Do you want to come?" Joey asked her.

"I can't get the window open," Belle said.

"Maybe I can help," he said.

She was right. The small basement window was painted shut, but he did have his screwdriver. It was a Philips. He looked around and walked to the cabinet on the wall, opened it, and found all kinds of tools, including a crowbar. On the top shelf was a gray case.

He pulled it down and found a pistol inside, just a .22 caliber purse-sized revolver, but it was loaded with four rounds. There was a small box of cartridges which he emptied into his pocket. He hid the pistol in his waistband, untucked his shirt, and grabbed the crowbar. In short order, he had the window open.

It was so small!

But not too small for Belle.

"Belle, I am going to lift you up so you can run away. First, where are we? I was blindfolded and got here late last night."

"We're on the Rez," she said.

"The Rez?"

"The Walker River Paiute Reservation," she said. He could tell his captors were making progress, and he needed to depart ASAP!

"Sweetie, are we in Nevada?"

She nodded. "Right in the middle."

"By Reno?" She shook her head. "Las Vegas?"

"No, we're outside Schurz, but there's not much here. Fallon is up the road about an hour by car, maybe less if my uncle is driving, but he's a bad driver. But, you could borrow my aunt's bicycle. It's behind the tin shed right there," she said pointing to the left behind an old elm tree. "If it's locked up, put in the number 1-3-1-3. You promise to bring it back?" He nodded and then helped Belle out.

She looked left and right and then motioned to him to come out and grabbed his hands as he squeezed himself through, but not before he had knocked over a can of varnish in the process. It spilled next to the water heater and ran toward the flame. Joey looked back, but there's nothing he could do.

He saw flames and smoke coming out the window as he ran around behind the shed, unlocked the bike, and saw Belle running up the road. She turned and waved, but kept going. He told her before she left to call the police; she said she would.

"Dial 9-1-1!"

On the bike there was a helmet with a red bandanna which he used to conceal himself, adjusted the seat, and started peddling behind the house on a trail surrounded by old, rusty trailer homes and an occasional unpainted frame house. It was a bleak, sad landscape here, and he vowed he would return with more than just the mountain bike. Behind him, there was a rising column of smoke, growing bigger by the second. He stayed on side roads and dirt paths, avoiding the highway. He knew they'd be looking for him, whoever they were. In any case, he knew that they were in Gunderson's employ. That guy was out of his mind!

But right now, Joey was happy that he was out of Gunderson's sight. He had been peddling for an hour-and-a-half now through sagebrush and mesquite, paralleling the two-lane Veterans Memorial

Highway, heading north toward Fallon, Nevada. But there was trouble ahead. He just passed the sign telling travelers that they were now coming up on Russell's Pass.

Maybe he should have just stayed behind and let his captors do whatever they wanted to him because this was definitely torture!

The trail of breadcrumbs Brady was following now had turned south from I-80 at Fernley and then south toward Fallon. Beyond that was Schurz and the Walker River Paiute Indian Reservation. Bleazard had dropped Brady off at a Big-O store where the wrecker had taken Joey's truck for tire repair, and he had continued on into the Reno Police Headquarters to check scanners and reports of any kind.

When Brady reported where the phone trail led to, he called the Sheriff's offices and police departments along the route. Then, he came across a report from the Walker River Tribal Police. He called Bleazard immediately.

"How soon will the truck be ready?"

Brady replied, "They're just mounting the tires back on right now. Not too long."

"Good," Bleazard said. "I'm heading toward Schurz, Nevada, the seat of the Walker River Indian Reservation. An Indian girl said a white man named 'Joey' helped her escape from a house that had caught on fire, and the man said he had been kidnapped; the report said he borrowed her aunt's bicycle and pedaled away."

"Holy Moley!" Brady said. "I'll leave as soon as they're done."

Bleazard continued. "Tribal police and the fire department are there now. I'm following the State Police there. I'll text you the address. I'll take the direct southeast route. You drive to Fallon and then south to Schurz."

❑ ❑ ❑ ❑ ❑

Blum read Brady's text message to Francine that they were on Joey's trail. It would be at least two hours before they would arrive on the scene. Marta had reported that her train was supposed to leave Brașov, Romania and was headed to the Tălăşmani Tunnel in Transylvania, final destination unknown, but somehow Blum believed it was linked to Salem Hot Springs.

"I would love to see the road and rail map showing how everything's connected," Blum said. "Somehow it's like the Chutes and Ladders game."

He changed gears and kept going. "I got this news from Martina. Her group is on a one-way trip! She said there were about 160 souls on four passenger cars aboard her 'Transworld Express,' speaking close to a dozen different languages."

"Wow!" Francine said.

They were back in the great room in the farmhouse taking a break after a busy morning online, checking and sending emails, and forwarding more recommendations up the chain of command. Francine now had the task of aggregating all the daily news–good and bad from around the world, but mostly bad–for Blum to read and then pass it all on to other interested parties.

She had finished cleaning up, wiped her hands, and sat down.

"You said you had something new for me," Blum said.

She smiled and then said. "Well, I could give you my aggregated 'wars and rumors of wars' daily briefing, but instead I've found something more fascinating and less dreary on a cable show called 'Legends, Myths, and Nonsense,' originally produced and funded by the Skeptics Society. Have you ever heard of Joseph Campbell?" Francine asked.

"Sure, his book was called *The Hero with a Thousand Faces*. An atheist, Campbell believed that the story of a son of God sent to earth to be its savior was somehow embedded in mankind's DNA, and in his own bizarre logic, found that somehow easier to believe than there actually was a God Creator," he said.

"He found dozens of ancient myths and legends that supported that story."

Then Francine explained what she found. "Well, what is weird is that in these legends there are also stories of divine destinations, places where the elect go. Quoting what I discovered, it says that 'the hero's adventure begins in the ordinary world. He must depart from the ordinary world when he receives a call to adventure.'

"With the help of a mentor, the hero must cross a guarded threshold, leading him to a supernatural world, where familiar laws and order do not apply. There, the hero will embark on a road of trials, where he is tested along the way. The archetypal hero is sometimes assisted by allies. As the hero faces the ordeal, he encounters the greatest challenge of the journey. Upon rising to the challenge, the hero will receive a reward or boon. Campbell's theory of the monomyth continues with the inclusion of a metaphorical death and resurrection. The hero must then decide to 'return with this boon to the ordinary world,'" she said.

"So, that's when they bring up Joey and Dana's TV appearances and conclude that they just 'borrowed it all from history.' Am I right?" Blum surmised.

'Exactly," she said. "Then the co-host goes off-script and says, 'Well, that's your theory: that it's all made up. But what if it's all actually based on real places and real events?'

"Then he quotes several biblical passages and argues. 'Look around; it's all happening right before our eyes exactly as it was prophesied. You sound like all the people who made fun of Noah just before they drowned!"

Blum laughed. "Yep, it looks like even the skeptics are looking for a little 'old-time religion.' Speaking of that, I'll bet Joey's been doing some serious praying himself over the past couple of days. And I believe that Brady will somehow be the answer to his prayers."

"Time will tell," Francine said.

Again, Francine the Faithful was proven right. After he had turned right and passed through Fallon, Brady was traveling south on the Veterans Memorial Highway when he passed a cyclist leaning against a telephone pole with a hand on the handlebars. The cyclist waved as Orange Crush with Brady inside drove by. Brady hit the brakes and flipped around right in front of Joey, exhausted and drenched in sweat, but at least he'd been rescued!

"How did you find me?" Joey asked, wiping his eyes on his sleeve.

"I think you prayed me here," Brady said. "There are cops at the house you burned down."

"Oh no! It wasn't on purpose. Burned to the ground?"

"Don't know. Wanna go see?" Brady asked.

"Let's sit down and think about it," Joey said. He threw the bike in the back of the truck and hopped in. "Got anything to drink?" Brady handed him a Coke Zero. It was warm, but Joey was thirsty.

"You know, it's a good thing I brought Bleazard with me. He flashed his badge around Reno and got some interdepartmental cooperation; the tribal police reported that a young girl called the police after a 'kidnapped man' helped her out a window.

"Then we put two and two together and after I got some new tires for the Orange Crush, I raced down here. Bleazard's probably already at the house."

"Call him and see what's going on. And, call Blum; he's probably worried sick."

Blum had been worried, but he had faith in Joey and confidence they were all doing the right thing. The world was getting darker by the minute, and more and more people were looking for an exit, some promised land. Corruption was rampant in the highest places everywhere.

He wondered, How do you fix all that? Blum didn't want to think about the consequences. Like everyone else, he had to have faith that Higher Powers have things under control.

With Brady at the wheel, they arrived on the scene with police cars and fire trucks everywhere. Six men were sitting on the lawn cross-legged with their hands in their laps concealing handcuffs and leg irons. Joey had told Brady he doubted he could ID any of the men on the grass. The house looked to be a total loss.

Brady told Joey to stay in the truck while he went over to talk to

Bleazard who was with two other officers and a middle-aged Native American woman. Bleazard saw Brady coming and excused himself.

They stood next to the pumper truck, talking quietly.

"How's Joey doing?" Bleazard asked.

"He's exhausted, been bicycling uphill for a couple of hours, but he's okay. He didn't get a good look at any of your suspects on the ground. Where's Gunderson?" Brady asked.

"Good question," he said. "Nobody's been Mirandized, but they're all as guilty as hell. They know it, and they know that we know it. He's not here, and we haven't talked to them."

"Joey told me a young woman was driving the car he got into, but he didn't see her when we drove up," Brady said.

"She's not the woman standing by the house," Joey said. And because the guy in the backseat put a hood over his head, he didn't see any of their faces, but he did see the hand of his captor. He had a Jersey or New York accent, and he's no Native American. Joey wants to talk to the owner of the house, and the Tribal Chairman, if he's around," Brady said. "And, he gave me this." Brady handed Bleazard the hood that Joey wore.

"Okay. I'll be right back."

Brady returned to the truck, found Joey asleep, and woke him up. In a minute, Bleazard re-turned.

"They're taking these lowlifes to Yerington, just west of here. There'll be a hearing at the Lyon County Courthouse in the morning. They'll spend the night in jail," Bleazard said to Brady.

"A Lt. Dodge will be over a minute to talk to Joey. The girl spoke with her aunt. She's the one over there. She works at the Pioneer

Crossing Casino in Yerington. She worked a night shift and came back when the house was on fire. She's the one who pressed charges on behalf of a minor, Belle. Belle was alone when the man came in last night with Joey. Belle is our star witness. She likes Joey. Let's stay overnight in Yerington and meet in the morning. I've booked a place in the Best Western."

"Thanks, man!" Brady said. Officer Dodge walked over to the truck.

"Are you Joseph Kunz?" Dodge said. "I understand you had a hard night. Can you talk to me in the squad car?"

"Yes, sir. May I first speak with Belle's aunt? I have her bicycle."

"Sure."

Joey exited the truck slowly. He needed a shower and a bed, but he grabbed the mountain bike and walked over to the woman standing next to the willow tree in front of the burnt-out house.

"Excuse me, ma'am?"

"Yes?" said the middle-aged woman wearing a Pioneer Crossing Casino golf shirt and a name tag that said, Shirley Fox. She tried to smile and held out a limp hand.

"You must be Belle's aunt. I'm Joey Kunz, and I spent the night locked up in the basement. She said this bike belongs to you. She's a sweet, brave girl." Shirley took the bicycle.

"Yes, she is! Thank you so much for getting her out of that place. I'm usually home by 1 am, but with all the sickness, I had to stay until 10 am. So sorry about what happened to you."

"I'm okay, but your house isn't. I'm going to take care of that," Joey said.

"Well, I think Momma did have fire insurance, buts it's kind of beaten up. I was planning on me and Belle moving. I'm all she has, and she's all I have."

"Let's meet tomorrow morning. We'll be in Yerington."

"That's good because Belle and I have to be at the hearing. You, too?"

"Yes, but I also wanted to also speak with the Tribal Chairman if that's possible."

She nodded and smiled. "Well, we're friends, and he'll be at the hearing tomorrow as well." Joey thanked her, walked over to the squad car, and talked with the officer. They set an appointment for tomorrow morning at the Courthouse at 9.

Brady drove the Orange Crush, Joey gazed out the window, and the two of them turned west toward Yerington for a much-needed rest.

❏ ❏ ❏ ❏ ❏

The first thing in the morning, Joey was in a small room with Lieutenant Dodge and an assistant county attorney. Bleazard and Brady were waiting outside.

"Tell us what happened two nights ago outside Reno," the prosecutor said. Joey mentioned the flat tires, the woman who offered him a ride, the man with the gun in the backseat, and everything that happened the next morning. But, the most revealing bit was the phone call from Gunderson.

The officer showed Joey a collection of cell phones. "Which one is yours?"

"That one," he said. "Where did you find it?"

"On one of the men sitting over there," he said, pointing at the hand-cuffed men sitting on the grass.

"He's not a Native American, is he?"

He shook his head. "Could you unlock the phone for us?"

Joey did so, and the prosecutor scrolled down his recent calls and found one that came in at 9:35 pm, and showed it to Joey. It was the last one on the phone. He called for an investigator to come in and spoke to him. "Go trace back where this call came from, please. And hurry back." Then, he asked Joey. "Who made that call?"

"It was Gary Gunderson."

"You're sure?"

"Yes, that's right after I had a gun shoved up against my neck and a bag placed over my head. What's more, this is not the first time that Gunderson came after me. Ask Brady Owens and Sergeant Bleazard outside. Gunderson was my boss, and he tried to pin embezzlement charges on me. When we confronted him with it and informed his father about his misdeeds, Gunderson came clean with the police. The charges against me were dropped. Then his father, Greg Gunderson, reimbursed me for my stock options, which his son had tried to invalidate. Long story, but it's all true. I thought we had seen the last of him. I was wrong. He's just a spoiled trust-fund brat who's never taken responsibility for anything he's ever done. One of his partners turned on him and gave us the evidence we needed to clear it up," Joey said.

"How much was your settlement with Mr. Gunderson Senior?

"Twelve million dollars. Have you found him?" The prosecutor looked at the inspector.

"Well, we think we know where he is. A private jet left the Fallon airport yesterday about an hour after the fire and flew to Mazatlan, Mexico. Extradition is spotty with Mexico," he admitted.

"What about the woman, the driver of the car?"

"Well, I was about to take you to a line-up? Want to look at some young ladies?" Dodge asked.

"Sure, but I have another idea. My attorney, who is also my superior in our campaign, sent us a text earlier that he has spoken with Greg Gunderson, likely owner of that plane, and the one who maintains his son's lifestyle. My attorney, Jonathan Blum . . ."

"Jonathan Blum, THE Jonathan Blum?" the officer said.

"Yeah, but maybe there's more than one," Joey said, trying to deflect attention away from his boss. "Anyway, we have a solution that is beneficial to justice, to me, and to the Walker River Paiute Tribe, as well as the family whose house burned down yesterday, which is my fault."

"You probably shouldn't admit that," the attorney said.

"Well, I knocked over a can of paint, as I told Lt. Dodge earlier, when I squeezed out of a window to elude my captors. I had blockaded a locked door in the bedroom where I had been left, broke through the wallboard into the adjoining furnace room, and helped a young Paiute girl get out the window. Then I followed her. That's when the fire started. That's why I want to talk to Shirley Fox, her niece Belle, and the Tribal Chairman later this morning. Then after that, and after Blum has spoken with Gunderson Sr., then I'll share the rest of my plan with you," Joey explained.

'Let's go to a line-up," Dodge said.

"My first one," Joey said. "Kind of like a beauty pageant?"

"This one is," the inspector said, grinning.

Five days later, Blum flew to Nevada to join Joey. Brady and Blea-zard had begun learning a new trade: farming. Blum was finally retiring as a farmer and returning to his home "in the hills." But today he was representing Joey in his efforts to settle his estate and the hearing in Yerington was going to be the capstone.

They were waiting at the Fallon airport to meet Greg Gunderson. First, they were driving to Schurz to meet the Tribal Chairman, Christopher Friend, who was going to give them a tour of the reservation and look at possible sites for a new manufacturing plant, a residential development, and a technical school.

Then, there was lunch at the Pioneer Crossing Casino and a chance to meet the tribal leaders to talk about economic development at the Walker River Reservation and other reservations in the West.

At 3 p.m., the County Commissioner, the mayors of both Yerington and Schurz, and the Tribal Chairman were in the commission chambers with news organizations from all over Nevada along with a few from outside the state.

Chairman Friend made the introductions, then explained the reason for the conference.

"One of the interesting aspects of living in the high desert, especially here in the Great Basin area of Nevada and Utah are wildfires. As you know, our native forebears thrived in this place by living on what nature provided. And to some, it looks barren. But, something interesting happens when a fire goes through an area. Environmentalists call them 'serotinous' cones . . . pine cones that hang on a pine tree for years. Some pine species have developed very thick, hard cones that are literally glued shut with a strong resin. But in a fire, they can be broken open and still survive.

"These pinion pines produce a staple that our people have thrived on for centuries, which is why we still celebrate the pine nut harvest every fall, even though lately the pine cone harvest has been a little skimpy.

"Why am I talking about wildfires and pine nuts? Maybe you know that we had a fire in Schurz over the weekend, and it involved a serious crime, the loss of a house, and criminal charges that I am told are being resolved with some guilty pleas. You can read all about it in the local paper. A victim in that episode and an interested party are here to explain how sometimes blessings can come out of bad beginnings, like pine nuts growing more abundantly after a wildfire. In view of that curiosity of nature, I'd like to introduce Mr. Joseph Kunz and Mr. Greg Gunderson."

The group reacted with some applause, but since many of them knew what was coming and were excited to hear the good news, they waited. Joey started it off.

"Hi, I'm Joseph Kunz. I've been in the news and created some controversy over my beliefs, but that's not what I'm going to talk about today. I have learned a few things in the last week or so. First, it's no fun to be kidnapped. Second, riding a bike up a mountain from Schurz to Fallon when you're out of shape is almost as bad as being kidnapped. But, the third thing I learned is that technology doesn't always benefit everyone. I arrived in Schurz in the middle of the night with a hood over my head.

"Then I met Belle and Shirley Fox and my eyes were opened. Large corporations build plants and factories and create jobs–good-paying jobs in faraway places while Paiutes, Shoshones, Utes, Navajos, Shivwits, Sioux, and others are most often bypassed and neglected.

"I think it's important that these cultures be preserved, that the languages don't die, and that the native people who live there aren't dependent on government handouts from the tribe, casino proceeds, or federal aid. So today, as part of my effort to liquidate my estate, I am granting approximately ten million dollars to the tribal economic development plan. It's a lot of money, but it's not nearly enough to do what really needs to be done. So, I asked a friend of mine, Greg Gunderson, chairman of the Gunderson Technology Group, commonly known as GTG, to help. I'd like to introduce Mr. Greg Gunderson."

As Joey sat down, he saw in the far back his old boss, Gary Gunderson himself, fresh from Mexico, sitting between Lt. Dodge and the assistant DA who had been able to extradite him overnight. Gary's father had repossessed the Gulfstream, transferred his son's trust fund into municipal bonds, and got an agreement with Mexico's attorney general to allow officials from the State of Nevada to bring his son back to the US.

For the first time in a long time, Gary Gunderson would take responsibility for his behavior in exchange for a liberal plea deal that Blum had helped work out on his behalf.

Greg Gunderson then detailed his contribution to the Paiute community that included the construction of a new factory and warehouse to make, inventory, and ship various computer and cell-phone accessories like bags, phone holders, covers, and other items that were originally going to be made in Indonesia. Its total, about $35 million in value. Its benefit would be 300 new jobs right on the reservation.

Item number two: With help from a friend in "Big Tech," a new Walker River Technical School was to be built on the west side of the Rez near a new subdivision of affordable houses. The school would probably employ at least another 200 people, Gunderson estimated.

Finally, Joey's last investment would be in a new home built at a more desirable location for Shirley and Belle Fox. Along with the house, Joey was funding Belle's college education.

After everyone cleared out, Joey said goodbye to Belle and Shirley, thanked the chairman and Dodge, and the DA. Then he and Brady walked to the truck. Bleazard and Blum were flying back on the jet. At the door of the county complex, Greg Gunderson hugged his son as Gary left with the officers. Greg waved at Joey, then turned and left.

"Let's hit the road, Brady. I'll drive," Joey said.

Thanks to Blum and Rachel, the sale on Joey and Dana's house closed. He kept his promise to Dana and had the landscaping finished. Loose ends were tied up, like student loans and mortgages, along with keeping promises, like the one he made to Dana to help Blythe, the singer, get an education and a decent place for herself and her mother.

Joey, Brady, and Blum had been stacking boxes, cleaning out the barn, and the cider house all day long while Francine was busy in the office summarizing reports on all their prospects as she called them, before a meeting at 6 p.m. They sat down on some hay bales to take a break. Joey felt the need to confess.

"I'm leaving naked, just like I came," he complained to Blum.

"I can't say it doesn't hurt because it does. Intellectually, I know it's an investment, albeit an eternal one. Still, I am tempted to look back, but then I remember Lot's wife."

'Or the story of Ananias and Sapphira," Blum added.

"What's that all about?" Brady asked.

"Kind of a sad but dramatic teaching lesson told in Acts, Chapter 5," Blum explained. "The early Christians in Jerusalem had agreed to pool all their wealth together to benefit the whole congregation, but when a married couple sold their land, they kept some of it back, hid it from the others. When they were discovered, first the husband and then the wife dropped dead. On the spot."

"That's kind of harsh," Brady said.

"By today's standards, maybe, but that's the problem, isn't it, Brady?" Blum asked.

"What is?"

"Today's standards."

Joey stepped in. "I've been doing a lot of thinking about meeting our own expectations of ourselves after having studied the Beatitudes these last four months. I used to think that when Christ taught the new order of things He replaced the harsher 'eye-for-an-eye" Mosaic Law with something softer, kinder, and easier.

"This law of performances that Moses got from Mount Sinai, those 613 commandments that the Jews were told to follow seemed much harder to obey than Christ's admonition to forgive your neighbor, turn the other cheek, give someone who wants just one cloak two. We focus on the eight Beatitudes, or blessings, that come as a result of living the higher law, such as '*blessed are the merciful, the peacemakers, the meek in heart, and those that mourn*' and so on.

"But, when we examine what is required of us in all three chapters of the Sermon on the Mount, we realize Moses's laws were the easier path. Just do those 613 things, and you'll be okay. Now we must focus on our intentions and motivations, not just on our outward performances."

"Like what?" Brady asked.

"Here's one that's been bugging me ever since I experienced Gunderson's wrath. Anger. Christ said whoever is angry at his brother without cause is in peril.

"Another one is, 'Agree with thine adversary quickly.' Or, '*Take heed that ye do not your alms in public.* Heck, I just did that with my speech in Yerington. 'Look how great I am!'

"This one is particularly hard for all of us, especially politicians and for me: '*Love your enemies, bless them that curse you, do good to them that hate you, and pray for them which despitefully use you, and persecute you.* Or kidnap you!"

Brady had been taking mental notes of this conversation and had one of his own to add. "And how about, '*Whosoever looketh on a woman to lust after her hath committed adultery with her already in his heart.*"

Blum stifled a laugh. "Yes, and that's the one that Jimmy Carter admitted to on national television, bless his heart. Of course, that was before your time. But, here's something you should never forget. The Master also said, *'Seek ye first the kingdom of God, and His righteousness; and all these things shall be added unto you.'* From what I see, you're all 'laying up for yourselves treasures in heaven,' just as He commanded. But we're all sinners, and but for Him and His sacrifice, we'd be doomed. He's the Good News!"

Joey smiled, and Brady gave him a back slap.

Blum looked at his protégés. "Well, boys, before we start lifting things again, I just have to ask you, Joey, how do you feel about Gary Gunderson now? After all, his plea bargain did give him a reduced sentence, plus a year volunteering on the Rez. I understand he and his dad spoke with you. What did they say?"

"He seemed sorry and contrite. And his dad looked happy and thanked me that his Prodigal Son had finally returned, but it's still too early to feast on the fatted calf. We'll see. As for me, I'm just glad it's over. Time to move on," Joey said.

"It is. Let's finish this up before Francine has her report ready."

Bleazard joined the four of them in the farmhouse. Francine had prepared a PowerPoint presentation, and Blum had a roaring fire going. She had decorated the place for Thanksgiving, and her sister and her girls were back in the family room watching a movie.

Very homey, Joey thought.

Francine started her slideshow. First came the theme, a scripture from Matthew. "Many are called but few are chosen."

"At first glance, the theme I've chosen might be a downer that somehow everything we've done has fallen short. Why can't everybody see what we see? Isn't it obvious?" Francine said. Jonathan and I have had many conversations about this. He's told me over and over again, 'You have got to take the long view,' and he's right," Francine said.

Up came another slide of a wide shot of innumerable people walking on a path, one after the other with the headline. "The Long Journey to Glory."

"We're all travelers on the path, some are farther ahead than others. The key is to stay on the path," she said as she changed to another slide with a graph of people who had been reached by various media, the website, the podcasts, the first TV interview, the Tulsa TV show, and thousands of emails sent out. Then she showed the number of invitations that went out, including hundreds from people in Salem.

"As I noted, many are called, but few are chosen. And of the many invitations that were sent to our respondents, only about a third accepted them. That's still a lot. And, they're from all over the world, as you can see," she said as her next slide came up

"Here is the schedule for actual departures from the train station to Salem Crossing over the next three months; the people who have settled their accounts and met the qualifications first will be next up. As you can see, here are the departure times and places. Jonathan has something to say." Brady had left a moment earlier to invite Francine's sister and girls to join the group.

As they arrived, Blum began, "We'd never have gotten this far without Francine's help sending out invitations, checking lists, and following up on inquiries. Since I depend on her so much, and since

I'm leaving too, her job is finished. So here's your family pass, Francine, along with the schedule and tickets for all of you! We all leave in three weeks." The girls jumped up and down, Francine and her sister hugged, and then they embraced Blum.

"Next up, since he will soon be a father, and he has done all that he can do, Joey is joining us too. Now as far as Brady and the Inspector go . . ."

"Hey, I'm retired," Bleazard said. "Just call me by my first name." They all looked around and then focused on Brady. Francine looked at him. "Okay, what is it?" Brady hesitated and looked at his old boss.

"It's Sergeant. Sergeant Bleazard," Brady said. They all laughed.

"You can call me Teddy," Bleazard said. "Like the bear. My real name is Theodore Roosevelt Bleazard like the guy on Mt. Rushmore, the one in the back."

"This man has a sense of humor!" Francine wisecracked.

Blum cleared his throat. Time to get back to business. Not everyone had a ticket . . . yet.

"Well, how about our officers of the law here? What about them? These two fine men are now in the apple business. We will be training them in the art and science of horticulture in the next three weeks as we wrap up business.

"Joey has made a generous contribution to our operating capital which should keep them going well past harvest time next year. Then there will be more invitations and more travel arrangements to be made. By then, these two men should be ready to join us, with spouses, I hope.

"We have a few loose ends to attend to in the coming days, Rachel being number one. That's all for now," Blum said as he concluded the meeting.

A few days later, Blum and Joey had matters to attend to at the Legacy print shop in town that was selling an old letterpress and several cases full of type and other equipment. Blum left Joey with the owner as he went to a lunch meeting.

"So, tell me where you want this shipped," Mallory, the owner, said.

"Here's the address. We'll pay for the crating, disassembly, and shipping to the site," Joey said.

"This is up in the mountains by that old rickety railroad depot. Really?"

"Really," Joey said smiling. "One other thing. I'm giving you another check for training here before I go."

"You're going to run this press? It's not that easy," Mallory said.

"Hey, I write code, and that's not easy either, and I made a lot of money doing it. Now I want to do something real that includes real handwork like artisans of old. How much do you want for ten days of intensive training?" The man thought for a moment, finding a way to make money from this foolish man.

"Four hundred dollars a day, not a penny less!" Mallory demanded.

"Okay," Joey said and wrote him a check for $4000, ripped it out of his checkbook, and handed it to him. "That's fair." He knew what Mallory was thinking. I should have charged a lot more! Joey was right.

"Can we start now?" Joey asked. "I can't return until my ride comes back."

"Why not," Mallory grumbled. "Put on an apron, or you'll ruin that fancy shirt. Follow me."

Blum was waiting at Luigi's, an old-style Italian restaurant that was big on portions and calories. Why not, Jonathan smiled to himself, I'm immortal! Rachel was late, just like the first time they met when he was with Walter.

He ordered a salad, some bread sticks, and a refillable Coke Zero with lots of ice. The place smelled like a curing house for ham, salami, and Parmesan cheese. The smell alone could fill you up, he thought. Some things about life in this Fallen World he would miss, but not Italian food. He had decided to open up his own Trattoria in Salem Crossing called "Giovanni's." He had equipment headed to the train depot too, along with several crates of big Parmesan cheese wheels, $800 apiece thanks to Joey's largess.

He was about to text Rachel when she walked in.

"Sorry. I guess I say that a lot," Rachel said.

The waiter came to the table.

"Rigatoni with butter and pesto sauce and a Pellegrino," she said. "With gas."

"You've been here before," Blum observed.

"Many times when I was working for Joey. How is he?"

"He's great. Got kidnapped. Got away. Now he's going into the printing business, buying himself a hundred-year-old letterpress with hand-set type. No desk-top publishing for him, no sir. Dana is getting big, twins, you know."

She smiled. "Yeah, I heard."

Their food came. They played with it, and then Blum pushed his aside.

"Rachel, what's going on? Walter is worried. We all are."

She looked around, tried to wash her worries away with the Pellegrino, then looked down for a moment until she felt Blum's penetrating eyes on her.

"I'm worried, Jonathan," she said.

"About what?"

"Everything. How I'll fit in with people there who are more suited than myself, more righteous than me . . ."

"That's not it, is it?"

She hesitated. "There's somebody else, somebody other than Tanner. And that person thinks we're all wacky, that the world is changing, that we're going to have a 'Big Reset' . . ."

"Well, he's right about that," Blum said.

"Unfortunately, I know that deep inside. But I can't stop worrying about all those people, millions, maybe billions of them."

"Like your friend."

"Exactly. I feel like Mrs. Lot leaving Sodom and Gomorrah. I'll probably look back."

"She's been in a lot of our conversations lately, no pun intended. Joey and I had a similar discussion a month ago."

"Wasn't that cruel, though, and painful for all of those people in those cities to be burned to death?"

"What would be more cruel, to allow hundreds, maybe many, many more of God's children to enter those places as innocent babes and then be subject only to evil, never being able to choose the good, because it was not available to them? They would not have been able to exercise their free will. Which is worse?'"

"I get that," she said in response. "But something my friend Garth said has been eating at me. 'Doubting believers,' he said. "Either God is vicious because He does not want to prevent evil, or He is weak because He cannot."

"That's a worn-out component of the old Atheist's creed, and it doesn't hold for two reasons. First, it assumes that God created everything out of nothing, including evil. That is the ex nihilio theory, which is largely discounted by many modern thinkers.

"I happen to believe that evil, like goodness, has always been here; it's not forced on us unless we are in a position like the children in Sodom were, meaning we have no choice nor knowledge of a virtuous alternative.

"Second, how can we appreciate or understand this 'virtuous alternative' if there is no opposite, no evil opposite? Isn't that why we are here, to gain a knowledge of good and evil and their consequences by choosing one over the other?"

Blum pulled a well-worn card out of the collection in his coat pocket. "I've had this for a long time; it was written by an essayist I came across years ago, and I share it with people like you who are perplexed by this eternal question. I'll read it to you.

"'*No virtue could exist without its corresponding evil. . . .. In a world without evil—if such a world be really conceivable—all men would have perfect health, perfect intelligence, and perfect morals. No one could gain or impart information, each one's cup of knowledge being full. The temperature would forever stand at 70 degrees, both heat and cold being evil. A world without evil would be as toil without exertion, as light without darkness, as a battle with no antagonist. It would be a world without meaning.*'"

Rachel pondered that for a moment and smiled. "I like that. Maybe you can make me a copy," she said.

"I can do that."

Blum could see that her wheels were turning, and so he waited. "But . . ."

"There's always a 'but' . . .," he said with a smile.

"But what about a place like Salem where evil is banned?" Rachel asked.

"Evil is not banned there; remember Lucifer took a third of the host of heaven with him when he rebelled against God, and, of course, he was indeed cast out, John, the Revelator tells us.

"No, our destination is not a place where evil cannot enter unless people bring it with them. So we choose carefully. People are invited who have demonstrated that they, like you, choose to leave it behind."

Blum paused as he reached in his pocket, "And, if you choose to be with us, then this, dear, sweet Rachel, is your get-out-of-jail-free card, your exit papers, your ticket to Paradise," Blum said as he handed her the ticket.

"Be at the mountain train station in 17 days from now at noon with three suitcases. We depart at 1 pm."

A 20-passenger airport van was parked in the gravel outside the cider house. Georgia, Francine's sister, and the three girls had the far back bench seat of the van and were playing a game. The girls had come to grips with the reality of no more screens, no video games, no text messages. They were getting ready for 1925 and A Return to Normalcy, the new reality, the new reset.

Everyone else was in the cider house. The press and its accouterments, Blum's cheese balls, seasonings and crates of pasta, the noodle machine, and the pizza oven had all been loaded up along with Joey's press and type box, in the big truck idling behind the van. Drivers were getting impatient. Inside, Blum was giving last-minute instructions to Brady and Bleazard; he had everything written down, manual-style, for them to follow.

This place was his baby. His mission in the Fallen World was coming to an end, and he admitted he was going to miss the Honey Crisps, the Jonathans, and, of course, cider season.

But Blum couldn't look back. He had to set a good example. Francine was the most emotional. She looked at Brady as if he were a little brother; no, more like a son. Bleazard, stoic as usual in his Abraham Lincoln visage, tall and stooped, seemed illuminated; the new Bleazard now with friends and purpose.

With wet eyes, the travelers got in the van. Brady and Bleazard went out to say their goodbyes as the vehicles pulled away.

Blum stood near the stairs of the last car of the mountain express looking at his watch again. The engineer blew the whistle two more times. Steam was pouring out from the locomotive. Joey walked over to the stairs.

"Jonathan, you've got to get on. The conductor is coming. He's shutting all the doors and checking tickets."

"Five more minutes. I know she'll come. I know it!"

The whistle blew again. Just then, a taxi van came screaming up to the back of the train. It was Rachel! Joey jumped out to help Blum grab her luggage. There was a tall, dark young man giving her a hug, then she came running. They finally helped her onto the car and wrestled her huge, heavy suitcases onto the train.

And running around from the side was Walter, tears streaming down his face. He jumped in last and shut the door.

No conductor needed.

They were leaving the Fallen World.

It was Monday, Memorial Day. Joey and Dana could see everything in front of them from their second-story balcony. She had just put the twins, Jonathan and Maggie, down to sleep; Dana needed some herself.

She stood up in time for the unfurling of the colors as the band marched up to the square where their old brick town home stood, one of four on the west side.

Despite the two sycamores in front, they could see Old Glory being brought in by the color guard as the marching band prepared to perform the "Star-Spangled Banner." She put her hand over her heart.

At that moment, Joey spotted the two men carrying the colors to post them in the center of the park near the bandstand below them: a tall redheaded lieutenant and a shorter black-haired sergeant.

As the anthem began, the sergeant saluted the officer and raised the colors, but Joey didn't see that.

He was already bounding down the stairs at full speed. From across the square, a slight Asian woman was scampering to the same spot.

They both interrupted the ceremony at the same time, one hurling herself at her husband, the other embracing his father. Dana watched from the balcony, Oma from the porch.

The twins were sleeping soundly.

The Judge, Walter, Rachel, and Tanner were coming over later along with an unexpected guest.

It would be a memorable Memorial Day in Salem Springs.

THE END

EYE HATH NOT SEEN, NOR EAR HEARD,

NEITHER HAVE ENTERED INTO THE HEART OF MAN,

THE THINGS WHICH GOD HATH FOR THEM THAT LOVE HIM.

1 CORINTHIANS 1:9

APPENDIX & AFTERTHOUGHTS

THE INVITATION is admittedly a work of fiction, but it is a reminder of other people from other ages who picked up and moved
to a New World where they were free to live, to worship and conduct
their lives without interference from an intolerant majority.

There is no "New World," geographically speaking, where
people of faith can flee to today. As for myself, I can see a dystopia
growing before our very eyes where a "system of class and caste" as
Calvin Coolidge warned about, is being forced upon us, and where
many leaders of this movement wish to impose their will by force.

This "Dark Force" is antithetical to the principles of faith and
hope upon which this country was founded.

The British faced a crisis of enormous proportions during World
War II. Right after his country declared war on Nazi Germany, King
George VI broadcast a message of hope to the British people, quoting from a dialogue between a man and the Keeper of the Gate of
the Year. He said:

*"I said to the man who stood at the Gate of the Year: "Give me light that I
may tread safely into the Unknown, and he replied: 'Go ye out into the Darkness,
and put your hand in the hand of God. That shall be to you better than a light,
and safer than the known way.' "*

I wrote this book as a reminder of what earlier generations faced
and how they mustered the courage and made the necessary sacrifices to win the day. What the Keeper of the Gate said rings true
today more than ever: Putting our hands into the Hand of God and

trusting Him is "safer than the known way."

THE INVITATION offers more than food for thought: It appeals to our "better angels" in a time when angels are hard to come by. In addition to the paperback E-book, an audiobook is in the works.

See the website **www.theshiningcity.org** for more information.

PRESCIENT WORDS FROM PRESIDENT CALVIN COOLIDGE

President Calvin Coolidge makes a cameo appearance in The Invitation when we are reminded of a speech he gave in 1924. In the address, he asserted that *"government rests on religion . . .,' the claim to the right to freedom, the claim to the right to equality, with the resultant right to self-government—the rule of the people—have no foundation other than the common brotherhood of man derived from the common fatherhood of God. If this faith is set aside, the foundations of our institutions fail, the citizen is deposed from his high estate . . . society reverts to a system of class and caste, and the government, instead of being imposed from reason from within is imposed by force from without. Freedom and democracy would give way to despotism and slavery. I do not know of any adequate support for our form of government except that which comes from religion."*

—President Calvin Coolidge from an address to the Holy Name Society, Sept. 21, 1924, Washington, DC. (Go to the website, www.theshiningcity.org, and read the speech in its entirety in Backstories.

Thoughts on Being of "One Heart and One Mind"

In The Invitation , the main characters are driven to find a place where the people are "of one heart and one mind." What is the significance of that? Christ charged His followers "to be one, even as the Father and I are one." That's a hard thing to do, and as the scriptures say, it requires us to be "meek and lowly of heart." John Stuart Mill in his small book, *On Liberty*, advises his readers to admit, "I could be wrong;" I think that's a step in the right direction. Coolidge says that the mind of man should ever be free and notes the importance of tolerating the opinions of others be-cause no one person has the corner on truth. In other words, seek for it, and em-brace it, no matter the source, and then follow it, and see where it leads. And, I hope, as you read The Invitation , you will find en-lightenment, amusement, a reward at the end, and food for thought that you can chew on for a while. I wish you good reading, no matter the book. And I pray for our country, that the United States may become one nation, under God, and indivisible.

For more details about John Winthrop and the Puritan settlement in New England as well as background on our 30th President, Calvin Coolidge, as well as his first inaugural address, please refer to **www.theshiningcity.org/Backstories.**

GM Jarrard

GIVING CREDIT WHERE CREDIT IS DUE

I must thank so many friends, colleagues, and organizations whose contributions—whether they knew about it or not—helped me research and write my book.

First, I thank my wife of more than 53 years, Christie Halladay Jarrard, for her patience and forbearing as I buried myself in the basement office, reading, researching, writing and rewriting the text, and spent money that should have gone to my upkeep during the past nine months.

Thanks also to my muse and mentor, book guru Karen Christoffersen at BookWise Publishing for editing, proofing, and guidance in helping get the book ready for prime time.

As noted earlier, I express my appreciation for the inspiration and spiritual context to the writers, directors and producers of **THE CHOSEN AND ANGEL STUDIOS** whose series on the life of Christ and his disciples gave me so much hope during the dark days of last summer as I began writing my story. I must admit that I borrowed their idea of "paying it forward" as part of the plot of **THE INVITATION**. And., I must credit my use of the "pay-it-forward" concept from the series as well as the use of the concept "to bring your own bread and fishes—God will supply the rest." When Christ declared to his people "follow me," as depicted in their series, He meant all of us. So, the ultimate expression of gratitude should go to Him.

In Chapter 21, I paraphrased many of the ideas and sources that I found in the YouTube series produced by Dr. John West and his colleagues at the **DISCOVERY INSTITUTE** in Seattle, Washington. Their work on Intelligent Design, the fallacies of Darwinism, and the work and writings of C. S. Lewis should be the focus of believers everywhere who see the Divine every day, from a sunrise to the smile of a child. I recommend you spend time looking at and reading their materials by visiting their website and watching their YouTube channel at https://www.discovery.org. It's very educational. A list of their resources is provided at the end of this Appendix.

Also, I borrowed ideas and writings from B. H. Roberts' works and his essay *"The Problem of Evil in the World,"* as well as from the works of C. S. Lewis, in particular, *Mere Christianity*.

Finally, a big thank you to my friends, family and business associates who let me twist their arms to read my very imperfect "Advance Readers' Copies" and help me find hundreds if not thousands of errors therein. In addition, to my book guru and owner of Book-Wise, Karen Christofferson, they include Don Gull, Jeff Kirk, Keri Lafferty, Jerry Johnston, Rob Bishop, Michelle Willis, Sharon Myler, Neil Smith, Vivi Underwood, and many, many others. And, thanks to you for taking a chance and reading this story. I hope it's worth your time and expense.

All the best,

Greg M. Jarrard

IF YOU WOULD LIKE TO KNOW MORE . . .

Scriptural Citations: Scriptures referred to in **THE INVITATION** as cited here are from the King James version of the Bible; in addition, I quoted a verse from the apocryphal book of Esdres. Here are those citations:

Matthew, Chapters 6 & 7 (The Sermon on the Mount)

Matthew 20: 1–17. (The Parable of the Householder and the Laborers in the Vineyard)

Luke 18:18–25 (Story of a "Certain Rulers" aka The Rich Young Prince)

Luke 24: 36–39 (The Resurrected Jesus Christ appears to the disciples)

John 21: 21–25 (Jesus with the Apostles at the Sea of Tiberias)

Acts 5: 1, 3–5 (Ananias and Sapphire hold back their offering, lie and die)

I Corinthians 1:9 (What God has in store for those who love him)

I John 3:2 (What is man's destiny?)

2 Peter 3:13 (Peter's promise of a 'New Heaven and a New Earth")

DISCOVERY INSTITUTE

Based in Seattle, **DISCOVERY INSTITUTE** is a non-profit education and research organization whose mission is to advance a culture of purpose, creativity, and innovation. Its Center for Science and Culture challenges scientism as well as exploring growing scientific evidence that nature is the product of intelligent design. The Center supports research, sponsors educational programs, defends free speech, and produces articles, books, and multimedia content. Learn about evidence that nature was intelligently designed, a portal for accessing hundreds of free articles and videos.

www.intelligentdesign.org

Explore **DISCOVERY INSTITUTE** and its programs and publications at its main website. **https://www.discovery.org**

Privileged Species

Join renowned geneticist Michael Denton as he investigates through books and videos how our universe and planet were fine-tuned not just for life, but life like us. **https://privilegedspecies.com**

The Magician's Twin Video Series

Explore the dangers of "scientism" and the abuse of science in this free video series focusing on the ideas of C.S. Lewis.

https://www.youtube.com/user/cslewisweb

The Magician's Twin Book

Explore C.S. Lewis's prophetic warnings about scientism in this book edited by Discovery Institute Vice President John G. West.

https://magicianstwin.org

Secrets of the Cell Video Series

Join biochemist Michael Behe as he explores the incredible nano-machines inside our cells.

https://michaelbehe.com/videos/secrets-of-the-cell

Science Uprising Video Series

Learn about the scientists who are challenging the worldview of scientific materialism in this fast-paced YouTube series.

https://scienceuprising.com

Darwin's Impact on Society in under 3 Minutes

In less than three minutes this video will help you understand the dramatic impact Darwin's theory has had on our society.

https://youtu.be/HzLkvoj5TTc

Darwin's Corrosive Idea

Learn about the influence of Darwin's theory on society and culture in more depth in this free lecture by Discovery Institute Vice President John West. **https://youtu.be/FWKKVL_Pkf8**

ABOUT THE AUTHOR

GM Jarrard is a writer, author, and an owner of a small ad agency that for more than forty years has focused on technology, health products, B2B marketing, and politics. He has written dozens of biographies, managed a publishing company, and worked as a copy editor at a daily newspaper in Utah. His podcast, 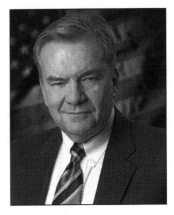 "Latter Day Radio," can be heard on Spotify, Apple Podcasts, Anchor.fm, and other venues where he frames his podcast with the phrase "Broadcasting from the intersection of faith and freedom" (also available at his website at www.latterdayradio.com).

Over the years, he has created paid political messages for candidates such as former Senator Orrin Hatch, former Governor Mike Leavitt, and Senator Mike Lee, among others.

He has lectured in Rostov, Russia to democratic party workers for the International Republican Institute, taught college courses in religion to young adults in Mainz, Germany (2015-2016), and completed a volunteer assignment with his wife Christie for the Kennedy Institute for International Relations in Geneva, Switzerland, creating materials to teach human rights in developing countries for the United Nations.

He lives in South Jordan, Utah with his wife Christie.

You can find more background information about sources, quotes, and other reference material incorporated into the narrative of this book at **www.theshiningcity.org.** It will be updated regularly with new material, particularly with new BLOG posts, so we suggest you check back periodically.

THE INVITATION TO THE SHINING CITY is also available as an e-book; go to Amazon Books to purchase it.

For more information, visit the website cited above..

THE INVITATION TO THE SHINING CITY is published by

Preservation Books, South Jordan, Utah 84095

www.preservationbooks.com

www.theshiningcity.org

Made in the USA
Columbia, SC
16 April 2022